RULED BY BLOOD

WICKED COURT
SHADOW CURSED

MAY SAGE

Ruled by Blood

Cover by The Illustrated Author Design Services
Edited by Theresa Schultz
Proofread by Cara Quinlan
Logo by The Book Brander Design
Interior Design by The Illustrated Author Design Services

NOBLESSE OBLIGE

WICKED COURT

Do not go gentle into that good night.
Rage, rage against the dying of the light.

—Dylan Thomas

Álfheimr
Niflheim
Álfheimr
Nithavellir

KREFERDOR
The Cursed Mountains
the Wilderness
Court
of Sunlight
Denarhelm
Olden
Bridge
Ljósálfar
Tenebris
Wicked
Court
Mithgarth

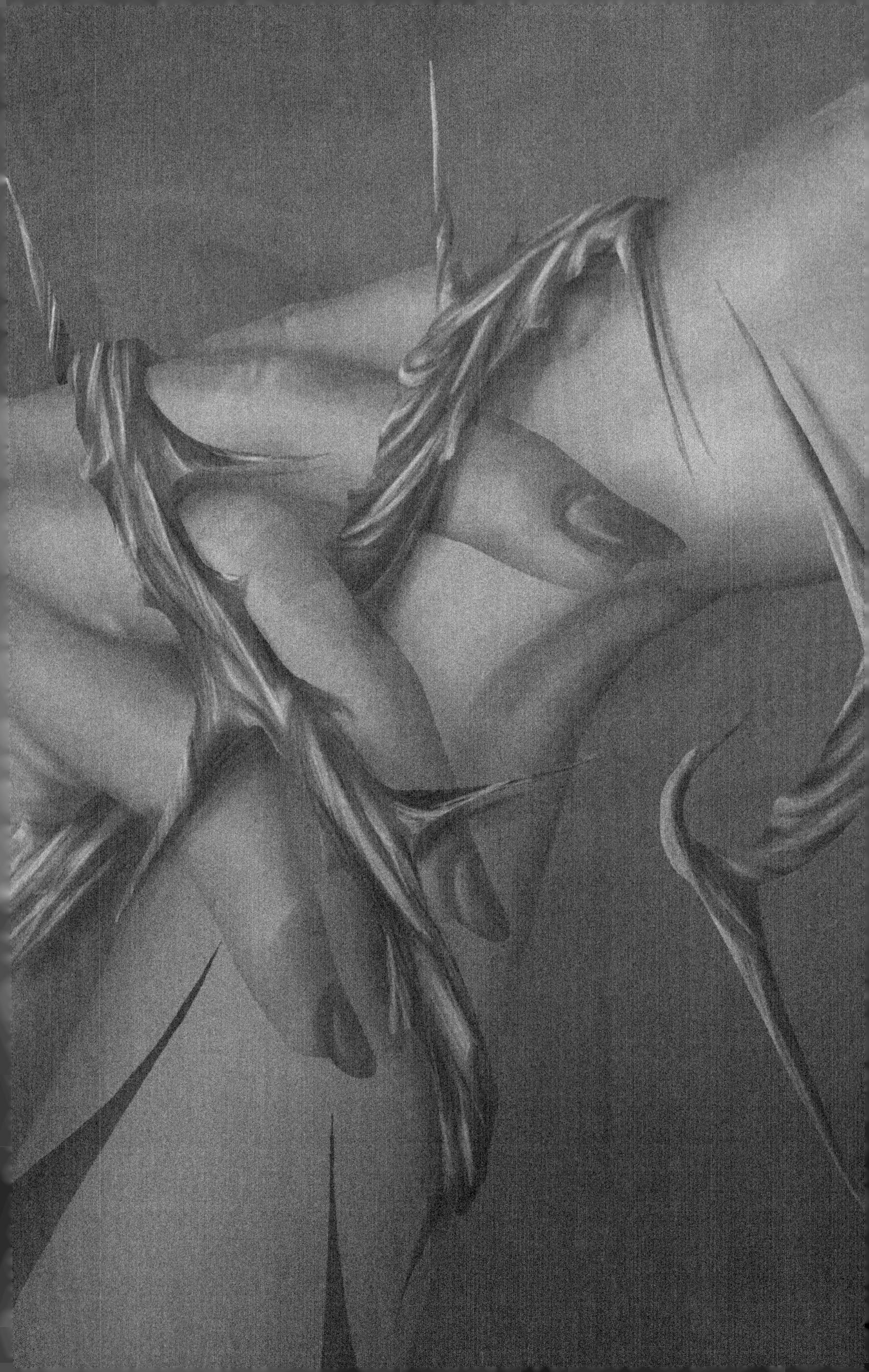

one
word of the folk

Every creature in the Murkwood wants to kill me—some for sport, others out of hunger or spite.

I leap from tree to tree, outsmarting the branches that slink under my footfalls to trip me up, all of my senses alert. I don't think the birch, oak, and old ash appreciate being trodden on, but they'll have to suffer it. The thick cover of their leaves provides a semblance of safety I can't afford to lose, and most of the things that wish to take a bite out of me are wingless creatures, bound to the moss covered forest ground.

The wilder dwellers of these lands could very well wet their teeth with my blood, if I get distracted.

The Murkwood's southern border sprouts at the feet of the Shadow Peaks and edges the seelie kingdoms. It stretches so far north part of the forest belongs to the Wilderness. The gods and monsters of that realm don't care much for borders. While their dislike for the ways of the courts keeps them off our homes, they can be found wandering our woods.

Occasionally, I wonder about my sanity. On such an icy night, close to dawn, I ought to be home, in front of a warm fire, not freezing my ears off in the single most hazardous place of Tenebris, hunting down a shade.

A *shade*! A careless chuckle escapes my lips as I jump to an old fir that seems less bloodthirsty than the nearby ash.

Once mortal, the shades were poor halfwits who'd sworn an oath to one of the darker folk; in payment for a favor, they surrender their soul. When the fae claim their due, the mortal victim turns into a shadow of a being, a creature of darkness with a tragic lack of personality. Shades serve their master until they're released. If the fae who own them die before granting them freedom, the shades turn rogue and roam the lands, wrapping whatever creature they come upon in their shadow, sucking the life out of them.

Shades aren't much of a threat to a gentry. Their prey of choice are rabbits and squirrels—a weaker puck, if they can get their hoods on it. They avoid the keeps, towns, cities, and courts for fear of knights and princes. The only place where they can be found in Tenebris is the Murkwood, as they instinctively travel north to reach the Wilderness.

If I die chasing a shade, my mother would fashion a spell to bring me back to life just so she could murder me herself. While recklessness is seldom lambasted in the house of Bane, stupidity is frowned upon.

Through the darkness, my eyes catch movements on my left, near to the ground. A swift shadow glides between bushes, parting trees, and I grin, following its progression as silently as my leather boots allow.

Finally.

There's no grand, heroic reason why I should want that shade. I went to work at sunset and did my chores on my way back; by midnight, I was bored enough to find my way to the Light Market. I talked to Khia, a round, barrel-tall salamander with blood-red hair and eyes. She's an unapologetic charlatan, but one

I happen to like. More than I ought to. Salamanders belong in the Court of Ash, fringing our southern shores. The source of their power is kept in their stronghold; living so far from the rest of her people weakens Khia so much I can barely sense any fire in her. If she's here, she was desperate enough to leave everything behind. That alone should make me wary.

It doesn't. I know a thing or two of despair.

Khia asked me for a shade's cloak. What she intends to do with it, I don't want to know. The folk don't come to me to be plied with questions about their schemes; if they intend to get tangled in misdeeds, they can justify themselves to knights or queens. I either choose to grant them the wish of their hearts, or I decline their request.

My answer is rarely no.

In my somewhat brief existence, I've built a reputation in certain circles; I am the gentry who can get things. All sorts of things—answers, rare items, spells. Whatever they want. And in return, I demand a boon of equal value. Or, if I can get it, an unnamed favor.

Khia is a valuable acquaintance; it pays to keep her happy. In the Light Market, she hears all sorts of things from all sorts of folk—whispers I might not have learned without her. I am a curious creature by nature. She's also one of the best at getting her hands on rarer relics, which comes in handy in my line of trade.

While she's given me dragon blood, selkie ink, and poisons aplenty, I've never extracted one single favor from her.

She's promised me one if I can get her that cloak by first light.

I need her oath. I need it like I need air.

Before the first oath I collected, I was nothing. I was powerless. Now I have warriors, pirates, thieves, princesses, and murderers who would have no choice but to come to my aid, if I demanded it. My friend Esea says I'm raising an army. She's wrong. I'm erecting a shield of flesh and bone before my meekness.

A shield I could never raise against the one enemy I'm truly fighting.

I unhook the thin glass vial at my belt, eyeing the tiny creatures inside. A flock of devases, mischievous as they come. I don't know how they ended up flasked; I doubt their innocence in the matter. They've tried their tricks on the wrong fae.

I bartered a sphinx pelt for them at the market, and promised to free them so long as they helped my chase tonight. From what I understand of their cacophonous chirping, they spent nigh on a decade in that blue-green prison. Needless to say, they were quick to accept the bargain.

It'd better be worth it. Without any fur over my shoulders, the bite of the wind is bitter.

When I open the cork caging them in, they burst out of the flask and shoot high in the starry night sky, their inner light glowing so much brighter than it had moments ago. Their airborne dance is beautiful; beautiful enough for me to gasp, although it looks like they might flee without holding up their end of the bargain.

But they are fae, and a bargain struck by the mouth of the folk is a law none of us can escape. They soar down to the trees, and fly north, faster than I could have thought possible, illuminating the night.

I half regret my decision to bring them with me. My eyes can distinguish most of what's in front of me, even in the dark, but I hadn't been able to see much of the Murkwood from my perches atop the highest trees. The creatures of these parts blend too well in the darkness. Now, I see.

I haven't ventured too far in the Murkwood; ten miles at most. I didn't expect the worst of the monsters to have crossed my path yet. And they haven't. I only see wolves the size of bears, serpentine dragons coiled around nearby ferns, ageless hags, bogles, and fachans. No nightmares, dragons, or anthropophagi in sight. There's that. They're known to roam these parts, too.

The entire silent forest seems to be watching me. I wonder if they're bored. I may be their entertainment for the evening.

Perhaps they've placed bets on when my surefooted run up here will ultimately end. Perhaps they're fighting to claim my eyes, lungs, and heart.

I follow the lights.

When I reach them, the shade is writhing on the mossy forest floor, desperate to rid itself of the tiny, bright fairies who coat its darkness. For a moment, it strikes me that forcing a shadow to endure light is rather cruel. My plan was clever; I couldn't have outrun one of them with ease, but as expected, it's stopped to defend itself against the devases. The shade is burning inside out, poor wretched thing.

The moment I get to the ground, I take my pouch of salt and throw it in a neat circle engulfing me, the shade, and all the devases, to give anything hunting us pause. Then I unsheathe my iron blade, hand on the wood and leather hilt. Once, the thing on the ground was a mere man of clay, a boring old human; now it's a creature of the folk, and like all of us, it fears iron. I see it still as the blade draws near. The shade half whines, half screams, stumbling upright to attempt to flee. It cannot cross the salt barrier either, trapped inside as surely as the other monsters of the woods are kept out.

I'm quick to end its suffering; my blade flashes to what would have been its throat if it had been shaped like a man, and cuts open the small bead of silver holding its cloak on its shoulders.

The shade stumbles back to the ground, the impossibly dark fabric in my left hand. Gazing down, I can only pity it. I've never seen a hoodless shade before; I have no desire to ever see one after tonight.

I know mortals—I've traveled to their lands more than most of the gentry care to. As I survey what's left of the shade, I cannot deny that though this thing walks in our world, it's still one of them in the end. A frail, emaciated, gray-skinned man with twig like limbs. All the blood and flesh seem to have dried up long ago, leaving nothing but bone and old wrinkled skin.

I could kill it. Without its hood, it can't glide in the night, and its one power, darkness, has failed it. I should kill it. Its life is so very wretched.

To me, even a wretched existence is better than nothingness, emptiness.

I crouch down on the balls of my feet and tilt my head to the side, watching it closely. There is a life of sorts left to it.

"Poor little shade. Do you recall the name you bore?"

It hisses and its few teeth flash in its cave of a mouth. I decide not to mention the virtues of brushing one's teeth.

"How would you like a bargain?" The offer crosses my lips thoughtlessly, carelessly—perhaps cruelly.

I laugh as the thing crawls away, desperate to flee. Bargaining with the folk is what got him in this state to start with.

I'm not accustomed to showing kindness. Kindness has no place in my world. I speak the words nonetheless, although there's nothing to be gained from them. "Son of man, servant of fae, you're free of every oath to the folk."

Dangerous words that I have no right to speak. This thing belongs to a master, and I have stolen it.

I can't say I care. The one thing that matters is that I have the power to do it.

I watch with interest as the creature changes, its skin regaining some color, its flesh padding with some muscle. In instants, I'm standing in front of a plain, naked, graying man, not unlike any I might have crossed paths with in the mortal realm.

The man continues his retreat, crawling away, fear in his hollow eyes. I stay crouched on my heels, unmoving. He mumbles, madness limning his every feature. Among the nonsense, I hear one word.

Royal.

Finally, I get to my feet, and lift the cloak in the air. "Thanks for that, human."

two
in the light market

I run, eager to leave the woods before the hungrier creatures of the night sniff my blood. I shouldn't have to worry about sluaghs and ogres this far south, and so close to daybreak, but I've been cavalier enough for a night.

Besides, I have to get back to the market. Khia was clear: she wants the cloak by first light. If I'm late, she could weasel her way out of our deal—or try to offer me a lesser prize for the cloak. It's her oath I'm after, and I can practically taste it on the tip of my tongue.

I'm almost at the edge of the Murkwood when I'm knocked aside by something heavy—and fast. I do what I can to keep my balance on the branch where I'm perched. While I don't fall, I smash face first into the trunk. Dizzy, I spin around to face my adversary, and groan.

Never mind staying on this tree.

I leap in the air, one hand clutched around the rough fabric of the magical cloak, the other gripping the first branch I can catch on my way down. It's thin, too flimsy to support my weight for long, and the effort is taking its toll on me.

Nature has made me agile, and fast when I need to be, but raw strength isn't my forte. I can't hold my body up with one arm for any extended amount of time. Pain already cripples my left side, stretching from my fingers to my shoulder blade. I feel my claws extend from my fingertips, burning my skin as they plunge into dry wood.

The damnable branch creaks, threatening to snap.

I glance up at my attacker. Two eyes, as bright as the moon, and a set of fangs flashes above me. It's a wyrfox, playful as they come. Its tail slowly bats from side to side, and I like to imagine that it smiles at me, its prey.

Long ago, gentries cursed some gray foxes, wild cats, wolves, bears, and birds to live as we do, long lives that can only end in blood. An endeavor to fashion themselves companions, I think. Some older families still have wyr familiars in their household, but now most of them live in the wild.

Foxes are wicked as cats and smarter than wolves. They're day dwellers, usually asleep high in the trees at night so as to not get eaten by stronger predators. I might have woken that one—or perhaps we're closer to dawn than I'd estimated. I have a human clock, somewhere in my drawers at home, but it ran out of battery at least twenty years ago.

By the looks of it, the wyr is young—in time, they turn black, silver-gray, or reddish-brown, surrounded by midnight-black fire. This one still has the gold coat of a juvenile, without so much as a spark around its fur. I can thank my uppity education for my ability to define the many things that endeavor to eat me on a daily basis.

The predator's youth isn't good news. An older wyr might have thought twice and decided that there were easier meals to be hunted. Young foxes are ludic in their murders. I watch it wiggle its back to adjust its position. I doubt it noticed how fragile my branch is. I doubt it cares. I have instants to make a decision.

Down, toward the ground and all its peril. My blood is air and water; the folk of earth are my natural enemies. Most of the forest is at an advantage on their land.

Or I can give the stupid twig a chance.

I grunt as I pull my body up with one arm, careful not to damage the cloak. The branch squeals in protest, but doesn't betray my foolhardy trust. I can count the times where my small frame has been an advantage on one hand. Tonight adds another instance. There's no doubt that, slender as we are, it would never have supported the weight of an average height fae.

Still, the branch can't hold me for long. Rather than finding out exactly how long, I fling myself as high as I can in the air. If I wasn't wearing a leather coat, I would have freed my wings. As we're late autumn, I'd opted to cover up—like an idiot.

I land on a stronger tree and run along its branches, then leap again, and run to another one. I can see light parting the boughs in the distance. I'm close. I focus on that, rather than on the gekkering and pawfalls closing in behind me.

I should be grateful that the wyr is a fox and not a cat; I'm the better climber. But it is faster than me.

I'm not inclined to hurt it if I can avoid it, but I'll most likely have to defend myself before I get to safety.

I near the last row of trees when it finally catches up with me. This time I sense it; I have mere instants to block its mouthful of sharp fangs with the leather cuff of my left forearm. I groan when the canines dig deep, feeling thick, hot blood ooze under my tunic.

I refuse to use the blades at my belt. The iron would kill the young wyr, now or later, by poisoning its blood.

Calculating my options, I choose the least lethal weapon in my arsenal. It might kill it too, but there's less certainty.

My hand rises, palm up, and I flex my fingers, as though I'm crushing the air in my grasp. A burst of bright green energy coats my palm, becoming brighter, greater at every moment.

And then I breathe, perfectly at peace for one precious moment.

Nothing quite feels like using my ability. I am myself for once. I am allowed to *be*.

The wyr's scream could have raised the dead, had they not already been lurking in the Murkwood. It stumbles back, losing its footing, and falls down.

I curse out loud. I'd never meant to force it to the ground.

I peep over my shoulder, to the path leading out of the forest. I'm *so* close.

"You're going to regret it," I warn myself out loud. My voice sounds incredibly like my father's just then.

I jump down anyway.

The fox falls on its side with a squeal. I join it a second later, on an elegant crouch.

The animal's golden ears are flat, and it recoils in fear. It ignores me, though I'm right next to it. The vulpine's eyes are fixed on the horse closing in between the trees, moving like a shadow. A colossal rider dressed in black mounts it.

The most notable thing about the rider would be—according to many—that it doesn't have a head. I would argue that the whip he's holding, made of a spine, is equally terrifying. I don't think it's given nearly enough credit in the descriptions I read back in my school days.

The dullahan's horse launches. I hold my palm, still filled with energy, between myself and the creature, pushing as much magic as I can muster away from me. Strands of light gather in my hand, and explode in a burst, blinding it.

It is never natural for me to *give* magic. I prefer to take it. But a headless huntsman won't be spooked by darkness; what horrifies the true monsters of this world is receiving healing energy, hence why they live in the night, avoiding the sun and all its light. I suspect that if I were to entirely heal it, it might just end up being a regular headless corpse.

The dullahan screeches, its horse bucking. Oh, it's pissed. Thankfully, it's also not able to run me—or the confused wyrfox—down, at the moment.

"Go. Back up the tree. And stay up there, you idiot."

Some fae can charm any animal, whispering sweet things in the ears of horses, dogs, and even grants. I'm most definitely not one of them. Even the tamest of horses at home stubbornly ignores every one of my commands. But the wyrfox isn't as stupid as I thought it might be; it climbs up the tree, slipping out of view, to safety.

I don't attempt to follow it. Down here, we had a truce of sorts while facing the dangers of the forest, but back in the trees, I am a snack.

So, I run on foot, reminding myself to take at least two pouches of salt next time I'm foolish enough to return to the Murkwood.

I EMERGE FROM the woods with a well-deserved limp. It'll get better soon enough—one of the perks of my kind. The bigger concern is the claw that pierced my skin when the wyr got to my cuffs. If it's old enough to be poisonous, I may be in trouble.

I ignore it for now. I can't do anything until I get home.

Once, Tenebris was divided in eight mighty courts, ruled by their kings and queens, then Nyx conquered them all. The lower courts—Stars, Storm, Silt, Irchor, Stone, Ash, and Mist—have retained their respective rulers, but all answer to the high court. Settled in the heart of the eastern mountains, it used to be called the Court of Wind. Now it's the Wicked Court, home to High Queen Morgana Lilwreath, Nyx's great-granddaughter.

The gentry can live forever, so one might have thought that a mere twelve hundred years after her conquest of the lower courts, Nyx would still sit upon her throne, but that was underestimating how bloodthirsty our kind can be, particularly when bored. Not one of our high queens has ruled more than three hundred years. To me, that makes the job particularly unappealing, yet there's always a fool willing to do it.

The Murkwood is north of the Wicked Court. The great palace carved inside rock and mountain stone never fails to exert a grimace from me when I approach. I hate everything about this place. Everything except, perhaps, its beauty. The fine, arched high columns, sculptures of the Old Folk, the slender shafts of the crossing tower carved in mountain stone, I can admire. Everything else about the court is derivative.

At the foot of the chain of Shadow Peaks lies Hardrock, the greatest fae city in Tenebris, and therefore, in the world. The immortals of Álfheimr have attempted to build some sort of empire, or so I'm told, but it is well known that the fae territories are superior to the rest of our continent. Our magic feeds the land itself.

The seelie kingdoms up north are still divided into minor courts, as we were before the days of Nyx. I understand that each of their kingdoms has its own settlement, but here, everything worth mentioning has been concentrated in Hardrock.

I fasten my leather hood around my hair, and make my way through the familiar paths. The roads are grass and moss, littered with groves and rivers. Even in our cities, we fae do not fare well away from nature. Farther up, closer to the queen's keep, there's a wide cobbled avenue for carriages and horses. The lords, ladies, kings, queens, and rich gentry of all Tenebris own manors either side of that avenue. Most use them occasionally, when attending revels at court. Others live here—the advisors to the queen, the courtiers who don't know the world outside of Hardrock. I try not to judge them. My own mother had been one of them, once.

I willfully avoid that path, though it might have been faster to reach the Light Market.

The market is south of the city, close to the Arm of Sea Harbor, where goods arrive at every time of night or day. It's so large, I used to get lost as a girl. Now, I know it better than the woods surrounding my parents' estate. Here, in the midst of chaos, where no one matters, I feel at home.

There's a very proper market somewhere in the loftier neighborhood, I'm told. I'd have nothing to do there. In the Light Market, one can find everything they want—sorcerers' staffs, enchanted jewels, cursed blades, sprites in search of a new household, brides, even human servants, for those who like to buy those instead of proper staff.

I grimace, seeing just such a trade take place in the main square. A different merchant gets to present their wares every night. I arrive late, and there's only three products left on the stage: two golden-skinned, strong, shirtless men, who look so alike they must be brothers, and a pale girl almost as short as me adorned with an indecent amount of bosom, proudly displayed in flimsy red silk clashing with her black curls.

The crowd is wild, bidding bags of coins for the three mortals, though they'll fade away in the blink of an eye.

Owning humans is a practice I can't condone. However plain and short-lived, they look and think too much like us to treat them like mere dogs or horses. I suppose that's why some fae relish making them heel. I don't see the point in bragging of holding power over such pitiful creatures.

They have their uses, though. A child of a human and a fae has the characteristic of a full-fledged fae, no doubt because their blood runs so weak. And their reproduction rate is much higher than that of our kind. Why, in a short decade, a mortal woman could birth ten infants—even, I think, ten at once. Fae are lucky to be blessed with more than one per century, if that.

Many heirless lords breed with humans to strengthen their bloodlines. The crown also sends knights to acquire children from the mortal realm once every century; the parentless, the poor starving urchins, the lost, those whose family sell or bargain.

I know that in some courts, they lure the comeliest maidens and send them back with pockets full of gold and faerie children in their bellies. Others keep them for a year and a day.

The children reared in the mortal world always end up seeking out the folk when they grow older. Blood calls to blood, when the blood is strong enough.

The seelie are rumored to trade changelings for human children that they raised in their court and married.

All this, I understand.

Human servants, not so much.

They're too awkward and untalented. Too slow and weak to be useful for anything other than breeding.

That may be why they're so coveted today. The men will plant their seed in fae ladies, and the girl will bear her master's child. That'd explain their manner of dress. I hope their seller thought to charm them to ensure they didn't die of cold, at least.

I take comfort in the knowledge that none of them would be here, had they not frittered away their freedom in a bargain. Although, our kind is known for tricking mortals into agreeing to what they don't understand, so the bargain may not have been fair.

What do I know? Perhaps they want to be here. Perhaps they'd like a faerie lover. I've been to Mithgarth, watching mortals from the shadows. They talk about us around bonfires, and while some shudder at the mention of the fae, others sigh wistfully and whisper that they wouldn't mind a wild night in the woods.

On closer inspection, I don't detect fear or displeasure from any of them. The men are smiling at the crowd, flexing their muscles. The dark-haired girl looks like she could be close to me in age; I stopped growing in my twentieth year, so that doesn't mean much.

They are no victim, and I, not a savior.

I doubt my assistance would be needed, if I could give it. And I can't. I'm too poor to buy them, powerless to stop the auction, powerless to help. I hate nothing more than feeling powerless, so I walk away.

My path takes me through the food stalls. Though most are closed this late in the night or early in the day, I still smell delicacies from every corner of Álfheimr. In the row of silks, there's cloth made by the elves. My favorite permanent stalls are in the row of steel, where we can find anything metal—enchanted jewels, charmed mirrors, and swords crafted by dwarves. According to the merchants. Most of them are charlatans, trying to pass horse-piss water as a remedy.

Catching the first rays of sunlight in the distance, I rush past all that and directly make my way to Khia's stand. The salamander is packing up shop.

I place my loot on the empty table between her and me, leaning in.

"One cloak, freshly obtained, as agreed."

Her eyes widen. Then I see her gaze dart west, where our sun rises every morning. Her lips purse. She knows I'm on time—barely, but on time nonetheless.

"How did you get this?"

I grin, giving no response. I sometimes ask myself what my acquaintances think of me. Am I a thief in their mind, or a broker, simply arranging exchanges between one source and the next for a price?

"I believe you owe me an oath."

She snorts, taking a little round piece of glass and placing it in front of her left eye to inspect the cloak—no doubt hoping for a defect that would mean she can start negotiating the price.

I try to keep my expression bland, though I have no idea whether there might be a wyrclaw tear somewhere.

"Mh." She's come up empty of protest. "All right. What do you really want?"

As if she didn't know. "Your oath."

She narrows her eyes, calculating.

"Your oath, or give me my cloak back."

The round little lady keeps pushing. "Catching a shade is impossible, especially for a wee thing like you. They're too fast. Who did you take it from?"

I sigh, irked now. "Your oath, Khia."

"If someone comes back for it—"

"Has anyone ever come for anything I've given you?"

She might not understand why, or how, but she knows I only deliver authenticity—and that, unlike many of her suppliers, I don't lead anyone crying thief at her stall.

"Fine, then. You have my oath," she grouses. I remain silent. She knows she needs to say the words. "Vlari, daughter of Mist, I swear to grant you one favor, should it be in my ability. I will obey your word until my debt is paid. Happy?"

I am. I really am.

But letting people know what matters to me is a weakness.

I have enough of those.

I point to the bag already loaded on her puck assistant. "Do you mind if I buy some starnuts before you pack up? They're just delicious."

I don't tell her nothing could sate me more than knowing she owes me.

three
blood of the heirs

By the time I make it home, my arm is throbbing. I feel faint, unsteady on my feet. There's no longer any skepticism as to whether the wyr was old enough to poison me. I mutter, cursing it—and myself, for helping it escape the headless huntsman.

The gentry of the folk don't get sick that easily—it takes spells and curses specifically made to weaken them. One of the many reasons why they're considered the superior race among the fae. They're also immortal, and better at magic than the rest of our kind.

My mother is a pure gentry; her lineage couldn't be superior.

My father, not so much. A common fae without any title, he has some sea blood from a nokk ancestor, I think, and there's plenty of sprite in him. Most sprites are common servants, when they wish to be useful, wicked ruffians when they don't. The only distinguished heritage he can boast of is that of his mother, a pixie of the seelie courts.

Her kind is known for their deviousness and their skills in the art of war. Like the selkies of the Sea Lands and the salamanders of the Court of Ash, they're almost as respected as the gentry.

While a child of a mortal and a fae is a full fae, those hailing from two different fae families tend to blend the attributes of both—hence why breeding with a lesser fae is more frowned upon than taking human partners, among the gentry. I have my father's weaknesses, hence my current predicament. Common fae don't tend to be immune to poisons or venoms.

Contrary to popular belief, I'm not ashamed of my legacy. No one who's ever met my grandmother would say that my father cursed me with weakness. His blood is a gift, just as well as my mother's.

For all that, I must admit, being sick has never been my favorite thing.

At least I cannot die of it. It'll pass eventually.

I drag my feet into the hall of our keep.

The Court of Mist has long ceased to function like a proper kingdom; my parents don't even hold the title of king and queen. The castle is in a sorry state, some parts of it in ruin. But it is home.

The carved white stone arches and massive, dusty halls darkened by ornate windows are part of me. I wouldn't exchange its drafts and mold for all the gleaming palaces in Álfheimr.

Hearing the distinctly faint sound of heels brush the floor from above, I straighten up, masking any trace of pain and weakness from my face. Only one person in this keep moves so quietly, like a shadow, and she will not take kindly to the state I'm in, if she discovers it.

Meda appears on the first floor, staring me down.

I tower over the woman in front of me by nigh on two feet, but when she glares at me, I shiver.

"I can explain," I blurt out.

"Can you?" My grandmother's quiet, melodious voice is a thing of nightmares.

Meda came to live with us as soon as I was done with school, some forty years ago. I'm her one grandchild, and she wanted to train me up.

She hasn't left since. Part of me wonders whether she was bored in the seelie realm. It could just be because she doesn't think my training is up to par yet.

She's quite the beauty, with her thick dark locks, so unlike mine. She wears a gown light as air, green like her eyes. She's in her three hundredth year, I think. It's hard to say. The pixie blood in her veins will always keep her youthful—even more so than the gentry.

Gentries age until they've grown into themselves; sometimes in their thirtieth or fortieth year, seldom earlier. I owe her my youthful appearance as well as my diminutive height.

In a few decades, I'll be able to make myself look taller, smaller, younger when I wish. I don't think I'll be able to age myself, even then.

I'm normally rather skilled in talking my way out of trouble, but the pain and the venom have dulled my wits. I can only manage to chatter nervously. "I was in the woods. There was a fox, and a headless—"

"In which woods, pray? I do not think I've seen foxes here."

I'm in trouble. A fool could ascertain as much.

"I know you like foxes, Meda. You wouldn't have wanted me to hurt it." That sounds reasonable. Flattering, even. She might fall for it. "So, to spare it—"

"You got careless. You let a lesser being, a mere animal, wound *you*. And you worried your mother by coming home later than you said you would."

I wince. Grandmother Meda is ridiculously fond of my mother; I fancy she likes her better than her own son—and definitely better than me.

"I heard there were less than a dozen wyrfoxes left in our realm; I simply tried to—"

"Ah. You were in the Murkwood, then. Interesting."

I bite my lips. As the wyr are wild creatures, they prefer to be close to their brethren in the north. She was letting me talk to give away what I had been up to, and it was working.

I decide to blame it on my increasingly throbbing headache. It had been years since I'd fallen for her simpler tricks.

"I just need to sleep it off. I'll be fine."

The air crackles, and I don't have time to blink before Meda launches herself at me. It's the second time I've been attacked tonight. This time I don't hesitate. My leather coat is on the polished floor, and I have my iron sword in one hand, a silver dagger in the other, holding them both firmly between myself and the scariest woman I know.

She's moving so fast I can barely detect her. There's little hope of anticipating her moves, yet I must try. Such are the rules of her game. I can manage the impossible, or I can bleed out on the polar flooring.

I stop paying attention to what my eyes tell me and allow myself to feel. Feel the pixie—her heart, her mind, her blade. My sword crashes against hers. I breathe out. Now that she's at a standstill, I see she's uncovered her wings. Delicate, diaphanous membranes, like a bright butterfly. Black and blue, they're the most beautiful wings I've seen in all my sixty-nine years.

"You came back wounded, Nevlaria." Meda snarls. "That means you need *further training*."

I'm in a world of trouble.

Pixies are naturally light and fast; using their tiny, light wings, they can fly at a speed unmatched by any other fae, which renders their fighting style deadly to even the strongest gentry. No one can maintain a superior speed for long, but a few minutes is enough to destroy whatever stands in their way.

My wings aren't nearly as fast as hers, but I unfurl them anyway, tearing the back of yet another linen shirt. I cannot win against her, but I can prevent her from beating me into a pulp if I fight fire with fire, like my life is on the line.

For the first time, I think that Khia's oath wasn't worth it after all.

I train. All morning, I train, right there in the main hall. Those among our household up so late go through great lengths to avoid us, taking longwinded passageways. She slices my limbs and kicks my stomach, punches my face. I manage to land two blows.

Finally, when the sun is at its apex, blinding me through the open archways, she sheathes her blade.

"Not bad."

I laugh, delirious, exhausted, and drunk on triumph.

Not bad, from her, is the highest of praise.

I smile on my way to bed, thinking I might just be a little insane.

four

screams and salt

Nevlaria Bane."

Ignoring the few sniggers that never failed to follow my name, I rose to my feet, eyes forward, inexpressive as ever. But oh, by all the gods on Eartia and beyond, why me?

Again.

I wasn't going to survive another humiliating presentation in front of the entire class. I was certain of it. At sixteen, I used to be a little dramatic like that.

The Ivies, Thorns, Windersts, Briars, Wilds, and Grimdales—my peers, my cousins—would mock and disregard me for long after that, though. And I bore it well enough, all things considered.

I was aware that my being called out was purposeful. Professor Hollowdale, our homeroom teacher, knew just what was wrong with me. If he was pushing me like this every week, it was because he'd been asked to. Ordered to.

His superiors wanted to ensure I was well leashed, that I wouldn't lash out under any circumstances.

Hollowdale needn't have bothered. I'd never risk the wrath of his boss. Even back then, I wasn't stupid enough to defy the unseelie queen.

So I stared on. When Hollowdale asked me to present my assignment, I produced a suitably weak, shapeless orb that earned me more derisive sneers from the back.

I tonelessly stated, "I chose to form a MoonOrb today, as they have the ability to absorb excess magic. I figured it may prove useful if any of the other experiments go wrong."

The professor smiled at me briefly.

It wasn't unkind. Hollowdale wasn't a bad person as such. I had to remember that when I was tempted to kill him.

MoonOrbs were the tools of children, one of the first tricks the fae learned when our magic manifested.

It was weak. Like me. Like the powerless creature I'd been turned into.

"Very well. If you'd place it on my desk, please. You'll get a B minus for your efforts today. Sylph Thorn."

Sylph summoned a WaterOrb, and three foot-long lake dragons burst out of it, gently gliding around the sphere. The class gasped in awe. I closed my eyes and breathed, controlling the wave of anger and resentment.

I had sea blood—I could manage a WaterOrb easily enough.

I didn't need to ace my classes. I didn't need admiration. I just hated having to hide. It wasn't in my nature. Nor was submission.

"You will make yourself invisible. You will make yourself irrelevant. I never want to hear anyone say your name in praise. If you fail in this, I will destroy you."

These words were planted in my mind. They'd only been uttered once, ten years ago, and still I heard them in my dreams and nightmares. I heard them when I breathed, when I bathed, and most of all, when I was humiliated.

I had a choice. I could be no one, or I could die.

I wished for a distraction from this. Something, anything had *to happen. Before I lost it.*

Just then, I turned before anyone else registered a change. An instinct deep inside me, not dissimilar to fear—only stronger—gnawed at my very soul.

He appeared at the door seconds later.

An older boy, almost a man. The fae's aging process can differ from race to race, but the high fae tend to reach maturity around the same time as humans. At sixteen, I—hopefully—wasn't done growing yet, but he was close to adulthood. It wasn't the only way he didn't fit in. His clothes were plain, even plainer than mine, although my family was poorer than anyone else admitted in this school. I wore a simple cloak and my black dress had seen better days, but they were silk and wool. His shirt was rough cotton, loose on him and faded gray, as if it had been handed down. His brown breeches were in a worse state.

What stood out to me wasn't the grubby attire, or the age.

It was his eyes. His presence. His aura.

I'd never felt a strength like this. Not once. Not even in the presence of the unseelie queen.

High Queen Morgana had power. She had all the kings and queens of the lower courts bowing down to her, she had terrifying familiars who'd tear anyone apart for looking at her with scorn, she had knights and sorcerers, and she had the crown that demanded as much respect as everything else. Removing all that, she was just one gentry, one woman. Beautiful and terrible and cruel, but no more than one person.

The boy? He was power.

This stranger could kill me. He could kill us all, I was certain of it.

For the first time in my life, I smiled at school.

"Sir Hollowdale." The headmistress, Fera Weathergreen, stepped close to the stranger, as if she didn't suspect he could snap at any moment and bite off her head like a feral beast.

I would have cheered him on.

My eyes stayed on him as she addressed our tutor. "This bright young boy is Rystan Drusk, the transfer I mentioned."

"Ah! Of course. Find yourself a seat, Mr. Drusk. Class, I trust you'll take care of our new student."

Sylph and the rest of the royals exchanged a glance. Oh, yeah, they'll welcome him. Bullying newbies is one of their favorite pastimes.

I smiled, guessing it would be fun to watch.

"VLARI."

I frown. No one called me that at school.

"Vlari!"

Cold. I feel cold. Why? It had happened in the summer.

"Nevlaria Bane, wake up this instant!"

A drop of water falls on my forehead, and I blink. My eyes finally open, to stare right at a fist sized hole in the ceiling.

Ugh.

I know better than to fall asleep on the left side of my bed. The roof has been leaking for about a year in that spot.

My father's shaking my shoulders, his claws digging into my arms. Through my blurred vision, I see fear in his features.

Oh.

I'd been asleep, and it had just been a dream. Well, a memory of that day. It's been what, fifty-some years? And I can't say I'd wasted a second of my life thinking about that day until now.

School had mostly sucked, it was over, the end.

As I relax, I feel waves of power radiating out of me. No wonder my father is agitated. I bite my lower lip and call my energy back where it belongs, sealed inside of me.

He sighs in relief, and hugs me close. "You wouldn't wake up. I tried the spells, and they didn't work."

I can practically taste terror on his skin.

What have I done this time?

My head's thumping, but with some effort, I sit up in my canopy bed and look down to the wooden floor. The circle I'd traced with salt all around me has been broken, as if a gust of wind had shoved it out of the way. Except my ornate window's closed, and the direction of the blast shows it's been pushed out from the inside.

From me.

Double crap.

I groan. "Tell me I didn't kill anything?"

He winces and I sigh.

"Nothing of importance, blossom." I can tell he's lying, but I choose not to ask.

The servants, the knights, and my family know better than to go unprotected while I sleep. They have wreaths of spelled thorns around their hands and neck, or enchanted jewels keeping them safe from my capricious fits. That doesn't mean I can't harm other things. Flowers, songbirds, wandering hobs and imps.

I should push, but I let him soothe me, caressing my back from the neck to the shoulder blades. The skin is always sensitive there, for those of us who grow wings.

"Do you want to tell me what happened?" he murmurs.

I don't have an answer. "I would if I had any clue."

I'd used my powers, that much is evident, but to what end? Did I just lash out for the hell of it, kill something because I could? Not improbable, though I should be beyond that. At sixty-nine, I'm hardly an emotional teen anymore. Among my kind, I'm considered an adult. Not a wise or an ancient one, but an adult nonetheless.

My father narrows his eyes. I can tell he doesn't quite believe me. Nero Bane is many things; stupid isn't one of them. He knows I have at least part of the answer. I should share my dream.

I don't want to.

I can't tell why. It just seems private.

A knock at my door interrupts whatever lecture he's about to give me. I have half a second to be relieved. Then, our one sprite servant announces that I've been summoned to court at once.

I can't say I'm surprised.

The unseelie queen knows everything. She's already heard about my transgression. Whatever spies she's planted in our midst have whispered in her ears. My using my power without her consent, outside of her control, will not be unpunished.

Which means that despite being careful for years, making myself insignificant to avoid her notice, I might die before the night is through.

I manage a weak smile to reassure my father. "It might be all right."

It likely wouldn't.

five
property of the crown

Tenebris is a kingdom of night; the fae of our realm rise with dawn and fade alongside darkness.

I'm supposed to start working at eight, in two hours, and on foot, the path leading from my parents' domain to the House of Frost in the Court of Storm takes almost as long. On an ordinary day, I would have made it on time, but there is not a single doubt in my mind that I should prioritize the queen's summons over trivial things such as earning my bread and butter. Punctuality has been drilled into me by my father as one of the simplest courtesies I should observe.

My mother had other teachings. Today, I am her child. I have to be. She's the only one of them who survived the Wicked Court. Assuming her careless, free spirit is a necessity. Yet, I can't help frowning, disappointed, frustrated with myself. "Can you send Lady Frost a note?"

My father nods, already on his way to his study on the other side of the house.

I alone reside in the east wing, for everyone's safety.

I hear his voice down the corridor. "And I'll ask Ciera to attend to you."

I don't realize my shoulders were so tense until they relax.

When I was younger, our sprites and imps helped me. Now, rushed as I often am, I've learned to take care of myself. Unlike many women of my station, I can dress myself just fine—even when I have to wear more elaborate clothing requiring corsets and other torture devices—but today, I welcome the assistance.

After the barest of ablutions, I slide into the fanciest of my work attire, a jade velvet frock with lace sleeves, and I rifle through my jewelry box to find a suitable trinket to slide on my wrists or fingers. I have many jewels, but most are made of broken glass, old oxidized coins, random shiny things I've found during my walks and gathered like a crow. Junk. At the high court, they'd be seen as nothing short of an insult.

I feel my mother's presence long before she enters my room. Her soft hand clasps my wrist, and cold metal catches my attention. I look down and smile, grateful. She's closed her golden cuff bracelet to my left arm, and she's sliding a number of rings on my bare fingers.

We are poor. We aren't permitted to look like it though. Not in the high court.

"You're a life saver."

"Oh, daughter mine. No amount of baubles will be enough to keep that pretty neck in one piece, if you go anywhere near the queen with hair like that."

Fae cannot lie. Most do so anyway; we cheat and deceive as well as our nature allows. Not my mother. Ciera Oberon Bane says things as they pass through her mind, without a care for what her audience makes of it. Some call her honest, others cruel. I know she can be both.

She's right, of course; my hair is a mess.

I'm not allowed to cut it without the queen's blessing, and she's never given it, if only to inconvenience me. The long tresses now reach the floor, when they're loose. Not one to pamper myself, I don't give it the care it desperately needs. On a normal day, I twist it into one braid and pin it at the back of my head, hiding the damaged ends in the knot. The hairstyle has another advantage: it conceals the shade of my mane at its tips.

Purple. If the folk saw it, it would spell trouble.

Rare are those who possess hair of that shade, and all belong to our line.

The royals like to pretend that I—and the rest of my family—don't exist. We're mistakes they're more than happy to forget. And everything about me allows them to do so. I am short. My eyes are sky blue, the one physical attribute I have inherited from my father. I have no evident mark of royalty; indeed, at a glance one might mistake me for a pixie, if not a common sprite, without a drop of gentry blood.

At the roots, and for a good three feet, my hair is silver-gray, washed out, without shine or thickness. It only turns purple toward the ends. The deepest amethyst, like the queen's eyes and nails. Like the royal blood. It marks me as one of them.

I hide it for their benefit as well as mine, on a daily basis.

There will be no hiding it today. The queen doesn't approve of much when it comes to me, but my hair is the one thing she's ever complimented.

After messing up during my sleep today, I need all the help I can get. If she's of a mind to destroy me, a reminder that I am family cannot go amiss.

My mother is magic. Her control over water has never earned her much approval from anyone; she's too weak to use her skill as a weapon of any consequence. Even so, it does wonders to my poor, dry hair, taming it into soft silky waves. Every time she cares for the mane, murmuring songs I remember from far away as she brushes it, I tell myself I should ask her to do it with some regularity. I wouldn't mind having nice hair, even if it's in braids. I wouldn't mind being cared for like this.

Regrettably, neither she nor I have time for frivolities. Tomorrow, I will return to my routine and forget it again.

As long as I am alive then.

I close my eyes, biting back all trace of rage or ire I might harbor in my heart. They're natural, for me more than most. But they're also my worst enemies.

I have to be no one. I have to be nothing. I have to be weak and emotionless when I face my maternal grandmother.

WE LIVE A three-hour walk from Hardrock. This morning, I had time enough to spare, but now, I ride one of the few horses we keep at the stable.

I take the cobbled avenue this time, unwilling to risk any delay. As I approach the imposing fortress carved into the heart of the Shadow Peaks, I pass magnificent beasts with coats of night sky, silver horses with eagle wings, and the odd unicorn, though they're known to be wilder than the fae.

I have Bess. She's brown and white and silly. We stop whenever she feels like it, she often trots backward, and I know better than to tell her when she's supposed to eat or drink.

I dismount Bess a little way away from the entrance, near a mountain stream.

"Spend your night as you wish, but don't wander too far." None of this sounds like an order, because it isn't. We have an understanding. She doesn't test my patience and I don't interfere with her life more than I ought to.

I walk up to the entrance of the royal stronghold, the hood of my cape low on my head. To get to the fortress, we have to cross a moat dug so deep there's nothing to see at the bottom except a thick mist. When the mood strikes, the queen opts to tie the wings of a fae and throw them up from the highest tower, instead of cutting off their head. The folk are easily irked, and easily cruel.

There are four gates in front of the bridge leading up to the fortress. A long line of folk waiting for their turns to be allowed in bars the first. They'll be given a chance to enter if and only if the queen wishes to see them tonight. More than often, she doesn't. The second is less crowded, reserved for those who have an actual reason for being here—an appointment, or an invitation. It's wide open, though somber goblin guards look down, their mouths peeled away from their pointed teeth, tasting the air as if they can sniff a drop of treason. The third, closed, is the gate of courtiers. They can enter as they please, though it's also guarded. The goblins on that side seem bored, half asleep.

The last gate might have appeared like an empty archway to an undiscerning eye, but I see waves of strange colors flowing around it, emitting an energy that calls to me. There's no guard; none are needed. Anyone who attempts to cross those gates without having the right to will suffer the most excruciating curses and die before they manage a couple of steps. An old spell, older than any living folk, I think.

I head to that gate and cross it, ignoring the eyes trailing me. As I pass through the energy barrier, a burst of unnatural wind pushes my hood off my hair. I can feel my face heat as I lift it down over my eyes again.

Another reminder I am royal after all.

The courtiers on the bridge slow down and part ways to let me pass, eyes trained on me. They're trying to place me. There are a few of us; I could be any of my cousins, any of my aunts. But I am shorter. They don't recognize me. Those who've seen me don't remember me.

I am no one.

The waves of resentment and disdain rising inside me come at no surprise. I hate and despise them all; the worms that follow wherever their queen leads. They'd do anything for the favor of royals. They're sheep.

I'm too quick to rise to anger, especially here. And I can't afford to be.

I keep my eyes forward, heading straight for the Hall of Crowns, where I've been summoned.

When I reach the doors, I finally remove the hood, letting it fall on my shoulders. I plaster the best smile I can manage on my face, and I clear my throat, turning to the stunned knight posted in front of the hall.

He doesn't seem to have any problem placing me. He's looking at me as if I am a shocking thing. Maybe I am.

"Nevlaria, for the queen, at her request," I tell him, with some authority.

As if stung awake, he shakes his head and rushes to open the doors. I hear him whisper to the master of ceremony on the other side. Then the sound of a wood staff hitting the paved marble floor three times stops all conversation.

"Your queen would like her privacy," says a voice I can't quite place, though I've heard it before.

I forget all things of the court, when I can manage to.

The doors open again, wide this time, and stay that way, as a swarm of courtiers hasten to leave before the queen grows impatient with them. Her orders are carried out with alacrity.

I wonder what she's done to deserve such obedience, such respect. Then, I remember how fast I've rearranged my life today, to get here as soon as possible, and I have my answer.

She's earned it through fear.

When the hall is empty of all save for the two figures at the back of the great room, seated on two thrones atop a golden dais, and the seven animals at their feet, I am announced.

Morgana could receive me in a private chamber, rather than empty the heart of the court to allow us privacy, but she likes to tower over me from her place of power. To remind us both of where we stand.

"Nevlaria Rose of the line of Oberon, daughter of Ciera, humbly presents herself to your majesties." I make no mention of my father, or the queen. Morgana doesn't recognize the Banes, and she doesn't recognize me. I don't get to claim her kinship. Instead, I name her consort, Alven Oberon, now at her side.

My grandfather nods in acknowledgement.

I walk forward, head high, and I can't help laughing at myself.

Humbly.

There's nothing humble about me today; I wear my best, my mother's best, and I behave like the princess I will never be.

But compared to the two gentry on the thrones, I am humble.

They're covered in gold, from the tips of their shoes to their heads. I understand the saying, now. Heavy is the head that wears the crown. It needs to be, with all that to carry. The queen's satin gown is a thing of wonder, stitched with starlight, or so it seems. Her familiars are all equally magnificent. A giant wolf, though they're rarely tamed, an ageless stag with antlers so large he'd had trouble passing through the doorway, a wyrcat, licking its paw of fae blood, a raven fixing me with its clever gaze, and the three serpents at her feet—one white, one evergreen, the last, dark as night.

Seven. She has as many as Nyx, a sign that the land has recognized her as queen and blessed her. Familiars increase the power of their lords, and stand alongside them in a fight.

I allow myself a second to gaze upon their magnificence before sinking to the floor in a well-practiced curtsy I never make use of anywhere except here.

I'm grateful for the Whitecroft education. I'd have no idea what to do here without it. My mother has always hated the stiff ways of the court—she wouldn't have taught me any of this.

Seconds pass like the first raindrops before a downpour; one at a time, soft and silent, promising sorrow.

Then she speaks. "Rise." Her voice is as beautiful as the rest of her.

I obey.

I should feel sorry for my tormentor. Her desire to destroy me is written on every one of her features, marked in her sneer, tattooed in her flesh. The one thing stronger is her desire to use me.

If I can be controlled, I'm an ace in her sleeve. The secret weapon that can change everything if there's ever an attack on her person.

Our kind isn't what one would call a peaceful bunch. The gentry live for centuries, and we're prone to violence. We've started wars for no other reason than shaking things up a little. Now that our courts are united, our enemy of choice are the seelie in the north—mostly because they're as resilient and powerful as we, so our conflicts are interesting—but we're not above waging wars on the Sea Lands, the immortals, the mortals, and even the Wilderness. Having someone like me to help can be useful.

I could have been, in any case.

Morgana Lilwreath willed it otherwise.

That her daughter had eloped with a common fae without a drop of gentry blood was inexcusable. The moment Ciera Lilwreath linked herself to Nero Bane, she ceased to exist as far as the court was concerned.

My birth changed things. Children of the high fae are rare enough to be celebrated, no matter their descent. And though the least of the royals, my mother was still a daughter of the realm. So, I was named right here in a shrine at the heart of the mountains, among the cries and cheers of the court.

It is said that Morgana smiled when she first saw me. I can't decide if I believe it. It's a possibility. Despite our difference in heights, I look like her, more so than my mother, or any of my aunts, uncles, and cousins. As a child, there must have been some hint of that.

Then I reached out to touch her hand. Instead of closing my fist around her finger as most children might have, I absorbed some of her energy.

I couldn't help it; not as a baby, not as a child, not as a teenager. I can barely help it now.

Power over life. Power over death. I was blessed with the very ability Nyx herself had wielded.

She rode to battle with her seven familiars, on the back of a giant wolf named Shadow, and it's even said she was queen of crows. Her power—my power—was enough to conquer all the lands she passed through.

As a child, I was fascinated by her. I remember studying each and every one of the paintings of her I've had a chance to come across. Even now, I can rarely resist a smile when I see her effigy. She was a legend, and none of her descendants had ever shared her gift.

Until me.

Morgana could have embraced me despite the threat I pose to the realm, to the court, to her rule. That's too much to ask, I guess. But I suspect that if she'd carried me in her arms and cooed at me back then, things might be different.

Instead, she drew a claw and branded a seal on my shoulder to limit my reach, sealing my powers inside me. The spell didn't last—by my tenth year, my power had grown beyond it. It still hinders me, causing me pain every time I slipped and used the magic in me, but I've grown beyond it. I welcome the pain, just as I welcome my magic.

Morgana has been shackling me ever since, one way or another. When her hex ceased to matter, she threatened my family, my home, our court and its folk. My life.

That never fails to work. I've learned to be polite, deferential, subdued. I've learned submission.

As she watches me from the dais lifting her golden throne, her purple eyes full of ire, I am the picture of affability. "It's been so long, Grandmother Queen. Grandfather."

The queen's consort smiles back.

Morgana doesn't. "Nevlaria." Her greeting is half curse, half insult.

My name was chosen by she. I'm not fluent in the old language, but it means something along the lines of Daughter of Nothing.

Girl of the Void.

I like it well enough.

"The knights alerted me of a disruption in the Court of Mist."

At her side, my grandfather inclines his head, ever so slowly, his midnight eyes fixed on me. I don't need him to voice the warning. I have to be careful about what I say now. Very careful.

It takes every ounce of strength I possess, but I manage to lower my eyes to my hands in submission, feigning shame. "I'm so sorry, Grandmother. I had a nightmare." I bite my lip. "I must have thrown a pillow down to the ground in my sleep, breaking the salt circle around my bed."

I've prepared many such excuses in advance, just in case anything ever happened. It's the first time I've had to use one in decades.

This one is the most appropriate today; it's formulated like a guess, which allows me to lie. Saying that I had no idea what happened wouldn't have gone well. Ignorance was dangerous. I didn't need her to tell me that.

The queen narrows her eyes. She's no more stupid than my father. Having a family made up of hundred-year-old wise creatures can be frustrating.

At long last, she speaks. "Do not let this happen again, Nevlaria. For your sake."

I won't.

I can't.

I like being alive, for some reason. Despite the shackles, the curses, the futility of it all, I want to linger in this world.

I curtsy, and start to turn my heels.

"You're not dismissed."

Of course not. My luck didn't stretch that far.

"You will attend Samhain at court this year."

I can't hide my surprise.

Save for the times when she has to lecture—or threaten—me, the queen generally likes me to stay in the Court of Mist, far from the high court. Now she's inviting me to a revel?

Not just a revel, *the* revel of the autumn. Samhain is celebrated throughout Tenebris. Everywhere, there will be feasts, dances, revels through the night and day. Wine and blood will flow like water down a stream, gentry and pucks will end up dancing naked until they all collapse. Most of the children of the folk were conceived on Samhain.

I don't know how the high court celebrates; I doubt it includes naked dances and drunken muddy romps with strangers.

"It's time you're seen and appraised here." The queen feeds a grape to the raven on top of her throne. "I won't have you sully our name cleaning up after lower-borns for much longer."

I work as an assistant, and she makes it sound like I scrub latrines. I bite my tongue.

And *seen and appraised*? What in the name of the gods does she mean?

Then it hits me. She wants to match me.

Of course she does.

A hundred years ago, she did it to my mother. The salamander the queen picked for her daughter was a brutal warlord who'd run through three wives in as many decades. While he hadn't actually been accused of killing any of them, I wouldn't have been surprised. But Morgana found him suitable, because he was heir to the Court of Ash and had an army nigh on as large as the royal forces.

I'd be sold like cattle too, if she could manage it.

I don't know why I didn't expect it. Naivety, no doubt. My entire life, I'd thought she'd want to use me a different way—for my power, not my flesh.

Morgana apparently had no issue killing two birds with one stone. I could be her weapon and her latest piece of meat for sale at the same time.

I feel like the human brunette on display in the market square this morning. I wonder how she'd managed to smile.

"I'm meant to be working on Samhain, my queen. I wouldn't want to disappoint Lady Frost."

The queen bares her elongated canines—two sets of fangs that she keeps hidden when she wishes to appear pleasant.

So, never in my presence.

"And you wish to disappoint me?"

Definitely the wrong thing to say. I'd had no response prepared for this specific situation.

To my surprise, Grandfather comes to my aid. "We'll talk to Lady Frost, Vlari." His eyes still convey a clear message to me: be careful. "I'm certain Her Grace will agree we wouldn't want you to miss your share of amusements."

I don't have a choice, and I know it.

I belong to the realm.

I belong to the queen, until my death.

Or hers.

six

matters of the heart

"Vlari."

Once away from the great hall, I run out of the royal caves like the devil's hounds are on my tail, eager to escape the court and everything it stands for. Not many calls could have halted my path.

Almost no one here would dare command me. They wouldn't even dare try here, for attempting to do so would be questioning our matriarch's rule.

The high queen leads the court, the realm, and her descendants hold the same status: we're the high heirs. The notion that the eldest male should be crown prince and inherit the rule of the realm simply because of the power of the Almighty Elder Penis is entirely mortal. Our kind doesn't calculate the worth of an individual based on age or sex. What matters is the extent of our own powers, intelligence, and influence. In reality, how much the queen likes or dislikes us also plays a great part.

At the moment, the favorite is my aunt Krona. I don't know her well enough to judge whether her taking the crown would be an improvement over Morgana's rule, and I may not have to find out. Two of the high princesses have already been murdered by one or another of their siblings. Krona might die, Morgana might choose another heir. I can't say I pay much mind to the machinations of the court. I don't think Morgana will let the crown pass on anytime soon in any case.

Technically, any one of us, descendants of Morgana, may be the next ruler of the realm. She'll name one when the time comes—or we'll get to fight for the throne if she dies without choosing an heir. Thus, it is understood that every single member of the court, save the queen herself, is below us.

The least of the royals I might be, but my birthright still buys me some peace here. By folk law, I answer to no one except the queen, and the queen is done with me.

I stop all the same, and turn to my grandfather.

Alven Oberon has little to no power in the high court. He is king of the Court of Mist, technically, but as he hasn't stepped a foot in his land for centuries, that power has evaded him. When he was chosen as consort to Morgana, the domain fell into neglect, as the queen took up all of his time. Before I was born, Alven gave the ruling of the court over to my mother. I often wonder whether the queen was angry about it, but it was his to give.

All in all, a high king consort is nothing; an elevated concubine.

I could leave if I wanted to.

I don't. We have a strange relationship, he and I. We both know his wife hates me. We're allies, nonetheless. As much of an ally as my enemy's partner could ever be.

And family. While I struggle to acknowledge Morgana and I share blood, there's no doubt of my kinship to the king, though I share no features with him.

His gaze hasn't changed since he stood at his wife's side moments ago. Stern, full of accusations and caution.

While Morgana's disapproval is born of hatred and mistrust, Alven only wears this look when I've disappointed him.

Alven and Morgana are married—not bound or mated. They have a hundred-year-long contract, signed for political reasons. They've renewed it three times. No mystical link binds their souls.

When Morgana decided to have children, she picked the most suitable partner to conceive them. Alven Oberon was a child of Skye, and she, a daughter of Nyx; the two most acclaimed unseelie queens in the history of our race. Alven also had the blessing of a human father, which meant that the likelihood of conceiving children with him was higher than with most gentry. Their union was born of greed and power, as many are in the royal family.

Alven never has—and never will—say a word against his wife. She's queen; he's the breeder she chose to bind herself to. But unlike his wife, he's shown interest in me. I know better than to trust him, but every time I've seen him, I've noted that he does what he can for my welfare.

I might be wrong. He might just be one of the many ways the queen keeps me under her control.

A hand on my hip, I glare. "What?"

I'm tired of being treated like I kicked a litter of puppies for fun tonight. I had a bad dream, that was all.

My annoyance only shows now because it's safe to do so. Alven won't slit my throat, or throw me down to crash at the bottom of the moat.

I'm a coward, and I hate it.

He tilts his head, gesturing for me to follow him.

I glance left, to the doors leading out to the bridge. So close. I could have been out within a minute.

With a sigh, I turn and follow after him. It would be foolish to sneer at my one ally here at court. A consort has no direct power, but who knows what influence he has on the queen, in the dead of night, when he whispers on her silk pillow? There's a chance that my continued survival is his doing—at least partially.

King Alven takes me through the corridors on the west wing, opposite the Hall of Crowns and to a network of smaller hallways.

The fae rushing past us are in plain uniforms, with caps and aprons. We're in the servants' quarters.

He opens a few rooms, till he finds one fit for his purpose: it's dark and empty.

He leads me in. I follow, eyes narrowed, my entire body ready to pounce or fly at a moment's notice. This is too strange, too outside of our usual ways. *What's going on?*

The moment we're alone, he shouts, "What in the name of the underworld do you think you're doing?"

I can only blink.

"An entire regiment of guards at the borders of the Court of Mist reported a potent energy shift at the property, miles away from the castle, Vlari!"

I narrow my eyes, my ill humor showing. "I didn't know a regiment *was* posted around our place at all."

I had been aware that I'd been watched, actually. My temper is flaring because I don't like to be lectured more than I have to.

Alven looks like he wants to throttle me. "No? It never occurred to you that our borders might be watched?"

I bite my lip. The Court of Mist is the westernmost land of Tenebris; it's logical that our army would be posted around us. The thought that my magic might have reached them, as far as they might have been, is chilling.

What did I do last night? I've never been more frustrated.

After a long interlude, he speaks again, slowly, with a visible effort to control himself. "If you ever need to use your power, you need to be smarter about it. A lot smarter."

Oh, bother. "I didn't try to do anything." I want to stomp my foot like a child, my irritation rising to an alarming point.

Now that it's clear I'm not going to be killed, I'm angry. At the world. At the realm. At *him* for being married to my enemy.

I keep it in as best I can. He deserves my screams. He doesn't deserve what will come if I don't control myself. I grit my teeth as I strain to hold myself back. "I have no clue what happened. *None.*"

My father, my grandfather, the queen. No one believes me. They think I'm trying to be clever, hiding my purpose. They might even think that a conspiracy is brewing. I *want* to be that smart. But I don't have any idea why my power surged last night. I'm simply not as devious as any of them think I am.

I just wish I was.

Alven is startled, speechlessly assessing me. I can tell he's trying to decide whether he should trust me on this.

I shouldn't begrudge him. While the high fae can't lie, we find new, constructive ways to deceive each other on a daily basis. Omission. Twisted words, skirting around the truth.

I've spoken plainly enough though. At long last, he nods to accept my version of the event. "If that's the case, then you need to learn to keep your heart much closer to your chest."

I don't quite understand what he's telling me, but nearly seven decades of acquaintance have taught me that asking for clarification is a pointless endeavor. He won't explain himself. For my sake, more than his.

Walls have ears in these finely carved, sculpted caves. Even in the servants' quarters.

My heart?

I didn't think I had one worth mentioning.

I leave court a lot more confused than I was when I walked in.

Granted, my head is on my shoulders. There's that.

I find Bess a few feet away from where I left her, grazing grass. She neighs at me, warning me against attempting to disturb her snack.

Everyone is ordering me about today. Even my damn horse.

I'M LATE FOR work, but I head home first, once Bess allows me to mount her.

I reach the beech woods surrounding the domain my parents claim, and leave Bess to find her way back to the stables; I don't have the time to head there and back on foot. I leap from tree to tree—my preferred method of transport if the woods allow it—to speed up my pace until I'm in front of the ancient, crumbling castle.

White stone in some parts, wood in others; there's even an iron tour from the old days when the gnomes and dwarves of the west used to live here. They moved to Nithavellir a few hundred years ago.

It's beautiful in its unapologetic oddness. And it's ours.

My parents wait for me in front of the golden gates, Nero holding Ciera's shoulder. They're an odd couple—she, a lithe beauty with sharp cheekbones and cunning eyes, towering over her mate by an entire head, though my father wears heeled boots. He's shaped like any sprite, thinner than the gentry, almost fragile compared to us, with hair and eyes the blue of the deep sea. Lady Frost tells me that in her circle, their story is considered romantic; the princess and the boy who could have been a servant. My father's a musician, to his mother's dismay. She prefers professions that require washing blood off one's sleeves on a daily basis.

One look at them, and I'm glad I've decided on the delay. They're a mess. Anxiety radiates from their every pore.

I leap from a twisted branch, over the gates, and land at their feet.

My arms circle their shoulders in a tight embrace that makes me feel like a little girl.

"I faced little threat today." A lie of sorts. They know it, I know it. This meeting could have gone a different way. No doubt the gallows were already ready on the city square. But the tongues of fae can often manage a lie or two, as long as we ensure we use adequately vague adjectives. What does little mean, at the end of the day? It could change from one person to the next. A little murder before dinner was quite more to contend with than a little salt on potatoes.

Little always lies.

"The witch wanted to know why I slipped this afternoon. I explained I slept badly. She invited me to Samhain." The condensed version of events makes them sound so inconsequential. I almost believe myself.

My father sighs in relief.

My mother doesn't. Ciera knows the woman who raised her. "Samhain?"

I manage a smile. I can't deceive very well with words, so I've learned to do so with my expressions instead, when the need arises.

"Indeed. It's just a revel—they have one every week."

"Samhain is *the* winter gathering for the court, Vlari. *We* don't get summoned for these things."

There are a number of celebrations at court, but the two that matter most are Samhain and Beltane. Every other celebration are festivals invented as excuses for opening priceless wine and dancing, whereas the two original fests follow the beginning and end of the harvest seasons. Celebrating them is essential to the welfare of the realm; during Samhain, the lords give back magic into the land to ensure that the crops and game survive the winter. In a land where magic and nature are so closely linked, it is ill-fated to ignore the traditions.

The royals haven't summoned my parents to court—not since my mother's marriage—and me? I am persona non grata, except for the occasional appearance, like tonight.

Trying to dismiss this was going to be pointless.

Thankfully, I had another way to evade questions.

"I just wanted to let you know I'm safe." For now. "I'm impossibly late for work."

I hug them, and turn my heels, ignoring my mother's protests. She wants to know what was going on.

That makes two of us.

seven
a wind of change

The duchess Lera Frost employed me without so much as an interview the moment I applied for the position of assistant in her household. This is the labor of sprites, imps, brownies, and pucks—rare are the gentry who ever covet such positions. Our kind are landlords, politicians, soldiers, not mere servants.

Daughter of a rich family, Lera Frost and her dowry caught the eye of Duke Genrion Frost, a commander in the queen's army, about two centuries ago. Back then, there were whispers about Genrion only liking her for her fortune, but they renewed their vows, though he'd already gotten his hands on all her money by then, so it must have been love.

Despite that, the gentry never quite accepted her, for the same reason they couldn't accept my father.

The difference between common fae and the gentry isn't so much in our physical appearance or abilities; most of us are winged, some are marked by nature, with horns or feathers on their hair, skin green as moss, and clawed feet. The real difference is that common fae are known to be blessed with little magic, while the gentries come from lines that have traditionally been granted higher powers. For that reason, some gentries thought it the duty of their kind to only breed with other gentries—or humans—in order to preserve our strength.

It's sheer nonsense. There are weak gentries and strong common fae. We're individuals, defined by our own abilities, not our race. I'm proof of that. Rystan Drusk is proof of that.

I like Lera well enough, and I sympathize with her ordeal.

She loves having me as her pet; none of her peers can boast of having their very own princess at their beck and call.

Not that anyone actually considers me a princess, but Lera likes it all the same.

She dismisses my apologies when I arrive four hours later than I ought to.

She's having guests today; her circle of powdered ladies, wrapped in silk and furs. Lera has me playing the harp while they have tea, though my skills are barely above passable with any instrument. She just wants me to be seen and heard.

I can't say I mind.

At my age, many fae live alone—in Hardrock, or in the lower courts, where life is cheaper. There are entertainments and friendships to be had, but I decided to wait at home for a while. My parents couldn't possibly manage alone, financially.

My mother has no trade. She keeps the house, and feeds us with her bow and arrows. Though a decent hunter, she doesn't have the physical strength to drag around enough substantial game or to sell it. She kills what we, and our small household of knights and servants, eat. Herself, my father and grandmother, me, one sprite, a handful of imp maids, a brownie, and three goblins—that's enough mouths to feed to keep her busy.

My father plays just about any instrument, though he's a master at the viola. He's often commissioned at social gatherings such as these, but his income is barely enough to keep the house, grounds, and take care of the small town around our keep. The nonessentials—such as roof maintenance—are neglected.

I'd feel guilty wasting money on a place of my own when they so desperately need my assistance. And I love the Court of Mist, fallen though it might be.

Needing the money makes any task Lera demands of me manageable. So what if I have to butcher another autumn ballad on that daft instrument? There are worse trades. My earnings paid for the renovation of the roof on half the house so far this year. Before winter's here, I should have enough to get the rest of it done, which will prevent me from waking up under two feet of snow again.

My apartments are in a deserted part of the house, away from any other living thing. For that reason, renovating it has been at the bottom of the list of priorities. I don't mind the rain so much, though I must admit I prefer when it stays outside of my bedroom.

I have other ways to pay for the roof—I could ask those who owe me favors to lend me the builders or give materials—but working is no hardship. What else would I be doing in the early hours of the night, when all those I frequent have trades of their own?

I could spend my time in the market, but I'd grow bored of it if I had nothing else to do.

"Does she sing, too?" Flora Hawthorn asks Lera.

I grit my teeth, expecting the answer.

"Oh, Nevlaria is a sweetheart. She does absolutely whatever you want her to do. Vlari, dear, would you sing for us?"

Of course I will.

I hum among the notes my inept fingers play, wondering what song I'm least likely to destroy.

No daughter of Nero Bane could have failed to understand a thing or two about music—I was born wrapped in piano sheet music and winter songs in the gardens. It doesn't mean that I'm any good at rendering it.

But she overpays, and tips too.

Long is the night where the maiden roams,
Long is the road, so far from home,
Dear is the river running down the mountain,
And sweet is the blood running 'round the fountains.
She drank at his neck,
Kissed his lips,
He took a promise,
Rotten at the tips.
Long is the night where the maiden hunts,
Steep is the wall to clawless hands.
Run, run, mortal man,
For fair is the maiden and sweet is the hunt.

Seasonal, if a little bloodier than most popular tales. I can't quite tell if it talks of a hag or a white lady—it could even be a siren. There's no lack of females fond of flesh in the Immortal Lands.

My ballad is met with applause, which means that none of them know a thing about music at all.

I plaster a smile on my lips and turn to acknowledge my audience.

Then my fingers freeze over the strings. So does my mouth.

At the door, there's a man I haven't seen since Whitecroft. A man I didn't think I'd ever see again.

He's changed in fifty years. He's always been broader and taller than most gentry, but now, he's ridiculous, his frame taking up most of the doorway leading to Lera's drawing room, his large shoulders considerably bulkier than anyone else in the room, knights included.

He wears black breeches that accentuate the line of his narrow hips and light flat boots so similar to the ones I favor, though his are encrusted with blue jewels at the ankles—sapphires, that he also wears on two rings and a heavy gold necklace at his throat. His long coat and vest are equally dark; one velvet, the other damask.

Drusk looks like a lord of Tenebris. I can't reconcile myself with this vision. It doesn't compute in my mind. He's Drusk, the boy who defies all authority, the boy who never tried to fit in. All had flocked to him despite his difference. Maybe even because of it.

I shouldn't be this shocked and disturbed to see him, but I am.

Last night, I dream of our first meeting, and freak out so much my power bursts out, and now he's here? It makes no sense.

The rest of the room notices him. "Oh, Drusk! Wilden mentioned you'd come by today. You're early. Come, sit."

He's here to see Wilden, the duchess's son. It makes sense that he would.

Rystan grins—or smirks—and joins the squealing ladies.

They don't even pretend to pay attention to me anymore. I stop singing, playing a low, slow song even I can't mess up, as they flutter around the newcomer like moths to a light.

Lady Molton squeals, visibly delighted. "We heard about the attack!"

Lera fixes her with one of her rare cautioning stares. "Such a shame."

Molton blushes and sighs. "Yes, all those people."

"You were heroes!"

I have no idea what they're talking about; I feel off balance. I don't follow politics closely, but if all of them have heard of something, it feels like I should have, too. Lera usually tells me whatever tidbits she hears from her circle.

Of course, it didn't help that I arrived impossibly late today.

"So very glad you're home safe..."

"How are your wounds?"

"You were so brave!"

It sounds like there was an attack. I can't help it; I'm interested. I want to join them. I want to ask questions. I'm a moth, and he's my flame.

I force my fingers to move on the strings again, slowly, and with more care than before. I give it all my attention, all my passion.

Even I, daughter of Nero, who's heard the best players in the land practice at home when they've visited my father, admit that today, I don't play badly, though I can't recall which song I pick.

To my shame, I still hear them. Part of me is paying attention to the ladies and their guest, refusing to let myself get lost in my song.

The dozens of ladies don't let him get a word in at first. He chuckles.

"You flatter me." His voice has changed, too, in all this time. It's lower. Darker. More indecent. "I did nothing beyond my duty. And I was lucky to escape the assault. I've been given the rest of the week to rest, and I'll return to my post shortly."

"Surely not!" Lady Frost exclaims, clearly disappointed she wouldn't get a lot of time to parade her newest treasure. "Wilden said you'd be around for a while this time."

"Indeed. I have to undergo some rehabilitation, so I've been posted at the royal keep, where I can get the care I need, and serve under the command of the king consort."

My fingers slip, gripping the wrong chord and bringing the attention back to me.

The first thing I see—the only thing I see—is his gaze.

That hasn't changed at all. His eyes are still dark and deep, midnight black with a hint of blue, like his hair. And as they did back then, they look at me as though I am a menace he intends to dispose of.

I can't blame him. I feel the exact same thing about him; from the very start, I'd detected that he was a threat.

I suspect he doesn't quite know what to make of it. I'm just Vlari—the weak, the meek, the irrelevant.

I feel my face heat as I mumble an apology for my slip, and resume my song.

Rystan Drusk. Back here?

That cannot be good.

At all.

I studied at Whitecroft from age fifteen to twenty-five, like any other member of the gentry. In the first years, I was mostly ignored, occasionally teased.

Rystan Drusk, age nineteen, joined us when I was sixteen, as his lessons, back where he came from, hadn't been as demanding as the ones we nobles undergo. He finished school in five years, leaving when I was in my early twenties. I heard in passing that he joined the army.

He was no one to me. I shouldn't be so rattled to see him again.

I'm not.

I've only spoken to him twice. He doesn't matter at all.

eight
air of madness
fifty years ago

I doodled in the corner of my long parchment sheet with my favorite purple quill to combat boredom, my ethnography test on seelie customs long completed.

I wasn't entirely certain why I remained in my seat. Habit, I guess. I was accustomed to being as unremarkable as I could manage in class—finishing my work in a few minutes when we were given an entire hour didn't seem incompetent enough.

As the hour had almost come to a close, and some of my classmates were beginning to leave, I was considering handing my work when I bristled in alarm, my head snapping to the windows.

An attack.

It didn't make sense. We were safe here.

Long ago, all the way back to the reign of Nyx, the queen built this place.

At the core of our very land, she built ley lines diverting some of the magic from the lesser courts, in order to ensure direct control over the provinces. Finding one spot where all ley lines converged, at the heart of Tenebris, she knew that no lord could claim this territory.

I wondered whether she'd considered moving her court there, but the Shadow Peaks have magic of their own, and I didn't think she would have liked leaving the ancestral home of her clan. Instead, she built our school. An establishment that didn't quite belong to any of the courts, standing at the edge of all seven soils.

It was guarded by knights, wards, and nightmares. Our lessons were taught by the fiercest heroes and monsters of legends. Nothing but the best for us.

Not just anyone attended Whitecroft. It is reserved for the children of nobles, rich gentries, and, occasionally, a few notable kids who exhibited uncommon powers. In my days, that only occurred twice—a girl who started before me, and Drusk, one year after.

I owed my place to my lineage—I was a legacy, and therefore, entitled to attend free of charge, to everyone's displeasure. Mine, most of all. I had nothing in common with the rest of them. Our family was scorned by the queen, which was reason enough for the nobles to detest the sight of me.

While I would have fared better at home, under the tutelage of our people, my mother had insisted that I was to learn alongside my peers. It might have had something to do with the fact that I never learned to curtsy or talk like I should in my childhood. My parents were too kind, letting me run free in the hob-infested shrubs and roll in muddy swamps with ballybogs. I even flew in the woods, uncouth as showing my wings may be.

It was rare for Ciera to ever insist on anything—trusting her reasons, I suffered through the scornful disdain.

At least, while no one liked me here, they weren't bold enough to tell me so to my face. They weren't bold enough to approach me at all. I outranked them. A fact that warmed my cold little heart when I despised them most. I outranked them, and they hated it.

Between the ley lines, the protection of the queen, the knights, and the actual dragon teaching there, the notion that Whitecroft could be attacked was inconceivable. Yet there was no denying it: a round shot wrapped in fire was headed right to us, at a considerable speed, as if projected from a cannon.

Whitecroft was built in a time when windows weren't considered fashionable—weathering the seasons, bitter or smoldering as they may be, was a show of strength, according to ancient nonsense. We had columns, alcoves, and archways leading right onto the playgrounds, the river, or the marshes, depending on what part of the keep we were in.

I barely had time to straighten up—Miss Moss moved like a tornado, placing herself in the way of the weapon. She caught it, and the flames disappeared. Only then did I realize it wasn't a cannonball at all—or an attack. Feeling foolish, I rolled my eyes. She was holding an oval, smoking leather ball in her grasp. One of the other classes must have been playing Kings out there—one of the stupider popular games our kind indulged in. They ran around a field with four goal posts with symbols of each of the four elements, and gathered points by throwing the balls inside nets—it could only enter them when the ball was charged with the matching element. I didn't pretend to understand more than the basics about it. Games might have interested me more had I been allowed to engage in them.

"Who threw this?" Our tutor spoke quietly, wrapping a threat around each syllable. I almost felt bad for the players outside.

Miss Moss was incontestably the scariest thing in Whitecroft.

I frequented more terrifying women on a daily basis, but to those who'd never shouldered the glare of the unseelie queen, the teacher certainly was formidable.

"Sorry, ma'am. I meant no harm."

I recognized the voice, and could practically see dimples flash all the way from my seat.

Drusk.

The boy spent a year in my class, catching up on the many things he hadn't been taught where he used to live. Then, our tutors bumped him up four grades. He was to graduate that year, though he was only twenty-four. He'd have completed his education in less than half the usual allotted time.

I couldn't pretend not to envy him. For that, and other things.

Like his freedom.

Drusk had an older power, just like me—a rare magic defying the logic of elemental sorcery. But his was praised, nurtured. Mine was all but snuffed out. He was a Myst, a shadow wielder. So long as he's in the dark, he can summon and control shadows, to conceal, transport, and yes, destroy too. I saw him set many things on fire when he concentrated too hard. Myst is a power with almost no limit, to those who can control it.

Our tutor's lips curved up. I hadn't been aware that Miss Moss could smile until then.

From the very first day, Drusk charmed the teachers, and the knights, and the pretty ladies.

The rest of Whitecroft knew his wrath instead.

I knew nothing other than what I'd observed from afar. He never so much as glanced my way. I wasn't pretty enough, powerful enough, interesting enough to command his attention.

"See that you improve your aim, Mr. Drusk."

She sent the ball back to him without so much as a detention.

I rose to my feet and silently handed her my paper.

I needed out of here.

Whitecroft had a boarding option, but my home was only an hour's walk away—and I couldn't imagine a worse fate than having to remain there day in and day out.

After unseelie culture, my class just had training, and I was excused from that, due to my "fragile constitution."

I was smiling and skipping on my way out, delighted to be done for the night, when I froze, shocked to see Drusk right in front of me.

I usually felt him long before I could see any part of him. Those of us blessed with magic have the ability to sense the energy of others like us. At school, I rarely noticed anyone, given the fact that many of us, descendants of old lines, wielded magic. My alert system was on overdrive.

Drusk was distinct from most; there was a boldness, a brightness to his soul, to his very aura.

Not today. I didn't need to wonder why.

His jaw set, lips pursed, and eyes fixed forward, staring at a wall he'd just punched, judging by the fist-shaped dent in the stone. He didn't notice me, lost in his rage.

I stood still for a moment, then decided to keep going, ignoring him right back. Catching the sound of my feet on the wooden flooring, he finally turned to me.

Seeing him step awkwardly and wince, I finally understood his anger.

He was hurt. Something was wrong with his foot.

Drusk wounded. The notion didn't quite compute. He was greater than life in my mind. The boy who could do everything effortlessly.

I should have relished his suffering. Weakness was shameful to him—unacceptable—that much was clear.

Instead of basking in his pain as I should, I walked up to him, stopping too close—closer than I ever was to anyone who wasn't part of my immediate family. That was the only way I could sense the extent of his wound.

He glared down at me, eyes narrowed, but didn't say a word. Neither he nor I knew what to make of this. We never interacted. I was shaking the status quo, our reality where he was the popular, beautiful genius, and I, a mess not worth mentioning.

Observing him now, there was no doubt in my mind he knew just who I was. He didn't look at me as though he'd never seen me before. He seemed to know everything about me—and he hated all of it.

I'd changed the game. I didn't even understand it.

"A sprained ankle." Those were my very first words to him. I just stated the obvious, hardly at my wittiest.

His jaw tightened. "Dekren tackled me. It's broken."

I had to disagree. "You wouldn't be able to put any weight on it if it were broken."

"That says how much you know about me, *princess*." That couldn't have been said with more scorn.

I couldn't tell whether I snorted or chuckled; something in between, half insulted, half amused.

I'd always been aware of him. Until that night, I hadn't realized he knew of me at all, but now it was plain enough: he really did. I'm the only princess in Whitecroft.

Well, he might have called all the girls he met that. I had no clue. I never took any interest in his method of seduction.

Not that he was seducing me. He still wore a sneer.

"Isn't that thing with the lords tomorrow? The evaluation." We were all getting tests that week before the midsummer break, but those in their last year at Whitecroft were in line for worse: their parents were coming to watch them perform, train, and fight. "How will you fare on your physicals, if your ankle is broken? Or sprained, for that matter."

His black eyes flashed, burning into mine. I think he meant to frighten me. Maybe I should have been frightened.

"I heal as fast as your kind." His tone was defensive. For a moment, I wondered what it would be like to be Rystan Drusk, a boy of common stock, without any official gentry ancestor.

His physical attributes made it clear that there was at least some gentry blood in him—he was too tall to just be a puck or a sprite, too slender for an ogre or troll.

It's not unusual for servants to have gentry features—lords of manors have been known to fool around with their maids.

"And my kind would usually get better in…a day or two? When's your test?"

I didn't know why I was pushing him. Why I was talking to him at all. I should be on my way home.

He gritted his teeth. "Tomorrow."

My eyes darted down to his lame foot. I let my mind brush his, evaluating him.

"I could fix it." The words might have been a whisper, softer than wind, but they escaped all the same.

Dangerous words.

Just like that, I'd defied the unseelie high queen's wish. I'd revealed my power. Part of it. There were other kinds of magic healers, after all. I hadn't expanded on the full extent of my abilities. Morgana would have been furious all the same.

I couldn't begin to explain what madness had seized me.

He focused on me, his sullen expression morphing to something else. Something a little like intrigue.

Lifting my chin, I repeated myself, louder that time. "I could technically fix your ankle—instantly. The question would be, what would you do for me in return?"

We were already too close, then Drusk took a step forward, closing the rest of the distance between us. His legs brushed mine. Tall as he was, he towered over me, but he lowered himself to gaze right into my eyes.

"What would you want from me, princess?"

Suddenly, I felt like the power had shifted. I wasn't negotiating anymore. He was. He had the air of a predator toying with its food.

"A favor," I blurted out, without thinking.

I couldn't come up with anything on the spot, while he was gazing me down so intensely. An unnamed favor sounded like a reasonable request in exchange for a service rendered.

I think I might have surprised him, somehow. Drusk studied me, as if trying to make sense of me. I itched to fidget under the scrutiny. Instead, I stood my ground.

I half expected him to negotiate, state terms, limits, or demand that I define the favor. To my surprise, he inclined his head. "You have my word. If you can patch me up reasonably right now, you'll name a favor and I'll do it."

That seemed too easy.

He was the strongest boy of his age, the most popular male at Whitecroft, and I, his polar opposite. Yet suddenly, he'd let me claim power over him.

Madness must have been catching.

I grinned.

nine

whispers in the dark

Drusk was the first one to owe me.

I made a bit of a mess of that specific oath—it might not even be binding, though no fae can easily weasel out of their word. After taking care of his tiny little sprain, that absolutely hadn't been a break, I returned home drunk on power.

A feat, for someone like me.

My constitution makes me physically weaker, and I hadn't yet learned to fight; my one skill, I wasn't allowed to use. I'd never known I could acquire a different kind of strength until then.

A week later, overhearing Sylph Thorn and Brenne Ivy whispering about blessed waters on our lunch break out in the grove, I rolled my eyes.

Blessed waters has little use, particularly for two girls of twenty, without so much as a drop of sea fae blood in their veins, but we'd learned that it was one of the ingredients necessary to brew amoria. A temporary love spell that would get any man kneeling at their feet, begging for their kisses for an hour or two, amoria was of little use against the gentry. I could only think of one boy they might want to spell—Drusk. They wanted his attention before he left our school this year. Winter had already given way to spring; summer would be upon us in no time, and Drusk would be gone by the end of it.

Thinking of him brought an idea to the edge of my mind—a silly notion that I half dismissed.

To my surprise, I said, "I could get you some."

The girls ate their pies near the grounds' well, a few paces away from my willow tree. I knew better than to approach that well; the hag at the bottom of it could get bored and decide to snack on any of us if the inclination struck her.

They heard me all the same.

I didn't think I'd ever talked to either of them before.

Sylph was my cousin, of sorts—the same way anyone with royal blood calls ourselves cousins, evoking a common ancestor so far removed no one cared who it was. I believed our link might have come from my grandfather's side. It mattered not; we were strangers, for all intents.

Brenne's family, the Ivies, married the ruling family of the Court of Ichor, a southern kingdom of warriors. She was considered a princess in her land. Though I technically outranked either of them, their families were rich and mighty, and mine, disgraced.

I didn't expect either of them to pay me any mind, but they stopped chattering, and turned to me. They both looked shocked that I'd addressed them.

Before they recovered, I clarified, "I could get you blessed waters."

It was easy enough, all it took was a drop of royal blood given freely, in a little fresh water—my blood, not Brenne's. Since the high court rose, the land and sea stopped recognizing the local kings and queens as true authorities.

Giving one's blood wasn't something to be taken lightly, but I didn't think either of them had the mastery of sorcery it would take to curse me, or bind me to them. Besides, there was no reason why they would have wanted to. Their one desire was to get the attention of whichever boys they couldn't have.

They glanced at each other. I took a bite of the black apple in my hand and shrugged. "Just putting it out there."

We were to return for our astrology lesson any minute; I started to walk back to class.

"Wait! Would you really get us the water?" Brenne never sounded that whiny before. "I'd pay anything."

Still facing away from the two girls, I grinned, hoping no man would ever render me quite so desperate.

"I don't need money." Neither of them believed that, but it was true. Having been raised on little funds, I'd never seen the necessity of piles of money.

Our house belonged to us, the servants working there and knights sworn to us were cared for, and we had plenty of food on our table. Imps and brownies made my clothes, my mother owned plenty of jewels. I didn't think I needed material possessions back then—the beauty of youth. And the roof hadn't fallen in yet.

"I'll do it for a favor."

They accepted. I remember chuckling to myself as I saw Drusk and one of his friends, a selkie boy I never got to know—he was older than me—trip over themselves to dance with the girls at the next school feast.

I provided little things that were in my immediate power to my classmates for months; they told their friends, who told their own friends in turn, that I was the one to speak to when they needed anything.

In time, I became someone. Not someone important, perhaps, but someone whose name they all knew. People said hello when we crossed paths, even outside of school.

And the next five years at Whitecroft weren't utter torture because of my newfound influence.

The last five decades were just more of the same.

THE SECOND TIME I spoke to Drusk was at the summer ball Whitecroft held before our holiday break.

I didn't usually attend dances. They weren't my thing. But the school asked my father to play that year, which meant that he knew the day of my end of year dance; he begged and pouted until I promised I'd go with him.

I let my mother knot my hair with wild flowers and I wore one of her dresses, as none of mine could even pass for appropriate, and I saw no point in wasting money on gowns that wouldn't fit me in a few seasons. I still had hopes of growing a few inches taller, or at least larger around the chest.

I got one out of two.

Her dress was a white lace and silk gown that reached her knees, but fell to the floor on me. We knotted a large belt at my waist so that it didn't look like a tent. The result was passable, like me.

I watched my father from the edge of the clearing where the ball was held, impatiently wondering when it would end, when something bumped into me.

I narrowed my eyes and turned sharply, half expecting a prank; no one had thrown something in my direction. What crashed on me was a person; a person too distinctive for me to fail recognizing him.

He was a head taller than the professor, so I was about half his height. My mouth opened, though I don't know what I would have said.

Then he laughed, and I understood. He was drunk. Of course; the wine had flowed like a waterfall for hours. Most of my classmates were in a worse state.

"The dance is that way," I told him, pointing to his friends at the center of the clearing.

He didn't so much as glance at them. "You're here."

The banal observation was born of too much flower wine.

"Why are you here, Nevlaria? All alone by yourself."

"My grandmother calls me Nevlaria. When I'm in a lot of trouble. I answer to Vlari." I didn't try to point out that my being alone was the natural order of things.

"You do?" He seemed confused, like he'd never heard it. Instead of returning to his friends, like he should, like I expected him to do, he extended his hand. "Well, Vlari. It only took five years for a proper introduction. Nice to meet you. Drusk."

"I know." Everyone knew him.

"You never told me how you did the trick. With my ankle."

"You never asked," I shot back.

He laughed. There was no scowl from him that night. No sneering. He'd have been charming, if he wasn't the most dangerous thing there.

"And you also never named the favor I might do for you."

"I will." I wasn't stupid enough to waste Drusk's oath on a triviality. I'd use it when I needed to, not a moment sooner. "When it benefits me."

His smirk was mischievous. "You aren't going to ask me to kiss you? To touch you? I could take you right here in the shadows, against a tree." He leaned in. "I think you might like that."

It seemed surreal, so I asked the only thing I could ask. "How much did you drink?"

He shrugged. "Enough to talk to you." The insult was accompanied with a careless smile that betrayed his nature.

He was all unseelie, like my mother, like the queen. The kind of fae who relished making others squirm.

"Evidently. Have a nice life, Drusk."

Now the smile faded. "Dismissed with such impetuosity. Very well, princess. I'll endeavor to have a nice life. Till we meet again."

He bowed low and stumbled back to his group, fading in the dark, out of sight, out of my life.

Until now.

ten
dodging tricks

I only worked for half a day, but when I finally get out of the Frost estate, I feel like I've never had a longer day in my life.

I rode Wena on my way in, mounting the first of our horses I'd seen in the estate, to avoid arriving later than necessary tonight. Though I asked the beast to graze in the field where the Frosts keep their stallions, I can tell she isn't here at first glance. My fat, short mare would be easy to spot among great warhorses.

I groan and consider walking home. Who knows where the capricious girl might be now?

It's almost dawn. The clouds gathering in the lightening night sky indicate it might rain any time. Deciding the night has been unpleasant enough, I opt to avoid getting drenched through on top of everything else. I trek the ground, yelling the horse's name. My favorite green leather boots get cold and muddy in the field. My memory might be failing me, but I don't think I've ever had a night quite this horrendous before.

"Wena!"

She likes the shade of the woods. Spotting hoofprints that seem far smaller than those of the great steeds of the Frosts, I approach a path cutting through shrubbery and ash. Then I stop and spin on my heel, lifting my blade.

Drusk was all politeness, all courtesy in front of Lera; now he smirks at me, as if he knows all my secrets. As if he'd spill them out for his entertainment.

This is new. I expect veiled odium from him—unless he's had as much wine as a pirate. I don't trust his good humor one bit. I fear there's a trick, a joke coming, and it will be at my expense.

The person I have been for five decades fades away. I'm an uncertain child, inclined to run away. I hate him for it.

I consider ignoring him. I should; it would be wise. He's here to mock or infuriate me. I would have, back in our school days. I might have, another night.

I've had enough of doing what I should for the foreseeable future.

"What?" My irritation is obvious.

So is his amusement.

Drusk is always intimidating. At dawn, he's something else, too. The light makes his eyes so radiant I can't deny it: he's bewitching. The pupils are the darkest of sapphires. I could get lost in their depths, drowning as if they were a bottomless sea. He's a beautiful trap. I remember how Sylph promised me whatever favor I named for a chance to get his attention.

I'm no Sylph, but I can't say I don't understand her. I'd quite like kisses from a stunning creature such as he—if he hadn't been so terrifying. And infuriating.

I shouldn't notice. We're fae; we are beauty personified. Nature unbound, in all her splendor. All of us have been blessed by the mark of wilderness. Mortals can waste away, watching the folk dance and sing. We have wings of rainbows, eyes of lionesses, and mouths the red of human blood. Each fae is stunning and terrifying in their own right, in their own way.

Admitting that I acknowledge and appreciate *his* specific kind of pulchritude would be giving him power over me.

If there's one person in the whole of Tenebris who should never be allowed to have any more power, it's him.

Or me.

"Nothing of note. I heard screams that sounded reminiscent of a banshee, and I was intrigued. I'm quite fond of banshees."

I couldn't tell whether he meant he liked bedding them, or eating their tongues. Perhaps both. "Well, no banshee that I've noticed around here."

It would have been rather difficult to miss a shrieking spirit of the dead.

"Then it must have been you."

I start to walk away. I won't be his entertainment for the night.

His steps join mine, each stride the length of nearly three of mine. "What's Wena?"

Where is that horse?

As Drusk is still following me, I sigh. "Are you that bored?"

His smile broadens. "I hear you're often here. Wilden has been so good as to let me use a room here while I acquire a place of my own—closer to Hardrock than my folk's house. We'll see each other daily. Can't we be friends, Nevlaria?"

"Not if you call me that."

It's not fair to take my irritation out on him, but I simply don't trust him, or his intentions. I can't think one reason why Drusk, *the* Drusk, would waste his time with me on his first day back from his assignment. He has friends. Everyone from Whitecroft is his friend. Those who aren't want to be. If he's here with me, it's because of some scheme. It must be. I don't know what he wants from me, but I can't let him think he might be able to take it.

Drusk chuckles at my side. "You know, I wondered if I'd dreamed that conversation."

Smirks, smiles, and chuckles.

Has the queen sent him to keep an eye on me?

I remember his mention of my grandfather; he's posted with Alven. Perhaps I should contact the king, ask—

I shake my head. Never have I contacted the Wicked Court before. I won't start now. It's not worth the trouble I could get in if my correspondence falls in the wrong hands. If Morgana learned I conversed with her husband, who knew how she'd react?

My one instruction from the queen is to be invisible. Invisible girls don't write letters to kings.

Keep your heart much closer to your chest.

I'd felt insulted by Alven's remark just yesterday. Now I wonder whether he knows me better than I do. I am letting my emotions dictate myself right now. The only thing that should move my hand is caution, when it comes to anything related to the queen.

Drusk is intent on small talk. "You told me to call you Vlari, have you not?"

"Look, I'm tired, and I need my horse. Can we do—whatever this is—another night?"

He redirects his gaze to the woods, past me, focusing on something that seems far away. And I see his eyes change. I see him change. Power gathers around him.

I should be afraid. I should be ready to charge. He is terrifying.

And I'm intrigued.

An instant later, my horse whinnies, galloping straight to me, as fast as she can go, as though she's chased by a horde of fire-breathing demons.

I only glance to her, before turning back to Drusk.

"What was that?"

He scrutinizes my sullen face. I wonder what he reads—hopefully, annoyance. I can't interpret his expression at all. The years have shaped him into too proficient a liar. "I'm not the enemy, Vlari. I don't have to be."

He's right. I'm treating him like he is a threat. It feels right to keep doing so. Safe.

I should thank him nonetheless.

My father would.

I'm still my mother's daughter tonight. "Aren't you? You want something from me. You wouldn't be here otherwise. Here's some news for you: everyone around me wants to use me, one way or another. I choose those I put up with. You're not on the list."

I still can't read him at all, and it's beyond maddening. His smile doesn't fade, nor does his good humor, and he isn't saying a word.

I'm not the enemy.

I don't believe it. He should be. That's the natural order of things.

Wilden was one of the popular boys. He ignored me at school, but I saw him snigger at many, terrorize the weak. He's learned to be a courteous lordling. I've learned to ignore that I detest the sight of him.

While they were part of the same group, Drusk was never one to tyrannize the other students. Maybe he just liked to watch and preferred not getting his hands dirty. Maybe he didn't like it at all. Either way, if I've managed to grow past Wilden's youth, I could be nicer to Drusk.

I don't want to. I don't have to. He isn't my employer's son.

I leap on Wena's bare back and trot away. "Thanks for freaking out my horse, by the way."

I should head home, but after tonight, I have a set of needs I can't fulfill at my parents'. So I head to the Thorns.

I DIDN'T GET my own Thorn until my thirtieth year.

Sylph and I learned to tolerate each other well enough, provided we were strictly business. She is someone—she attends court regularly, never wears the same gown twice, and takes a different lover to bed every other day. Her merriments are foreign to me.

Once, visiting their estate, I met her younger sister Mephesea, who'd just finished school. Esea is another socialite, and it all ceased to matter somewhere along the way; she's a delight. We've laughed like children well into midday more times than I can recall.

Esea has no concerns like mine; money isn't an issue among the Thorns, and she doesn't need to work. But unlike me, she has a patriarch invested in everything she does, and very little freedom for the important things in her life. She can't live where she wants, practice the amusements she likes unless they are approved, frequent the friends she prefers, and of course, she won't be allowed to get married or bound unless her uncle approves it.

I think I'm the lucky one, even with the threat of Morgana in the corner. At least she leaves me alone on a daily basis. Or she used to; her summons changed much. Who's to say what'll happen at Samhain?

I was approved by Vikro Thorn, so I know I'm welcome at the Thorns', at any time of the night or day.

My frequent visits allowed me to become acquainted with another Thorn—Sylph and Esea's older brother. I make my way toward his chamber first.

Dekren and I have an easy understanding. We like each other well enough for an hour or two, and then, we both like to part ways as friends. He's a delight that has allowed me some divertissement for years.

I knock at his door. There's no answer. After a moment of consideration, I push it open. It's still early—I can wait for him to come back. He gives me free rein of his rooms whenever I wish.

Inside, I wince and laugh all at once; Dekren was in, after all, and not alone.

To my surprise, I recognize his companion, spread out on his silken bedding. The human girl with black curls and heavy breasts; bare in the starlight, I note that the cleavage was just as spectacular as it seemed to be.

The girl lifts her head when I enter. Dekren, head between her curvy legs, doesn't stop his affair.

She waves at me as I walk backward to get out of the room.

"Sorry," I murmur. "I'll leave you to it."

She mouths something I read as "*Do you have to*?"

It's all I can do to keep myself from laughing out loud as I close the door behind me. Dekren is a competent enough lover overall, but his mouth has never been his strongest point.

Commiserating with the mortal, I cruise the familiar corridors.

I wonder if Dekren bought the girl. It doesn't sound like him. I can't imagine him stepping a foot in the Light Market, for one. He's also never wanted for female companionship. He's the son of an earl, nephew of a duke of the Court of Stars. Even if he'd had the face of a troll, he would have been pursued. As it turned out, Dekren was quite the beauty—he had an almost feminine air, with his long red curls and his tall, thin frame.

I knock on another door, and this time, I am bid to enter.

Her sitting room is empty, and one glance to the bedroom shows the covers undisturbed. Going farther inside her apartment, I find Esea is in her bath, head thrown back in bliss.

Esea is a tall ethereal beauty, and though she's young, her skin is already marked by thin, intricate designs that spell out the story of her life. A rose, for mourning, a wolf, for a battle, double lines linking them.

I've never asked her what happened—it's not considered polite. After certain ordeals, the gentry of the unseelie court emerge with these drawings on our skin.

I don't have a single one on me. Maybe there's too much pixie, seelie, or sea blood in me. Maybe I just haven't achieved anything yet.

I merrily barge in. "How's the water?"

"Perfection." Nothing else would do for her. She sighs and bats her long lashes. "You wouldn't *believe* the day I've had."

Esea is pretty as a button, loving and beloved by all.

She's also incredibly dramatic.

I can only smile. She doesn't have any occupation, other than that of being her father's daughter. She stays at home, meets suitors, organizes balls, and, occasionally, shops.

"Tell me," I say, getting undressed to join her in the pool.

Her bathing pool is the size of my entire room; we've fit twelve in there before.

Her day is interesting—and also, reassuring.

My life seems to have taken too many unexpected turns these last few hours. Hearing her tale is a reminder that the world is still spinning as it should, despite my misadventures with shades, wyrs, queens, and Drusks.

She's met one of the men Vikro is considering for her, and he sounds as dreadful as can be for a woman like her. She's a bronze-skinned beauty with hair like the waves of the sea. Earth and water blended in one beautiful creature.

"He's ridiculous, wearing mustard yellow and green *and* gold. Not to mention it clashed with his hair." To her, no sin could be greater, no doubt. She's laughing at herself while talking.

What I love most about Esea is that she realizes just how silly she is.

"What was his hair like?"

"Red. He's from Ash. I think he's part salamander, part gentry. My father and uncle don't care. He's a *prince*." She couldn't say it with more contempt. "That's what matters to them. Getting a crown for the Thorns."

Listening to her woes, I truly start to calm down. This is what I needed. A reminder that being angry and frustrated and powerless isn't mine exclusively; I share these blessings with the world.

"You could marry me," I offer, playing with the bubbles and giggling with her. "That might be helpful, actually. Grandmother dearest might be thinking about matching me."

Her jaw hit the floor. "No! Truly?"

"Tell me all about it." I wince in distaste.

"Yes, tell us."

I crook my head to the side, noticing the newcomers in front of the bathroom door.

Dekren is holding the human's hand. They both got dressed—he, in a robe, and she, a satin gown the exact shade of her hair.

I can only stare in wonder. They're already finished? I can't have left them more than half an hour ago.

They slide in the pool with us.

"The queen wants me at Samhain. She says she wants me *appraised*."

"Ah. I know that word. I hear that word every other night."

The siblings grimace. Even the human is nodding. "She's definitely going to get you a suitor."

I close my eyes.

They jest about their ordeal because they know that, overbearing as their family may be in their desire to induce them into matrimony, their hands will never be forced.

The queen commands all—she's ordered some of her own children, even those she likes, to wed. With me, she'd do so with delight.

I decide I don't need to ruin our good humor. One change of subject comes to mind. "I saw Drusk tonight."

Esea gasps. "The Drusk? Sylph is going to go crazy!"

I can only laugh.

"She already knows he's back," Dekren says lightly. "He came to see me, before going to the Frosts'."

I'm reminded Dekren and Drusk were well acquainted, back in the day—they finished school together.

I frequent far too many of Drusk's friends.

Esea ignores her brother. "Tell me everything. I want to gloat at Sylph."

I do, though there isn't much to our encounters.

WHEN I'M FINALLY home, far too late, I lie in bed, rain on my face, motionless, frustrated with myself.

I am curious.

I am intrigued.

I am not myself at all.

I should have asked Drusk about the attack. I should have asked what he needed to recover from; he looked well enough. Damaging gentries for longer than a few days isn't easy, but Drusk isn't only a gentry—and someone managed to hurt him.

Most of all, I am haunted by one question. If he was in so bad a state that he needed an extended recovery, why didn't he ask me for help? He knows I can heal.

I don't spare a second to bask in my fear of the queen before fading into sleep, my mind full of the dangerous boy I have always been fascinated with.

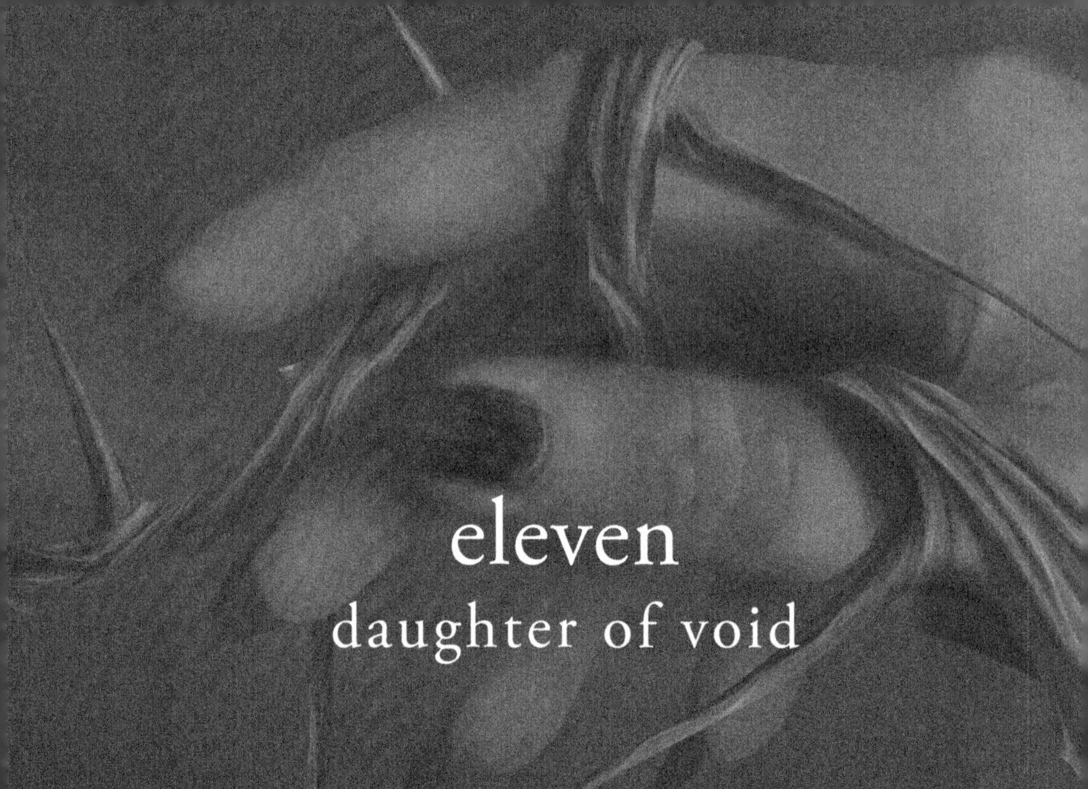

eleven
daughter of void

I don't see Drusk the next day, or the day after that. It was foolish to assume that I would; he has a position at Hardrock—soldiers and guards aren't known to keep the light, indolent schedule of the gentry—and plenty of acquaintances to visit in all courts.

My mind eases with time. I'm glad nothing changes for his being here. I don't feel childish or confused or out of breath again.

One week passes before I catch a glimpse of him, and when I do, I successfully avoid him.

Part of me longs for a confrontation. I need to shout and clash against him until he or I breaks, until I understand why he affects me so. I recognize this as the impulse of the darker, stupider beast firing the soul of any unseelie.

I work five days, and the sixth, after Meda's brutal training, I'm at leisure to wander the market, striking little bargains and hearing tales.

I'm surprised to find Padetra's stand set up. She's an infrequent vendor, usually brought by the high tide every other full moon.

Padetra and her crew travel the edges of our lands, stopping at every harbor to acquire anything she thinks she can sell.

She's by far my least favorite market dweller—not because the strong, small, graying woman is mortal, but because she's utterly uninterested in bargains, preferring cold gold coins in her palm. And yet, I never can stop myself from stopping by when she comes to us.

She's a window to the rest of the world, bringing dwarven iron, elven silks, the magic of the gods themselves, the sweetest plums, and drawings of cities I'll never see, worlds I'll never know. I hear she even ventures to the Wilderness, under the protection of one of the untamed tribes.

Today, she's escorted by a boy who looks to be my age; his sun-kissed skin and bulk mark him as one accustomed to labor, but I notice his eyes above anything else—so like Padetra's. Her son, or grandson perhaps. I smile at him, as I'll no doubt have to deal with him directly in a decade or two. This stand was minded by Laurelei, Padetra's mother, before she passed. Such is the nature of mortals.

The boy reddens to the tips of his ears and blurts out, "May I help you?"

Before I can decline his assistance, the old human croaks a laugh. "Oh, I don't think so. Never let this one sweet talk you, boy. She'll have you dancing to her tune in no time. Get the rest of my books!"

He rushes to obey.

"You're making me sound like such a temptress." I'm not displeased at that notion, and I must show it, because the merchant laughs.

"I think not, but the boy has a soft spot for little, helpless girls."

I grimace at her assessment of me, wishing I could unsheathe my blade and show her just how helpless I am.

I'm not without pride. Thankfully for her wrinkled neck, I'm well practiced in hiding it. "You have books?"

I've read precious little. Books are costly, and purchasing them is never a priority in the Bane household. In my school days, we were given textbooks, poems, and spellbooks for our studies, and I don't think I've touched more than a handful of volumes since then.

"You have money?" she returns.

I do, but it can't be squandered for my amusement.

I don't give an answer, looking at the trinkets on her table. One curved dagger with a black edge and a wooden hilt, and a goblet carved in bone catch my eye first, then I frown. Underneath the goblet, there's a thick leather-covered book locked by a heavy silver chain.

I like books well enough, mostly because they're the kind of luxury I don't have access to, but this one enraptures my attention at first glance.

At the center of the embellished cover, one signet has been stamped into the leather. It's a V, with the left branch smaller than the right and at a deeper angle, and with a line crossing through the middle of the letter. Splitting it like that makes it look like V.N.

It's mine. V for Vlari. N, for my full name. I've signed like this as long as I could remember. I've never seen anyone else write like this, but here is my mark, sealing a dusty manuscript that looks older than any of the courts.

I push the goblet aside and take the book. It's heavy and smells rotten, moldy and foxing on the borders. I bet half the pages have crumbled away. I can't tell: the book is locked tight.

"Hey! No touching if you can't pay." Padetra is grouchy as ever.

"How much?" I counter.

She isn't impressed. I often browse her stand, but I've never purchased anything from her. "Too much."

She doesn't bother adding *for you.*

"What, my gold isn't good enough for you?" I unhook the pouch at my belt and the coins inside jingle.

She considers me, eyes narrowed, trying to gauge how much I'd be willing to spare. I replace the book where I've taken it, nonchalant as I can manage to be.

"Five gold coins."

I laugh. That's all I can do. Yet, my spirit sinks. I expected her to overreach—the Light Market is a place of bartering—but if she starts at five gold coins, there's no hope of lowering her expectations to a price that I can afford.

The repair of the roof will cost me ten gold coins overall, because all I need to purchase is the materials; with the help of some villagers who'll trade their assistance for a few coins, our sprite can handle the work if he has what he needs.

I have eight gold coins; I'll have eight more in a week when my wages are due. I can spare the money, but I know I shouldn't. I have to buy a dress for Samhain, and so many other practical things.

I know what my father would say. That the roof isn't my responsibility at all; that he'll have the money by spring. By spring, there will be another emergency, and I would have spent the winter wet and cold in the east wing.

I know what my mother would say. That a daughter of hers should think to please herself, first and foremost and at any cost. She's never been one for responsibilities. She loves her life exactly as it is now, or she would change it. She loves hunting, and keeping a house away from court, and above all, she loves my father.

I lift a brow. "What book could possibly be worth half that?"

She cackles like she's never heard a more diverting joke. "That says how much you know of the old world, girl. Let someone who can appreciate it buy it."

There's a finality to her words. Despite myself, I'm enthralled. I need to know what's in this book, just as much as I needed Khia's oath a week ago.

We unseelie are creatures of desires, intense, burning wants that overcome any sense. The most powerful of us are least equipped to deal with denial, and though I'm well leashed, my spirit burns as bright as any unseelie lord out there.

I've learned to hide it, and to satisfy it in secret, but I know that if she looks into my eyes now, she'll see me for what I am.

Thankfully, she doesn't.

I contain myself and force a smile. "Two."

"I think not." She takes my measure, and narrows her eyes, understanding I am serious about purchasing this musty book. "Four. That's my last call."

"Two and ten silvers."

"I can get four at *any* market in the capital." We stare at each other, unblinking. Though she is mortal, I can't deny her will is as unbending as that of many folk. Finally, she grumbles, "I can let it go for three."

I sense she won't lower it any more than that, and while three gold coins is more than what I've spent on myself my entire life, I can't help considering it. My book beckons me—for it is already mine, in my mind at least.

"Well, then you're going to have to open it, first. Let's see what I'm buying."

She's no fool; sensing a trick, Padetra makes me swear I won't steal it, or memorize it, or curse it. The word of a fae is binding, as we cannot tell lies. I fantasize at least half a dozen ways I can still inconvenience her if I have a mind to, but I'm more interested in peeking at the book than I am in being a nuisance today.

She fits a silver key into a small lock and the book opens with a click. I draw it to me, rapturous. She peeks at it over her stand; until now, I don't think she's had the curiosity to open it, only interested in its value.

I tilt it at an angle to prevent her from spying on me, mostly out of spite.

I read the first page, stare at it for the longest time. There are only a few words in it, but they shake me like nothing has before, not even Drusk.

Journal of Void, it says, in elegant, flourished handwriting scribed in red ink that smells faintly of dried blood. Not one word is the least bit faded, as if a spell preserved it.

And I don't doubt it did, not when I read the name of the writer.

Nyx.

Daughter of Maeve.

Underneath, her hand has signed it, her hand exactly like mine, with that strange V.N.

I don't question whether it's genuine. I know it is. I feel it. It *tells* me so.

It is my book. It was meant to get into my hands.

I give her the three coins in haste, before she thinks better of it and demands five again.

I'd pay anything I have for it. One look into my eyes and I feel like she might discover it.

twelve
a fairy bargain

I barely sleep for days, reading Nyx's journal every moment that I don't spend serving Lady Frost.

It seems to be an account of her life on a day-to-day basis. Her handwriting and style are both formal and elegant, though occasionally she's blacked out one word, or ripped out pages.

I like to think it was her who ripped them out, anyway. If someone else did, I'd hunt them and rip off their head.

I've never felt closer to anyone in my life. The Nyx I've admired for so long was a girl once. In this book, she's younger than me; she started writing it after her schooling was over.

She spoke of the Court of Wind, and I can't recognize even a shadow of the Wicked Court in her words. This land was ruled by her mother Mab to be a hub for the arts—musicians, painters, sculptors were welcome at court along with the gentry. I read of peace and beauty in the very halls that now terrify me.

What mystifies and arouses me is the way she talks of her power, as if it were nothing at all; an inconvenient, seldom useful, hard to cultivate gift.

She calls it Void, and now her title makes sense.

I'm shocked to realize that she used it for more than I could ever have thought possible. Nyx didn't only kill a butterfly to bring life to a flower as a young fae. She learned to weave spells with her gift. Enchant twigs so that they could sustain the life of its wearer even if they were grievously injured, and gifted them to her favorite knights. She used Void to sustain spells indefinitely, drawing on her energy to anchor them. How I wish she detailed the spells in the journal, but she never did, using the pages to recount her days and share her frustration with the world. Simply knowing it is possible to mold my abilities that way makes me ache to try, but I don't dare. The queen's spies could sense me again, and there would be no saving me this time.

After another week of work, and sleepless days lost in the book, I wake up to a shrill cry. Stumbling out of bed, I kick at the salt circle on my floor and blink to force my eyes to see clearly through the drowsy haze.

I settle, confused. Rattafer, one of the housemaid imps, round and with leathery pink skin, is shaking what appears to be the carcass of a squirrel, and yelling at me.

"Never have I seen such disrespect for my profession! The lady of the house will hear of this, mark my word! Food on the couch? Do you know how hard it is to get blood out of crushed velvet?" She's prone to anger, but I don't recall having seen her quite so irate before.

I groan, willing my body to let go of alarm.

No need to question why she'd think I'd snack on raw squirrel—I like a fresh kill as well as anyone—the question is, what was it doing here in the first place? I certainly haven't brought it upstairs.

I glance at my couch, nestled underneath my open window.

Strange. I would have sworn it was closed before I went to bed.

Ignoring the sniveling horned imp cleaning up and muttering curses, I endeavor to get ready for the night ahead—my one night off this week.

We're one week away from Samhain now, and I can no longer ignore that I need to prepare for it.

I paid for the repair of the rest of the roof when I got my wages three days ago, prioritizing a dry bed over everything else. It leaves me with little in the way of funds; certainly not enough to afford the kind of gown I ought to wear for a court fete.

Part of me wonders whether I should choose my simplest dress, and stay at the edge of the celebration, ready to fly away at the first sign of hostility. Part of me craves that safety. I won't. Acting like a spineless shrew would do nothing but brand me as a weak thing, easy to manipulate, easy to break. I cannot afford for my grandmother to see me that way.

I cannot afford for anyone in the court to see me that way.

Asking Esea for a gown is an option—she certainly has many to spare—but we look nothing alike. I'd be quite ridiculous in anything she owns, unless I have imps rip it apart and adjust it. No gown deserves so little respect.

I tip my leather purse over my bed and count my marks: three gold coins, ten silvers, and a handful of coppers.

I don't need much; I'm fed and housed and cared for at home. I don't have any expensive habits to sustain. There's enough wine in the cellar to last a hundred years, if I was inclined to drown my sorrows. I can spend it all. But it won't get me far, especially if I'm to get shoes, too. And I should.

I decide to just buy the fabric; Nerella, the long-clawed puck who serves as my mother's maid, can sew well enough to fashion me a gown. And no one will pay attention to my feet. I can wear some of my own shoes. Never mind that I only own three pairs, all of them ankle boots.

Mounting Bess, I coax the beast into taking me to Hardrock, the pouch of coin tied at my belt along with my swords.

Outside of the Light Market, I don't know the city as well as I should. I only lose my way twice before finding the street of cloth. I've never had cause to wander this way before.

I don't even think of entering the velvet-clad store of the dressmaker, Ma'am Rolo, who is so well renowned that even Esea and Sylph don't make a habit of commissioning her; they each own one gown made by the dressmaker, and they treasure them so well they've never worn them. Both hang on the walls of their parlors, enclaved in glass, like pieces of art.

Rolo would demand at least a liver, if not a heart. Lower down the long street, there are more modest stores. The windows show drapes that look pretty enough.

I wish I knew a thing about clothes; new clothes. I've had little occasion for purchasing or ordering any in the past. I only require of my outfits that they keep me warm and cozy. On Samhain, I need it to keep me alive and free.

"By Nyx!" The voice is deep and suave and low. I'd know it anywhere.

I stop before thinking better of it, though at least I don't turn to face Drusk.

What is *he* doing here?

"Do my eyes deceive me?"

I hear his steps getting closer to me. Itching to run away or turn around, I do neither, feigning interest in the display of furs and silk.

"Princess Vlari. On the streets." He makes it sound like I'm too good for walking in Hardrock, as if I'm a pompous noble—the kind who orders dressmakers to their homes and wouldn't think to join the people for an hour or two.

He's either teasing me, or he doesn't know me at all. The latter, I expect.

I lift my gaze to the sky, willing the stars to give me strength to deal with him.

I've managed to avoid him for the last three weeks. When I sensed him, I reminded Lera of an errand or two she'd meant to have me carry out for her. Now he's here, standing right in front of me. Too close. His scent is so distinctive and heady. It's fresh, almost sweet. I catch notes of wood, moss, and rain. Maybe a drop of blood.

I lift my hand to his chest, at eye level with me. I mean to push him back a foot or two. But I keep my palm there. "That's near enough."

He seems to find my obvious discomfort amusing. "Has anyone ever told you how unpleasant you can be, Vlari?"

Not to my face.

"And yet, you keep bothering me. What does that say about you?"

I'm so distracted I don't even feel another intrusion into my personal space until it's too late; I catch the sound of a clever blade cutting my purse off my belt.

I turn on my heels, tense, and prepare to pursue the thief. Facing him, I stay right where I am.

It's a blue, wrinkled imp of a tender age—no more than a boy, who hasn't even grown horns—wearing rags, his pale green skin caked in mud.

He must be no older than eight, and he is far too thin for my liking; like a twig ready to snap.

I know hunger. Not like some—not like the boy—but some winters, when our crops wouldn't grow and my mother couldn't hunt every day, we did get hungry enough for me to begin to understand.

Three gold coins might have bought me fabric for a passable dress and a pair of plain enough shoes, but for him, it's a month of food in his belly—he could even stretch it to the whole winter if he's careful.

"Want me to get it back?"

I forgot all about Drusk. He's frowning, watching the boy go. I wonder what he thinks of him. Whether he regards him with pity or contempt. I can't tell from his expression at all. Whatever it is, it feels cold.

I shake my head. "No. It was nothing of consequence."

I can say it because it's entirely true to me. The dress, the nonsensical feast I don't want to go to. I'd attend in rags, if it was unlikely to ignite Morgana's wrath.

"Well, it'll certainly make your trip in the street of cloth less productive. Let me lend you whatever you need for today."

I refuse, reluctant to owe him anything if I can help it. Besides, I couldn't afford to repay him until my next wage day, which I won't earn for weeks. I'll borrow one of my mother's dresses. I'm so short, it'll be like I'm playing dress-up, but I can't say I care. Nerella'll adjust it.

I could ask my parents for money, too. That option makes me feel uncomfortable. I mean to earn my bread and my fineries. It's all well and good for the Thorns to leech off their parents—they have enough money to go around. Mine don't.

Sighing, I resign myself to making my way back to the Light Market. I'm owed dozens of favors after all. I'm sure they can glean me a few yards of velvet or satin.

Drusk's not done with me. "I insist. And I do owe you, if you recall."

Ah! He aims to exchange the oath I've extracted from him for a few coins. I think not.

I face him directly, staring right into his annoying face, gritting my teeth. "I said *no*. Nothing could induce me to relinquish the power I hold over you. *Nothing*." I mean every single word.

I expected to make him angry, but instead of displeasure, I see eagerness, rapture, excitement flare in him. I've set a challenge. He may just be bored enough to rise to it.

"I used to think you were hard to understand. Different from the rest of us, somehow." The next step he takes brings him back in my personal space. I refuse to budge, knowing he wants to see me step back, show fear. "But you love power as much as the next gentry, don't you, Nevlaria?"

"How would you know? You're no gentry." I can tell I've succeeded in hurting him, and for a moment, I'm glad of it.

"And yet I have a better position than you. More money than you. More friends than you, *princess*."

"If only I were interested in position, money, or friends, I might envy you."

I turn my back on him and stride toward the market, certain he'll give up this time. Which shows that I don't know him any more than he knows me.

"Aren't you spending Samhain at court?" he calls from where I left him.

Word apparently travels fast.

I ignore him.

"If you wanted a dress today, I could have one made for you. For a price."

Damn him. Now I'm curious again. What could he possibly want of me? It shouldn't matter; I won't let him spend his money on me. Yet I can't help myself. I turn back to him.

He doesn't need prompting to state his offer. "Let me escort you."

I laugh at the sheer absurdity of the notion. It's all very scandalous, and stupid beyond measure. Me, on his arm? Me, at court, with Rystan Drusk?

"I can wear something I own."

His gaze takes me in from head to toes. I internally wince, knowing what he sees.

I'm in brown leather breeches, green boots, a tunic, my leather coat, and a cloak—my standard ensemble when I'm not working. I have half a dozen such outfits, in various shades of browns and greens. He's never seen me in anything but this gear, or the faded, plain dresses I wear at the Frosts'.

"You absolutely cannot wear something you own."

"Have you taken an inventory of my wardrobe?" I question. Never mind the fact that he's right.

"I may have served at court for all of three weeks, but I've seen enough to understand they wear something extravagant for lunch. And brunch." He considered his words. "And tea. For dinner, they're in gold and silks and velvets. This season's, not the last—otherwise they're mocked mercilessly. Something tells me you don't enjoy being mocked."

He isn't telling me anything I'm not already acutely aware of, but I bristle all the same. "Then you'll understand why I prefer not to talk to you."

I start to walk away, and predictably, he chases me. "You think I jeer at you?"

"Frequently."

Drusk's smirk only serves to confirm that impression. I walk faster.

"Let us make a formal bargain. I hear it's your predilection these days."

It's my turn to laugh. "Right."

The one thing fae love above all is bargains. We bargain with mortals, with dwarves and gods. There are no rules, other than the fact that we have to win. No pleasure is near as exquisite as tricking another fae.

As a teen, I'd offered something he needed, and he'd agreed to my terms without questioning them. I'd give him my heart on a silver platter before I'd make a bargain with him on *his* terms.

"A simple, straightforward one. No tricks."

I snort.

"Don't you want to hear about it, at least?"

I shouldn't. He'll make it sound reasonable, maybe even desirable, but he is going to trick me, I am certain of it.

I make the mistake of turning back to him and looking right into his dark blue eyes.

Suddenly, I want to hear it. Nyx wouldn't let him go without at least knowing what he has to say.

"All right." I'm all business. "State your terms. This is not an agreement. I only offer to hear you out."

I shouldn't even do that.

Drusk takes a long time to think of his words, which only serves to make me more suspicious.

"You, Nevlaria Bane, will take me to Samhain with you next week, and in exchange, I, Rystan Drusk, will buy you a dress for it. Whatever dress you desire. This is the full extent of our agreement and I swear to uphold it unless death, or you, release me from my word."

I turn the words around my mind, over and over. They're ironclad and simple, unadorned with fairy mischief.

There are too many words, but all sound good and simple.

What does he want? How could he have tricked me without my knowing? And he must have.

Bargains that seem to favor one side over the other tend to have hidden traps, but however much I try to decipher hidden meanings, this one seems fair. Equal.

Drusk would never be invited to attend a high court celebration like Samhain; it is the affair of kings, queens, princes, and princesses, where only dukes and high lords may stand witness. It's the heart of the royal court, where blood matters more than worth and deeds. The one way he can join would be as a soldier guarding the gentry, and even that honor might be hard to achieve.

If he wishes to go, he'll have to accompany someone. I'm his ticket. He's willing to pay for the entry.

I see how it might benefit him to go with me, rather than a gentry he might have to flatter for tedious hours.

Now I think about the consequences for me.

The queen will be furious.

She wants to wed me to whomever she'll profit most from, but if I arrive with a man like Drusk at my side, I doubt I'll get any interest. Alone, I'm an opportunity—a weak, poor, malleable princess many might wish to own, a prized possession. With Drusk, I'd be a wild card, someone who doesn't mind associating with dangerous men—with the wrong men.

I'd wanted to go showing strength, using a pretty dress that didn't let me be unnoticed. Instead, I could show power. I could show Drusk as my ally. A pretty lie no one would question.

We can use each other.

So I say, "And shoes. You're buying me shoes, too."

Part of me feels like I've taken leave of my senses.

The other part is looking forward to Samhain now, despite all its dangers.

The queen, the lords, and Drusk.

thirteen
thorns and silk

We end up at Ma'am Rolo after all; not by my will. Drusk asks me which designer I favor, and when I come up blank, he recommends her. "I hear she's the best."

"That also means the dearest."

He shrugs that off. "It sounds like my problem, not yours."

I glance at him, wondering at his magnanimous generosity. I've never had cause to think soldiers earn quite enough to squander their gold in such a manner.

Ma'am's twig-limbed brownie assistant greets us, and after opening an account in Drusk's name, quickly ushers him to what she calls the husbands' cafe. They're to be given as much wine as they need to forget that their wives are spending their fortunes next door.

It's all very scandalous, to me at least.

Then I'm taken to a large room closed with blood-red velvet curtains, where assistants undress and measure me.

I peek at the numbers scribbled on their sketches and sigh. I'm four foot nine, still. I hold myself straighter, imagining that I might earn the last inch that would bring me to a more reasonable height.

The high fae females stand around five foot ten on average. Of course, the pixie females are often under four feet in height, like Meda. When my father didn't inherit her legacy, she generously passed it down to me.

I wish certain bequests could be returned.

I'm served wine and taken to a room with an endless supply of fabrics; lace, silks, velvets, embroidered satin, of all colors and weights. I'm overwhelmed, hardly knowing where to look, touching everything, finding a new favorite shade at every turn.

It's just as well I can't afford to buy from stores like this; I'd waste my life away in here.

I want everything. Having to settle on one piece of cloth seems an impossible feat, until I see it.

A midnight-blue tulle with gold thorns embroidered all along its length; no roses, just the thorns. It's beautiful and prickly. It's harsh and soft all at once.

It's me.

I rush to it and touch the cloth. It's softer than it appears to be, and warm enough for a winter night.

"This."

The assistant tells me I need to pick a plainer fabric to complement it; I find blue velvet, and next, I'm taken to Ma'am Rolo herself.

While I'm surprised, I hide it well. I tower over her, and the slightest wind could blow her away. Ma'am Rolo is a pixie, or something close to it, though she has eyes of sea and the long limbs of a spider. Her lumpy trumpet nose and big eyes without pupils, stuck inside of her skull, suggest imp ancestry. Her skin is the green of moth, and she has long white hair braided at the back of her head.

I expected a sprite. That a lower fae has managed to rise as the best-known dressmaker in Hardrock is no small achievement.

"Who are you? I know your kind."

I'm too stunned to reply immediately.

"Nilieth, Nilian, Niligan, Morigan…"

"Vlari." I introduce myself, cutting her off. I don't need to be reminded of the names of all my ancestors. "Nevlaria Bane."

She nods like that makes sense to her, and takes notes in a small notebook she keeps close to her.

"Yes, yes. The youngest born. I'm glad to see you, finally. I've outfitted every woman in your family, you know. Everyone since Nyx herself."

Now knowing how old she is, I don't need to wonder how she knew what clan I belonged to, though the purple in my hair is knotted away in my hairdo.

She could probably smell my blood a mile away. "Even my mother?" I ask, curious.

Ciera doesn't talk of her time at court; what I've learned, others have told me.

"Every woman." Ma'am shrugs, eyes measuring me.

If she's used to the lithe Lilwreaths like the queen and her daughters, I must be a disappointment.

"At least you're interesting." I know better than to take her assessment as a compliment. "Now, answer. What do you like most about yourself?"

I'm confused.

"A heartbeat per answer is all you're permitted to think. I don't have time to waste."

I say the first thing I can think of. "My eyes?"

"Mh. Hence the blue. Yes. It'll do. Do you have a pretty back?"

"I can't tell, I've only ever seen myself from the front."

She keeps shooting questions. "Your bosom satisfies you? How about your bottom? Your legs? Arms? Fingers? Chin?"

I feel like I've been interrogated by a formidable general by the end of it, exhausted and self-conscious. I'd never thought that I needed to pay that much attention to my features until now.

"When do you need the dress?"

"For Samhain. I know it's soon, but..."

"It'll be ready. I'll have it delivered to you. Next." And I'm dismissed.

I return to the entrance to find Drusk, who also survived the husbands' lounge.

"That was stranger than expected," I tell him.

He opens the door for me, and we leave the store together.

I don't know what to do with him now that he's served his purpose, though his presence isn't altogether unpleasant.

To fill a comfortable silence I don't know what to do with, I speak. "Are your wings getting better?"

He glances at me, eyes narrowed. Wings are private things; our one true vulnerability, as they're fragile and slow to heal. Speaking of his arse would have been less uncouth.

I've never been one for polite nonsense though. "I figured anything else would have healed by now."

It had been two weeks since he'd come back, and there was no need of his returning to his battalion; it must have been his wings.

After a time, he nods. "Slowly. A tear can take years to mend. I won't be able to go back to the front until after they're well. Unseemly as uncovering wings might be in the courts, many of the defense maneuvers we practice need fully functioning wings."

That explains his being here for an extended time. I'm surprised how easy it was to get the answer I wanted. I'm used to everything having to be hidden, concealed.

I muse at his world, so different from mine. He isn't afraid of showing who he is. He isn't even afraid of his weaknesses.

"Do you want to? Return to the front, that is."

He laughs. It's humorless, almost harsh. "An interesting question."

I want to push, but for once, I don't make myself disagreeable.

"This is me," I say, indicating Bess, making a fool of herself next to a fancy black warhorse who doesn't spare her a glance.

I laugh, seeing her neigh and bump into him.

The horse keeps ignoring her; there is even a unicorn strapped next to her, for the gods' sake. Can't she tell she doesn't have a chance?

"Me too." He points to his mount, the stud that dwarfs my silly Bess.

Of course.

We trot down the road leading east of the city.

"You still live at the Frosts'?"

"Not quite. I was given chambers at court. I just don't like them much. And Lera's cook makes me buttercakes."

He seems so very normal today. I can't trust it. I feel like a trap is closing around me. That there's a joke going on and I'll be the victim, when the game comes to a close.

"I don't. Want to return to the front. Not truly. But I also don't have much of a choice in the matter."

"How so?"

"I had a different fate. I was going to be a farmer or a servant, like my parents. One day, I was fighting against some town boys who were bothering my sister, when I caught Genrion Frost's eye. He saw what I was capable of. And he sought to use it. I was young—too young for his armies—so he put me through school, helping me and my family out. When I was old enough, I was expected to enlist. That was the bargain. And I wanted to."

All in the past.

"What happened?" I need to know. He could have a bargain out of me just to spell it out.

Thankfully, he doesn't demand it. "The army. The gentry see it from the strategy board, and suffer through one or two days of fighting a month. I saw it from the trenches. I saw it in the cold mud. I saw friends fall—friends I cared for. I don't particularly wish to see more of it. But someone has to do it. And I'm better than most. When I'm healed, I'll go back. It's my place."

All of a sudden, I'm angry, frustrated, at him and myself, though I can't pinpoint the reason why.

I'm glad we're at an intersection I have to take north; the Frosts' is south of our lands.

"Until Samhain, then? If not before."

I'm working for the next three days. I might see him then, but I wish I wouldn't.

I can only take so much of Drusk without drowning.

He nods and turns his impressive horse south.

Something bothers me about the entire situation; about him. Always has.

And I still can't pinpoint what it is.

fourteen
vines and roses

My dress is delivered one night before Samhain, while I'm working. I'm glad it got here in time—one less worry to mull over before attending the Wicked Court—but I don't unwrap it, too eager to get back to Nyx's journal. It'll be waiting on the morrow. That's what matters.

I'm almost halfway through the journal. My ancestor is in her fiftieth year now—so young for a fae. Something tells me I'm drawing close to the moment that changed everything, the moment when she became the ruler of legend.

Strange that history hasn't bothered to remember why a princess of a minor court might have decided to take over all others. They took it for granted that it was greed, the power-hungry nature of the court fae, but everyone has a story. I love learning hers.

Nyx's mother Maeve was neither seelie nor unseelie, hence why she'd chosen a court so close to the northern kingdom. She was born of the seelie queen Una and King Lin, the old lord of the Court of Wind, though they hadn't been wed. Their passionate and short affair resulted in a boy and a girl—twins, which was rare enough for the fae.

Una claimed the boy, Tharsen, and Lin took Maeve, who was never meant to rule; he already had two sons, both born unseelie.

All that mattered to Maeve was indulging in the arts, the beauty of nature, and the wilderness. When her elder brothers murdered and cursed each other, there was no other alternative than to elevate Maeve to her father's throne. She accepted the duty, but never took to it.

Nyx was impatient with her mother's caprice, and her utter unsuitability as a ruler. Despite all that, Nyx adored her mother.

Maeve sounds like my mother; a free spirit not fettered by any kingdom, any crown. I see no ill in my mother's ways, but I could imagine what it was like for Nyx, who was interested in intrigues and politics. She craved sitting on the throne. She had the power and inclination to do it well.

And she would. Maeve had been wiped away by history. I've heard her name in passing before, though no one has ever said a thing about her. Even her twin, Tharsen, is more renowned, though he was raised up north in the seelie realm—and then banished to the wilderness for his crimes.

I want to know how Nyx had come to succeed her mother. Had she been given the crown? Had Maeve died? That I have no idea how it had all unfolded seems preposterous. They are my family. This is the story of my lineage, my house.

I need to know. It seems important.

"Oh, no. No, no, no."

I haven't heard a step, but Meda is standing at my door, baring her teeth as she approaches my reading nook under the window. "You, young lady, are going to sleep!"

I've never had cause to be this annoyed with her. "I'm no child."

"Then you ought to remember you're entering a lion's den in less than twelve hours, and you haven't rested in days. Do you want to put your family through the pain of losing you? You might have said so before. I wouldn't have bothered wasting my time training you, ungrateful, ridiculous girl!"

I'm seething, which is never a good thing.

Anger is a familiar companion, and I am so accustomed to it I could mold it, modify it at will. Not tonight.

I see a glow of greenish magic crawl from me to my grandmother's feet, slithering its way to her. I enjoy what I see in her eyes: fear.

"You forget." I hold my chin high, and bare my teeth. "None of your lessons were ever needed. I can vanquish any enemy with ease."

These are my words, and they aren't.

Nyx has never written them word for word, but I feel her influence in my turn of phrase. That's strange enough to spook me into letting go of my magic, but I keep glaring at Meda.

To my surprise, she nods with what I interpret as amusement. "Finally. Some teeth. Bring them with you tomorrow night. And now, sleep. Child."

She's right; I am childish, irritated by nothing more than the truth. I should sleep. The very real threat of Morgana's wrath matters more than the shadow of Nyx. I have to remember that. Yet part of me doesn't want to. Lost in Nyx's world, I start to understand how irrelevant Morgana truly is. She's ruled for four hundred years, and she has yet to have achieved anything of note; she's another Maeve.

I sleep, dreaming of long-forgotten times, of carpets of moss and garlands of wildflowers hanging on the pillars of great halls, now covered in silk and tapestries. I like to think I might have liked Nyx. She would have understood me. Her violet eyes are fixed on me through my dreams.

WHEN TWILIGHT COMES, I struggle to roll off my bed, and Meda's words come back to me. She's right; I've barely slept for days, and I'm weak. I can't afford to be.

I frown, glancing at the book on my bedside table. The book that's worth more than all my belongings combined—except for the dress I've bargained for with Drusk. I'm sure he's spent more than three gold coins on that.

I bite my lip, shaking my head. I'm not reading it tonight. I shouldn't read it tomorrow, either.

I've heard of books with curses woven inside the binding, hexing anyone who reads them. I don't think the journal is one of them, but it has a strange effect on me. A pull at my heartstrings. I want to believe it's because I love reading, and I haven't had many occasions to, but there's more.

A problem for another time. Tonight is Samhain, the end of the harvest season, the start of the darker part of the year, where our kind thrives.

And I will attend the court celebrations.

With Drusk.

I bathe and wash my hair, brushing it while it's wet. My mother's care three weeks ago is long undone; my ends are split and the tresses have lost their shine. I'll have to braid it.

I approach the dress naked, unsure of what underthings would fit it best. Unwrapping the brown sack, I stare in disbelief.

The gown is a soft cloud of gossamer from feet to waist, with two panels of my blue velvet fabric embroidered with gold thorns splitting at my thighs—everyone will see a lot of my legs under that daring cut. The velvet bodice has a square neckline and a low back, but there's blue lace stitched with diamond stars from the throat to the sleeves. I'll be covered from ankle to neck, and not covered at all, all at once.

I have my answer. I can't wear anything under that dress.

When I slip it on, I find that I don't need to; Ma'am Rolo made sure that my breasts are supported. I could run in this dress. Or dance until I ruin my satin slippers.

I'm observing my reflection in the heavy marble mirror on my wall, trying to stand in a way that makes me look as though I belong in this piece of art. As it catches the moonlight, the color changes to a dark purple. I smile, and find that when I do, it doesn't look so wrong on me.

I'll have few reasons to smile at court. Hopefully, I can also pull it off with a scowl.

I catch sight of a smudge on my left shoulder and rub it. To my surprise, it's not fading at all.

I turn my back to the mirror and twist my neck to look at myself.

Right between my shoulder blades, there's a dainty rose with bright red petals, and vines or thorns reach my neck on either side, their branches and thorns extending to my shoulders. I don't know what to make of it. Flowers are for mourning, and I've had no cause to mourn anyone at all, yet the mark is there. Since when? I can't tell. I'm not sure when I looked at my back last.

Footsteps approach, but I don't let them disturb me.

"Mh. Finally bothering to dress as befits your station, I see."

I don't think Nerella has ever come to this part of the house.

The long-limbed puck with nimble twig-like fingers has served my mother since long before I was born. I've never asked, but I think she used to attend court with her.

She's never been fond of me. Nerella likes pretty dresses and complicated hairstyles, and I have time for neither.

"Don't get used to it." She snorts at my quip. "Did Mother send you to me?"

"I sent myself. And a good thing, too. Now, sit."

I do as I'm bid, settling on my dresser, and without a word, she gets to work on my hair. I let my mind wander as she works while humming a soothing tune.

Dusk gives way to night before she finishes taming my hair. "There. That's the best I can do."

The best she could do was braiding a crown around my head, fixed with one of my mother's silver diadems, and taming the rest of my hair into soft waves. I look tall, older, wiser, and crueler. I could kiss Nerella for her magic.

As I don't think she'd appreciate it all that much, I say instead, "I owe you a favor."

That amuses her. "And you'll remember it. Now, be quiet, I need to do your face."

By the time she's done with me, I'm not myself—Vlari is gone. I see Nevlaria, princess of the realm. Good. I'll need her tonight.

fifteen
queens and pawns

I didn't expect Drusk to come here. We haven't clarified the technicalities of tonight, but I thought we'd meet before Hardrock. Yet when I walk down to the entry hall, I find him there, in the sitting parlor, conversing with my father.

I didn't even think he knew where I lived. That we reside in the Court of Mist is common enough knowledge, but he's never been here.

I can't reconcile myself with the tableau: Drusk and Nero, chatting comfortably. I can't imagine what they might have in common. One, a soldier, the other, a musician. I still and eavesdrop on them from a distance.

And look.

Drusk wears a navy double-breasted coat similar to any of his usual outfits, though it's embroidered in gold, just like mine. His shirt is satin, underneath. The only marked difference is that his hair is better combed than usual.

Men's lives are so simple.

"It's been too long since I've eaten a good gruel. My wife is very much about meats. Raw meats, if she can get them, and cold meats. So is my mother. Come to think of it, the only person in the house who will eat anything other than carcasses is my Vlari. She loves flowers, best. Candied violets, and poppy petals. I think she'd like gruel."

Drusk chuckles. "I can't quite picture it. I thought I'd eaten enough gruel for the rest of my days—there wasn't much more in the front. But when my father makes it, it's something else."

"It's home." Nero nods, like he understands only too well.

I wonder about what it's like for a man like my father to have married Ciera Oberon. His mother is here now, but I don't think he knew her well, in his youth. She reared him, and as soon as he was old enough, let him make his way in the world. They were too different for Meda to know what to do with him.

"You're very welcome any day, sir, if you pass our way at dusk. We don't live far, just a few miles south, at the border of the Court of Stone's domain." He casually waves southward. "My father makes enough for ten guests, and the door is open to any who wanders in."

"A generous offer. I'll take it, too, when I've had enough of boar and venison. We—"

Whatever he's about to say dies on his lips as he sees me.

I walk toward the hall, self-conscious under his scrutiny. I wonder what Drusk thinks of the dress, of the hair, of the dusting of shine around my eyes and the blush of my cheeks.

All he says is, "Handsome dress."

This feels more like a compliment to him than anyone else; he's happy with his purchase. I want to kick his shin. "What are you doing here? I thought we'd meet in town."

He shrugs. "I figured you wouldn't want to ride all the way and risk ruining your gown."

I hadn't even thought of that—credit to how little time I spend in pretty clothes. "Oh."

My father gets to his feet and hugs me as I approach. "You're beautiful, blossom. Dance, sing, and make merry tonight."

I know what he doesn't say in front of Drusk: that I should do my best to enjoy myself rather than spending my time worrying over what the queen has planned for me.

"I'll try."

He squeezes me harder before letting go.

I'm about to ask if Mother intends to see me out, when I feel her presence come from the grand staircase. She's also in finery; the Court of Mist will celebrate too, although it won't be a grand affair—just dances and songs in the woods, around a bonfire.

Drusk looks from her to me, and seems confused, as though he doesn't quite understand how such a tall, ethereal fae could have birthed me.

The desire to kick him increases.

Ciera is also paying attention—to him, not me. "That's a striking man, daughter dear." Her voice is silk and shadow. "Why ever would you keep him to yourself?"

I grit my teeth. I've explained that an acquaintance is escorting me tonight; I told both of my parents it was just a bargain. Why is she embarrassing me like this?

"He's not mine to keep. Drusk, if you're ready?"

"Oh, no, I think not. You'll introduce your escort to us, Nevlaria." She seldom uses that tone; the voice that reminds me she's been raised a princess of the realm, and could well wear the crown.

It's going to be a long night. "Rystan Drusk, my parents, Ciera and Nero, lords of the Court of Mist. Mother, Father, Rystan Drusk, soldier, wielder of Myst. Who's absolutely no one to me." Not a friend, nor an enemy. "Now we're going to be late."

His dark horse is strapped next to a brown mare; they pull a small black carriage without banner—it's a simple conveyance, well made. The driver is a pale green-skinned pixie, to my surprise—there aren't many pixies south of the border. I'd never seen one before my grandmother came to live with us. He nods at me in acknowledgment as Drusk holds out his hand nonchalantly to help me in.

Inside, I find the wooden bench covered with thick, plush furs, and the windows hooded by velvet curtains.

Our old carriage is in such a sorry state, entering the luxurious vehicle furthers my feeling of having disguised myself as something else, someone else tonight.

"Ready when you are, Pirrin!" Drusk calls to the pixie, and we're on our way, in silence.

We drive past the clover fields and haunted groves until we reach the Court of Stars, and then through the lakes and murks.

We're minutes away from Hardrock when he says, "You've never attended court, have you?"

A loaded question. I evade it. "I've been to court."

Always on a summons, meant to answer for my principal crime: existing.

"Mh. Your parents seemed wary."

I bite my lower lip, not wanting to get into the details.

"We could choose another way to make small talk, if you wish. Let us talk of music, dances, books, and lovers."

I'm comfortable with none of those subjects. "It'll be my first Samhain at court. My first celebration. The queen doesn't favor my side of the family. If you hoped to get her attention, that's not going to happen while you're with me."

"I care little for the whims of queens."

He's so nonchalant that I believe him.

"Then why did you want to be here?"

Drusk hesitates. "Do you know what it's like to be there, and yet not exist? I suppose not. Even if no one speaks to you in a room, they know you. They know your name, your status. Soldiers without great names are invisible. I thought it'd be entertaining to cavort with my superiors, and spit in the face of their disdain when they try to will me back into nothingness."

I blink, incredulous. Then a chuckle escapes me. Drusk seems to understand I'm not laughing at him. He grins back.

"That sounds marvelous. You'll dance with queens and kings and princes, and they won't be able to say a thing at all about it."

"And princesses. I shall dance with some princesses, too."

THE GATES ARE wide open, and a crowd of sprites, pucks, and imps trample all over themselves to get inside the cavernous halls. I'm stunned and confused; I would never have thought that Morgana would invite the common folk.

"They're to remain in the halls—the court assembles at the summer palace tonight."

I try not to resent Drusk for knowing what I didn't.

"Why have we come this way, then?"

The summer palace is on the other side of the mountains, on the waterfront.

"Following the peaks would take a whole hour. The king advised me to pass through the palace. Though that's hardly likely to save us time."

I peek at the merry, slow-moving crowd through the window—then, I draw the curtains back to talk to our driver. "Would you mind sticking to the left line?"

The pixie glances back at me and nods. I've seen carriages pass through the royal gates; it should let us all through safely as long as it senses my presence in the back.

I close my eyes, and expand my mind, hoping my idea isn't about to cost two horses and two fae their skins.

I am here. I belong here. Let me through.

Welcome back, mistress.

I jolt, surprised to have heard an answer clearly in my mind. A strange answer; these gates have no reason to see me as anything but a visitor. But I feel the magic wash over us as we pass through the royal gates safely, ahead of the crowd.

In front of the crowd, we dismount and join the mayhem.

I've never been anywhere but the hall of crowns—and the servants' quarters where Alven led me on my last visit to shout at me—but Drusk seems comfortable here. He stuffs his hands in his pockets and offers me an elbow. I hook an arm through, and let him guide me. The crowd parts with bows and greetings that aren't all for Drusk.

I know these people, I realize. They're the merchants and clients at the markets. While they might not have seen me like this, in a fine dress, painted like a doll, they know and respect me enough to let us go easily forward.

We pass a hall of thorns—great marble columns trained with thorns and roses—a hall of art, with sculptures of naked fairies painted black and gold. Next comes the great hall. I finally understand why the queen thought nothing of inviting the entire town; five thousand fae could comfortably fit in here, and maybe a giant or two. The hall is lit with millions of candles and trapped devases gleaming like starlight over the dark ceiling. Large tables have been pressed against either side of the walls, and piled up with a feast of cakes, candies, meats, and wine. Mostly wine.

I wish we could stay here, laughing and dancing with the folk, but Drusk leads me out of the hall, through a sinuous passage that opens to the eastern beach.

Sea air crashes into me from a distance. The waves are dark and violent, hitting the white-columned open-air edifice where we're headed.

"Why do we gather here in the winter?" I muse, confused.

Holding the summer solstice here, I would have understood, but I'm frozen to my bones.

The path to the palace is covered in moss and white flowers. When we reach the first pillars, I'm relieved to find the air perfectly warm—the open hall is wrapped in a spell that makes it comfortable as a summer night.

We're announced at our entry, and I try to shed all traces of fear when the throng parts to let us approach the queen.

I thought Morgana richly dressed every time I saw her, but today, in a high-collared white gown stitched with starlight and strands of white gold, she's a vision, gold speckles on her cheeks and throat.

In contrast, Alven wears black, his eyes dusted with coal.

As Morgana watches me with her cold eyes, I curtsy deeply.

She says nothing, does nothing.

"Rise, child. Rystan." I'm shocked my grandfather has intervened, but I obey all the same.

Finally, Morgana says, "Enjoy the festivities."

I am thus dismissed.

Her look promises reprisal, vengeance. She hates what I've done—the dress, Drusk. But she doesn't seem inclined to exact it here, in front of all her court. I breathe out. It'll be just fine. When I'm confronted, I can feign ignorance, innocence.

"I think I need warm mead after that," Drusk says, chuckling. "The queen has never seemed this icy to me."

"Mead sounds great, *Rystan*." I'd known that was his name, of course, but everyone calls him Drusk.

Along the open arches, there's eight long tables laden with food and wine; he finds a large lead pot of scented mead, and serves us both goblets. I wrap my cold hands around it, and sniff it. Fresh spices, honey, and brandy.

"I haven't poisoned you, you know."

The thought hadn't occurred to me, but I say, "Better safe than sorry."

I take a sip. It's warm, rich, and delicious.

Drusk fixes me with a stare and starts a retort, when he's interrupted.

"By the underworld, I didn't expect to find you here!" I tense as Dekren approaches.

He's accompanied by his human beauty—still with him after four weeks, to my surprise. Dekren embraces Drusk, who doesn't seem to mind, and kisses the top of my head.

"If you've ruined my face, I'll tear you to pieces." Nerella worked hard to smudge shadows on me.

"Such sweet things she says to me," Dekren coos, before taking Drusk aside to whisper in his ear.

I grin at the human, and lower my head in a brief greeting. "Nice to see you dressed." And it is. She wears a beautiful red gown that emphasizes her very unfaelike assets. I can only admire her curves, her sensual ways.

"Likewise." Her laugh isn't silly or childish or cruel like mine; it's a lush, dark purr that promises another kind of naughty things. "You look quite magnificent out of the bathtub."

"That would be considerably more flattering if your kind couldn't lie." She's easy to speak to, and fun. I'm glad of the distraction her presence provides from the constant conflict with the queen, and with Drusk, too. "I don't think I heard your name."

I'm stunned to realize I've already finished my drink. I know better than to take another one right now.

The woman lifts her brow. "My true name?"

I blink in confusion. To my knowledge, humans only have one name at all.

Unless—

"You're a changeling."

She nods. "Indeed. I was brought here in exchange for the queen's daughter."

I'm flabbergasted. The queen's? None of it makes sense. Morgana had a daughter, a young one?

"You don't know?" The human takes my arm, and we start to walk about the room. "Forty years ago, they took me from my village, and brought me here. The queen's blessed me with charms so that I don't age."

I can't question her word; there's no cause for her to lie, when finding out the truth would be too easy. And there's no reason why I would have known—I don't concern myself with the affairs of the court. If she's been here for forty years, I don't doubt her presence was quite scandalous at first, but time would have lessened the rumors.

"Then why..." I look about us, checking if anyone can overhear us.

Everyone can. No one is paying attention, though.

"Why were you at the market?"

I don't spell it out—why was she selling herself at the market.

She laughs and counters, "Why were you?"

I don't point out that only one of us was being sold.

"I like it there," she tells me unabashedly. "I enjoy getting out of the keep, right under the noses of my guards. I enjoy doing wicked, terrible things Mother would disapprove of. And I certainly enjoy getting screwed for coins. It beats getting screwed for politics."

"The queen—" I can't finish my thought.

"Makes me bed whoever she wants for her advantage? Yes—hence why she gifted me youth, I think. Currently, the Frost boy. After I've given him a child, it'll be someone else."

I'm speechless, horrified. That's far worse than any treatment of a human I can think of. I don't ask if she's already bred children with other lords. I don't need to.

We've circled back to our corner of the banquet. To distract myself, I clear my throat and interrupt Drusk and Dekren's tête-à-tête. "Is your littlest sister here?"

Dekren grimaces. "I'm not either of my sisters' keeper, but I've never seen them miss a revel since youth. I'm sure they're about. Probably deeper in the castle."

I'm glad to have something to do—being here in this hall, full of laughter and music and dance, I don't quite know what to do with myself. This isn't my world.

"I'll try to find them, if you don't mind," I tell Drusk. He's my escort, after all.

"I'll be here."

I nod, and walk away.

The human stays by my side. "I still don't know what to call you."

We're family of sorts—both stuck in the queen's web. I should know her name.

"Lily. And you're Nevlaria. My niece, it seems."

Though I was almost twice her age, she was right.

"Vlari."

She hooks her arm through mine, and I let her, walking down the length of the summer palace, past the great hall, to drafty yet warm open chambers.

Some are occupied by dancers swaying to the distant sounds of the horns, flutes, and strings from the great halls, others, by gamers around card tables. I glance inside and fail to find any familiar faces, but Lily greets dozens of people.

There's no door barring entry, but as we go farther in the belly of the castle, I see lovers bent over chairs, taking each other wildly against walls—others flogging each other and screaming for more, naked in the moonlight.

I'm about to turn back, when I spot Sylph in a room filled with barely covered bodies, where everyone touches, tastes, and takes one another.

I wouldn't have thought the proud Sylph likely to join in something debased and carnal like this, but I suppose everyone here is proud. Everyone here is a lord, or a queen. Maybe she was even told to engage in this gathering, like Lily.

Or she could simply like it.

It's Samhain. The common folk let their wilder side free. Why would I have thought the gentry were any different? Anything they do, we do better.

"Do you mind if I take leave of you?" Lily asks me.

I turn to her, and see raw need and desire in her every feature.

I laugh. "Of course. Enjoy."

I've never been affected by the seasons, the festivities. When I want release, it's simply for the sake of it, rather than the will of nature.

Lily tears at the openings of her dress, eager to reveal her flesh.

I keep walking the hall, less awkward now that I'm alone. I don't feel like a voyeur; they're the ones displaying their pleasures.

Esea is in the last room, a smaller hall that leads right to the shores. In the distance, waves crash against limestone. She plays the harp while a gentry touches her breasts.

"Am I interrupting?"

"Hopefully," the lord replies.

Esea grins. "Never. I heard the Sea Lands are coming tonight. They like an entrance—I figured I'd get the best view!"

I join them, sitting on a low bench.

The Sea Lands is an old court, older than any of ours; they were there before our kind came to Álfheimr, fleeing the devastations of our Isle, in the north. They've claimed a stretch of unseelie land in the south, and seelie land in the north. When they need to deal with us, they make us come to them. Their gracing us with their presence here seems unlikely, yet fascinating.

If Morgana manages a true alliance with the Sea Lands, she'll be known for it throughout history.

I hope she doesn't.

"And you are?" the gentry asks me pointedly, throwing rank in my face to assert his dominance.

"A princess who could have your hands cut off for speaking to her so," Esea tells him. "Which would be a shame. You're quite good at this."

She's toying with him with so much ease, I can only admire her.

The man takes it as an invitation to take his seduction one step further, and slides his hand under the cloth of her bustier. She moans in approval, but I doubt she's that impressed. She doesn't so much as miss one note.

My eyes go to the sea—fierce and magnificent. I don't know how long I spend following the waves.

"There you are." I blink and look up to Drusk.

Esea has stopped playing altogether; instead, I hear her panting. She's spread her thighs and let the fae put his head between her legs. She must be fond of him; I know she doesn't take many lovers—and that none of them have had the pleasure of entering her. Her uncle has forbidden her to waste her virginity until he finds her a husband, archaic fool that he is.

"Done with Dekren?" I ask.

He joins me on the bench. "He had news from the northern borders. More attacks. Not the sort of thing you'd want to be bored by at a party, I'm sure."

I can't tell if he's condescending or thoughtful, but he's right. I don't care to hear about the northern borders. It's the affair of the queen. Unless something concerns the Court of Mist, it's not my problem.

"Esea said the Sea Lands were invited. I guess she was wrong."

"Not necessarily. It's early yet."

It doesn't feel early. I laugh. If half of the guests are already naked now, this revel is going to end in a veritable orgy.

"Look!"

There is a light in the distance, right above the waves, bright and warm.

I glance back at Esea. She can't miss this. "Mephesea, look! I think the Sea Lands are here!"

She focuses her gaze on the door while her lover keeps pleasing her. Her panting and moaning grow louder.

I laugh along with Drusk and return my gaze to the sea.

The waves part, rising higher than ever before, high enough to top the Shadow Peaks, and the shadow approaches. A castle, I realize. A castle riding the sea like a ship. The songs of sirens drown the silence of the night. I can only sigh. "I've never seen anything quite this beautiful."

"I have."

I turn to Drusk, curious, but he says nothing else. "Well?" I prompt.

His smirk is wicked and full of secrets. "Oh, I think not. You'll have to use your favor if you want to know."

"Never."

Drusk gets to his feet, and extends his hand. "Come. We don't want to miss the sea."

sixteen
will of the sea

The halls have different lovers, and singers, and players, and the revel is in full swing when we return. Lords and ladies smell of sweat, wine, and sex as they dance in circles or pairs to the sound of a mournful ballad.

We reach the great hall instants before the Sea Lands lords enter it.

At the fore are two women, one dressed in a tight translucent coral lace gown, the other in soft seaweed green, wearing richly embroidered breeches and coats—their two queens, mated a thousand years ago.

The one in lace has sea-blue hair cut short, the one in green, long gray-white curls, thick like seafoam. They both are stunning, willful, playful, and fierce.

Two men follow them, dressed in one or the other of their colors. Their consorts, who fathered the children trailing behind; five princes, seven princesses. Most are older than any one of us.

I've heard that their court is both seelie and unseelie. Watching them, I don't doubt it. They seem cunning, calculating, cruel—the best and worst of the folk.

My grandmother was foolish to call them here. Anyone would be foolish to attempt to bargain with them.

Or desperate.

"Darya." Morgana greets the red queen, then turns to the other. "Tasi."

"Morgana," Tasi says, slowly and softly, as though tasting it on her lips. "It has been long since we've walked on land."

I notice that they aren't walking on land at all, though. They're standing in a puddle of water that follows them everywhere.

They don't trust us.

"Where is the child?"

Morgana looks around, until her eyes find mine. "Nevlaria."

It's a command.

The queen says my name like it is a curse, a veiled threat coated in hatred. I stiffen, and in the cavity of my chest, I feel my heart speed, like it did when I was running from the wyr, like it does every time I face a danger.

I had a plan then. Now, I don't. There's no escaping this predator.

What was I thinking? The dress, Drusk, all of it. I should have thrown myself at her feet and declared myself her creature. I should have thought of nothing but to live. Survive her. Outlive her, until I have my freedom. Someone was bound to stick a dagger in her throat or poison her, some day. She is too wicked and cunning to live peacefully.

She is another Nyx.

And I?

You will make yourself invisible. You will make yourself irrelevant. I never want to hear anyone say your name to form a praise. If you fail in this, I will destroy you.

Irrelevant. Invisible. Weak.

I am nothing.

Drusk's grasp tightens on mine, and my gaze slides to our fingers. As I stare, the inner voice screaming for my attention, telling me who I am, what I should be, is lowered to a whisper and then tuned out entirely.

This. His grasp. That's solid and real.

I look at the queen, feeling his hand, focusing on it, until I have to let go.

Then, I walk down the hall to stand before her, next to the sea queens. I fall to the ground as elegantly as I can manage.

"This is my granddaughter," Morgana says.

I understand then.

She wants to sell me to them. To the sea, where I will be torn apart. Where I will no longer be a problem for her. She's bartered me for an alliance that will render her more powerful than my ability ever could.

My heart beats at a thousand miles an hour.

No. She cannot. I cannot.

If I'm right, I'll never again see the Court of Mist. I'll never see my parents. I'll drown underwater for the rest of time. I admire the sea folk, but I cannot think of a worse fate than to end up with them, away from all I love, all I am.

I have to prevent this somehow. Convince them to abandon the notion.

The sea queen with gray-white hair touches my chin, forcing me to look up from my deep curtsy. "Your mind is waves of shadows, child. Shadows and terror. Pray, what do you fear?"

I look down the depths of her tumultuous eyes. "You."

She laughs, pleased. "A smart girl. Good. Dance with my near-son."

She doesn't tell me which son she means, and it doesn't matter.

One of the men detaches himself from the rest of her retainers, approaching me. He gives me one hand. I rise to my feet, glancing at Drusk in the distance.

Never have I wished for someone to save me. Never have I thought of such a thing. Meda would be appalled if she suspected I might, but I think it all the same.

I want him to come here and pull me far, far away from the magnificent sea prince.

He takes after the red queen. His hair is a bright blue, and he dresses in bloodred and gold. He's tall, and fair, and strong. The sort of prince any girl might dream of.

He's my nightmare.

He bows to me elegantly, and music starts promptly. Enchanting music that's not of this world.

"I don't know how to dance to this." I take his hand, seeing mine trembling.

The prince laughs. "You don't need to. All you need to do is relax. Are you able to, landling?"

I don't think I could. Especially not when he pulls me close and puts his hands on either side of my waist, guiding me.

"Don't fret. I won't marry you."

I release a breath. "Sorry, I thought—"

"Your queen wants you to. My mother wants me to. I won't."

I eye him mistrustfully.

"You're too small, dainty, tiny, weak. You would break in the Court of Bones. I need a wife strong enough to bear heirs."

I guess I should feel insulted. I'm relieved. "Glad we agree."

"Unfortunately for you, that means Queen Tasi will want you for Kaito, instead. He'll take you, and gladly break you. His court prizes pain above all."

"And what does yours prize, sir?"

He grins, showing sharp canines. "War, my lady. And they call me Lind."

"Vlari."

We sway in silence that ceases to become uncomfortable as time passes. He seems quite adamant that he doesn't want me. If we're cursed to be with each other, at least we'll be equally displeased.

"Why have your queens agreed to this? It's not like the Sea Lands to come here—or seek a land bride."

I'm surprised he answers truthfully. "Times are changing. There are forces that seek to control both land and sea. It is a time for alliances."

"If only alliances could be had without throwing daughters into the mix."

"And sons. Let us not forget the sons."

We both laugh.

The next song is from our parts, and the rest of the court has joined.

Lind bows, and I am relieved to be released so early. I don't look at the queen for approval, slipping away from the great hall.

Someone catches my hand just as I return to the corridor leading to the antechambers.

Drusk.

I'm unreasonably irritated at him. "What?"

He shoves his hands in his pockets, shrugging. "I thought you might want to dance."

"I never attend royal revels, Drusk. I can't dance, and I hate it." And I couldn't stay there another moment.

"You didn't seem to hate it just now."

I glare up at him. "They're selling me to the Sea Lands. They want me to marry that scary guy—or his scarier brother—to seal an alliance. I'm good at pretending. I still hate everything about tonight."

He glances back at Morgana, seated on a dais, lording over the rest of the court. Then, he takes my hand, and leads me away from the hall, farther in the corridor.

"They wouldn't." His lips purse in one slim line.

"Morgana is *queen*," I remind him. "High queen, in fact."

"No one can force another fae to marry. Not since the reforms."

I snort at his mention of the law. "No, I guess not. She can only torture, behead me, and take everything I love from me until I agree."

A mask of fury has contorted Drusk's features, drawing his upper lip over his teeth. "She can't. She wouldn't *dare*."

I'm stunned that he managed to say the words; they're an outright lie. He must believe it.

I could tell him Morgana has already done worse. She's stripped me of everything I should have had. She's made me feel like every day could be the last, my time a gift of her grace.

"It doesn't matter." I walk down the corridor, heading back to the last chamber, where I'd found some peace.

"It doesn't matter?" he echoes, in utter disbelief.

"Yes. And there's no point worrying over what cannot be halted."

"So you've given up. You've given up your freedom, just like that." He seems incredulous, disappointed. Furious.

I'm angry, too. How dare he judge me, when he's never had to make himself small just to survive? "You have no idea what you're talking about," I manage through gritted teeth. "None."

I'm glaring up at him, facing his rage head-on. My anger and his are a living thing, as tangible as our magic. I half expect to see it.

"You could get married." His words stun me, entirely unexpected. "To someone of your choosing, before there's any oath or agreement binding you."

I have nothing to say, at first. Then, I chuckle, rolling my eyes. "Right. Because Morgana wouldn't find my lucky new husband, rip him apart, and do as she pleases in any case?"

"Not necessarily. She didn't do it with your mother, right? I think it might be perceived as lack of propriety by other lords."

Wanting to argue, I ponder his words, letting them marinate.

How would Morgana react to my slipping through her fingers? Not well, that's for sure, but would she spill blood over it? She hasn't with my mother, and she was more invested in marrying Ciera well. In my case, she just wants me away from her—preferably kingdoms away, buried in the undersea.

I remember I jested about marrying Esea a few weeks back. Maybe I *should* have.

It'd be dangerous. For me and whatever fool I link to my fate.

As seconds pass in silence, I start to accept there's a degree of wisdom in Drusk's words; at least, they aren't complete madness.

I could ask Dekren, though I don't think I'd like being under the thumb of the elder Thorn. Besides, his uncle Genrion would never allow it without the queen's blessing. Perhaps Wilden. I wouldn't mind being a Frost, and I doubt Lera would see any objection.

I titter, a wild idea crossing my fancy. "And you owe me a favor. I could shackle you."

"I can't say I dislike shackles, ordinarily, but in this matter, I think I'd rather remain free to make my choice, *princess*. You'd have to seduce me. *Very well.*"

"Or make some amoria." He's easy to tease tonight. Easy to speak to. I don't know what has changed, but I can't deny something has. "I recall that worked on you once."

"Once. Never again, princess. You'll have to ply me with kisses and promises."

I laugh again. "Kisses and promises are all it'd take to risk your neck?"

"I risk my neck most days. Give me half a reason, and I'll do it again. Gladly."

Perhaps it is simply that I now stand in my enemy's palace; in the wake of Morgana's presence, I feel that he and I aren't antagonists after all. We aren't allies either. We're something else, something I can't define. We clash, but I am not scared of him. I don't think he wishes me ill.

I could be wrong. I decide to let time tell.

"Enough foolishness. Let's find somewhere to wait out the rest of this nightmare."

Drusk offers me his elbow, and I take it. We walk in pleasant silence, leaving the revels behind.

seventeen
thread of blood

I wake well after twilight, my head heavy with dances, honey mead, the sound of violins. Despite the already growing headache, I'm smiling like an idiot.

I did it. I survived Samhain. I may not even have angered the queen last night. I haven't spurned the man she obviously picked for me; not exactly. He seemed to have understood I have little interest in him without my having to delineate. But I only danced with him once, before disappearing with Drusk. We talked in the antechamber until the end of the revels.

At my window, there's another carcass—a rabbit, this time. At least Rattafer didn't find that one soaking my bench. I may have gained an enemy daring enough to enter my room, but it's not a very smart one, if they think I will be spooked by a little blood.

I don't bathe, needing to exert myself after the stress and worry that has preceded the revel. I leap out the window and extend my wings, like a wayward child.

My night clothes, like most of my undershirts, are cut to allow for their size. I wouldn't be the first fae to spread her wings during a nightmare—or a very nice dream, for that matter.

Some of the gentry, descendants from the old air courts, bear the wings of great, proud birds. The lesser fae are of different stock; we have insectile wings. The wings of beetles or mosquitos, for the imps and bogs blessed with the ability to fly. I've heard that some sprites can have dragonfly wings. For pixies, it's either moths or butterflies. Wings that fly as swiftly as those of a tiny little butterfly, but as tall as a pixie's—they allow us to move too fast for even the folk to see, here and there in the blink of an eye.

Flying isn't what one would call a civilized pursuit. It is the affair of war; the soldiers of the crown learn to defend our land by any means, spreading their wings to protect us if they must. It's also the affair of lovers, fleeing in the dead of the night to protect each other's secrets.

I don't think I've ever been taught how to fly, but I've always known how. I've always craved it.

Tonight, I give in to the longing. I glide along the dark sinuous forest at the border of our land—near Mithgarth. I soar above lakes and groves, hills, and burrows. I let myself breathe, truly breathe.

I'm alive. I'm alive, and yesterday, I was in control. I may still manage to control my fate, despite the shadow of the queen. And if she marries me off to the prince of the sea, well, I'll be far away from her, down under water, where she can't reach. Lind didn't seem cruel, or smart enough to get in my way. He was enjoyable, even.

And malleable. He's afraid to break me; I could manipulate him to leave me alone.

It could be worse. Everything could be worse. But the very thought of being dragged to the sea makes bile rise in my throat.

I cannot submit to that fate. I will not. Drusk is right, I can weasel my way out of it.

And if I keep thinking about Drusk as a potential victim, more the fool I. He's clearly said he didn't want me. I could still force his will because of the favor he owes me, but I won't condemn us to a century of misery. I have to ask a friend.

Someone simple, willing, and easy.

The last things I desire in a companion, but this union would be about survival, not desire.

Drusk would not be malleable. There would be no making a toy of him. Toying *with* him? Definitely. Not against him.

I'd never break Drusk, even if I tried.

And I wouldn't. I'd know better.

I don't think he could break me either. We'd challenge each other.

Inside the heart of every unseelie fae, there's a wickedness, a desire to take and twist and set things on fire. I've felt it all my life. I've snuffed it out.

With Drusk, I take. I twist. I burn. I scream and insult. I let myself be who I could have been without my bonds.

And he likes it.

I'm swaying through the clouds when I see a fire in the woods below. A wild, reckless fire, destroying everything in its wake. It's close to home.

Spotting movements through the foliage, I plunge down. If there's wingless folk or beasts down there, I can be of assistance. I can help put it out, too.

As I near, the sound of steel crashing against steel, screams of battle, and the smell of fresh blood hit me. This is no ordinary fire. We're under attack.

I let my wings retract under my skin so that they don't burn, and land high on a tree, close to the fire. My eyes pierce the smoke and flame, and I see them. Soldiers in foreign colors, screaming with vigor and cheer as they cut through folk.

Common folk, not our knights. They're slaughtering defenseless people.

I leap to the ground and contour the fire to meet them.

My heart sinks. Now that my vision isn't hindered, I see hundreds and hundreds of soldiers—if not thousands. I can't quite believe it. If all the courts were to raise one army, they'd have fewer warriors than those in front of me.

I advance all the same, though I'm just in my night gown, without any weapons or armor.

I'm almost at the edge of the village they're slaughtering their way through when I hear horses approach. I spin on my heel, adopting a defensive position, but I recognize the riders.

"Meda." My grandmother leads our knights.

"Mh," she says, eyeing me with something that looks a little like approval. "Looks like your training didn't quite go to waste."

"Give me a sword. I can help."

"You can help evacuate the nearing villages, and the woods," she counters. "Someone must, and you're not dressed for war."

I want to argue, but I don't. She's right, someone must, and it's logical that the someone should be me. I'm faster than the rest of our knights, and less schooled in the way of battles.

I rush to all of our nearby settlements, screaming at the top of my lungs to get the folk moving. "Where to?" they ask. There's only one place defendable here—our home, so I tell them to go to the Court of Mist.

I tell myself Meda will win, that she'll push them back, but there were so many soldiers, and fierce as she is, she's just one person, with a dozen knights.

After making my way through every village, I return home, passing through the forest, to get whatever animals I can find to move the right way.

Hundreds of paws follow my steps. One catches my attention, smoothly running in the shadows of the branches overhead.

A wyr. They don't live here, so far from the Murkwood. It's a wyrfox, not unlike the one I saw a month ago, though older, as it's entirely black.

When it leaps at the last row of trees, and lands right at my feet, I realize that it's not like the one who'd tried to eat me. It's the very one. I recognize his essence, and his eyes.

Then I think back to the random carcasses on my windows.

I shake my head, confused.

I saved its life in the Murkwood. It could be feeling grateful, but it's not in the nature of a wyr.

Watching him, I understand. "You're mine."

I've been given a familiar, though I'm no one to the land—not a lady, or a true royal.

I don't have time to wonder at it.

"Well, if you understand me, get in the house. Stay safe." And it must understand me, because it obeys my order.

I've only reached the threshold when I feel a sense of panic explode in my chest, knocking me over.

I can barely breathe. I can barely think. My head is on fire, and the pain in my side, right under my ribs, feels like I've been stabbed with iron.

I'm dying. I must be dying to feel this broken.

Nothing has hurt me, hit me, but I know that something inside me, a huge part of my soul, has been destroyed.

I need to go. I know exactly where, and at the same time, I don't know at all. I can *feel* it, a thread pulling me like I'm fish on a line.

I don't have a choice. I follow it.

eighteen
court of wind

I run.

I run fast, staying low on the ground. My feet hit the mossy forest floor, and I think of all of my grandmother's lessons, everything I've heard the Whitecroft tutors tell other students—those who were allowed physical exertion.

The first lesson in war was simple. Never be taken by surprise.

We would have been wiser to expect an attack at all times. Be prepared for it. Dressed for it. Armed for it.

I'm in a stupid flowing night gown, and without so much as a sharp knife to protect me.

Taking to the sky is too risky; their archers *might* be poor marksmen, but my wings would make for a big, bright target.

My heartbeats thunder in my ears as I hear marching soldiers all around me—their steel and iron clashes, closing in.

I have to get where I should be. I *have* to. I can't die now. I'm not permitted to.

I could have died yesterday, but I didn't. I could have died a month ago, but I didn't. If the queen of Tenebris hadn't ordered my end, these idiots aren't allowed to commandeer it. The fact that there is an entire army of idiots is irrelevant.

I will not fall.

Not here. My journey can't be over, because I am needed elsewhere. I have to get *home*.

Not to the Court of Mist, not to my parents.

Somewhere else is calling me. Crying for me. Screaming my name, so loud I can't tune it out.

Vlari. Vlari. Vlari.

I belong to that voice, and I have to get there.

Now.

My next footfall doesn't hit where I expect it to; tripping forward, I roll over the asphalt of an evenly paved road. Though familiar, it takes me a while to realize where I am.

In Hardrock; right in front of the queen's keep, at the edge of the drawbridge.

Nowhere near the forest. Nowhere near home. I turn around, dizzy and confused. Everything around me is clouded over with a dark, thick mist.

I cough, bringing my sleeve to my nose to protect my airway.

Myst.

I'd been transported here, right to the gates of the castle, but the warded gates would have prevented anyone from appearing inside.

There is only one person who could summon me like this: Drusk. There hasn't been another Myst in generations; it's assumed he is the only one alive.

The thick fog starts to dissipate. I turn on my heels, looking for him, but he's nowhere to be seen.

Over the beats of my heart, I start to hear the racket of a battle; steel on steel, screams and battle cries, explosions.

What is going on? That an army has reached my home in the west makes sense, but how could they have gotten here, to the heart of the unseelie territory, so fast?

There are only two possibilities. They've either come from the north, through seelie land, or from the east—the sea. They couldn't have done that without the blessing of the Sea Court.

I think back to yesterday. Why had the queen invited the sea folk at all? She has nothing but contempt for anything, anyone who isn't gentry.

I start to understand the pattern of events that brought us here. Events I'd shown no interest in.

The attack Drusk survived. The uncharacteristic diplomacy. It has all been because of this—because we've already been at war, though she hasn't warned any of us.

And now, Hardrock is burning.

I spin around to face the royal caves, residence of the queen, of the gentry. If I pass through those gates, I'll be safe, and I am so very close.

But the city is burning.

The Light Market. The street of cloth, with Ma'am Rolo's store. The residence of the Frosts, and the Thorns, and everyone else I know. Everyone else who owes me. Everyone I own.

My city.

My *people*.

Folk I've talked to, bargained with. Folk I like, folk I enjoy teasing, folk who delight in teasing me.

They are the ones suffering down below.

A scream pierces through the cacophony of the battle, through the darkness, louder than a banshee's screech. A scream carrying words in a tongue older than me, older than the queen and her keep. It takes a while to realize it came from me.

Come to me, it said, both to my friends and foe. A threat and an invitation.

When my lungs are empty of air, I finally stop, my throat burning. I'm out of breath, and I take a second to still myself.

A second is all I have.

The city is quiet now, and all eyes are on the castle.

On me.

I'm stunned by the realization I've just doomed myself. Given away my position, and dared anyone to come get me.

I could still fall back. Ten steps are all it'd take—I'd reach the doors.

The first wave of armed soldiers wearing foreign colors bawls out, darting to me. I can't even tell how many of them move.

Ten steps.

Safety.

That's all it'd take.

While I deliberate my next course of action, I realize that while numerous, my would-be assassins are…slow. Awkward.

Human.

I've never hated humans; not like some of us do. I pity their short lives, their lack of wisdom, their obsession with a level of perfection most of them will never come close to reaching. And I don't hate these soldiers either. They're cannon fodder. Underfed, underqualified, sent to be slaughtered while their lords reap the reward. Hundreds of thousands of them were sent to die today, to kill a thousand fae. To eradicate the Wicked Court.

The Court of Wind, home to Nyx, home to my blood.

When the first human reaches me, swinging his great sword to strike me, I'm still in the same spot.

I lift my hand right as his blade falls down.

My fingers close into a tight fist and I smile.

The human screams, but not for long.

I'm not trying to make them back down as I did with the wyrfox. I'm not after his suffering, or his submission.

All I claim is his life, and that of all of the others running up the drawbridge, in one simple, decisive movement of my hand.

They collapse as one.

An explosion of energy bursts into me, almost strong enough to knock me out.

So many lives. So much…

Power.

I've taken their power.

I smile.

I take the sword that would have cut me in two from the dead man's grasp. It's a plain, uneven blade without much grace—I doubt it's even been named. It'll do anyway.

Ignoring all of my instincts that scream at me, demanding I return to the castle, I make my way down the bridge, to the city.

My call has brought more than enemies toward the castle. In the chaos, I see folk, trying to fight their way through the human army.

There's too many of them, and as they mingle with fae, I can't use my power again. It doesn't matter. I have a sword, and thanks to Meda, I know how to use it.

Meda. I think of home, for one moment—of the army heading for them. But being distracted on the battlefield is one sure way to end up dead. All that matters now, here, is the next human at the point of my blade.

Screams. Blood. Sorrow. For every fae they kill, we destroy ten of them, but each fae life means something to me. The humans are just puppets of blood and flesh, invaders I refuse to see as more than inconvenient fleas.

Yet, I'm losing against them. I'm losing the people. My people. My folk. They're more mine than they've ever been Morgana's. She isn't the one who goes to markets and negotiates with pucks. I am. Some of them owe me, others respect me. I know them, and they know my name.

Throwing myself in the middle of a fight is no strategy at all.

We need an exit, and there's only one place to go.

"Not bad, for a gentry!"

I spin around, finding a small, round fae surrounded by a ring of fire.

I laugh in relief. Khia. I could have kissed her.

"Not bad for a salamander," I echo, screaming to be heard over the mess. "I need to call that favor."

Khia's beady eyes widen. "Now! You want a favor, now?"

I parry the blow of a man and swing my sword down—then, spotting the four closing in, stomp my foot hard on the ground, letting go of some of my energy.

I turn back to Khia, rather than watch them fall. "I need your fire, on either side of this path, from the drawbridge to the town square. Keep it going as long as you can. We can defend the entry point, and only let the folk pass through."

She seems stunned—shocked that I'd asked for something that wouldn't just benefit me, I think. But she shakes her head.

"The gates are closed. We'd have nowhere to go, and they could blow the bridge with their catapults."

Of course, Morgana had left Hardrock completely defenseless.

Coward.

I try to think. The gates predate Morgana—they predate the Wicked Court; they'd been in place in Nyx's days. I doubt she could have controlled their magic. If she's disabled anything, it's the manned gates on the right; those the people who want to beg for an audience use.

"I'll get you through the gates," I say, letting no doubt into my voice.

God, I hope I'm right.

"Just blaze a path."

She nods, done arguing.

Her hands lift above her head, and I leap to her side, blocking a sword meant for her, pushing her back through the wall of fire she's erected.

As I hoped, the humans scream and rush out of the way. No one much likes the idea of being burned alive, but the folk can survive a burn or two. I slice my way through the soldiers, to reach the start of Khia's blazing corridor. To my surprise, three boys and two girls are already in place, their weapons in hand.

They let the folk walk in, and throw arrows or daggers at any human getting close.

This might just work—as long as I can get the people inside the castle once they're on the bridge.

I raise the sword that doesn't feel so awkward now, ready to strike any soldiers who get too close.

"We're good here!" The imp who screams at me can't be much older than a boy. "Go get the others to safety!"

I hesitate, because if we don't hold the entry, there's no point trying to siphon our people through.

"My wife's on the bridge. And my ma. And other folk's mas and sweethearts. Go!"

I nod. He's right; I can't be in two places at once, and the only thing no one else can do is open the gates. "Hold this entry," I tell him.

No need to spell out what will happen if he doesn't.

I run up the scorched path. It's less than half a mile long, but by the end, I realize how tired I am. Drained.

My kind isn't meant for long battles. Duels? Yes. We can fight, and win. But pixies aren't known for their endurance.

At the bridge, and out of the fire, I will myself to regain speed. Now isn't the time for weakness. Any weakness.

Tomorrow, I can think about the thousand times when I could have failed, the million ways I could have fallen. Tonight, I have to ignore the odds, and think of nothing but the next step toward safety.

Toward home.

I am home.

I belong here.

I am of this court, and these are my people.

Open.

Open, open, open.

Let us through.

I pass the left gate first, not letting myself doubt my right to be here, my right to bring the entire city through the gate.

I turn back, seeing a little girl walk in first. Her wings are out, and folded behind her—moth wings, brown and droopy, but not unlike mine.

Let. Her. Through.

Yes, mistress.

I hadn't realized what was talking to me when I'd been in the carriage, begging the gate to let Drusk and his footman through. Now, outside, I feel it.

The wind.

The young fae steps forward and comes out the other side of the gate unharmed.

I let out a breath I hadn't known I'd been holding.

This is working. Good.

I take the next step, knowing the night is far from over.

We've left our attackers, and entered the home of my enemy.

The halls are dark and silent, when just yesterday, they were lit with thousands of fae and candles, alive with music and laughter.

"Where's ev—?"

I shush the speaker with one move of my hand.

I could have assumed the court had evacuated, by air or boat, but this is no mere absence. I feel them. I feel the aura, the essence of the entire court—all the gentry, advisors, artists, dancers, servants who belonged here.

They are still within these walls.

And at the same time, not at all.

If this weren't a sufficient indication of what occurred here, the stench of blood would have been enough.

I take a torch on the right wall and light it against the cavernous stone. "Keep going right ahead," I whisper. "Through each hall, never turn. You'll reach the sea, on the other side."

I'm not speaking to anyone in particular. There are hundreds behind me—let one of them hear it. Let all of them hear it.

I don't tell them what they can do at the sea. I don't mention that our assailants could have come that way—their ships might still be docked there.

And thankfully, no one asks.

"What are you going to do?" someone asks—a child, I think.

Another answer I don't want to give, but at least I have one. With some effort, I force it out, turning back. "I have to lead."

As long as I can.

We advance through the dark hall, and then the hall of crowns. It isn't until we've reached the hall of revels that we're forced to stop. The great white stone doors that had been wide-open yesterday are closed, and barricaded.

I don't have time to ask for help; half a dozen lads—a troll, I think, four imps, and a brownie—push them. The troll takes one side himself and the other five manage to move the other.

My stomach sinks as soon as the doors are ajar. By the time they've managed to push them open, I'm gagging, hand over my mouth to stop myself from vomiting.

I see the little girl who's almost my height step forward, and I grab her hand, pushing her back to the rest of the crowd.

No child should see this. No one should see this.

In the hall of revels, the entire court has been slaughtered, sliced through and bled like common game after a hunt.

At least a hundred gentry—most of our nobles. Above all, on a raised dais where the queen oversees her parties, she, her daughters, and her sons are standing all together, held in a mockery of a formal presentation. They're all scorched black, burned alive by an enchantment.

As I watch the ashes of the woman who's terrorized me my entire life, I am too stunned to move, or think, or feel.

Dead, dead, dead.

Morgana is dead.

Her heirs are dead.

And I would have been dead too, if she'd favored me.

Perhaps I'll be dead soon. It would be foolish to assume that I can fend off a thing that could have torn through the court.

"Run." The first time I say it, it's barely a whisper, but I clear my throat, and I say it again. "*Run*. Now. Before they sense us."

They don't question me. I've led them this far.

I allow myself to take the time to concentrate, sensing the presences around me. I barely scratched the surface earlier, because I didn't have the time or inclination to define just what was here with us—and how many of *it*.

I'm not stunned to feel immortals. Not the folk; the descendants of the gods.

Though we'd only faced humans, I would never have thought Mithgarth capable of attacking us—and reaching the heart of our kingdom—not by themselves. Of course, there are plenty of humans in Álfheimr. That they'd be used as soldiers to slaughter the common fae while the immortals took our court—our courts—made sense.

I refuse to think of my parents. They could take care of themselves, and unlike me, they had a Meda to defend them.

Seeing that I haven't moved, the troll turns to me and growls, questioning.

I wince at the noise. "The invaders are upstairs." What were they doing upstairs? The court and the queen's quarters are all on the same floor. On the higher levels of the keep, there is nothing but stone, to my knowledge. "They're…focused, but if they feel us here, they'll kill us. *Run*."

The troll doesn't like that idea, I can tell. It tilts its heavy jaw toward me. Then I get it. It's asking what I'm doing.

Fair question.

I'm being insane. Stupid. Dangerously arrogant.

Rather than attempting a response, I kneel on the smooth floor, drenching my nightgown in fae blood. Sweat and mud and blood. The garment is having a hell of a night.

I hold my arms to my sides, palms facing up, and let go of the energy left in me. Not my own—I have little of that. The energy I've stolen. The strength and lives of the hundred humans I took on the bridge. I release it. I direct it. I force it to enter the broken bodies of the folk at my feet.

Then I sense it crawling to the dais. Crawling to the queen.

I call it back, and redirect it where I want it.

I will save her court. They're folk. They're the gentry of our people, and if we're at war, I'll need every single one of them. The old and wise, the strange and cruel, the young and brave.

But not her.

Never her.

She can rot until I am broken and join her in hell.

Part of me thinks about the others on the dais. The aunts I don't know. The cousins I've never spoken to. I don't know if I can help them—not as they are, burned to a crisp, and if I could, it would take too much from me.

Before I've made a conscious decision, I find that I'm empty.

Void.

The energy I've taken has been given again.

And the court rises.

They're stunned, confused, shocked. All of them are looking right at me. I can tell, they know that whatever happened, I caused it. I did this. For better or worse, we are linked together in a chain of power and obligation none of us understand.

I get to my feet, clearing my throat. "The people are heading to the summer palace. Go. I won't be long."

I'm not done here; I can feel it.

nineteen
the queen's plans

I don't know what forces pushed me to walk through the castle room after room, despite the danger, despite the fact that the people, in dire need of help, are making their way down unfamiliar halls, to an uncertain future, but I refuse to question it.

I'm no more familiar with the court than any of them; I've never even stepped upstairs before.

I find studies littered with books and maps, laboratories with potions still cooking up. It seems I've entered the functional, military part of the court—where the leadership sleeps, eats, and works for the queen.

In one of the larger rooms, there's even a chair grand enough to pass for a throne. In front of it, a table carved in oak wood is painted with the largest map of Álfheimr I've ever seen. Various figures on the board—an eagle, a wolf, a sun, among others—make me think of a child's game; I had figures of wood just like these growing up.

Upon closer inspection, I understand this is a game, all right. One not meant for children at all.

Feeling I'm alone, I risk taking a moment to myself to approach a table. I know nothing of war; a glimpse at my grandmother's plans might enlighten me—or give me an idea as to what I can do next.

The sun is at the heart of the seelie kingdom, right on the spot where the Court of Sunlight should be, from what I remember of my lessons. The wolf is in the wilderness. On the forbidden mountains to the north, there's a white crown. I remember the legends of a prince cursed to sleep forever, right there.

Tenebris has far more figures than the other kingdoms. On the Wicked Court, there's another crown—black, with a green stone. I've seen it on many of Nyx's illustrations; I glean it represents the queen. A flame for the Court of Ashes, a snowflake for the Court of Storm, a sword for the Court of Ichor, an ax on the Court of Silt, and a rock on the Court of Stone.

The Court of Mist has two effigies; one is a star, and the other, the only character I see on the entire board. The others are symbols meant to represent the courts, but this is just a girl.

That tiny doll-like model seems to have been carved in a different wood as the rest of them. Maybe at a different time. Stunned, I realize it's me.

I don't have time for this. I don't understand any of it anyway.

Just as I'm about to move, I pause, my eye catching the shine of a thin blue line running right through the court on the map.

It's not water; the sinuous river running from the ocean to the heart of Tenebris is south of Hardrock.

My fingers trace the line; it's minute and discreet, but I can feel it underneath my fingertips. It stops on a familiar point. My eyes widen, taking it in.

Whitecroft; my old school. It's the ley line—one of those Nyx built to connect the courts.

My mind rushes in a thousand different directions, calculating, analyzing, remembering details.

I know I have to make time for this. I have to understand it. I have to use it.

I let my mind widen again, though I'm playing with fire. If I can sense the intruders, there's a chance that they might sense me right back, but I need to know if they're close.

I feel something else. Someone else.

My head snaps to my left, out of the room.

Drusk. He's here, I can tell. And he isn't alone.

Has he betrayed us? Is he with the invaders? That would explain how he alone survived the fight at the borders.

I'm torn between the map and getting to Drusk.

I'm always inclined to believe the worst of him. There's a chance he isn't against me, and if so, I need him by my side. Drusk is a better defense for our people than a dusty old map could ever be.

A curse escapes my lips. I turn back to the map, memorizing every single detail I can commit to memory one last time, before getting out of the room.

Friend or foe, Drusk is a key element I cannot afford to ignore.

Silent as I can, following shadows, I let my subconscious lead me to him.

I reach heavy golden doors and sense him right on the other side. Drusk, and three others. Fae, from what I can decipher. Tensing, prepared for a trap, I push against the cumbersome owl-faced knob.

On the other side, Drusk grips his sword in a defensive stance, holding his wounded left side, hand thick with blood. At his flank, two other knights mirror his position. I'm so relieved, it takes me a second to see they're protecting something on the floor.

Alven's bleeding out on the polished marble, a dagger in his chest. I don't ask why it hasn't been removed—it would have killed him instantly.

I can't help chuckling, walking into the light. "Looks like I won't have to kill you," I say casually.

The knights have lowered their weapons, but Drusk hasn't moved an inch, his intense gaze biting into me.

I ignore him, circling him to kneel next to my grandfather. My hand presses against his chest.

Alven groans, protesting against my ministration. "No. The stone. Take—"

"Shush." He can tell me all about stones after I heal him.

I've used up all of my stolen energy downstairs, but there's still enough of me to help him. I feel my palms tremble, and I wince as pain slices through my chest, right where he's been stabbed. I pull the dagger out, stifling a scream.

My heart beats fast in my chest, as if stunned it survived the pain.

I can wonder about it tomorrow, and the day after.

I rise and extend my hand to help Alven up. "I can't heal you all the way through."

I don't elaborate on why. He winces, but gets to his feet anyway.

"We have to go. Those who killed the court are—"

"Upstairs." Alven tilts his head toward the ceiling. "Sealed for now, but that won't last long. We had them chase us to the dungeons, and locked the keep down. They'll find a way out, though." His gaze cuts through me. "You've seen the court?"

"I helped those I could." I'm not answering the question he hasn't asked. He wants to know about his wife, his children. His family. He wants to know if I've helped them.

And when I tell him I haven't, he'll hate me.

I don't let guilt weigh me down. I rush out of the room and return to the war chamber; if I have a few moments while the enemies are in the dungeons, I need to use them to study this map.

"Wait." Catching up with me, Alven hands me a flat rock. "You need this."

I nod, pocketing it without sparing it a glance. What I need is a plan. "Do you know if the army came from the coast?"

One of the two knights I don't know, a tall gentry with silken white braids knotted to her back, points to the northern borders of Tenebris, right next to the Murkwood.

"No, they attacked from the north—I think they entered through the seelie kingdom, staying close enough to the borders to avoid their scouts or ours."

I nod. "Then we can evacuate the city by boat."

"Not without help." Alven shakes his head. "We only have two ships."

"Let me worry about help." I point to Whitecroft. "Tell me about this. Tell me about the ley lines."

My grandfather frowns, perplexed, but he answers all the same. "They were built as a way to control the minor courts. The strength of the courts—their lands and burrows, their lakes and rivers—is harnessed by its lord, hence why the kings and queens of the lower courts are more powerful than their subjects. Holding the position is enough to be able to draw from their court's strength. Nyx's ley lines limit the strength at the core of the court, and redirect it through the lines."

Instead of leading to the Wicked Court, the seat of power Nyx held, she'd made them converge on Whitecroft.

I think back at the book that had so fascinated me. I think back at the powerful and power-hungry girl who'd written it.

She would have dearly desired increasing her strength, but she didn't.

I'd loved and admired the girl because the one thing I've read between her elegant lines was unconditional dedication to the unseelie folk. She'd been frustrated by her mother because she valued strength; the strength to protect her people, to stand between them and any enemy, should they be the seelie realm or the other courts.

Nyx wasn't quite good, or evil. Something in between. She played by a different set of rules, and what mattered to her wasn't propriety. It was results.

Suddenly, I understand. I don't need to read it. I know why she united the courts.

And I know what we need to do next. "Is there any paper?"

Familiar with the war room, Alven finds a roll of parchment I fold in two, again and again, before ripping the corners until I have eight uneven pieces.

On one, I write *Whitecroft* and hand it to the knights. "Can you copy it five times?"

I don't stop to see if they've complied, writing the sixth note to my family, and the seventh to the Court of Sunlight. They ought to know strangers are trampling their land—that's assuming they haven't given them the go-ahead.

The last, I hack in two, and address one to a friend, the other to a quasi-stranger.

That's the best I can do. I don't let myself believe that it's not enough.

"Can you send these to the courts?" I ask Drusk, pointing to the seven identical words.

He lifts the hand that's not holding his side, and the pieces of paper disappear in a poof of thick smoke. While he makes it look easy, his wince betrays the effort it costs him now, because of his wound.

Knowing I'll need him again, I press my hand to his, and let go of as much energy as I can spare. Pain slices me, making me stumble dizzily. I've never been this weak.

Drusk moves to help, but Alven is faster.

My grandfather holds me up. "That was foolish. Careful, child."

"I am," I reply.

I know better than to try to give more than this. I am a Void, empty without my power. If I give too much of myself, I'll die.

"You don't understand. You have to save your strength. You could be the last of your blood left, if your mother was taken."

I glance up to him.

He knows. He knows I haven't saved the royal family—my family, and his.

And he doesn't seem to judge me for it.

I decide to process that later, shoving it down along with any other feelings I don't have time for right now. "Are there ravens, eagles? Something that can carry messages."

Drusk steps forward. "I could—"

I hand him the note for my family. "You can send that to the Court of Mist. For these two, I can't use magic."

Alven whistles low, holding an arm up.

Within moments, I see a dark bird approach in the distance. A raven with all-knowing, clever eyes I've seen before.

I'd always assumed it was one of Morgana's familiars, but if it had been, it would have died along with her.

It lands on Alven's shoulders, talons digging into his flesh.

"Tell him where he needs to go. He'll reach them, or die trying."

Hopefully the former.

I help Alven attach my messages to his bird, and hope flies out of the keep.

Then, we run.

twenty
child of the blood

The court and the rest of Hardrock have made it to the summer palace when we emerge from the cavernous halls.

Alven, Drusk, and I look back to the castle as one, each one of us feeling the same thing: a wave of fury and strength approaching us with a roar.

The immortals have freed themselves from the dungeons. "What now?"

I look at the ocean in the distance, dark and violent, just as dangerous as the enemy behind us.

We don't have a choice.

I turn back to the keep, lifting my sword.

Alven shakes his head, and hands me his. "If we're to meet our end here, let it be said that the last queen had a decent weapon, at least."

We don't need a grand coronation to know that the crown has passed on to the next heir of Morgana.

I hiss, "My *mother* is queen, Grandfather."

Ciera is alive. She has to be. I'd know it otherwise; I'd feel it.

Alven shrugs it off, as though his daughter's life doesn't matter. As though nothing matters.

He's lost much today, but I can't forgive him his indifference. I need him to care. I need every single one of the fae standing at my side to care enough to give the folk behind us time to get away. I don't have the strength to shoulder this burden alone, not now, after using so much of my energy.

I'm just a pixie, small and ephemeral.

Feeling a hand on my shoulder, I glance to my left. Drusk smiles at me. It's not a nice smile; there's something absolutely wicked about it.

He smiles as though we're about to play. As though he can't wait for the fight to come. It's just a game, and he intends to win it.

To my shock, I smile right back.

"You're insane. Both of you." The male knight hadn't said a thing until now.

I wonder who he is. If he's about to die next to us, I should know his name at least.

I'm about to ask, but the immortals are upon us.

There are only three of them. That's enough. It was enough to annihilate the court. It was enough to burn my grandmother alive, along with all her present children.

The first immortal is a colossal man with long dark hair, dressed in thick layers of silk and velvet. He has the bearing of a king.

No, not a king.

A god.

Part of me wants to run. I ground myself, jaw tightening. This is my land, and we don't worship any god but death here.

At his side stand one man and one woman, each almost as terrifying as their leader. The woman is smirking, her eyes fixed on me. To my shock, I realize she's not just one of them. The elegant curve of her ears and something in her violet eyes betrays her. She's one of us. Not just a fae—a descendant of Nyx.

Family.

It hits me. Lily. If Lily was a human changeling brought to the queen, it meant that the queen had sent her daughter to the human realm. The child of the blood has come to reclaim what belongs to her.

I start to understand why the royals were burned. They hope to replace our ruler with her—the immortal's pawn.

Over my dead body.

Which is probably the plan.

The man on the left resembles the leader; he must be a son or a brother.

I don't know enough about them. I don't know enough about the world as a whole. I want to scream at myself for letting everyone, everything, shove me in a little box where I wasn't allowed to be noticed, wasn't allowed to ask questions or see the rest of the world. I'm utterly unprepared to face them, because I know none of their weaknesses.

Drusk steps forward, intending to lunge, but I grab his arm, pulling him back. He looks down at me. "Not now. This is a game of patience."

We have to buy as much time as possible. I don't say it out loud, for fear of the enemy overhearing us. If they did, they could attack right now to avoid giving us what we need.

He nods, and steps back closer to me.

I redirect my attention to the trio. They've slowed down.

"Well, it seems we have another one." The dark-haired immortal speaks low, his thunderous voice cruel. "Where were you when we burned your loved ones, cockroach? Hiding, I'd wager."

I have to fight a grin.

Wherever they're from, leaders love to hear themselves talk; especially when they've won. He wants to give a speech, and I cannot say how much that pleases me.

"Who are you? What do you want?"

Speak, speak, speak. I have to goad him into telling us all his evil little plans.

"I am the emperor of Álfheimr, child. For too long has your little forest rebelled against our rule. You steal men and women who belong to us. You keep the resources and magic of our lands for your own uses. You will bow to our rule." He glances to the girl at his side. "Not you personally, perhaps."

No, he intends for me to be buried deep underground or washed away by the sea first.

"I still haven't heard a name."

The son, or brother, doesn't like my tone: his lips bare a set of white, sharp teeth. The self-proclaimed emperor doesn't seem to mind. "I am Kraver Vikus."

He seems smug about it, as though the name itself should have me quivering in fear. And perhaps it would have, if I'd had any idea of the history of his land, his rule. Instead, those two words evoke nothing in me. They're simply the name of my enemy. I commit it to memory. Enemies define us just as much as our friends and lovers. More, sometimes.

When I don't react, the emperor narrows his eyes dangerously. I can tell the time for speeches is over. He starts to move, and I brace myself.

Just a little more strength. Just a little more energy. Just a little more time. I can do this. I think it over and over, as though hexing myself.

Before Kraver attacks, a horn sounds in the distance.

Now, I laugh, relief crashing into me so hard it almost knocks me off balance.

The others glance back, but I don't need to; I sense the ships' approach. I feel the storm rage harder, pushing them toward our shores.

"How in the name of Nyx have you managed—"

"A pirate or two owed me." I shrug. "And now, I owe the Sea Lands."

Bargains and oaths have always been my currency of choice. I admit, I didn't think we'd get a response this fast, but with the Sea Lands' help, any ship could have crossed the ocean in a matter of instants.

Sending Lind a message was almost an impulse, driven by despair, but I'd guessed he would have been our best chance. He'd meant it when he said he wanted alliances. And he's apparently not against an alliance with *me*.

The girl at the emperor's side screams obscenities, pointing to the ships. Kraver doesn't seem to care. "We'll kill them regardless," his carelessness seems to say.

I grant he might, but we have hope, and I refuse to let go of it. I don't know the extent of his powers. There's a chance he might not be strong enough to kill us—all of us.

I look at Drusk, first, then my grandfather, and the two knights. "Hold this line."

From the corners of my eyes, I see them all nod.

Whatever the cost, the immortals aren't going through until the folk are safely ensconced on the dozen ships.

It is only three of them. We can do this.

Kraver waves his hand.

The ground beneath my feet shakes and roars—I'm propelled feet backward, hitting my head as I fall.

I try to get back to my feet and am squashed down again, so hard I feel blood in my mouth.

The four others at my side don't seem to fare any better, and Kraver advances, smug and infinitely powerful. He doesn't even seem to strain under the effort.

Drusk reaches out to his Myst; thick fog coats the ground around the three immortals, starting to engulf them.

My eyes barely catch the movement, but the man next to Kraver leaps in the air, and lands right on top of Drusk's wrist, crushing it to the ground.

The emperor and his pawn keep walking to the shores, ignoring it.

Drusk screams as the bones break, then screams again when the immortal kicks his head. He draws his wings out—great and dark, with a powerful span—and blocks the third kick, wincing. With great effort, he manages to get to his feet, and calls to his power again.

The immortal groans as the Myst attacks his body, eating at his flesh like acid. For one wild, wonderful second, I think Drusk has gotten the better of him.

Then the god leaps in the air, breaking out of the dark shadows around him, and lands right on top of Drusk, pinning him under his booted foot. A malevolent smile crawls on the corner of his lips. He's enjoying this. Pain. Causing it—even receiving it.

The immortal takes his sword in two hands, and draws it back, ready to swing it.

I don't know how, but I manage to force myself to dig into my already-exhausted magic, and drain him of as much life force as I can steal.

Feeling the violation, the immortal stops mid-swing, turning the full extent of his wrath on me, his face contorted in a mask of pain and fury.

Dragging his sword behind him, he advances leisurely toward where I'm still lying on the ground, mere feet away.

I barely notice him, my mind foggy, confused.

Moments ago, I couldn't hope to stand. All I had was bravado. Now my limbs feel weightless, the pain I'd felt when I'd taken on the wounds of others a distant memory.

I look at the smug immortal closing in, rising to a crouch and then standing to face him.

His grin tells me he loved kicking Drusk and he's going to delight in what he plans to do to me. I'm his favorite kind of prey; small, dainty, female. Weak, to him. He plants his sword deep in the ground, eager to make the torture last.

He doesn't understand I'm not the victim here. He is.

When he's close, he grabs me by the throat, lifting me in the air, and I let him. I want him close, easy to reach. "You're nothing, compared to us."

I could laugh. He means it as an insult, but I have been nothing my entire life. That is my normal. It is in my nature, as a Void. Hold no power, no good or evil.

I am what I *take*.

"What does that make you, handsome?" I whisper to him, before shoving my hands right at his face, and sucking every last drop of strength from him.

I feel him writhe. His hand leaves my throat to battle against my arms, but I'm holding on to his soul, not his flesh. And I am ingesting it.

The man screeches, finding his effort pointless.

Behind me, I feel the immortals approach, but I don't fear their immense power, not anymore.

I have it.

I only let go of the first immortal when he's nothing but an empty shell. He falls at my feet, lifeless.

The two others lunge at me, and I lift both hands, beaming.

I start to suck on them, too. Why stop at one, when I can be three of them? When I can be a god.

I'll never again have to be irrelevant, or invisible.

I take, and take, and take.

I feel my hair against my cheek, dark and lush purple to the roots, as it was always meant to be.

Now it's my turn to bare my teeth, claws extended.

"Nevlaria!" My name sounds like a faraway echo. Why would I pay attention to Alven? He is nothing now. "Their army is coming. We have to go!"

Let them come. I'll destroy them. I'll absorb them all.

"You're going to succumb to madness if you don't let go now. Voids are dangerous because of it. The power is addictive. Please, Vlari. Let go!"

He just wants to control me. Use me. I extend my hold to start absorbing my grandfather, too. I'll never let go of the power. I need it more than I need to live.

More than I need anything at all.

"Vlari."

I pause, glancing back.

Drusk is struggling to stand, using his sword as a walking cane.

He's hurt. Badly hurt.

"The ships will leave. Come on."

I can't let go. He doesn't understand, and he should. He should be on *my side.*

He reaches out with one hand coated with his dried blood.

He almost died today; not once, but twice—at least.

And he needs my help. So I let go of my three victims, slowly, detaching myself from their life force.

When I've severed the connection, I stand there, stunned at what I'd just done—what I would have done if I hadn't let go.

I can't understand it. And I don't have time to try.

I rush to Drusk, placing my palms either side of his head and healing every crack, the internal bleeding, the wound I couldn't entirely close before. I need to let go of this energy. All of it. Before it consumes me.

On the ground, the emperor and the girl I am related to are barely breathing, struggling to recover from what I've done to them. The emperor's hair has lost all its shine. It's white now; silver-white. The girl is something close to a corpse.

But they're two immortals and one gentry of the folk. They'll recover.

Part of me wants to ends this. Shove a sword through both of their chests and be done with it.

I don't. Maybe because of what I've just done, maybe because I know that if I kill the ruler of Álfheimr now, we'll always be at war, until the blood of all the folk has been spent.

I run to the ship, avoiding the eyes of my companion.

I don't understand what happened tonight.

I don't recognize what I've become.

A sea-worn kul with blue-green shining skin and long knotted tresses helps me on the closest ship. "That was some magic, lass!" He laughs, good-humored. I don't read any judgment from him; I shouldn't be surprised. Grogan is a water spirit known for their cunning, wickedness, and malevolence.

He's unseelie, just like me.

"Where to now?"

There is only one place where we can go. "Whitecroft."

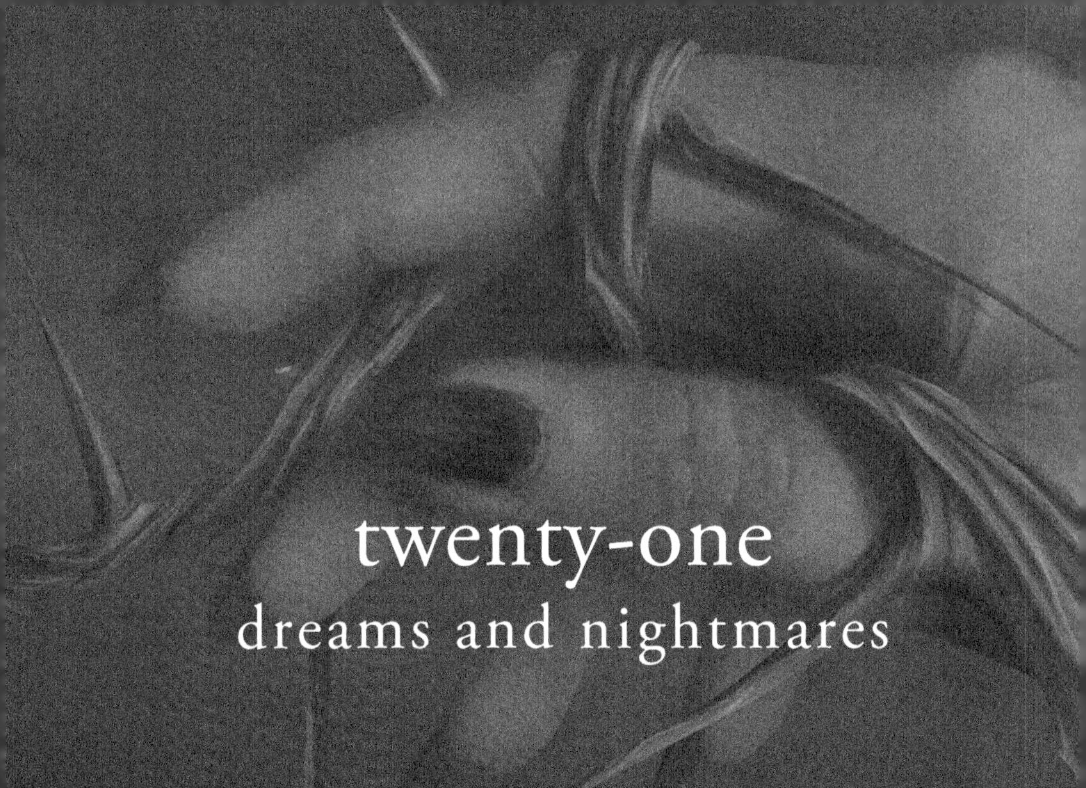

twenty-one
dreams and nightmares

We sail peacefully along the river. I remain on the deck, watching the coast for any sign of the immortals following. None do. They're recovering, assessing their next move, no doubt.

I'm not naive enough to think that a little display of power on my part has sent them running back home—though that would be awfully convenient.

Their army came from the east, and they've managed to take the Wicked Court in the west, too. I've only saved half of Hardrock, at best.

They're here to stay, until we push them back.

The white stone building appears in the distance. I didn't think I'd ever return. I certainly didn't think I'd smile, seeing it again.

Drusk comes to stand next to me, and my smile falters.

"Really?" He rolls his eyes. "You're terrible for a man's ego, you know."

"Your ego doesn't need stroking."

He smiles. "I'm going to be gallant, and refrain from saying the millions of retorts that have suddenly burst into my mind, princess."

His silliness manages to exhort one short laugh from me.

Then I remember the screams. I remember the feeling of invincibility when I'd sucked on the immortals—on my grandfather.

I remember I liked it.

Drusk leans forward on the polished wooden beam painted black, watching the dark river below. "Do you think there are selkies, this far from the sea?"

"Probably not. Kappas and nokks, maybe, though they know to stay away from a kul's ship."

He glances back at me. "How did you manage to get a favor from him?"

I shrug. "He's fond of hats, and doesn't like to go on land. Anyone could have made the trade, but merchants don't like to go on his ship—and he doesn't trust his crew to pick a good hat."

Drusk blinks. "The salvation of the court was due to a hat trade?"

Smiling is a little easier now. "I spent most of my money on a book, just a few weeks ago. Who are we to judge what others love?"

"And you love books." That seems to surprise him.

I don't hear any scorn, so I reply. "I guess. It might have been that book in particular. I think I love making bargains, more than anything else."

At least, I used to.

Now, all I can think about—all I love—is raw power. Nothing else compares.

"Make a bargain with me."

Drusk has managed to surprise me again. I frown. "About what?"

"I don't know. Anything. What would you want from me, princess?" It's the second time he's asked me that, and fifty years ago, I had no clue what to answer.

Some things haven't changed, after all.

"That's not how it works. If you want to bargain, tell me what you're after, so I can find a boon of equal value. Should I heal your wings?"

I don't think the energy I shot him with earlier would have been enough to completely mend broken wings.

I should have offered weeks ago, but I hadn't. While I never voiced why, I knew the reason. He'd said he was supposed to return to his post when he was better—and he didn't want to.

I'll bet that's why he hadn't asked either.

"They're fine," he replies, looking up to the sky. "They have been for some time. I was scheduled to get back to the army in a few days."

I try not to feel wounded that he hadn't thought to mention it until now. It felt like something we might have discussed yesterday.

I shake the disappointment. We aren't friends. He owes me nothing but a promise.

"I want you to tell me what happened a month ago," he says, his intense dark blue eyes, so like the sky, now fully focused on me.

I'm confused. "A month ago?"

"When my company was attacked. I wasn't just attacked. I wasn't just wounded. I died, Vlari. I could feel myself leave this world. There was nothing, no pain, no light—just darkness. Then I saw you, right in front of me, and I was back. In pieces, broken wings and all, but back all the same. Everyone else was dead around me. When I told my captain, they sent me straight to the king consort, who made me swear—"

"Not to tell a soul," I guessed. "Not to tell the queen."

The night I'd awoken after using so much magic the queen's men felt it—without realizing I had.

Keep your heart much closer to your chest.

Alven had known what I'd done—though I hadn't. I think back to the flower in my back. A mourning mark I'd not understood.

My heart speeds in my chest, thundering, as I finally connect the dots. My mouth hangs open.

"How did you do it? Why?" Drusk's voice is gentle at first, but the last word has another note; an edge of despair.

And I know. I know why I saved him. I know why I could always find him—why my soul had recognized him before I'd even set my eyes on him, the very first time we met. Why he alone, not the voice of reason, not the screams of my kin, had pulled me out of the darkness earlier.

Drusk was mine.

Against all logic or odds, rare as they are, fate has given me a soulmate, with a strength to match mine and more kindness.

I grin. "Oh, no. You'll have to figure that one out yourself."

He sighs. "That's not fair."

"Who told you I was fair?"

Grogan gives orders to dock the ship in the harbor. In the distance, I see torches and fairy lights; some of the courts have made it here, at least.

I'm too impatient to wait; I leap to the shores, and run all the way to the school.

Nero and Ciera are the first to greet me—they aren't in a better state than me, covered in human blood. My father hugs me, and my mother kisses the top of my head.

Someone clears their throat; I smile down at my grandmother, who stays at a distance, no doubt for fear of signs of affection.

I know better than to try to get a kiss or hug from her.

Behind them, some of the knights guarding Whitecroft stand guard, stiff and formal. I eye them with approval.

"How did it go?"

"We had to drag her away from the humans." Nero sighed, helplessly. "She was cutting her way through most of them, but they outnumbered us. We did what you asked."

I smile gratefully. "Did the other courts make it?"

"Storm, Silt, and Stars are here, so far. We were all attacked at the same time. Stone and Ashes are on their way. We haven't heard from Ichor."

That's more than what I hoped for. "I take it you have a plan? We have a better chance standing together, but if the Álfheimr forces were strong enough to take the courts separately, they might cut through us."

"They won't have a chance. Come. I don't wish to repeat myself."

I walk the familiar drafty halls, heading to the headmistress's office, fairly certain that the lords have chosen to retreat to the most luxurious chamber in the building.

Lera Frost and her husband Genrion are huddled in an armchair, near the roaring fireplace; their son Wilden chats with Dekren Thorn. The head of the Thorn family has taken a seat on the headmistress's chair, behind the desk. To my relief, both Sylph and Esea are here. I smile at my friend, glad to see her safe.

I have seen the other lords in passing, but I'm not overly familiar with any of them.

They all rise as we enter the room.

I don't let my discomfort show.

"My ladies. Is it true, then? Is the queen gone?"

I nod.

"I heard something else." Vikro Thorn narrows his eyes. "I heard you brought some lords back to life. Is it true you wield this power?"

To that, I make no response, heading to the fire. I reach out, warming my hands.

"Then why didn't you bring the queen back! We're under attack! We need her strength to keep together."

"Sir." My voice cuts through his tirade, coated with all of my power, hitting like a whip.

Angering me isn't wise. Not today.

Never again.

"You're standing before your queen. When you ought to be *kneeling*."

I turn back to him, staring him down, despite my small stature and his great height.

The entire room watches me, various degrees of shock registering in their gaping mouths and wide eyes.

There's nothing but silence. As they stare at me, I feel the current in the room. I feel the air and the earth under my feet respond to my command.

I feel that the land has recognized my claim, and so have they.

I turn back to the fire. "I meant my mother, Genrion."

I am in no position to hold the crown.

I cannot lead them well when everything in me wants to succumb to darkness, to take lives. Lives of folk, and men, and gods.

Like Nyx, I desire to protect Tenebris.

That includes protecting them from me.

"Lord Thorn meant no disrespect, my lady. We were unaware that Void had returned. And if indeed—"

I hear others enter the room; more lords, alight from the boats. I close my eyes, willing my strength to stay with me just a little longer. Then, I speak.

"I let the hag die because I wanted to, and because I could. I brought the court back to life because I wanted to, and because I could. Controlling me will never be within your abilities, my lords. Now, if we could move on to more pressing matters."

I ask about each court—the number of folk they've brought with them or left behind. Which of them can fight.

I estimate that half of Tenebris is with us. Some of those dwelling in the north fled to the seelie lands; in the south, others asked for asylum from the Sea Lands. In the west, a few have gone to Mithgarth.

"We need to send scouts to learn the extent of the human army—and how many immortals are with them," I say. "And in the meantime, we ward Whitecroft."

They exchange glances, either unsure about taking orders from me, or doubting the viability of my plan.

"Whitecroft is the intersection of Nyx's ley lines. The power of all courts converges right here. We can use it to shape our wards into impenetrable walls. The Álfheimran might raid, and destroy our land, but as long as we're all here, we can prepare. Wait. And when we're ready, retake Tenebris."

There is a problem with this plan; it will work considerably less without the other courts. Stone, Ashes, and Ichor have to make it before we close the wards.

Before Kraver finds us and sends his army in earnest.

"That could work," General Frost says, somewhat reluctantly. "Though maintaining a ward like that will take a considerable amount of energy."

I close my eyes, feeling the strength of the gods I've stolen. The strength of a thousand fae.

"That won't be a problem."

twenty-two
sleeping beauty

Unlike one certain infuriating princess, I help the crew land the ship before returning to Whitecroft. Then, when folk and gentry from other courts arrive by land and water, I help them too, carrying wounded through the hall to lead them to the infirmary.

The walls feel smaller than they did back when I'd been a student here, for a mere six years. Six good years. Some of the best, frustrating as they might have been.

I'm stunned into place, spotting familiar faces in the crowd gathered in the courtyard.

My little sister is the first to spot me. "Rystan!"

She drops the pegs she'd been holding to help Ma put up a tent, and runs to hug me. I hug her right back, numb. I hadn't let myself hope, or even think of them, for fear of giving into despair, but they're all here, along with hundreds upon hundreds of folk.

Not just the gentry; sprites and imps and brownies and hobs swarm around us, mingling with the wilder, more dangerous of us. I spot a white lady, and shiver.

At least they'll be useful in the battle to come.

As my family fusses over me, forcing a bowl of broth in my hands and a blanket over my shoulders, I try to look for Vlari.

I usually try to look for Vlari, if I have any reason to believe she's near.

I can't find her.

I try to focus on my family, asking about their escape, but my mind is on a delicate, tiny, sassy, and fierce princess.

"We heard the court sound the alarm bells in the distance, but we were so far." My father sighs. "I was about to lead the family east when a pixie covered in blood found us. She told us to go with her, and, well, I wasn't about to argue with *that*."

My sister giggles. "Mera looks feral! She's amazing."

Count on my sister to admire brutality. We are definitely related.

"And the pixie brought you here."

They nod. I am rather bewildered, given that I know no pixie; I can't think of why one might have helped my family. I'm grateful all the same.

I can wonder about it tomorrow.

Right now, I need to sleep—and find Vlari.

Not necessarily in that order.

I struggle to keep my eyes open, but when a burst of light flashes through the sky, cloistering us in a sphere of bright energy, I stand to attention, recognizing the energy signature behind that magic.

Whatever it is, it comes from Vlari, of that much I am sure.

Sleep is the least of my concern now.

"I have to—I'll be back."

I leave my baffled family to rush inside the school, toward the source of the magic. It's shooting upward from the inside of the building, and covering the school—the entire ground.

Wards.

Wards so powerful they feel like physical walls of energy, pulsing with life.

I practically trip, walking so fast I run right into Alven.

I don't even think to apologize. "Where is she?"

The king consort—former king consort—smiles at me. I don't understand why it looks so sad.

"Calm down. You can go in, in a few moments."

"Where is she?" I repeat.

This time, it sounds like a threat.

Alven is no useless sprite. Not only does he outrank me, he's also ten times my age; there's a chance that if we fight, he'll wipe my face on the marble floor. Especially now. I'm too tired for a brawl.

I'll still punch him, if he doesn't answer.

I don't quite understand my urgency, but I feel like something fundamental is wrong.

My family is safe. We're all safe.

Why does it seem like we lost?

I lost.

"Right here," he said, pointing inside the professors' dining hall. I'd snuck in there a time or two to steal wine and fairy fruits.

I move to enter, but he holds my arm. "Patience. The queen's with her, now."

The queen.

Her mother, I glean.

Vlari is chatting with her mother. That is all. I shouldn't be this agitated.

But I can't calm down, whatever I tell myself. For one, I can hear no words. I can hear nothing at all.

Four heartbeats; three strong, the other one, slow and weak.

Vlari's presence is there, there's no mistaking it.

But it feels wrong.

So wrong.

Finally, footsteps approach.

The queen is the first to come out, her beautiful face wet with tears. Then comes her husband and mate—the common fae I'd chatted with when I picked up Vlari.

Had that just been last night? It feels like a thousand years have passed since.

He is crying too.

The last to exit is a pixie, unfamiliar, unlike the rest of them. No tears from her, but her eyes look like they might set fire to heaven itself.

A fierce pixie.

I stare at her, my mind starting to connect the dots.

Vlari hadn't just written a word to her family—unlike the rest of the courts. She'd sent a few words. I'd taken it for sentimentality.

She'd sent her after my people.

Where was she?

The queen stops right in front of me. She's almost as tall as me, standing far above her husband.

It occurs to me that I should kneel, or at least bow my head.

Before I can attempt either, she stretches her elegant hand and touches my shoulder. Then she attempts a smile through the tears.

I stumble away, toward the door.

Pushing it open, I freeze. My very blood freezes.

Vlari's lying on a bed, eyes closed, as though in a deep sleep, her loose, dark hair falling to the floor. There's something at her feet; a fur, I think at first, but I see it rise and fall steadily along with her heart. A wyr, black as night, wrapped in shadow, curled up to keep her feet warm.

I only have to see her to understand there is no waking her. No amount of shaking or screaming her name will work.

She is under a curse of her own.

"What has she done?"

I don't recognize my voice. I don't recognize myself at all.

"What needed to be done. We'll be safe here, as long as it takes."

I watch helplessly, not attempting a word, a step. I can't. I can't. I can't.

I should have died tonight. I should have died a month ago. It would have hurt less than this.

"She's gone," I say.

Her life isn't extinguished, but there is no waking from curses such as these. North of here, in the wilderness, a prince has been asleep for a thousand years, guarding his mountains.

Alven shakes his head. "No, she's very much here. Her consciousness remains with us. There's more strength in her than in any one of us combined. She can wake herself, as long as she does so before her mind falls to the darkness."

I force myself to look away from the sleeping princess, and face the old king. "How long?"

I don't need to elaborate.

"It depends on her strength, and on her desire to hold on. Thankfully, in her case, we have a physical indication as to the state of her magic."

I look at the long hair sprawled on the bed; dark like heart's blood, rather than silver-gray, as it had always been, for as long as I've known her.

"When her hair is back to normal—" I don't finish the thought.

Alven is less kind. "She'll be too weak to come back." He repeats, "She's given us what we need. Time to regroup."

At what price?

All of us, the seven courts, for her life.

It seems like a fair bargain. I'm not surprised she's taken it.

I hate her for it.

I hate her with all my heart.

And I'll hate her a thousand times more if she lets herself die.

I turn back without entering the room.

"Drusk—"

I cut Alven off. "If anyone's looking for me, I'll be training the folk."

epilogue

The girl ran as fast as her bare feet could carry her, without daring to look back. She could hear her pursuers closing in, laughing as they chased her. It was a game to them.

Another arrow flew past her ear, drawing a line of blood.

So, so close. To death and salvation both.

She saw the dome of light in the distance.

She'd never been there, but she knew it. All the folk knew it.

Before she was born, years ago, there was a battle, and a curse, and a princess.

It sounded like a fairy tale, but she believed. She had to believe. If she didn't, she'd just curl up and let the huntsmen kill her and cut off her ears, like they did to all the folk they could get to.

Her feet hooked on a treacherous, sinuous root, and she fell down, chin first, hitting her head on a rock. Crying, she kicked at the root, hurting her ankle in the process.

She managed to get back to her feet, and kept going toward the light.

She had to get there. She just had to.

The huntsmen drew near. She willed herself to keep going, without looking back.

So very close.

The wall of light was just on the other side of the marshes, when the hooves of a dozen horses reached her.

The laughter made her want to weep, so she closed her eyes. She wouldn't give them the satisfaction of crying, or begging.

"This one is courageous."

"And pretty enough. Maybe we should have fun with her, first."

Sera lifted her blade to her own throat. Better to die by her hand than submit herself to being tortured by them.

They laughed harder, thoroughly entertained.

Then their laughter died in their throats.

A bright light coated in shadow had appeared between the men and Sera. A shadow with the shape of a short girl. She felt like a ghost, a spirit, but when she lifted her hand toward Sera's blade, it flew to her grasp. Ghosts, if they existed at all, couldn't hold weapons, as far as Sera knew.

The spirit threw the knife at the closest man, and lifted her grasp—answering her call, the blade sliced each and every one of their throats, so fast they didn't have the time to release one scream.

The specter drew the knife back to her, before tossing it at Sera.

"Go on, before something else catches your scent," it said.

And without another word, it disappeared, returning to shadows.

Sera drew a breath she hadn't realized she'd been holding, and rushed toward the light.

The moment she approached the dome, a doorway opened up in front of her, letting her through Whitecroft.

She fell to her feet, tears on her face.

She'd made it.

She'd made it.

Somehow, she was alive.

But the rest of Tenebris was still in darkness.

Someone offered her a hand, and she took it. Looking up, she found herself facing the scariest man she'd ever seen. There was no hint of kindness, no light in his blue eyes. If he'd once known happiness, it had long been extinguished.

"Are you hurt?"

She could feel her lips trembling. Rather than attempting to speak, she shook her head.

He nodded, waving toward one of the eight buildings behind him.

They were strange halls—most recent, except the largest one; the one from which the blinding light warding the territory was shooting out.

"Choose your court. You'll be cared for."

Sera had been courageous enough for a day—courageous enough for a lifetime—but she found it in herself to speak to the terrifying dark fae nonetheless. "What about the girl of light? The pixie with purple hair. She helped me get away. Is she still out there?"

The colossal gentry spun on his heel, every single one of his features alight with something that could only be fury.

There was only one pixie with purple hair in the whole of Tenebris, to Rystan Drusk. And she had been comatose for a decade. "What did you say?"

deleted scenes

I should have died a month ago.

I was going through the motions. Doing my duty, fulfilling my responsibilities. Earning cash to put food on the table for my siblings and my parents.

I'd been gifted with a power that couldn't be wasted; I made use of it to protect my home and provide for my family. Dreams and hopes were distractions I seldom indulged in. My one fantasy was *her*.

She was suitably unattainable, and therefore not worth pursuing.

But now, I'd spoken with her. Touched her. Teased her. I was under her skin. My time with her felt like a beginning.

And I was about to be slaughtered with the rest of the court. There was no denying it.

We were trapped in the royal keep, surrounded by an army, pursued by gods. They'd killed most of the guards. The reinforcement was a day away at most. By daylight, the immortal warriors would have killed us all.

I followed my liege on autopilot, doing my best to stop thinking. Stop existing. If I allowed myself to take a moment to ponder my mere thirty winters on Eartia, I'd think of her, and I couldn't bear it. I couldn't even bring myself to formulate her name in my mind.

Grayish hair, dark in places and violet at the tips, she bore the mark of a royal, though no one treated her like it. No one but me.

Beneath layers of sophistication, silk, perfume, and badges announcing pompous titles, I'd always been the boy from the murk, and she, a jewel of the realm.

We may be fae, but our story wasn't a fairy tale. She'd marry a duke, a prince, a foreign lord. Not me. Never me.

Not now, in any case.

The one light I clung to in my darkest day was the fact that she wasn't here. She wouldn't die along with me. She'd live. She'd live. She'd live.

Nothing else mattered.

King Consort Alven led us through a maze of secret corridors hidden inside the walls of the keep. We'd already asked. They didn't lead out.

Though wounded, the king kept going. I could smell an abundance of royal blood in the air. He might have lived a little longer if he'd cared to stay still, but he'd been adamant. We had to get to the treasure room. We *had* to.

I didn't bother asking why. I wasn't one to sit still if it could be helped. Despite the substantial wound in my side, I followed.

My partner, Pearl, wasn't so amenable. "Why the treasure room?" she'd exclaimed, baffled. "That dreary old room, of all places!"

The king could have ordered her to shut up and follow him, but that wasn't Alven's method. His wife, the unseelie queen, had been the iron fist of the power couple ruling over the Shadow Peaks.

"Because," he'd replied, though forming words took some effort with the gnarly gash in his stomach, "there lies the one hope this kingdom still possesses."

Hope.

I had none.

But if the kingdom could somehow hold, then *she'd* be safer.

I shuddered to think what could happen to her, if our world fell to the rule of the western gods. She had a better chance of surviving than most, whatever happened. She'd never been pampered, unlike the rest of her kin. And though she hid in the shadows, she was strong. Resilient. I focused on that.

Nevlaria Bane *would* survive.

We reached the treasure room at last, walking in through a pivoting door hidden behind a dusty tapestry. I couldn't say I'd spent a lot of time in this room; I'd never been much of a history lover. Everything here had a tale, long forgotten, or written in schoolbooks I no longer remembered. I eyed the swords and armor displayed behind gold and glass cases. I had to admit, they looked considerably more practical than what I was wearing; dark training gear and a simple short ceremonial sword.

We hadn't expected the attack. It had come out of nowhere. I still couldn't understand how the thousands of soldiers had breached our wards.

I didn't suppose it mattered, in the end.

Alven didn't reach for the sword of Titania or the shield of Mab. He didn't even make for Chronos's cape, rumored to have the ability to manipulate the fabric of time.

Ignoring the impressive heritage of his people, he walked to a plain wooden case in a corner. It looked old; older than anything else in the room. I didn't think I would have even seen it, had the king not stopped right in front of it, and placed his bloody palm on the translucent case.

The glass surface vanished at his touch. Inside lay a single stone, purple like his royal blood. It should have seemed boring. Cheap, even. There wasn't any shine to it, and its shape wasn't as well defined as that of any jewel on the king's throat, fingers, or clothes.

But it wasn't plain, nor simple at all.

"What is it?" Pearl asked, as Alven pocketed it.

The king was already rushing away, walking as fast as he could, though he was leaning forward under the pain.

We should have gotten him to a healer.

"Your Highness. If the queen is dead…"

"You'll trust that I know that my own wife has passed to the underworld, Drusk," Alven replied lightly.

I swallowed hard. He was right. Though the king hadn't been the queen's fated mate, they'd formed a bond. Any fae would have felt the death of their partner through their link.

"Well, in that case, you're king. We should get you to safety."

Somehow. Whatever safety meant.

Flying away wasn't an option; any enemy attacking fae would have posted archers to pick them off the moment they tried to escape. And as the wards of the court were known to be unbreakable, the palace was situated at the very center of the city. Which meant that getting out of here was nigh on impossible, without encountering countless soldiers. A glance out the window revealed just how many immortals were surrounding the keep.

The king shook his head. "No. Help is coming to us."

That notion was fanciful, at best. Delusional.

"I'm sorry?"

The king kept going; toward the main exit, it seemed.

The treasure room led right out to the great hall. It'd be swarming with enemies.

"We should return through the passages. Sir!" Pearl cried, almost pleadingly.

She froze in her steps, along with the king and me, because the heavy white carved doors were already opening. From the hall.

We were doomed.

Or so I thought, for a moment.

Then I wished we were.

Because the horror waiting for us was worse than certain death. Even in the poor light and despite the distance, I couldn't mistake the person who stood in the doorway.

Five foot nothing—shorter than most high fae. Grayish hair, purple at the tips. Eyes of emerald, beautiful and filled with secrets.

Nevlaria. The girl of my dreams, now starring in my worst nightmare. And she was covered in blood.

NOBLESSE OBLIGE

SHADOW CURSED

Whatever our souls are made of,
His and mine are the same.

—Emily Brontë

one
shadow of tenebris
drusk

Once, the fae woods were alive with malice, laughter, and schemes, but gone are the days of the folk. Trolls and boggarts no longer hunt shadows of the night. No hag wanders the darkness, lying in wait to ensnare a maiden and eat her heart whole. The goblins returned to their hills, and the aven hide in burrows.

Tenebris is a land of men.

For now.

The bodies of the four mortals at my feet incite no feeling in me. No excitement, no contentment. I remember I used to enjoy causing pain to those I deemed deserving of it. I loved the hunt. I even loved the kill. Such is the nature of the blood running through my veins; beneath layers of sophistication, we unseelie will always be instruments of chaos and destruction.

Now there's nothing but a void. An emptiness. I killed these mortals because they were in my way. I killed them because I had to, without feeling a hum of pleasure or desire.

One of the most inconvenient human qualities is that they tend to swarm like locusts. Destroy a handful, and a dozen pop up in their place. Before I have time to wipe the blood off my sword, I sense company nearing. I curse under my breath, unhooking my bow from my back to shoot the mortals approaching from a distance.

"Look up!" Iola yells behind me.

I don't bother. The day I can't feel an oncoming gunshot is the day I'm no longer Rystan Drusk. The gunpowder humans use stinks of charred metal, and the air around it vibrates in an unnatural way.

I don't know where most of my heritage comes from. What I do know is that Mysts are the children of the air. As its master, I am one with the night.

Before the human weapon finds its way into whichever piece of my flesh it would have lodged, I disappear into the shadows.

I reappear next to Iola and Erdun, a few hundred paces ahead of where I was. "Do you have it?" I demand.

My companion nods, pointing to the satchel on her hip.

"Go, then," I say. "I'll delay them."

Iola frowns, and then shakes her head. "We can't. Lesson one: no one is ever left behind. Remember?"

The thing I forgot is that today is her first mission outside of the walls of Whitecroft.

Erdun laughs, tugging on Iola's sleeve. "That rule applies to everyone except him. Come on, greenie. He's Shadow. He'll be fine. The faster we are, the sooner he can join us."

Shadow. That name almost manages to get a reaction out of me, but I ignore the chill running along my skin.

Iola lets the other ranger tug her forward, and they start their run to the southeast, only looking back once.

I'm glad I included her in today's rescue. She may be greener than some, but she's ready. And the gods of heaven and hell know we need as many rangers venturing beyond our sanctuary as possible, if we're ever to reclaim what's ours.

Ten years ago, when Tenebris was invaded by human scum led by a traitorous usurper, I volunteered to train those who wanted to help. Our army was all but decimated in the attack preceding our retreat. While naturally agile and stronger than any mortal, the folk weren't fighters, per se, and they knew nothing of discipline. I used to be a soldier, in another life. I figured my training should be passed on.

Almost a thousand folk have suffered through my lessons. They hate me, curse my name. One or two have begged me to kill them when I work on their endurance. But unlike the hotheads who believed they didn't need any training, unlike the few soldiers who came with us, every single one of them is still alive today.

I haven't taught them obedience or any such things the armies used to require of me. I taught them to survive.

They're each a bit of hope for our kingdom. For our race. If I can do nothing else, I'll endeavor to keep hope alive for those who still have some.

My actions don't matter; I realize that. There are a hundred thousand humans in our lands. More arrive every day. They've cut down woods and built settlements through our home. They've claimed it. They even renamed it. No trickery, no spell, no curse can will that many mortals into nothingness, and those are the true weapons of the folk.

It'd take a miracle to claim it back, with so few warriors among us.

I've long since ceased to believe in miracles.

I wait in the shadows of my Myst, invisible to the eyes of any fae. As humans are blind at the best of times, they see only a fog in front of them, and don't even sense that anything is wrong until it's far too late.

I let them approach, silent and immobile. I am a spider, and like the insects they are, they're too easily caught in my web. When the dozen men are within reach, I strike, turning the world into fire all around me, scorching their flesh with blue flames. They dance all around me, tickling my skin.

The humans scream—some have the presence of mind to roll on the ground, others run away. None of that will help. They'll stop suffering if and when I allow them to.

I hear the rest of their regiment advance, entirely focused on me rather than following after my companions. That's the way I like it.

My parents and sister unfortunately don't see it in the same light. The last time she shouted at me, Ma called me suicidal.

She's wrong…and right. I'm not suicidal. I am already dead, the heart in the cavity of my chest long frozen. I care for them still. I care about the future of Tenebris—for I'll never call our land anything else. I care about making the humans pay for taking our lands.

For all that, passion, desire, enjoyment have left me. I am a shell of the man I used to be. I'm sorry it pains my family. I'm not sorry it has turned me into Shadow. A monster who can put himself in the line of fire without a care. I am a weapon; one of our only weapons in a losing war.

The humans rush to aid their companions, and fire extends to the rest of them as they enter my web.

"Stay away from the monster—we need to kill him from a distance! Archers, lances, on my command! The sorcerer—"

Monster. I suppose that's what I am. Not because of any of my abilities. I'm a monster because I can take lives without letting it matter to me. I'm a monster because I don't feel. I'm a monster because of her.

I move too fast for any mortal eyes to see, taking a small knife I made a week ago in my grasp and throwing it. The leader's words die when the blade sails through his throat. Watching him fall off his black warhorse, the lieutenant at his side freezes in horror, realizing his commander's death means he's now in charge. Which would make him the next corpse on the blood-soaked moss.

If I were still who I used to be, there would be another knife flying through the night. I'd kill for the sake of it, again and again.

But it's a pointless endeavor. Crunching locusts is a child's game. More will spring up in an instant. What I need is for them to leave, ensuring Iola and Erdun's safe return.

I let him choose his fate, watching him as he stares at me, sizing me up.

"Fall back! Fall back to the Court! On my lead."

Some mortals are smarter than others.

I retract my fire, letting those who aren't yet dead extinguish. Burning them wouldn't provide so much as a smidgen of satisfaction or entertainment, and it wouldn't do to use up more energy than necessary.

Myst, like any power, is taxing on the mind. I'd hate to have to sleep before the end of the night. It'd worry Ma and Neb. Besides, I mislike fatigue. There are always things to do in Whitecroft. Young folk to train, fields to plan, swords to sharpen.

Pa understands, I think. He doesn't say much, unlike the females in my family, but sometimes, I catch looks he sends my way when he doesn't think I'm paying him any mind. He touches my shoulder for too long, or sighs when he watches me.

That's worse than shouting. I see him mourning his son, though I'm right in front of his eyes. He knows part of me is gone, buried inside Whitecroft Hall.

Buried right next to Nevlaria Bane.

I don't know why I took the loss of Vlari so hard. Perhaps she represented amusement and freedom to me. Perhaps it's something else entirely.

I make my way back to the dome of light stretching over hectares, engulfing all of Whitecroft's extensive grounds under Vlari's protection.

I would never have thought that Whitecroft was intended to be used as a fortress. It was nothing but a school for the richest of the folk, or the gentry with lines dating back to the Old World. Pretty, ill-defended, but overall useless. Vlari's spell turned it into the most impregnable area of Alfheimr. Our enemies tried everything. Magic, explosives, armies. Our walls are only opened to the folk.

As I approach, the shimmering golden barrier parts right in front of me to let me pass. I never quite understood how it works. The others say that sometimes, the walls remain closed; it generally means there's an enemy nearby that they need to dispatch before being allowed through. The spells woven into our shields are quite beyond me.

They've never failed to open for me. Perhaps because no enemy is stupid enough to follow me.

Seconds after I'm allowed in, I see the wall open again at my right, a few paces away.

Frowning, I approach it.

There should be no other party of rangers coming in tonight, and my companions should have arrived ahead of me.

No enemy has ever made it through the barrier, but I am on my guard all the same.

Someone comes through—almost a child, not much younger than my sister. I only have to take one glance at her to know her story. She's emaciated, out of breath, and her dilated pupils betray the ordeal she's been through.

She's one of the courageous souls who have managed to make their way to us by themselves. Over the years, the ranger parties venturing outside of Whitecroft have managed to rescue a number of folk, bringing them to us, but rare are the fae who've made it on their own.

None of them were children as young as she.

"Are you hurt?" I ask her.

She's unlucky I'm the one who found her. I've never been accused of gentleness. I read fear in her eyes as she takes me in, and I don't attempt to defuse it.

I don't detect any wounds, but I don't like making assumptions.

The girl shivers, but she shakes her head. I'm glad of it. I'm capable of administering basic remedies when the circumstances call for it, but I'm not much of a healer.

She needs something warm to eat, and a place to sleep. She probably also needs someone to speak to, and that someone isn't me, so I gesture behind me. "Choose your court. You'll be cared for."

The lower kings and queens of Tenebris have found refuge in Whitecroft, with a part of their courts. As we could hardly all fit inside the building that used to be our school, we've built seven halls, with small but comfortable apartments, each representing our seven courts. Ash, Mist, Stars, Storm, Silt, Ichor, and Stone. Whitecroft Hall itself houses the royalty, and whatever is left of our government—the leaders of our armies, our politicians, our lawmakers.

The one good thing to come of our ordeal is the fact that we aren't defined by where we were born. Not anymore.

Before, a fae born in the Court of Stars could only join another court if the king or queen requested it. For the first time in generations, we've been able to choose where we belong.

My family was born at the border between Stars and Mist—technically on Stars lands. They've chosen to remain with the Court of Stars, in order to be close to their friends.

I haven't chosen. Not officially. I sleep in my parents' quarters, though my position means I could have an apartment of my own, should I request it.

Requesting lodgings would mean actually picking a court. A lord. I can't bring myself to kneel to anyone. I don't believe in the lords of Tenebris. Had they been powerful, we wouldn't be stuck behind these walls, cowering before mortals. I don't trust them. I don't respect any of them. None of the elders, none of the queens, none of the warriors saved us.

Vlari did.

Vlari, who's little more than a child to the folk. As the gentry don't fade with age, we're considered too young for responsibility under the age of a hundred years. Vlari wasn't even seventy when she placed herself between us and immortals, with none of the lower monarchs by her side.

Just me and her grandfather. Another lord I don't quite trust.

And she paid for their inability to protect us.

I don't think I can ever forgive the kings and queens of Tenebris for their helplessness. Their weakness. They've lost my respect, and how could I serve a leader I don't respect?

I can only kneel to a power greater than my own.

"What about the girl of light?" the child asks, making me stop in my tracks.

A girl of light? I try to make sense of the words. I might have been too quick to dismiss her injuries. It sounds like she hit her head too hard. Before I can ask a few pointed questions, the child carries on. "The pixie with purple hair. She helped me get away. Is she still out there?"

I turn to face her, watching her eyes, scanning for the first sign of a lie.

And suddenly, the void is gone. The emptiness, the lack of feeling that has been my constant companion. I am fire. I am rage.

If she's lying to me, I'll take great pleasure in making her suffer.

A *pixie*.

Pixies are creatures of the seelie courts. The legends say that they're the children of gentry and the shy folk of the wilderness, given the beauty of one race and the bloodthirsty ferocity of the other. They moved to settle south of the wilderness centuries ago, and bowed to the high queen of Denarhelm. When the line of the queen failed, they founded a lower court.

There may be a handful of pixies scattered across Tenebris, but I know of only three within the walls of Whitecroft. A full-blooded female. Her half-blood son. The son's daughter. A quarter-blooded pixie, yet so dainty and small her origins can't be denied. She blends the features of a gentry with those of the pixie, managing to look almost innocent, like an ingénue. A neat trick for the most powerful fae among us.

Only one of them has purple hair—violet at the tips, gray at the roots.

The shade of the royal line, running through the entire bloodline of Nyx.

Vlari.

I say one word to the exhausted, terrified girl I can't bring myself to reassure. "Talk."

two
stone cold
drusk

I move like a puppet held up with strings, going through the motions. I call guards and send them out, because it's protocol. Then I wait. For endless seconds, minutes, or hours, I wait. Then I listen to them, nod, and return to my base.

I teach the folk at the edge of the marshes. I chose the spot knowing I'd stay out of the way—nothing flourishes so close to the damp swamps, except for kappas and redcaps. It's far enough away from the halls to avoid accidents when our lessons don't go according to plan. That is, every other day. Accidental fires and explosions are part of our routine.

One day, months into our confinement, a building popped up overnight. I still don't know who is responsible for building it. My students, any of the lords, the high queen herself. I never bothered to ask. It's a simple one-story structure with a few studies, a library, and a large training area—useful for our purposes.

One day, a general walked in and asked me which of my students could be sent out of Whitecroft. We'd survived a few years rationing the extensive Whitecroft pantry, thanks to the way of the folk with nature. Give us one dying apple tree, and by the end of a song, it'll bear a hundred ripe fruits, sweet to the tongue and ready for picking. For all that, we needed seeds, for hay and wheat. We needed pigs and horses. Our healers needed some herbs, too. The task had been taken on by knights at first, but some never returned, and those left weren't enough to provide for everyone in our fortress. Our city.

I selected my best students and accompanied them. Daunting as the first excursion may have been, we all returned, with as much as we could carry, riding stolen horses. It wasn't hard to whisper in their ears and convince them to leave their mortal owners behind. Humans have never quite understood the way of beasts.

Now, Whitecroft is independent. My rangers are efficient at what they do, and we no longer need to leave for food or cattle.

We leave for hope. We retrieve spells, enchanted stones, crystals, that the high lords study in search of a way to save us.

It all feels so useless to me, but every time the rangers leave the barrier of Whitecroft, the folk sing and pray for us. We give them something to hold on to. Even I know that's important.

When I reach our base, Iola is beaming with pride at having completed her first assignment successfully. She holds a grimoire in her hands, almost reverently.

Part of me wants to tell her it won't do any good. That nothing in these moldy pages will save us. That nothing can. I feel like lashing out, hitting something, spewing venom.

I feel like *me*. Who, and what I used to be. Rystan Drusk. Not his shadow.

And I know why.

"Is everything all right, boss?" Erdun seems unsure how to approach me, sensing a difference in me, no doubt.

I didn't know him before Whitecroft. As a rakshasa, I think he was half-wild—living on a diet of sprites stupid enough to wander into his territory, more often than not. Now, he stands awkwardly, upright on his four limbs, his pale gray skin covered in soft fur. His mouth is filled with sharp fangs, his amber eyes circled with black shadows, and his flat pink nose gives him a feline air.

I suspect he favored the shape of a tiger in the past.

Most of us aren't what we used to be.

I nod curtly, and see him hesitate, as though he'd like to press on. He daren't.

"Report," I tell Iola, though I don't need it. I was right alongside her for most of our mission to the Court of Mist.

Vlari's home. Where she grew up. For years, it had held untold mysteries. I'd have given everything I owned for the pleasure of a visit. I listened to every rumor, read every line I could find about the northernmost unseelie kingdom to the west.

I snuck inside her manor without so much as thinking of her today. Without seeking her rooms, or recalling the one time I crossed the threshold, so long ago, introducing myself to her parents before escorting her to a ball.

A lifetime ago.

This early afternoon, I was still dead. Still unfeeling. Still unbreakable.

Now, I question everything.

I've always needed answers; the reason I hadn't sought them until now was because I suspected they wouldn't be ones I want to hear.

The semblance of a decision starts to form at the edge of my mind, but I allow myself a few moments to ignore it. After pretending to listen to Iola, I serve myself a bowl of stew, and push the broth around my bowl until there's no delaying the inevitable.

I stand, bid my companions a good night, and mechanically walk to the one place I've avoided for ten years. The one place that's been drawing me in.

I stop in front of gates manned by a mammoth of a moss-green-skinned troll and a stockier, shorter boggart with pointed teeth smeared with blood. Neither of them could have posed much of a threat to me, but they're certainly suitable guards. I suspect one would think twice before approaching them with ill intent.

There are thousands of folk in Whitecroft. I suspect I've encountered them both once or twice around bonfires, but we haven't been introduced. If they know who I am, they also know I don't have any reason to be here, at the gates of my old school that now serves as the high queen's keep. I'll have to identify myself and state my purpose here.

My name opens many doors; since the lords of the realm have started coming to me with assignments, the folk see me as someone of import, someone worth befriending. That said, I don't think either of these guards will be much impressed by me. And what is my purpose, exactly? Demanding answers of the high queen? Asking her how her comatose daughter could have possibly come to a sprite's aid? Shouting, stomping my foot, threatening until I am heard?

I feel powerless. A state I've grown accustomed to, of late.

I glance back, hesitant to turn around.

The troll lifts the heavy, sharp lance in his hand, and hits the ground twice with its dull end. "Rystan Drusk at the gate," he grunts out loud.

Then to my confusion, he and the boggart at his side both step aside, parting ways to let me enter.

When we first arrived at Whitecroft, the old school was the only edifice in the territory. The high queen, as well as the lower kings and queens of each court, took up residence here while we built more lodgings on the grounds. Now the only resident in these walls is the high queen, Ciera Bane. Vlari's mother. Though no one but her family lives here, the hall is a constant buzz of activity. It's where our war council is held, where the leaders decide on rations, work schedules, and ranger patrols.

I don't approach Whitecroft Hall—ever. Not once in ten years. That means anyone can simply walk in. I dislike this notion.

There should have been questions, possibly a few threats. At the very least, they should have asked their superior whether I'm to be allowed inside. I scowl, concerned by the lack of security in this place. What if I were a spy?

As I pass the two brutes, it strikes me that if entry were that easy, there might not have been any guard at all. I realize I've been cleared to walk in the royal keep ahead of time. Someone already authorized my access.

I could have come here any time, any day. As if I were welcome within these walls. As if I had every right to stroll right through the gate. As if I were part of what was left of the high court.

I'm flabbergasted, and irritated. With the guards, and with any of the lords who could have given them the order to let me through. The high queen. Her father. Her husband. Most of all, I'm annoyed at myself, because if I'd known I could have walked into Whitecroft Hall any time, without having to scramble for a justification, I might have done just that before today.

As soon as the thought enters my mind, I know I'm lying. There's a reason I've avoided this place, and it has nothing to do with the ease of access.

Spotting a gaggle of imps and goblins bearing the midnight blue colors of the new high court planted along the walls, I nod in reluctant approval. There's clearly enough security. Part of me wonders if they'd be better assigned outside of the hall, but I'm glad they're here, guarding the most precious thing in the land.

Walking the paved corridor feels strange. The grand white keep and its arched halls has been a looming, threatening shadow for so long. I kept my back to it, pretended it didn't exist. Pretended that the one woman I've ever truly desired isn't inside, cursed to sleep her life away.

The halls are still vaguely familiar. Long ago, I studied in the chambers now converted to studies and grand meeting rooms. I've screwed the sons and daughters of the noblest of families in almost all of the chambers on the first and second floors to pass the time between classes. Yet, they've changed so much in ten years, part of me doesn't recognize them at all.

Lavish tapestries adorn the once-bare walls; sculptures of great kings and queens of old have been carved in blocks of marble and trunks of ash. In the chambers left ajar, I glimpse more changes. Gone are the desks and bookshelves full of tales, spells, and manuals. There are elegant velvet sofas, harps, and heavy desks instead.

I imagined a temporary, hasty, makeshift travesty of a true royal keep, but my old school has morphed into an edifice worthy of the new high queen. Thus appareled, it's easy to remember our first high queen, Nyx, had Whitecroft built herself.

The one thing that hasn't changed since my school days is that my mind was, and now is, entirely fixated on one person within these walls.

At the gates, I'd wondered at my purpose here, but now my steps aren't hesitant. I stride through halls and corridors, passing arches and manned terraces. I slow as I approach what used to be the professors' dining hall, and come to a stop at its entrance.

The door is new. A carved, painted wooden piece of art, it features butterflies, beetles, and a stag painted black and red. The artful carving describes a story, a tale of sorts. I wonder if I can recognize it. I inspect each minuscule detail, as if they matter. They don't. It just gives me something to do.

I can't open the door. Not yet. I just need a moment to contain myself, to prepare for what I'm about to see.

My worst nightmare and sweetest dream all wrapped in one haunting vision.

There are twelve guards around me. None of them pay me any mind; I may as well be invisible. Concerns about the casual demeanor of the guards around Whitecroft spike again. Though I can't say I care too much about the rest of the keep, this specific room ought to be protected by mistrustful, bloodthirsty knights. They should be threatening me. Demanding my purpose. Shoving me away. No one does. No one says anything at all to stop me, much to my annoyance. I would have been grateful for a deterrent.

Can I be here? Can I do this? The last time I entered this room, I broke. I lost something of myself in there. I'm not sure I'm willing to endure that again. I want to turn back, but I know I can't. I have to understand.

A child has made it from the realm of Stars to our sanctuary. It's not unheard of. Our patrols outside our gates have indicated that the self-appointed queen of Tenebris, the usurper, rules with an iron fist, sequestering the folk to their homes inside gated villages and cities, patrolled by her army of human swine. They're quick to draw their iron swords and turn them on the innocent, the weak. Those who hope, those who dare, try to run away and make their way to us—we're the last of the true courts.

Few manage to escape. Rude, crude, and weak as humans can be, they have the weapons and the manpower to run down an untrained fae. Iron-tipped arrows. Explosives. Horses they ride to death and then replace without blinking.

The child shouldn't have made it. She was smart; she took the road through the marshes, and the humans don't tend to patrol the swamps as much as the other paths leading to Whitecroft. However, she probably hadn't had any clue how to hide her tracks, and naturally, the humans had cornered her.

That should have been the end for her. We should have found her broken, defiled body on our next patrol, left to be eaten by worms and fiends. But the girl was saved. Somehow, she was aided by that purple-haired pixie specter.

I have no explanation, no farfetched theory. I have nothing but confusion, rage, fear, and worst of all, hope.

A specter able to hold a blade? I can't make sense of it. The guards I sent out after hearing the girl's tale found five human soldiers whose blood fertilized the earth. Each of their throats had been slit. The implication is staggering. Confusing. Terrifying.

Something happened, and the answer lies behind these doors.

Ideas swarm around my mind, each wilder than the next. I need to understand. If I don't know what's going on, I'm going to succumb to the depth of the madness that threatens to pull me under.

I push the doors.

The room, bathed in darkness, comes to life before my eyes. A green fire starts to roar on the adjoining wall, allowing my eyes to take in every detail.

I don't move or breathe for several moments. Then I force myself to walk in.

This chamber has changed too. The heavy, large four-poster bed made of oak is new. Next to it, there's a round, three-foot-tall table, upon which a vase full of fresh flowers provides the only semblance of decoration, and an armchair. There's nothing else at all in the room.

It looks like a tomb.

In a way, it is.

I let my eyes slide to the bed last.

She's on top of the bed, wrapped in layers of silk. Her skin looks pallid. Seeing the wild cascade of waves around her, I tighten my fist. The long locks are half white.

From the tips to the middle, her hair is dark purple, but the rest has returned to a luminous silver-gray. I've always known her like this. The color of her hair has been a fascination of mine. She's beautiful, unique, and delicate beyond measure.

But now that I know what it means, those strands of silver terrify me.

The dark blood violet is the color of the strength of her bloodline. As it has half faded to silver-white, it means she's lost energy. Lost *power*.

I should have expected it—it's been ten years. But seeing it makes me realize our days are numbered. In ten years, half her energy is gone. In another ten, she may be entirely taken by her own curse.

I try to distract myself, closing my eyes. When I do, I see nothing but her, as she used to be in our school days. Remote, indifferent to all, especially me. Proud. She used to tie her hair in complicated knots that completely hid its color. I loved her hair. It was striking, and looked so soft. I've always wanted to touch it.

I want to turn back. I *have* to turn back. I should never have come here in the first place.

Instead, I take one step, and then another, until I stand right next to her.

Curled up on the bed next to her, there's a bundle of black fur I mistake for a throw until it breathes, its chest rising and falling. I blink, watching the creature raise its head and set its fiery eyes on me.

A wyrfox. I've never seen one this tame—or this close.

The way it looks at me suggests that if I made one wrong move, my fingers would be gone.

I ignore the underlying threat, redirecting my attention where it belongs. As I approach, the fox hisses like an angry cat, and leaps off the bed. The wyr slinks back to the shadows of the night, hopping off the window.

"Vlari." I didn't mean to say her name out loud. I haven't—not in ten years. But I call to her today.

There are plenty of things I want to say. *Stay with us. Stay with me. Come back to me.*

I kneel next to the bed, a hand hovering over hers. I daren't touch her. I don't want to feel how cold she is.

How *dead* she is.

Vlari has sacrificed her life's energy to power the wards that have saved our people. Almost half of Tenebris is behind the walls of Whitecroft, safe from our invaders, thanks to her.

And we're losing her.

I let my hand wrap around hers. My eyes fly to my grasp.

She isn't cold at all. She's warm, and her pulse feels strong.

I look to her serene face, taking in her long-lashed closed eyes haloed by gray shadows.

Then, progressively, she disappears, fading away before my very eyes. I don't understand. I don't understand anything at all.

I get to my feet, ready to call the guards. There's sorcery at work.

Instead, I freeze in shock.

Vlari is standing right in front of me. She isn't wearing that dreadful dress at all; she's in green pants, with her leather boots and a loose linen shirt tucked at the waist.

And she's grinning at me, as if everything in the world is fine. As if this makes sense.

"About time you came to see me."

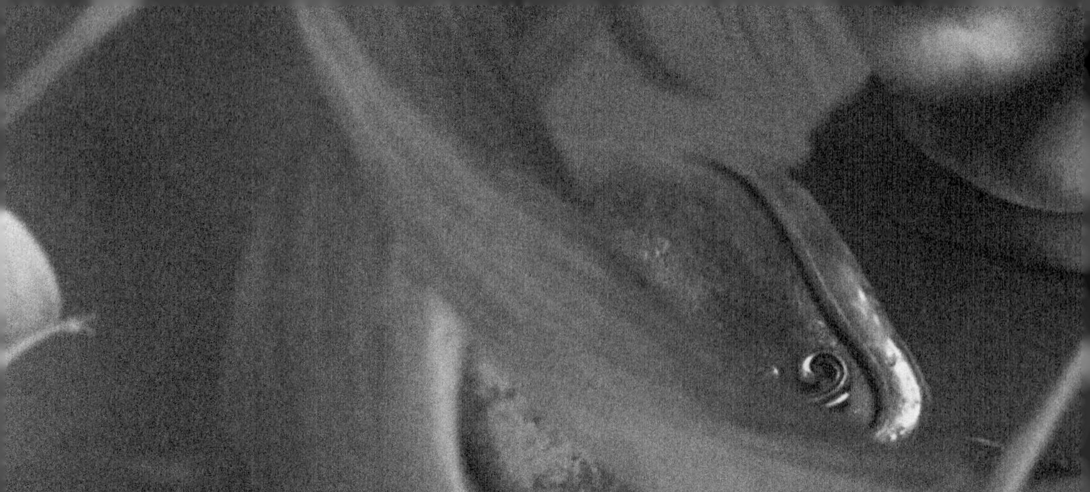

three
promises
drusk

The sound of my heartbeat resonates in my ears. i can't speak. I can't think. I can only stare and gape.

"I'm still asleep," she says next.

I give up trying to make sense of any of it. I take a seat on her bed and close my eyes in an attempt to banish the migraine brewing after all this confusion.

"You're in my mind right now."

I sigh and give up, opening my eyes again. I have to look at her, illusion or no.

"So, I'm dreaming?"

She shakes her head, and waves around the room. I notice it isn't quite the one I walked into. It looks like it had when I last saw her here ten years ago—with the professors' chairs scattered around the walls and fireplace, bookshelves, a desk. "Not at all. If anyone walks in, they'll see you next to me, your hand in mine. I suppose you'd look peculiar. Like a statue." She grimaces. "Sorry. It makes you rather vulnerable, you know."

I want to tell her I don't care.

I keep my mouth shut, letting her go on. Letting her talk.

Letting her be alive.

I missed her voice. I missed seeing her, and she was right there. For an instant, I pretend nothing else mattered.

"Pulling you into my mind doesn't cost me much energy when I'm touching you," she explains. "I was so very bored until I worked out how to do this. I could feel Mother brushing my hair, and I wished I could speak to her. Then, suddenly, I was doing just that!"

I can't begin to untangle my emotions, or make sense of them. There's some anger, directed at myself, at her mother, at the world. And at Vlari herself.

No one told me anything. No one told me she could *talk*, that she was awake—that she was fine. And no one had told me what she'd planned before she cursed herself. I didn't get to say goodbye because I hadn't mattered to anyone in charge. I hadn't mattered to *her*.

If Vlari had asked her mother to get me here, I know the queen would have done so. She hadn't. She hadn't cared to see me.

All the rage and sorrow muffled under the pile of ice that has surrounded my heart surfaced.

I *hate* her.

I hate her and all I can think about is touching her. Marking her. Pressing on her skin hard enough to leave bruises, so that she can feel me and remember me.

She tilts her head. "Pixie got your tongue?"

The pixie got my balls and crushed them in her grasp.

When I fail to respond, the teasing grin fades. She sighs. "How are you doing, Drusk?"

I'm a wreck. I'm undone, and moments away from exploding.

Gritting my teeth, I reply, "Fine."

Fine means nothing. That word is so hollow we folk only use it when we want to lie.

She lets herself down on one of the chairs near the fireplace, and taps the one in front of her, inviting me to sit closer.

Maybe I'm just dreaming. Maybe I've gone over the edge and this is what madness looks like.

"Come on. Tell me. Only one of us has a life. Entertain me. We used to be friends."

I feel like she's slapped me, insulted me.

"Friends?" I laugh. We were never friends.

We'd been a great deal less, and almost more, but never friends.

"Friends don't disappear without saying goodbye."

Her gaze, set on me until then, slides to the fire.

I don't know what I expect. An apology? No, that isn't her. That isn't us. We are unseelie. What we choose, we own. When we're wrong, we own that too.

"I couldn't." That's all I get from her: two words, delivered with an indifferent shrug. Then, she smiles up at me. "But I'll make it up to you, I promise. Now, tell me how we're doing. Here, beyond the walls. I can't observe everything in Whitecroft, and my parents are being unbearably tightlipped."

I want to shake her, scream at her, and demand more—more than this, her cavalier attitude.

The truth of the matter is that Vlari wouldn't understand the root of my sense of betrayal. She never saw what she meant to me. She might have glimpsed through the cracks, but my secret has remained concealed under layers of petty games and mocking smiles. To her, we *were* friends, or something close to it. I was a man she could flirt with when she felt like it. I was almost a stranger.

I force a deep breath out and shake my head. "Almost every fae inside these walls has received combat training—some only at a rudimentary level. The courts haven't forced anyone to take up arms; we need farmers, cooks, and healers, too. Those who wanted to—the majority of Whitecroft—have joined the ranks of our forces in one capacity or another. I train the youth for a year or two before sending them to their lords. The best recruits, I keep. They become my rangers, and travel out of Whitecroft when it's necessary. As of now, we have seven thousand soldiers and thirty-two rangers." I pause, then correct myself. "Thirty-three, counting the latest recruit. Another dozen in training. Between our magic and our agility, we assume a fae counts for ten human soldiers. In case of an all-out war, there will be terrible loss on both sides, and we can't guarantee we'll win with those numbers. We need another three or four thousand trained soldiers. Or a considerable amount of magic on our side. In five years or so, the younglings who'll come of age may make up for our numbers, but humans reproduce a lot faster than we do. And let us not forget that they have the support of the immortals of Alfheimr."

For the first time, Vlari interjects, rather coldly. "Let us not," she echoes.

She gestures for me to continue.

"I believe we need to get more of the folk outside our walls in here. There are another ten thousand of us out there in the rest of Tenebris. If they could come, we'd have a better chance. We could use air surveillance to see any weakening in the humans' defenses, and when there's a chance of taking a village, or even a farm, we could take it. I've mentioned it to Frost. He believes it isn't worth the risk."

Vlari's expressionless, taking all of that in. I doubt everything I tell her is news, but if her parents have sheltered her, she'll still learn a thing or two.

"Whitecroft is almost at full capacity—we're going to need more lodging. We've planted the greenhouses and we hunt the grove responsibly, but even so, food will become a concern within a year or two. We ration what we can. Meanwhile, the bitch daughter of Morgana has taken residence in the Wicked Court. She's having trouble commanding the folk—only a handful have bowed to her, and there's no gentry lord to back up her claim to the throne. The others hide. She opened the borders to

Mithgarthians, and as they've all but destroyed their own land, they were more than happy to come here. Tenebris has truly become a human realm. Still, she rules, thanks to her army of mortals. When the fae refuse her tribute, her soldiers descend upon the groves and take what they see as their due."

"Does the bitch have a name?" Vlari has fire in her eyes.

She looks like if she could get out of this room, she'd be out for blood. She can get in line. There are thousands of us who'd love to sink our claws in the usurper's throat.

"According to your grandfather, she was named Violet at birth. Who knows what name she uses now?"

Violet was a changeling, given to a human mother in exchange for a mortal girl Queen Morgana fostered.

I never quite understood the purpose of such an exchange. In the old days, the fae gave humans a sickly, dying child and took a healthy one in its place, but of late, those who took changelings had a tendency to give away any child of theirs.

I suppose Morgana believed she had enough heirs to secure her bloodline. How mistaken she was. Now, all of them have perished, save for Ciera and Vlari—the two members of her family she cast away.

Humans have uses in the fae world. For one, while a fae could try for centuries before being blessed with a child, humans are a lot more fertile. Their bloodlines are so irrelevant, their spawn with fae blood have all of our strength, and almost none of their weaknesses. But for a queen from an unusually fertile line to give away a fairy child for a human daughter? I see no sense in it.

"Violet." Vlari rolls each syllable around her mouth softly, almost lovingly. "Of nothing," she translates from the old tongue, before chuckling. "She was judged useless before she said her first words. No wonder she wants us all to suffer. Perhaps we should meet for tea and converse about the thousand deaths Morgana deserved."

I know little of the old unseelie queen, Vlari's grandmother. I'd been aware of the fact that Vlari's side of the family was disgraced since her mother married a common puck, against Morgana's wishes, but I'd only started to glimpse the deep-rooted hatred between them at Samhain.

The only Samhain that mattered in my life; the first and last time I'd escorted Vlari anywhere.

The queen had attempted to throw Vlari at the ruthless Sea Lands Court, exchanging a granddaughter for an alliance. I'd seen nothing but callous indifference from Morgana. No, not even indifference. The high queen had seemed *pleased* to see Vlari panic.

And the next day, Morgana was dead.

It's just as well. I imagine that if things had gone another way, I'd have ended up executed for butchering a high queen.

I circle back to the matter at hand. "Violet's stolen from, tortured, and murdered our kind. You do have odd taste in tea companions, princess."

Vlari grins wickedly. "I didn't say I wouldn't poison the drinks first."

I chuckle. It's odd to my own ears. Unnatural. How long has it been since I laughed at all?

I don't need to wonder.

Ten years.

"Mother says you've been invaluable."

I'm surprised her mother has said anything at all about me.

"I haven't seen her in a long time," I admit.

Not since I'd seen Vlari herself, ten years ago.

The queen doesn't step out of her keep. The folk are invited to feast with her on the celebration days, but I've never bothered to go.

"She keeps me informed about all my friends," Vlari says, shooting another dagger straight through my heart. "But nothing else at all. She doesn't want me to worry, but I should like to be kept informed. Thank you for the actual news. I do catch a few things here and there, but I can't concentrate too often. It taxes me."

Remembering the reason for my visit, I ask, "How does it work? I heard what you did earlier, to help a girl outside the walls. You were there, Vlari. *Material.* Holding a weapon and all."

Vlari shrugs. "I wasn't truly there. My body hasn't moved in years. But yes, if I concentrate enough, my mind can go anywhere in Whitecroft. The council rooms, bonfires." She grins. "Or I could spy on lovers, I suppose." She sighs. "It takes up a lot of focus and energy, however. I like to watch the borders sometimes. I spotted the girl, and I wanted to help. It was instinctive. But I've been exhausted since. Exhausted, yet asleep. It's quite the conundrum, isn't it?"

I can't wrap my mind around any of this. What I do know, however, is that we can't afford for her to waste her energy in any way. She can't rescue little girls or spy on lovers, not if it costs her weeks, days, even hours.

I remember what her mother said about the curse. If Vlari loses her strength, she won't be able to pull herself out of eversleep.

Since the beginning, nothing has mattered more than strengthening our ranks so that one day we can take back Tenebris. The moment we cease to need this sanctuary, Vlari could wake up. Stand before me, flesh and bones—not just some mental illusion conjured by her mind.

Then, I'd kiss her. Or throttle her. Probably both.

"Promise me you won't do it again. Promise me you won't waste any energy."

She laughs. "That's not how it works, Drusk. If you want my oath, you have to pay for it."

Bargains again. She's as fond of them as ever.

There's no price I wouldn't pay to ensure she remains safe, so I reply, "Name your terms."

She makes a show of thinking it through, lifting her eyes to the ceiling and humming as she pretends to ponder. I can tell she already knows what she wants. "All right. I want your time."

I blink in confusion.

"If I can't hop outside of these walls, I'll be bored to tears. I'll give you my word I won't, so long as you promise to come here and entertain me. You could read me books, or inform me of what's going on. Do we have a bargain?"

I could laugh. Nothing would have stopped me from coming back here every day, perhaps several times, now that I know I can get to see her. Talk to her. Touch her. Instead, I pretend I'm put out, letting my shoulders sag and sighing. "If I must. I'll entertain you as well as I'm able, and your mind will remain right here, in this room."

"I vow it," she says. She changes the subject, then. "You know, I hear my mother has a mind to make a lord out of you, for your services to the realm. She would have, already, if you weren't avoiding her." There's no accusation in her tone, but however she phrases it, it's still a question.

A question I can't answer.

How do I tell her I hate Ciera, and Nero, and everyone else who allowed her to save their lives? That I would have rather died on a battlefield ten years ago than let her fade into nothingness and condemn the rest of us to a gilded cage? I'm not one to spell out my feelings, and it won't start today.

"I'm not adept at playing with queens and princesses," I hedge.

That much is true enough.

Vlari replies, "Well, let us cut this visit short, then. My mother is on her way."

I don't have another moment to say anything at all.

The next instant, I'm back in the cold, empty room, where Vlari is still a pale, breathing corpse.

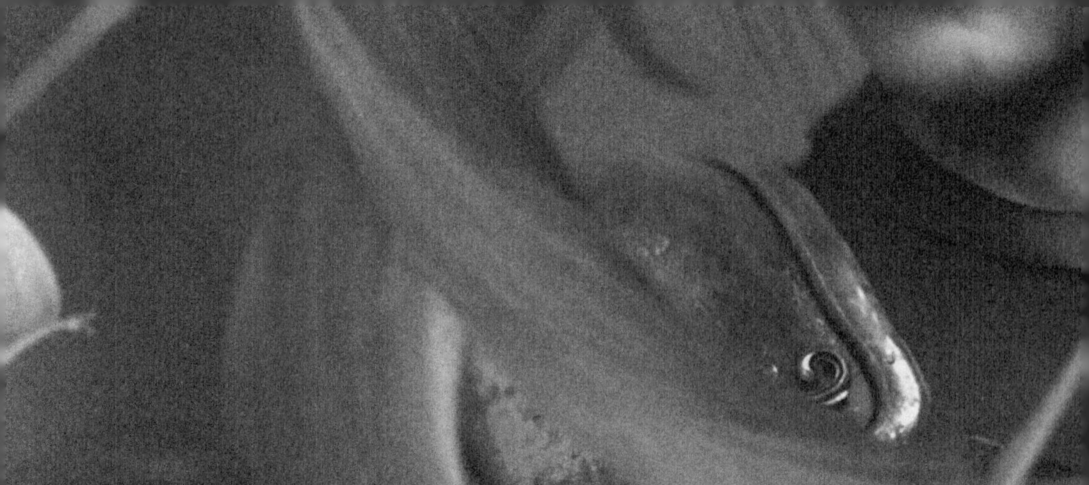

four
worth the risk
drusk

What we were after wasn't in that book," Lord Liken tells me.

I wish I could summon an appropriate level of disappointment, but I'm too used to hearing these words. The gentry send us to risk our skin out of the walls, and it always ends up being for nothing.

Nothing other than fooling the folk into believing that our lords have a plan. That they're doing something.

This status quo is no longer acceptable. I can't stomach their incompetence anymore. We need to act, now. We needed to act years ago.

"I see. And do you care to share what it is you're looking for, exactly?" My words are sharp as a blade.

The gentry looks at me with what I read as a certain level of curiosity. It may be the first time I've questioned what he tells me.

Lord Liken, king of the Court of Stone, won his crown by blood. He and his warrior wife Ina killed the despot ruling over the land southeast of Whitecroft, and none of his predecessor's descendants dared dispute his right to sit on its throne.

He isn't what I would have expected, when I heard of him. Instead of a dark general like Frost, or a cunning fox like the lord of Ichor, Velas Liken is a soft-spoken, lean fae almost as young as I, though he has seen his hundredth year. His long red hair denotes salamander blood, I think, though he has the appearance and aura of a gentry. I read intelligence in the depths of his coal-black eyes. Intelligence, and perhaps more than his fair share of cruelty, barely hidden under his languorous ways. There is no doubt that he belongs here on unseelie soil.

"A way to close our borders to Alfheimr, so that the humans cannot call for reinforcements. In the old days, we were able to produce shields as strong as the one our crown princess currently powers, albeit with the help of elemental stones charged with magic. If we uncovered this knowledge again, we could first awaken Nevlaria, and use the stones to protect Whitecroft. Then, cut off Alfheimr from Tenebris. That would ensure that no immortal comes to the usurper's aid, and that they don't get reinforcements."

I am too stunned to retort. Not only because Liken has answered me honestly without more prompting—because this plan could work. Would work. We may lose many lives if we were to fight hundreds of thousands of humans with less than ten thousand fae, but here on our land, protected by fae magic, we would be victorious.

And more importantly, Vlari would be free.

How is it I never knew that was the object of our research? I would have been outdoors every day with my rangers if I'd thought that was in the cards.

"Elemental stones?" My voice is mechanical. I'm taking in one piece of information at a time, willing myself to understand.

"Stones infused with raw elemental magic. There is one at the heart of each court, created by the first lords. Some of us had the presence of mind to bring them with us."

I think back to that day in the high court. How desperate Alven Oberon had been to retrieve what I dismissed as one broken piece of jewelry—a bright green stone. I remember his words. *"There lies the one hope this kingdom still possesses."* Had it been one of the elemental stones?

"The book you need. What does it look like?"

Liken shrugs. "I don't think any of us were alive the last time it was used. At first, we thought it could be here, as Nyx might have built the shields around Whitecroft with it. But there are many other possibilities. And one..." He scratches his hairless chin. "One may be complicated. The bridge leading to the Wicked Court, with its three doorways, was most certainly created using its magic."

"So, there's a chance that it could be in the Shadow Peaks."

Where the usurper lives. Unfortunate as it might be, this theory makes sense. The Wicked Court, formerly the Court of Wind, carved deep in Hardrock, had been Nyx's home, her stronghold. If she was the last known fae to have that book, it makes sense that she'd have kept it near.

"Could we attempt to create the wards without it?"

Liken winces. "We could, but what if it doesn't work? We'd risk everything, and Alfheimr would take the opportunity to swallow us up. We either need the book, or someone who knows the spells. No one within our walls is old enough to remember the time of Nyx, except maybe the hag in the well. But she knows nothing of spells, and she cares little for our plights."

The hag in the well.

I almost smile.

In my school days, there had been plenty of rumors about the well at the edge of the grove behind the fields we used for our sports. In a land with warriors of legend teaching spoiled, overindulged sons and daughters of princes and knights, where our literary instructor used to sing for gods, the hag was known as the oldest, most wicked thing. Naturally, it was the fashionable sport to tease her, try her patience.

We were told she once ate up a gaggle of princesses in retaliation. In my school days, she never showed. She sleeps for hundreds of years, only coming out when she's ready for a hunt.

Beautiful one moment, old crones the next, her kind roam till they find their perfect prey: an innocent girl whose heart they can carve out and eat to feed their immortality.

I once threw a nest of wasps down her well. As that elicited no response, I concluded she was a myth, or if she once was real, she could have left these lands for one without so many bored and indulgent kids nearby.

"I see I've lost your interest." Liken seems amused. I suppose he talked to me, but my mind is elsewhere. "Very well. I'll gather what knowledge I can, and come back to you when we find another old library for you to raid."

"Yes, do that," I reply.

He touches his fingertips to his brow and bows gracefully, before turning his heels.

I stop by the weapons room to collect the bag I bring with me to any raid outside these walls, then I draw deeper in the ranger headquarters till I reach the training area. Two novices circle each other, one with a broken nose, the other a bleeding mouth. They're overseen by the best trainer they could possibly have, me included: Neb. Though she's twice as vicious and three times more agile than any other here, she hasn't earned the title of ranger, and if I have anything to do with it, she never will. She belongs here, where she's safe.

My sister glares at me from across the circular room. She has other ideas.

I ignore her, catching Erdun's eye instead. I tilt my head toward the exit; he follows me out.

"Well?"

The rangers are always eager to hear of what the lords have to say, though their answer rarely changes.

I realize that for once, I can give them some hope.

I won't.

I haven't heard of the plan to shield us, which means it isn't common knowledge, with good reason: should our enemies hear of it, they'd attempt to thwart it. They'd burn any old books they could lay their hands on, and call for reinforcements early. They may even attempt to build a portal between Alfheimr and Tenebris, risky as that may be. We can't chance it.

"No luck with that book. I've had an idea, though. I'll need backup."

"I can call Iola, or Nebula—" Catching my look, he's quick to backtrack. "I think Winse is available, too."

I shake my head. "You'll do. We aren't going out."

He's intrigued, but he follows me silently through the old field, now converted into a dark, handsome stone building housing the members of the Court of Ash, which is half composed of salamanders.

Black and red eyes follow us as we head to the glade.

The well, circled by stone, waits for us in a shadow of a willow. I approach it, and look down to the black pit. I can't see—more concerningly, I can't feel what's at the bottom. This is a place of shadows—it should feel like my dominion.

It really doesn't.

I undo the leather bag at my back, then retrieve a thin spider-silk rope, handing one end to Erdun.

"You're going down there?" He looks and shivers. "That doesn't look good, boss."

"That'd be why you're here." I hook the other end of the rope to my belt and tie four knots, to be safe. "If you hear me call, if I tug three times, or if an hour has passed, pull me up."

Erdun has backed me up a dozen times outside the walls, but now he swallows hard. "What are you going to do down there?"

I hop at the top of the circular stones. "Get answers, one would hope."

“Or lose your head,” he mutters.

“Or that. A call, one hour, or three tugs,” I remind him, before jumping down into the void.

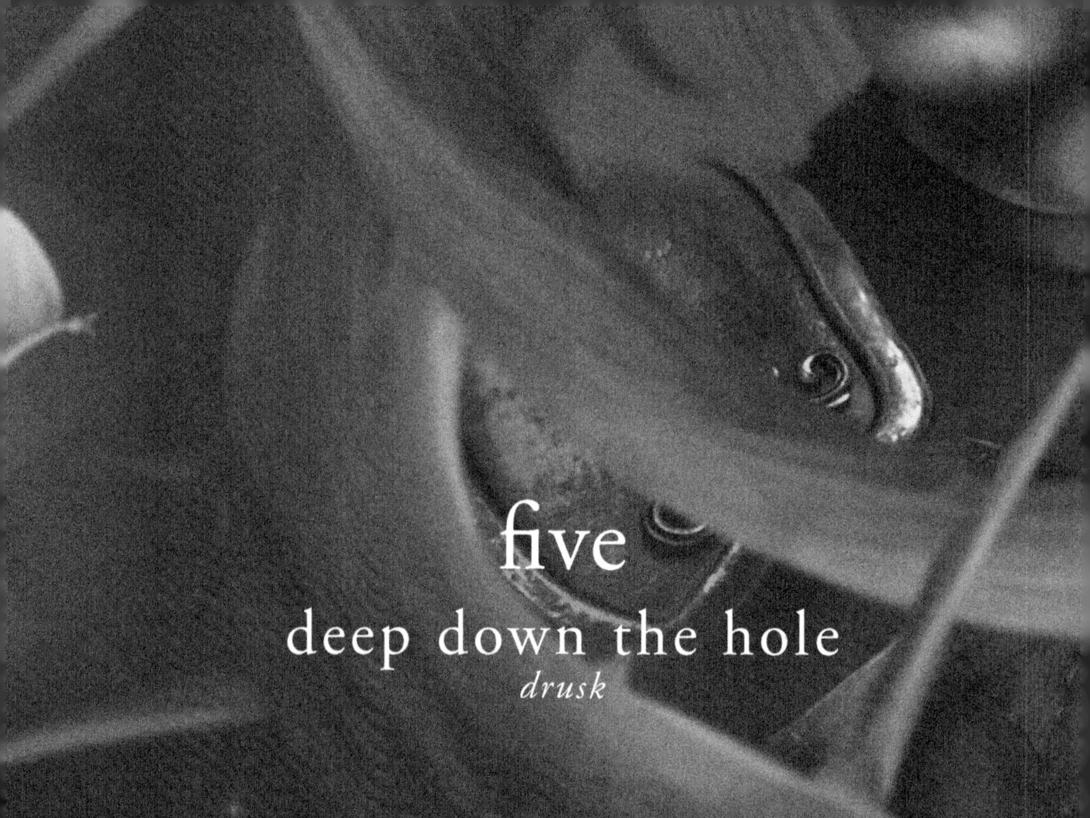

five

deep down the hole

drusk

I fall, and fall, and fall, for so long I have to wonder whether I'll ever stop falling. There's a spell at work; until the master of this hole wishes otherwise, I'll keep falling.

Eventually, my feet hit the ground.

I've never been scared of the dark. When my eyes can't adjust to it, I still feel what's lurking around me. Darkness is shadow's friend. But now, I feel nothing, see nothing. My hair bristles at the nape of my neck, alerting me of danger close by.

"Who, say, come see old Traffatel," a frail, weak, high-pitched voice calls. From where, I can't tell.

I itch to pull the sword at my side, but I know it's of little use today.

"They call me Drusk."

"Do they now?" The voice changes, now stronger and more seductive. "We've heard of a Drusk, have we not? For years and years, we heard whispers. The girls talk. He sends their pretty hearts aflutter."

I lift a brow. "You've heard of me charming girls? I need to work on my reputation."

"Well said. I am in danger of being quite charmed, too."

A light appears right in front of me, held in the hand of a beautiful lady in a dress that seems to have once been white, though its lace is marred with dust and blood.

Her white hair is so long it surrounds us, covering most of the floor, but there's no other sign of age on her smooth, spotless skin, except perhaps the shadow of her pale eyes. Her ruby-red lips stink of blood.

"You flatter me, ma'am."

"I suppose I must. Now, tell me, little Drusk, what is your name?"

My heart rate increases, catching her meaning. I pretend I don't quite understand her. "Rystan, after my grandfather."

She smiles, her lips parting to reveal a mouthful of sharp, stained fangs. "Now, now, let us not play games. You know what I ask."

She wants my true name.

"And you know I'll die before I place myself in your power."

She tilts her head. "Yes, I believe you may. But will you treat your pretty, pretty princess's life as callously as your own, I wonder?" The hag changes, her skin graying, her spine hunching, and her hands wrinkling. "You come here, into my domain, knowing that I've outlived the first of your line, knowing that I may devour you, because you're desperate. Because you're powerless. Because you're weak."

I can't naysay her, so I offer her nothing but silence.

"I heard you boys talking upstairs just now." Her eyes trail up to the ceiling of her cave. "I hear everything. I know of the spell you so desire. I know of all the ancient curses. I know every word that has ever been spoken in this land, since the days of your olden queen. And I will give you the enchantment. I will let you go free, whole, and in one piece. All I ask in return, weak, charming boy, is your true name."

Entering into a bargain with one such as this creature is madness. I should tell her to be gone, tug on my lifeline and get the hell out of here.

I can't force the word out.

Every fae is born knowing their true name, and knowing that it is a secret that must never be spoken. Fae children do not cry, for fear of ever speaking it. It is our one treasure. With it, we can be commanded to do anything—throw ourselves from a tower, into a pit full of poisonous snakes, kill our lovers and mothers, aid our worst enemy.

It cannot be worth it.

It cannot.

"Give me your name, boy. I will speak it but once. When you're alone and no one can hear. And in exchange, I'll give you the tools to save your kingdom."

I think I hate her.

"I'll give you a favor, then, without the name."

The creature cackles, and the sound surrounds me, coming from all angles, even underneath my feet.

"Oh, I think not, dear boy. I wish to hear you speak it. Humor an old crone."

I've been tortured before. In training, while in the army, and once by seelie lords who caught me north of their borders. I let them slice my wrists and throat, providing a diversion while my men infiltrated their camp to free unseelie folk they'd poached on our land.

Yet never have I suffered like this. My entire body protests against what I'm about to do. I'm fighting every part of me, including the power of Myst, rising within my chest, burning me from the inside.

"Shadow King."

I will have to kill her one day. Pour lava down this well and seal it shut.

"My name is Shadow King."

The first time I knew true fear was when my men started to call me Shadow. That they may have guessed even part of my name was a terrifying prospect. I chose to embrace it, if only to show that it meant nothing. But I am Shadow—though King is a bit of a stretch.

"It has a nice ring to it."

I don't know how I stay on my feet.

I'm empty. I'm powerless. I'm weak.

Hell if I'll let her see it.

"The book your leaders seek is buried with Nyx, in the valley between seelie and unseelie land, deep in the Murkwoods. It is of little use, for I can tell you each detail for that spell. Only the true owner of a land, a castle, or, say, a kingdom, may cast it over the entire territory."

"So if it's to cover the whole of Tenebris—"

The hag's stained fangs flash. "The high queen has to be the one casting it, holding the very heart of Tenebris in her hands. Tears of an enemy, blood of a friend, and a sacrifice of one the caster loves need to be buried along with four elemental stones—water, earth, fire, and air."

"Sacrifice?" That's an ancient word, from an ancient time, when we used to slaughter beasts, men, and folk in the name of power. No spell we rely on these days requires sacrifices.

But I'm not asking about modern magic.

The hag grins wickedly. "No one cares to recall how Queen Nyx's mother was killed, now do they?"

I know I hate Traffatel. She's enjoying this far too much.

But she's answered my question, so I thank her, before feeling my belt for the rope I need to tug on.

I don't need to look down to realize it's been cut when my hand can't find it.

"You said you'd let me go."

She clicks her tongue. "I never said when."

This time, I do reach for my sword, gripping it, though I don't draw it.

She laughs again. "That's unnecessary, pretty boy. I don't like your kind. Too rough. I much prefer the hearts of maidens. Soft and sweet and filled with hope. I am quite the scholar, you know. Why else settle here, of all places? I do love teaching children lessons. Yours is that you're far too easily trusting." She reaches upward, and my rope appears in her hand. "On your way, Shadow King."

I take the rope, and tug on it. On the surface, Erdun starts to pull me up. I climb along the walls, my hands finding cracks in the mold-infested, spider-filled, bone-littered well.

Only when I can see the sky do I realize the hag has used my name, wasting her one chance at commanding me.

Though I know better than to think it wasn't intentional.

six
fire and water
drusk

Still reeling from my encounter with the hag, I should have taken a moment to calm down, collect my thoughts, ruminate over the ramifications, and most of all, think of the price I paid. I said my name out loud. Though it may not cross Traffatel's lips again, she knows it. She knows me.

I realize that's the least important thing today.

I have the spell Liken wants. I have a tool we may use to end this invasion, and free our kingdom.

"I was scared for a moment," Erdun tells me. "The rope felt so light I thought I lost you."

I don't tell him he did.

"I'm here. You did a great job. I have another one for you. Recall all available rangers back to base."

Curious though he may be, he doesn't ask me why, nodding before drifting back to town.

For my part, I do the only thing I possibly can do. I head to Whitecroft Hall.

The two guards posted, a troll and a salamander knight dressed in the finery of the Court of Ash, aren't the same as those I encountered yesterday, but they also wave me through without question.

I turn to the knight. "Where might I find one of the high queen's representatives? I need to speak to the crown, in private."

I may be familiar with the old building, but I have no clue how they've organized it now. The only room I know is the one they set up Vlari in.

The knight turns to his companion. "Can you handle the door for a moment? I'll send someone to take my place."

The troll grunts his acknowledgement.

"If you'll follow me." The salamander is all courtesy, though I imagine I see some animosity in his amber eyes.

He's covered in silver and gold, heavy armor encasing him from the tip of his helm to the pointed toes of his boots. One of the reasons I never wished to be a knight is the outfit. Plain soldiers fare much better, donning supple leather and the occasional breastplate.

I suppose it must be difficult for him to appear anything but antagonistic in this metal casket.

We head toward the old assembly room on the ground floor, behind the grand staircase leading up to the higher floor. The knight could have just told me where to go, but I don't point it out.

When we arrive at closed doors, he tells a guard posted next to them, "Take my place at the gate for a few, would you?"

The guard, another salamander, pretends to sigh, though I can tell she seems excited at the prospect. There must be more to see at the gates than in a random corridor.

She rushes to the entrance, and we walk inside the assembly room, which is filled with at least a hundred folk. Ash folk, stone folk, star folk. Folk of meadows and castles. Gentries with great names and little sprites. They all wait in line to see the queen.

I wince. I told the knight I wanted to speak to a representative to avoid just that.

Before I can protest, the guard tells me, "This way."

We pass through the mob. I notice the crowd eyeing me with anything ranging from curiosity to hatred to awe.

We take a small unadorned door away from the great entryway leading to the queen's hall.

"We've met before, you know," the knight tells me.

I shrug. "I've met many a folk."

The polite thing might have been to ask for his name, but I've had enough introductions to last me a lifetime.

"And there's no cause for you to remember me," the knight guesses. "But I wouldn't forget you in a hurry. You were accompanying the Frosts to the Ash Court, years ago, during our tournament."

I laugh.

Then I'm not surprised he remembers me.

The general let me enter the tournament. I wiped the floor with a knight or two and brought a fat prize home. The thousand coins fed the whole village for a winter month or two.

While I don't make a habit of giving away everything I earned, I have always been painfully aware that it wasn't possible for my entire family to earn in a month what I make in a week. My mother was a servant in a white lady's house. My father's forge was one of the best in our court, but what he earned was nothing compared to my potential. My family only allowed me to bring food, occasionally, and some treats for my sister whenever I felt like it. As I had nothing and no one to spend money on, my earnings have piled up for decades. The few times when I earned a prize, rather than a salary, I was permitted to share it.

Hence the reason why I never refused to enter a tournament. And why I never lost.

"Did I wound your pride?" I asked as we cross another doorway.

That would certainly explain the layer of disdain I thought I could read from him.

"Only my wallet. I had a wager placed on one of your opponents. I learned to make wiser choices, after. This way, if you please."

I've never been to this part of the keep. The carved and sculpted walls seem out of place, far grander than any other room. When we pass black marble columns under a painted archway, I still. "These are the queen's quarters."

No one else could claim chambers so fine. Plush velvet throws and low chaises make the area look comfortable and relaxing, but in no way less regal.

"Indeed. You wished to speak to her, did you not?"

I frown. Everyone wants to see the high queen. It doesn't mean that we can or should.

The knight answers the question I haven't asked. "The high queen gave orders some time ago. The members of her high court are to be admitted at any time, and command us all, it seems. You aren't liked for it."

I blink. "I'm a member of the high court?"

That was news to me.

"There are so few, it's easy to remember the list. The queen's family, and you. That's it. As I said, you aren't liked for it."

I suppose I wouldn't be.

It astonishes me that I was included, when I never knelt to Ciera.

"This way. The queen will join you as soon as she's able."

I'm ushered to a study with bookshelves full of colorful spines. Too restless to claim a woven wood seat, I opt to inspect the books, pulling one here and there.

They aren't spell books, or memoirs, or even dull historical novels. These are stories. Human stories, printed by the hundreds.

I'm astonished to find them here.

"My greatest secret. I am a lover of adventure. Just not when it happens outside of the safety of these pages."

I turn to find Ciera standing at the doorway, hand in her husband Nero's grasp.

She has always looked the part of a queen, but now she wears a crown that looks too cumbersome on her pretty head.

"Your Highness."

I know protocol dictates that I get to one knee. I don't. She doesn't demand it.

"Come, sit. I am glad you came to us. Is your family well?"

I don't have the patience to stand for small talk. "I went to see the hag just now."

Ciera's eyes widen, but I see no recognition on Nero's features.

And no wonder. While Ciera was educated here in her days, Vlari's father, a commoner like me, knows nothing of Whitecroft. "There's a hag in a well, at the edge of the grove. She's been there for a long time. I thought she'd have some advice."

"Oh, I never doubted old Traffatel would have plenty of advice." Ciera shakes her pretty head. "But I never would have sent someone to their death to find out what she'd deign to tell us."

I don't point out that this makes her a weak ruler. She doesn't need to be told that.

"You were reckless, Drusk, but I can see you're well. If you've come to us, then I take it what she had to say was helpful?"

"The protective spell we need to close our borders. I have it."

I repeat the hag's spell word for word, and let them take it in. Word for word.

Tears of enemies, blood of friends, and a sacrifice of one the caster loves needs to be done and buried along with four elemental stones—water, earth, fire, and air.

To me, that was the important part, but Ciera says, "The queen must be holding the heart of Tenebris?" She sighs in relief. "Thank the gods, we do have the heart."

"Your Grace?"

"It was taken out of the Wicked Court by my father—with your assistance, unless I'm mistaken."

I wouldn't have guessed that the heart of Tenebris would be an actual object, rather than a fanciful notion about her popularity.

Was that the stone we'd retrieved?

"As for the four elements, we have air and earth, but fire and water…" Nero winces.

"We can ask Ash. Creating an elemental stone isn't easy, but with so many salamanders here, they should manage. Water is another matter. Do you think the Sea Court would speak to us?"

The queen and her mate whisper among themselves—I can tell I'm no longer needed.

"With your leave, then—"

Ciera's head snaps to me. "You have to stay. The lords will need to hear it all."

My lips thin. "I'm sure you can relay the information." Too late, I remember to add, "My queen."

She's displeased with me, but I can't bring myself to care. I bow, and I get out.

Already, I am tired, weary, and reeling from the day's events, but I have a promise to keep.

From the royal quarters, Vlari's room is close, but I lose my way once or twice in the unfamiliar passages. Soon, I'm back in front of the red door.

This time, I push it open without hesitation.

seven
a taste of history
drusk

I slid one of my sister's books into the inside pocket of my cloak this morning, knowing where I'd end up going sometime today. To Vlari's chamber.

She's been changed into another dress, and her hair is braided today. I wonder who's caring for her. Her mother? Her father? A servant?

The thought of anyone undressing her and taking liberties with her body while she sleeps unnerves me. She's so vulnerable. No woman has ever held more power in her grasp since the day of Nyx, and yet, she's as defenseless as a puppy. Someone could hurt her. Touch her. Steal a kiss.

I clear my throat, stepping forward.

"I believe we had a bargain. I certainly hope you've kept your end of it, princess."

A cold silence is the only answer I receive.

I start to read. Nebula is fond of great tales of warrior princesses and cursed knights. This book tells the story of a war I can't remember hearing of; the kingdoms are unfamiliar, but I recognize some names. Names of legendary folk, long buried. This is a story from the Old World, before our kind left to find a land more suited to the needs of the folk.

Alfheimr, our people called it, when they reached it. They were accompanied by three immortals, a thousand folk, and a hundred human servants.

This was supposed to be our world. Now, some three thousand years later, one of the only two fae kingdoms on our continent has been taken by mortals and traitors.

I wonder what Alara the Great, Conqueror of Death, Mavlan Spire, Air Whisperer, and Landrag Vern, Master of Darkness, would think of us now.

I can't say I pay any mind to what I read, until a line catches my attention.

I frown, silently reading it again, and then a third time.

Sir Vern melded the darkness so well, he could drown souls in its depth.

I would have dismissed it as more inane lyrical nonsense had I not done just that, again and again. Taken someone's body and mind, and contorted it under layers of shadows.

They're talking of mysting.

I'm stunned.

When Gendrion Frost found me in my village and told me the power I wielded was called myst, he mentioned no one had seen a Myst for an age. If books ever existed on this power, they'd long been forgotten. I was trained alone, in an experimental way. My tutors had no idea what I could do, what my limits were. I'm still not quite sure of the bounds of my power.

Yet this tiny pocket book printed not two winters ago mentions myst, under the surface. I am sure of it.

I close it, and turn it around, checking the attribution.

"*A History of Fae*, by Marren—79 AE."

It's a print of a book written not even a hundred years after our arrival in Alfheimr.

I catch a movement right in front of me, and lift my head.

Then I still.

Part of me wants to scream; the other could jump in elation.

Vlari's right in front of me.

She's also on her bed. She hasn't pulled me into her mind, this time. She's appeared here, in this world.

"I thought we had an agreement." My voice is dry, but firm.

"I'm within these four walls." She shrugs, callous as always.

I can't even be mad at her twisting our deal to please her fancy. I would have done the same in her shoes.

"You've found something, haven't you?"

I don't reply at first. I'm too busy looking at her, taking her in, wondering if I can touch her. Feel her.

At long last, I turn the book around. "See this line? I believe the author was talking about a Myst. This person—Vern."

"The Master of Darkness," she says. One of us was paying attention, at least. "The title would certainly fit. Isn't that what you do? Mold darkness to your will?"

It sounds like an oversimplification, but I nod all the same.

"And this could be a Storm," she says, pointing to a line on the opposite page.

Spire was "bidding the sky above to answer his commands." Storms are another lost power—air mages with the strength to command tornadoes and lightning, when ten regular air folk would have to use all of their power just to bring a little rain during a drought.

The sky, like the sea, had a will of its own, and did not care to bow to the desires of most of the folk.

"The Master of Death could be a Void," I say.

Her eyes widen with an eagerness I share. Hearing of others who may have been like us is a strange thing, in a world where I've taken for granted that I am alone.

"Well, keep reading!"

We're both enraptured with the rest of the tale. While it occurs to me that I should tell her to rest her mind, I'm glad to see her in front of me, and I'm selfish enough to prioritize my enjoyment over her safety. She's followed her part of the bargain, and stopped herself from roaming Whitecroft with the power of her mind. I faced a hag who could have been crunching on my bones by now. We're both due for some reward.

At the end of the overlong chapter, I know it's time to end this. Part ways. Return to my parents' quarters and get some rest. I'll need it for what is to come.

I remain silent and unmoving, unwilling to voice the word that must be said. Goodbye.

How I despise that word. Loathe it.

"Will I see you tomorrow?" she murmurs.

If the sun rises in the east. If the ocean's capricious, and the desert cruel.

"If I can." I leave the book next to her pillow and walk away. At the door, I hesitate. "Have you heard that your mother has made me part of the high court?"

"Has she, now?" Vlari's secretive grin exasperates me. I suppose we're not past this nonsense. Teasing each other. Keeping secrets. Hiding.

"I'm told it's a small court. Just the family. It seems odd that she'd think to add me. I've only met her once."

I don't ask whether Vlari told her mother to include me. It seems too obvious. The question is, why? Did she suspect I don't feel like I belong to any of the lower courts? How could she? Even Vlari doesn't know me this well.

"I can't claim to know what happens in my mother's mind, but when immortals fell on us, you were protecting the folk. If I were to hazard a guess, I'd say that probably branded you as someone trustworthy."

So few words, yet so many twists of the tongue. I roll my eyes. "You know, if you don't feel like answering me, you could simply say so. There's no need for tricks."

She beams. "And what would be the fun in that?"

eight

the price of time

drusk

I go back the next day, and the day after that. I must be a masochist to submit myself to that brand of torture. She does nothing but plague me, make me crave her, and drive me closer to madness.

I need her. I need to be far away from her. I need to taste her. Part of me wants to kiss her unmoving lips, but I've never been much of a necrophile.

I could take it up, though.

I've buried myself in my work over the last decade. Everyone is used to seeing me enter base at dusk and remain there until darkness fades on the horizon. In the last week, I've barely stepped foot there, taking reports when I pass by some rangers on my way to Whitecroft Hall. It's not like any of us have a mission. The lords and ladies are in constant meetings, arguing the best ways to use the information I came up with.

I'm restless, and the only thing soothing me is her. She's the worst kind of poison, a drug I can't help going back to though I know it's killing me.

Vlari is hardly calmer. I've updated her on everything I know. She has her ideas about our next logical course of action.

War.

Right now.

Without preparation, without seeking the elemental stones, without worrying about the usurper, without a scheme.

"I'm just saying, worst-case scenario, we lose. All the folk are dead. The land has been razed. At least they won't be stuck here, suffering a slow death." She sniffles. "I should never have locked us away."

I grin. "You're bored."

"*Terribly*." She pouts. I never knew she was quite this bloodthirsty.

"I must be dreadful at entertaining you."

She eyes the book in my hands meaningfully. "It's not about me, though. We need to *do* something. I should wake up."

She's so, so cruel. Hearing her say those words hurts more than a knife to the chest. Because she can't, and won't.

"If you do, the dome will fall. The scouts patrolling around us will notice right away, and there'll be an army on its way here within the hour. If you do, there's no stopping our destruction." I hate that I have to be the voice of reason. "We need to be ready."

She sighs, defeated. "Read me another book? This one really is awful."

I comply.

FOUR DAYS LATER, I'm surprised to enter Vlari's room and see a girl on the single chair. She's brought a lute with her, and she plays our princess a cheerful song.

It occurs to me that I do know her—she's one of the Thorns, Dekren's younger sister, Mephesea.

I move to return to the door, but she turns to me, abandoning her instrument. "Don't leave on my account. I'm about to go."

I hesitate, not wanting to cut her visit short, but Esea is already packing up the lute.

"I didn't know you played," I say.

I have seen her many a time in passing. Her brother was my friend back when we attended school here, and we did stay in touch. He was a little indulgent for my taste, but I appreciated his easy laughs and easier jabs.

We lost him in the Shadow Peaks.

Vlari brought many among the court back to life, but there still were many casualties when the usurper attacked. The royal family. Many guards. And the boys who liked to hide in the shadow with a lover or two weren't in the hall when Vlari used her power to revive our people.

Dekren may have survived it, but I've heard he was at court that day, and as he's not with us, the chances that he might still be breathing are slim.

"I didn't use to." Her smile is filled with sorrow. "We've all had to fashion ourselves into something else, here."

I find myself touching her shoulder as she passes me. "It was quite beautiful," I tell her.

I see others in the next few days. Old acquaintances, strangers of low and high rank alike. A lord she saved in the halls. Though he never knew her, he tells me he comes and kneels in front of her every new moon, to thank her for the time she gave him. A chambermaid who used to polish the polar flooring of Vlari's old home. Meda, once. Nero, twice. I do remind him he's welcome at Ash if he ever fancies a bowl of gruel.

It is unavoidable that I'd meet the high queen, given how much time I linger in her daughter's chamber, but I am never prepared. What am I supposed to tell her? What if she bans me from this room? I never know what to expect of Ciera.

I come in one day to find her brushing Vlari's hair. My princess is dressed in a simple gown of blue gossamer, not unlike what my own mother could have worn on a special occasion. There's no heavy, antique crown on the high queen's head, and she wears little jewelry at all, save for a gold wrist band.

My eyes linger on the bracelet. I hadn't noticed it before. I've seen ones just like it, though made of copper—on each of my parent's right wrists. They're seals, the kind that one exchanges in their bonding ceremony.

Most fae are long lived—some, entirely impervious to the passage of time. As such, our kind often form alliances for a hundred years or so, rather than lifetime commitments.

My parents decided to bond for life. It's less uncommon among pucks and sprites. The great gentries almost never bond, unless they've found their own mate. Yet I know this is a true seal. Ciera and Nero must have chosen to bond. I don't think they are true mates. For one, finding one's true mate is incredibly rare, but when we do, our skin often bears the mark of it. Ciera's exquisite gowns reveal most of her throat and arms—I've never seen a mating mark. They voluntarily linked in mind, body, and soul until the death of the flesh, which means that when one is killed, the other will soon follow to the grave. Unseelie folk, wild folk, shy folk, elven kind, and seelie often live a thousand years without experiencing a love like that.

I'm half tempted to ask what made her, a princess of the realm, favorite of her mother back in the day, decide to throw everything away for the love of a common fae. But I know. Insanity. She's completely mad.

Does it run in the family?

I hide a smile.

The moment she sees me, Ciera's eyes brighten.

"Rystan. Wait, I hear you favor Drusk?"

I shrug. "The high queen may call me as she pleases."

Her laugh makes me think of her daughter. "Why, I never knew you could be charming. My daughter doesn't speak much of her friends."

I attempt no answer.

Her smile drops and she sighs, returning to her brushing. "I owe you, Rystan. More than I should say. We all do."

She isn't the first to express some gratitude for the role I've taken upon myself—training the folk. I never sought gratitude. I saw something that could prove useful, when I was feeling utterly helpless, and I chose to do it to retain some sanity. That's all.

But she isn't talking about the rangers.

"Do you know how it works? Her hair." She's looking down at her daughter.

I shake my head. "I've always known her to be silver-haired, in our youth."

"She never was," the queen tells me. "Vlari was born with a full head of violet curls. I meant to call her Hyacinth."

I grimace, making the queen laugh again.

"Nero had the same reaction. Either way, we never had a choice. My mother saw her and decided her fate."

Her hand glides along Vlari's skin, and pushes fabric down her shoulder. That feels like an invasion. I want to tell her to stop.

"Just there," Ciera says, brushing the back of her shoulder. "That's where my mother branded her with old magic. A rune that sucked at her power. Sucked at her very life. All those of our line have an amethyst streak, inherited from our ancestors. And the moment Mother branded Vlari, her hair turned silver at the roots. You know what I noticed, right then? My mother's violet eyes were brighter. She wasn't only crippling my daughter. She was channeling her."

If I could bring Morgana to life right now, I would, only to ensure she suffers greater torments before extracting the last ounce of life from her.

"I vowed I'd find a way to end her rule. I vowed death and violence. But these things aren't in my nature. Most of all, I vowed Vlari would never be used again. Yet, we're doing that right now. Sucking at her life to protect ourselves. To maintain our power."

If she's hoping for me to disagree, she'll be disappointed.

"That's why I intended to wake her on her birthday, no matter the cost. She'll be eighty come midwinter, you know. And as we approached it, I saw her life draining before my eyes every day. I saw that if I would not condemn us all, I'd have to condemn my daughter instead."

My jaw ticks. "We still have time." I move closer, eyes on the soft locks. "She's still fine. Conscious. Fighting. Is she not?"

She has to be. We talk every day, and she has said nothing of her strength waning. I haven't seen or sensed any difference in her.

To my shock, the queen drops the brush next to Vlari and rushes to me. I instinctively move into a defensive position, but before I entirely shift to one side to protect my heart, she's thrown herself at me, arms around my shoulders, and her seemingly frail arms are squeezing me to her.

I'm astounded, confused, and honestly, concerned. For one, what if her bondmate enters and misunderstands the situation? I consider prying her off me, but she's *the* unseelie high queen. And she's Vlari's mother. It seems like she needs comfort. I can attempt to provide it, pretending it's my sister in my arms. With great difficulty, I force my arm to circle hers loosely. She sniffles in my grasp.

Oh, lords of all woods, I am dreadful at this hugging business.

"We do." The queen bobs her head up and down, as ungracefully as she's able to. "We do have time, now." Finally, *finally*, she moves away from me. "She was fading. Her slumbers lasted longer. Most days, she barely breathed, and she was cold. So very cold. Now, look." She's pointing to Vlari's hair. It isn't much different from what it was when I first saw it a week ago. Half silver-gray, the other half a deep, dark purple.

Reading my confusion, she clarifies, "We had less than three inches of color. My daughter is strong, but even she needs anchors. Things to hold her here with us. Friends, people to entertain her. Hope."

I practically growl. "Did none of her friends come?"

I pause, wondering if Vlari has friends at all. The Thorn girl, Mephesea, comes to mind. "Didn't Esea come?"

The queen nods. "Occasionally, and it helped, of course. But she has no one else. A decade is a long time to hold on to just a few threads. I don't think she was giving up. I think she was truly falling into the claws of deep eversleep, though I doubt it was of her own volition. She was fading."

I don't say anything. I can't. The guilt eating at me doesn't allow for a word to cross my lips. I could have come earlier. In my anger and cowardice, I didn't think about what her eversleep was like for her. All that mattered was that seeing her was too painful.

"And yet, she used some energy. To save the girl…the child, a few weeks ago."

I'm redirecting my anger at Vlari, because if I don't, I'm going to hit something.

Ciera sighs. "She said the child is brave. That she deserves a chance. I think she knew she was almost gone, by then. She may have wanted to do something good before leaving us."

I can't breathe. The queen should have just stabbed me in the heart.

She takes my hand, her palm hot against my icy skin. "You brought her back to us."

"How long?" I clear my throat. "How long do we have, now? Given her energy level."

Ciera smiles at me. "Years. We have years, Rystan. I can't tell you how many, exactly, but she's well now."

I remember how to breathe again then.

We have time.

I glare down at her body, stalking to her with a burning rage I can't contain. She was going to let herself die, and she didn't so much as tell me. I need to shout at her.

The sound of a frantic set of footfalls rushing toward us distracts me. I unsheathe my dagger and return to the door, positioning myself in front of the queen, though there are plenty of guards in the corridor.

Instants later, an imp in a page outfit appears, out of breath, wide eyes still open in shock.

"Your Highness—" The dainty, light-green-skinned imp is breathless. "You're needed in the war room at once. We have had news."

Queen Ciera's violet eyes cut through me.

"I'll stay with Vlari," I say, my words concealing my rage. She and I have a matter or two to discuss today.

The queen squeezes my arm, and follows the page out of the room.

I sit next to Vlari, and take one of her hands.

As the seconds stretch, I half expect her to take the coward's way out. She has to know how pissed I am. But reality fades, and she pulls me into one of her visions all the same.

Looking at her, I find that I'm incapable of saying anything at first, taking in the fact that she's right here in front of me. Almost alive.

"You were dying."

She sighs. "My mother can be dramatic."

"You were *dying*."

She doesn't seem to get it.

Silence looms as she stares at me cautiously, and I do my best not to snap.

If I let go of whatever control I have left, there's no telling what I'll do. Quietly, I ask, "Why didn't you wake up?"

She takes a moment before answering. I know she's thinking of a way to make her response sound better. "If my energy were to die down in eversleep, I think I could still power the ward for a while. Years, maybe. They say the Cursed Prince in the Wilderness still retains his power, though he's been in eversleep for thousands of years."

"You decided to stop caring about your survival based on *tales*." Never mind control. I'm shouting. She deserves to be shouted at.

She waves her hand. "So what? My life against that of thousands of folk? It's not like many people would actually care if I wasn't around. You would have forgiven me, eventually."

I could throttle her. I want to. "They have to. I don't."

She seems amused, as though she knows I'm talking utter nonsense. As if she knows I'm twisted around her littlest finger. "You would have."

That's new.

Vlari has never given me a reason to think she was aware of her hold on me, not even once. Even when I was weak enough to let her glimpse just how deep my obsession with her ran, she'd gloss right over the knowledge, reading something else instead. Teasing, cruelty, indifference. She's never acknowledged any awareness of my feelings.

Now she is implying she knew.

She knew I loved her.

"You would have understood I did the right thing. You would have admired me for it. And when Tenebris was ours again, you would have danced to songs about the sleeping princess at the heart of the ley lines. In a thousand years, you would have told your grandchildren you knew me."

I've never known such fury. "Don't." I can't deal with this. Her flippancy. Her indifference to death. "Don't you dare do this. Don't you dare give up on life."

"I'm not. Obviously. I mean, it was the best solution at the time. I'm too far from fading away to consider it again. And you have come up with an alternative solution I like a lot better than turning into a statue."

How can she be so very cavalier? "You're a corpse. You can't move. You can't touch, or feel, or see, or dance in the rain. Why don't you seem to care?"

She shrugs. "I'm a pretty corpse, at least. Mom's brushing my hair every day. It used to be so dry. I doubt it's ever been nicer."

I think she's doing it on purpose to provoke me now. "Why?" When she doesn't reply, I clarify, "Why don't you care at all?"

Her gaze evades me, gliding toward the fireplace. It's lit up and burns bright green in this vision of hers. "I suppose because this isn't much worse than what my life was before. I was going through the motions. I was powerless, frightened, and useless. Now I have a purpose I can embrace. I have little regret."

My anger dissipates, replaced by something worse. I don't think my heart can take more of this battering.

For so long I'd been intrigued and fascinated by her. I wanted to see beyond the mask, understand her, know what her life was like.

Now I find she had nothing. Nothing to hold on to, nothing to make her live.

My princess used to be a void.

"Please." My voice is barely above a murmur. "Please, talk to someone before risking your life like this again. To your mother. To *me*. You matter, Nevlaria. You matter to this world. You are more than a power source to protect the rest of us. Don't take it upon yourself to shield everyone. Not ever again."

She doesn't say a word, visibly disagreeing with me.

"You don't need a purpose. You just need to exist. Life doesn't have to have a grand meaning."

"I know that. I existed for decades. Now, this is who I am. The shield of Tenebris. Just like you coined yourself the shadow, I found a role that suits me."

"No one asked you to shield us. If you hadn't, we would have gone to war, and we might have won. The usurper had fewer human forces on our territory at the time. Either way, this would have been over by now." I don't quite mean that, but it feels good to say it all the same. "Next time, let the folk decide what they want to do."

"If I had, the folk could have tried to change my mind, and they'd be dead. I don't have to give anyone a choice. I am the heir to the crown of Tenebris. This is *my* fight."

I see it right in her eyes. What she is. What she may become.

She's the true queen. It doesn't matter that her mother wears the crown. She was the one who'd saved the folk, defeated our enemy, and brought us to safety.

The fact that she didn't have to justify herself, and that her orders were law, shouldn't bother me.

It didn't.

My jaw tightens. "Why didn't someone—anyone—tell me you were able to communicate, all these years? If we're *friends*, as you pointed out."

"Did you ask?" she asks, eyebrows raised.

Of course I hadn't. I didn't speak of her to anyone, and I avoided her family like the plague, as everything about them reminded me of her.

"You forbade them. You told them to hide it from me. You wanted to *punish* me." The wild accusations spill over my lips like vomit—I can't keep them in.

Her leveled gaze is the picture of indifference, as though my words roll off her. But I didn't miss the fire in the depths of her stormy eyes.

I was right. By all gods and demons, I was right. "You punished me because I wasn't playing your game, and supporting your decision to abandon us." I step close to her, leaning forward to reach her face. Now, I whisper. "You wanted me here, and when I didn't come, you lashed out like a scorned lover. Very mature, *princess.*"

She says nothing, and doesn't move at all.

"You had no right. We aren't lovers. We'll never be lovers. Because. You. Left. Me." I enunciate each word to make her feel just how profoundly they are engraved on my soul.

"I have every right," she replied. "Besides, don't you remember? You owe me a favor."

I'm stunned again.

She's absolutely unbelievable.

"Rystan Drusk, you gave me your word you'll do any task I ask of you, some sixty years ago. So, you'll forgive me, and that's the end of it."

Infuriating. Manipulative. Proud.

She's been sent by the deepest circles of hell to test me, I know it.

I can't believe she's given up her power over me now, after all her grand declarations about keeping me under her control at any cost.

She's freed me and shackled my hands in one go.

Because if I have to forgive her, then I'm back to being hers, unconditionally.

And I have no choice at all in the matter.

"You're a monster."

She grins as though I've complimented her. Maybe I have.

I close my eyes, and force myself to let go. Of the darkness, of the pain, the betrayal. Of the feeling of unworthiness. The fact that she's shown me my will would never matter to her.

I let go.

I forgive her.

And I close my mouth on hers.

Only, where her lips should be, there's nothing at all.

She isn't here.

She's asleep, and slowly dying.

I'm kissing her for the very first time, and I don't feel her under my skin.

nine
will of the queen
drusk

I should feel guilty about yesterday's outburst, but I don't. I'm on the defensive when I walk through Whitecroft Hall, half expecting to be told to clear out, but as usual, no one attempts to get in my way.

When I reach Vlari's room, a chaise has been moved next to her bed, and there's a fresh bouquet of flowers on her nightstand.

I make my way to the chaise, and drop on its plush crimson velvet. I can imagine falling asleep on it; it's a considerable upgrade to the cot I use at my parents'.

I take in Vlari's serene expression. She hasn't moved at all, though her hair has changed. Today, she's under a blue silk throw.

I could take her hand, get to talk to her, but at what price, and to what end? She shouldn't be draining her resources just to have a chat with me.

"I considered bringing you a book on the Cursed Prince, as you're evidently fond of children's tales, but instead, I thought you may benefit from a lesson in curses, instead." I'm petty, and I don't care.

I read aloud, barely taking in a word, flying through lessons in spellcasting, faerie tongue twists, and other tedious things I learned long ago.

My choice of book wasn't just born of anger. It occurred to me that while I've been guided through my discovery of Myst, Vlari has never had the chance to study her power. No wonder she was riveted by the possible mention of a Void in my sister's book. I've taken the knowledge for granted, but it's all new to her.

She can bring gods to their knees, but she has no clue about the limits of elemental magic.

She needs to know it. She needs to understand what is likely to suck her energy, and how to control herself.

Not that she cares about her own safety, but if the day comes that she chooses to consider it, she'll have the basics.

The manual takes us a week. I don't touch her. I don't want to speak to her. I can't leave her alone either, though.

When I finish reading the book, it's too bright out; the sunlight prickles my eyes, nearly blinding me.

"That's it." I yawn and stretch my arms over my head.

In a week, my anger has receded. I've taken in what she revealed about herself, accepting it—even the parts I loathe to consider.

She used to be alone. She used to feel hopeless, maybe even depressed.

Never again.

Now, I'm desperate to see her again.

I give in, my hand closing over Vlari's. "Any requests for tomorrow?"

She doesn't pull me into one of her visions this time, but I hear her loud and clear in my mind. "More of the same would be great. Lessons in magic may be boring, but they're useful. Thank you, Drusk."

It has always been strange to hear her call me Drusk. Unfamiliar. It's the name I used at school and in the armies, but to my friends and family, I've always been Rystan. Yet I've never asked her to call me that. I suppose I want her to come to the decision on her own.

"You're welcome."

I return to my parents'. My life has begun and ended with Vlari for weeks. I've barely seen my family. I make a mental note to spend the morning with them, before collapsing.

MY SISTER STUMBLES in my room at twilight. I blink the moment she advances, my instincts alerting me of a potential threat.

She's changed in ten years, even I know that. She's strong enough to do damage when she aims to.

I can't say I like it.

"The queen sent two pages! She wants you."

I suppose I'll have to spend time with my family another day.

I groan, sitting up. I've survived on a few hours of sleep here and there for years, but I've been exhausted on twice as much of late. My body is reaching limits I didn't know it had. Mental exhaustion.

"Can I come with?"

A rebuttal is ready on my lips. Nebula asks this very question every other day, and the answer is always no. She can't join raids outside Whitecroft. She can't fight in tournaments. She can't apply to be a palace guard. She can't be in danger.

Not only because I'm worried about her safety—though I am. Our parents already have one child bleeding for Tenebris. The second should get to enjoy some peace.

However I can't imagine that a meeting with the queen would place her in much danger. Like I was when I first enrolled at Whitecroft, and even later, she's fascinated by gentries. Their bright armor, clothes stitched with gold, and pointed shoes embroidered with hexes blind her. In time, she'll learn what I did. They're the best and the worst of us, stronger and weaker all at once. A prince of the lower court may raze an entire city in a fit of wrath, but they'd be hard-pressed to manage one day of hard work like our parents do. Accidents of birth may make them richer, indolent, but the common folk are the heart of Tenebris.

For now, Neb is still captivated, and I can't find a reason to deny her this one indulgence. "Sure."

She gasps, flabbergasted, then squeals. "I need to get changed!"

I laugh at her candor, dragging myself out of bed. I wash and get dressed in one of my ten near-identical black tunics and breeches, fitting my sword in a leather baldric I seldom wear. It's less practical than my other belts, hindering my movements as it does. Again, I'm assuming there'll be no fighting near the queen. I may have grown more trusting than is wise. By the time I leave the room I claimed—the smallest in my parents' quarters—I find the two pages seated in the living area, munching on fresh buckwheat rolls.

I eye my father, rolling my eyes. I favor my mother, save for the dark blue hair. Both of my parents are several inches shorter than Nebula, and she only reaches my shoulders.

That there's gentry blood in our veins is obvious—my power cannot come from the lines of the little folk. We don't know whose, because we haven't asked. Neb is too nice to bring up the subject. I simply don't care.

Da's rules of hospitality are so well engrained in his psyche, he'd invite the usurper for tea, if she ever dropped by. Those who knock at his door are his guests, and guests must be fed. The pages eat gratefully. No one starves at Whitecroft, but the rationing has been hard on some. An extra mouthful is a treat. My family gives away food where we can. Every new moon, a knight drops off the same pouch of gold I earned as a soldier. Here, it's a fortune. Most of the folk barter what they can—grain for leather, silk for wood. A gold coin is worth ten times more than it used to be.

I wonder when they'll realize it should be worth nothing at all. At least until we're out of this prison.

"Ready!" Neb screeches, running back in the kitchen.

My eyes soften. It's been a while since I've seen her like this. She used to wear pinks and blues and greens, with backless cuts and scandalously slit skirts that drove my parents close to the edge of madness. I've nearly murdered plenty of fellow soldiers for looking at her. Recently, she's been in leathers, always ready for the worst, like the rest of us.

Today, she's opted for a dress I've never seen: a blue silk affair with long sleeves, gathered at the waist and falling in soft waves that would have looked regal had her skirts not ended around her mid-thighs. She's wearing flat-soled boots that hike up over her knees, blending practicality with her sense of impropriety. I love it.

My father swears under his breath. "If your mother was here!"

Neb isn't one to be shamed. "She isn't." She winks at Da, and we exchange a grin.

I may have to stab a few fae today, but she's certainly old enough to decide what she should wear.

"You're meeting the *queen*!" I didn't think Da's pitch could reach so high. When I say nothing, he looks to the pages for support, but the sprite and his goblin companion are suddenly fascinated by what's left of their rolls.

"Well, I haven't had time to sew anything else, and I'm *not* going in leathers."

To end the pointless argument, I clear my throat. "When the high queen calls, we're supposed to answer. We're late enough. No time for an outfit change. Let's go."

The pages jump to their feet, visibly as eager to get going as I am. "This way, sir."

They lead us to the riverbank leading out to the Arm of Sea—the path we sailed to reach Whitecroft from the Wicked Court.

I stiffen. The bank is included in the protective walls Vlari erected, but all the same, everyone gives it a wide berth. Dozens of guards survey the area at any given time of the day and night, and we've taken care not to build too close to the sea.

Water is a temperamental element, and none of us land folk can boast to completely understand it. Some of us have a certain degree of sea blood, but true naiads, nixies, and merrows belong to the Sea Lands. Their allegiances change with the tide.

We don't have a clear agreement with the Sea Lands. The old high queen did attempt to form an alliance, predicated on her promising Vlari to one of their princes. That agreement was never sealed, and what's left of it died with Morgana.

Yet we need them now.

I find the queen right in front of the water, peeking down to the bottom of the river. Her mate grabs her by the middle and forces her to take two steps back. I shake my head.

One carefree queen. One caitiff consort king. Their reign wouldn't have mattered much during times of peace, but now, our leadership could determine victory or chaos.

The pages bow low. My sister curtsies. I incline my head.

The queen either fails to notice or doesn't care. Her attention is all on Nebula. "Oh my!"

I've never seen my sister blush so deep. I can tell she's reconsidering her choice of clothing. Then, the queen rushes next to her, and takes both of her hands. "The cut! The stitching! I've not seen the likes of it in—" She blinks. "I've never seen the likes of it. Who did this?"

I've never known my sister to stutter, but she does so now. "I—I did, ma'am. Your Highness."

"You?" she repeats. She takes a step back. "Turn, child."

Neb does just that, awkward as ever. "Oh, my," she repeats.

I wish I could record this instant and replay it on loop every time my little sister annoys me.

"I am—that is to say, I was—helping my mother in her tailor shop. Since I was little."

Our mother used to serve as a maid to the daughter of the Duke of Derfort. When I was born, my father cared for me as she kept working from dusk to dawn. It is rare for fae to have one child in a hundred years—in a thousand years, sometimes. Ma birthed her second in less than ten years, and then she knew she had to step away from the post, to care for us. She and Da put all her pennies and favors to good use until they had enough funds to open the shop.

Ma sews. Da forges. Nothing very grand, but it put food on our table in our youth.

"Now, I train with my brother. For the war to come," she adds, standing a little straighter.

The queen snorts. "Oh, I think not. No, no. Talent like this? Your hands aren't made for fighting."

I could kiss the high queen right then, awkward as it may have been, given the fact that I'd much rather kiss her daughter. If she asks, I'd even bend the knee.

To ensure I cannot be faulted as an excellent sibling, I point out, "Neb's one of the stealthiest fighters I've ever trained."

When Ciera's eyes fall on me, they're cold, determined. Regal.

So, there is a Lilwreath hiding under the surface, then. Perhaps not a queen, but a strong soul all the same.

Too bad the fate of Tenebris doesn't move her as much as that of one skilled tailor.

"No. You will give this girl to me." It's an order. Ciera is unyielding.

Part of me wants to laugh. Beneath cloth and decorum, stripped of our courtesies, we're beasts, as simple as wolves. And Ciera is not at the top of the hierarchy. Not even close.

I don't like the way she's talking—as though Neb is some commodity that is mine to give. But she's already turning to my sister. "There are different ways of fighting a war, child. Your brother's rangers and my father's soldiers are invaluable. But say, if we send a thousand soldiers into fire without any protection, what then? We do not treat the folk the way human barbarians do their forces—like cattle they're willing to sacrifice."

I still, understanding her meaning. Neb, however, doesn't.

For years, I've served in the military. As a foot soldier, I was given ten fabric charms—a small bird at the heart of a tree—that I had to stitch to my uniforms. They served to reinforce the fabric of my clothing, preventing arrows from hitting true unless they were shot from too close. When I made it to captain, the charms grew bigger, and were accompanied by a stamina charm—a lute.

I never paused to think about who had made them. That they were special and precious seemed obvious. Not every piece of clothing can easily be coated with charms. Cheap, common cloth will lose them.

The queen means for my sister to serve as one of the royal seamstresses. A considerable upgrade from what she was doing before. And more importantly, this occupation will keep her out of harm's way.

"She's talking about the charms you and Ma sewed on my uniforms," I clarify.

The queen nods, eagerly. "It's grueling, boring work, but terribly essential. We only have three seamstresses capable of such work—me included, and I haven't been able to spare much of my time."

I don't know why, but I expect Nebula to reject the prospect. She's had dreams of battles and blood for years now. To my relief, she nods. "I'd be glad to help however I can."

Ciera squeezes my sister's hands. Now that she's won that battle, she turns to me. "We've been trying to reach the Sea Lands, but none of the merfolk have approached us—not even a kappa. I fear, as they know we stay away from these parts, they've grown out of the habit to swim the river. I'm afraid we'd have to venture out to the sea to reach them."

"Couldn't we send a bird?" I ask, for the sake of it. If she wants my rangers out, out we will go. But I've relapsed into the habit of questioning things, and I don't particularly want to let it go.

"If we were willing to risk it being intercepted," Nero says. "It's safer to give a message to a merfolk directly."

I concur, but I mislike the notion. Whitecroft is right at the heart of Tenebris—the coasts are farther away than we've ventured in ten years.

I'd have to head such a mission, that's for certain. It wouldn't have mattered a few days ago. Now, the thought of going so far from Vlari for an extended time makes me pause.

In the end, there's only one answer I can give. "I'll gather a team, and leave at once."

The high queen touches my forearm. She's a tactile person, to my surprise. Vlari never seems to need touch like this.

Or perhaps she does. Perhaps she loves contact, and quite simply never bothered to get it from me.

"Wait a moment," Nero says. "Not questioning your rangers in the least, but for a journey such as this, it may be wise to bring a few knights with you. Some seasoned warriors."

I wince. "With all due respect, knights come with cumbersome, noisy armor that would either slow us down, get us spotted, or both. Our aim isn't to fight anyone if we can help it."

Generally, the rangers only get noticed after we've stolen something the humans guard. As this mission doesn't require us to retrieve any artifact, we might go unnoticed.

After thinking for a moment, the queen suggests, "Perhaps not knights, then, but someone with defensive magic? In case the need arises. I will feel better if you're well-guarded, Rystan."

She speaks as though we're friends, and she cares for my welfare.

"I can take care of myself, Your Grace."

"Be that as it may, your power is a weapon, not a shield. If you're attacked by hundreds, or thousands, you'll be glad to have some help—if only for the sake of your rangers."

She has me there.

I can take care of myself. But what of Samael, Iola, Hayles, Erdun, and whoever else will accompany me? They have little magic to speak of.

Perhaps she does have more power than I gave her credit for, after all, because while I don't like the idea of bringing anyone but my men with me, I incline my head. "As you wish. I am to leave within four hours; your mage will be expected at our base when possible."

She doesn't ask why I need this long.

I leave my excitable sister to chat with the artful queen, and return to Vlari's chamber.

When I arrive, I'm not alone.

ten

out of breath

drusk

It's late enough in the day that the rest of Whitecroft Hall starts to wake. I hear servants and lords stir around me, reviving fires, preparing or eating their breakfast.

I've had little sleep, but I need to see Vlari more than I need another one or two hours in bed.

I'm annoyed I'm not the first to arrive. I'm not in a mood to socialize—I'd prefer to have her all to myself this evening.

There's a fae next to her—someone I've never met. It's not saying much; I don't know everyone in Whitecroft, but most of them are familiar to me, by sight at least, or by their smell.

This stranger stands out in several ways. He wears heavy padded leather that doesn't quite look like the kind of craftmanship I normally see. Even his way of standing is different. He looks like a gentry, yet he almost slouches, his eyes drifting from one side of the room to the next.

Shifty. He's shifty.

"Who are you?"

He looks between me and Vlari, in a way I can only deem calculating.

Vlari's dark fox, that hardly ever stirred before—other than baring his teeth and hissing at me—is sitting on her stomach, his bright eyes fixed on the stranger. His tail flicks the air in annoyance.

I step inside, lifting one hand and gathering Myst in my palm. "I said, who are you?"

By this point, it's of no importance. If he meant no harm, he would have answered the first time around.

I step toward him, each move calculating. He's a lot closer to Vlari than I am. I need to reach them now.

The stranger moves faster than I anticipated, plucking a ball filled with black liquid from inside his cloak.

He throws it on the floor and breaks the glass under his heel. His enchantment spreads, rendering the room pitch black. This is no natural darkness, and I can't dissipate it with my power. Now blind, I have to rely on my other senses, but the intruder doesn't make a sound.

There's only one thing I feel, one thing I am certain of: Vlari's location. I can pinpoint it exactly in the dark room, though nothing else is clear.

I stumble as fast as I can, making my way to her. Something solid blocks my path.

There you are.

I sense an attack just in time to stop his approaching arm. A blade bites into my face, cutting my cheek. He has a knife or a dagger in hand.

My heart stops, not because I've halted a deadly blow. Because I understand the point of his weapon. This wasn't meant for me. His blade was intended to end up in Vlari's heart. This is an assassin.

I don't think I've ever known true rage until now. I believed I did a time or two, but the pure, undiluted hatred and fury poisoning my heart blinds all needs but one. I have to kill this scum. I have to make him suffer. I have to send his soul to the deepest of hells.

I kick and punch, screaming the vilest insults. His blade slices my arm, then my leg, and finds its way into my shoulder, but I don't feel any of it.

The assassin curses and attempts to step out of my reach, lunging to his left, toward Vlari's bed. Now that he understands I'm not easy prey, he's trying to carry out his mission and get away.

I think not.

His spell has started to dissipate, or perhaps my eyes have become accustomed to complete darkness, because I see a blur of movement. I lunge toward it, knocking him down with my body, and I pin him under me. The man thrashes to escape, but I'm heavier and just as well trained as he—this close, he has no chance of getting out from under me. Or so I think. Then he manages to kick upright. I wince as another blade gets lodged in my back. His boots are fitted with knives, too. He kicks a second, then a third time to get me off him. I try to keep him pinned, but when his knife hits the side of my ribs, he manages to weasel out, then jumps out of the way.

A low growl resounds in the darkness, and the assassin curses—I hear him kick and thrash. "Get off me, beast!"

The wyrfox. I mentally praise it for giving away the assassin's location. Thanking the laws of decorum for dictating that I should present myself to the queen armed, I unsheathe the sword at the end of my baldric, and launch, blind though I am. My sword crashes against metal—the iron cuffs at his wrists. I punch at eye level, my right fist hitting the target.

With a grunt, my target retreats. It's too late. Silent as he is, and despite the darkness, I'm too practiced in the art of violence to let him fool me. I swing. My blade slams against his with enough force to hurt. I shift my weight and kick low, where I imagine his arm is. Bingo. The assassin loses his footing, tumbling either backward or forward—with enough fracas to give away his location again.

I see a light from the corner of my eye. Someone's opened the door, holding a torch. The uproar finally alerted the useless guards. It's not much light, but it's enough to see what's going on.

For me, and for the assassin.

We both assess the situation in one glance. He's far too close. Vlari's bed is right next to him. I'm standing on the other side of the fireplace, several paces away. The four guards rushing in have barely left the door. They might as well be miles away.

In a split second, the assassin comes to the same conclusion as I did. He's not getting out of this room alive—but he can still carry out his mission.

As I pounce, Myst in one hand, my sword in the other, the assassin lifts a dagger in his fist, and plunges it down toward Vlari. Her heart, her throat. I can't tell. I can only stare. I can only despair.

In the instant it takes for his swift, agile fae hand to slash the air on its way down, I see her, the very first time we met. She was already turned toward the door when I entered the classroom. She scrutinized me, having recognized me as a threat right then.

That's when I knew her for what she was, not what she pretended to be. No one else knew that I was dangerous on my first day—they soon learned, after I proved it, but Vlari? She didn't need any demonstration of power.

The others smirked and whispered, mistaking me for prey.

Vlari? She smiled. Not at me. Not with me. She smiled, because she thought they were fools to cross me.

She turned back right away, so she never knew, but I smiled back.

That's all it took. Right then, I knew I'd be here one day. Protecting her, no matter the cost.

And I failed. I failed. I failed in the worst possible way. She was mine to protect, and I didn't do it. Not for ten years. Not in the last weeks, when I could have dragged a cot into this room and remained every hour, ensuring no one dared threaten her. And worst of all, not today.

I hadn't even believed that a threat could come to her.

There isn't enough time to move. My Myst is going to wrap around the assassin's mind and crack it like an egg when it reaches him. I will make him suffer fire, ice, and madness. My blade will sink in his guts and twist, so he bleeds out slowly. But it'll be too late. I don't have any other power in my possession. I am weak. I am worthless. I am nothing at all. I scream her name, my voice saturated with so much anguish I can't even recognize it.

She can't die. She can't. I don't think of Whitecroft. I don't think of the folk. I don't think about the fact that she's the only thing keeping us safe. I think the entire world would be pointless without her in it. I think that if she takes her last breath, it will be mine, too. My Myst keeps crawling to the assassin. I'm ready to obliterate each and every one of his cells.

But nothing I can do will prevent his blade from taking the one thing I've ever desired from me.

I see a lance and an arrow fly through the room. The guards were quick to attack the murderer, but their weapons will also hit too late.

I didn't think a second could last an eternity, yet here we are. My entire life could have passed in the endless instant it takes for the dagger to descend on Vlari.

Just as it aligns with her breast, Vlari blinks. Blinks. The sky-blue eyes that remained shut so long, eyes I never thought I'd see again at one point, open. The air around us crackles, suddenly charged with an energy strong enough to make mountains quake. The assassin's arm stills for endless, precious seconds, and Vlari shifts on top of her bed covers. The blade falls, slashing a handful of silver hair, before piercing right through layers of silk and linen. It plunges inside her soft mattress.

The assassin curses, stepping back to dodge the lance. He snatches the wooden hilt midair and twists it in his hand, ready to attack again. By then, I'm on him. My Myst and my sword are both at my disposal now, but he's mine. He's not going anywhere. I don't want it to end fast. This poor excuse for a fae needs to *suffer*, in the worst of ways. Body, first. Then, I'll get to his soul. My fist collides with his jaw, and withdraws to hit again, and again, and again. When my hands start to hurt, I keep punching. When his nose and my knuckles bleed, I strike, and strike again. Letting go of the weapon, he blocks the fiftieth punch, hiding his face behind his arms like the coward he is. Fine. That's just fine. I start kicking instead, screaming, yelling.

He almost killed Vlari. He almost killed *me*. I saw her die in my mind. I felt my very soul shatter. I kick everything, blind by a lust for blood no unseelie has ever tasted. I need more. More suffering. I'll take everything he can give me. All his screams.

"Drusk?"

The only thing that could have possibly pulled me out of the haze of violence in my veins is her voice. It's weak, and cracks on that one single word, but it's hers all the same. I look up. She's standing right next to me. Her hand rests on my sleeve, and I'm done.

I'm just done. With everything.

I freeze.

She's here. She's here, in person, touching me.

The assassin looks between us, and glances at the door.

I laugh. He thinks he's going out of here in one piece? My Myst is all around us. The only reason I haven't sent him to hell yet is because I want to hit him some more.

I start to send the dark cloud of magic to him, but Vlari shakes her head.

"Don't. Let me. I need—"

I nod.

Whatever she needs.

Vlari strolls to the coward backing up against the wall. "There's nowhere to go," she whispers. "You're mine now."

The man freezes, enthralled, ensorcelled by her bright blue eyes. Her small white arms wrap around his shoulders in a hug that could almost look gentle. Then he starts to scream as she sucks the life out of him, a serene smile crawling on her dry lips.

A few inches of silver hair turn purple, and she lets go, his body falling with a numb thud.

It's over. It's over. She's fine.

She's here.

In front of me.

Awake.

I think. Is she awake, or have we been pulled inside her head again all along? Is this a dream? It could be. I've never had nightmares so horrific or dreams so sweet. I can't make sense of anything. I feel faint all of a sudden.

I'm forced to remember I was stabbed like a pin cushion.

I don't think I care.

In fact, I know I don't.

I step over the corpse to Vlari, taking her chin in my hand. She feels soft and warm and real.

I have questions. I have many things to say. None of them seem important right this second, though. I bring my lips to hers and taste her for the very first time.

Except it doesn't feel like a first kiss at all. It feels natural. As though we've done this every day since the beginning of time. As if kissing her is as simple as breathing. As if it's the natural order of things.

I can't get enough. I need it more than air and water. I can't let go. So, I don't. I lift her in one arm, and she wraps her legs around my torso, climbing me like a vine. I feel my wounds burn as though someone poured salt on them. She's healing me. Part of me wants to stop her, to tell her to save her energy. But save it for what?

She's here. She's awake.

The implications are terrifying. It means Whitecroft is no longer protected under her shield. It means the army of thousands of humans can fall upon us now. It means we may all die before the night is through.

I care for none of these things. I don't care there are guards. If this bothers them, they can go.

We tumble to the floor, next to the corpse that doesn't even exist in my universe right now. I wince and she chuckles around my lips. All that matters is her, on me, with me. Wearing far too many clothes.

She thought something along the same line, because she closes her little hands on my lapels and tears my coat apart, exposing my torso. Buttons roll in various corners. Her hands glide on my skin, setting it ablaze. My hips lift to grind against her.

"Ahem."

I think I could literally murder whoever's disturbing us. At least, I might have, if it had been anyone other than Ciera.

The high queen grins from the door, one eyebrow raised.

eleven
under the stars
drusk

Vlari groans against my chest. "Mother."

"Daughter," Ciera echoes, smirking. "You came back to us."

The queen looks close to tears. I pray that she spares me the hugs, at least.

I gesture for the wide-eyed guards to take their leave, in order to give them a moment of privacy.

"I did. And now we're without protection."

I can't believe she dares sound put out about the fact that she returned to us. To me.

There never was a day as joyous as this, as far as I'm concerned.

"You're not returning to eversleep." I think I growl. Actually, I know I do. "Not for all the shields and weapons wielded by the gods themselves."

We'll manage without her sacrificing herself.

To my relief, she nods in agreement. I exhale, my shoulders sagging when the tension leaves my muscles. She's not leaving us. I can bear everything else.

"I had enough energy to create the shield and maintain it after sucking it from the immortals and Violet. I wouldn't risk it now." Vlari seems to be under the impression she needs to explain why she isn't returning right back to her comatose state. I don't think her mother or I would let her if she tried. "But Whitecroft is compromised."

She looks to the high queen, who nods in agreement. "Your father and I were visiting each court hall when we saw the dome shatter. Nero remained behind to reassure the people. I rushed here. I thought..."

She doesn't spell it out. I'm grateful. What she thought almost came to pass, and I'm not ready to dwell on it.

Vlari almost died. My Vlari.

I don't want to remember the way my heart and soul threatened to break. I'm willing to ignore the memory of the physical pain, and the deeper wound inflicted on my mind.

I caress her arm, and to my wonder, she doesn't push me away, doesn't say a word against my touch, accepting it.

"We have to act to avoid mass panic, and to protect this place as well as we can now." Vlari gets to her feet, dusting off her light blue gown.

Part of me wants to tell her how little I care for the folk's opinion. I almost lost her. I need her all to myself, if only for another moment. I wish I were that selfish, but I can also imagine the hysteria. A real threat looms in the distance without our barrier.

I reluctantly rise too.

"Could the air folk forge a golden dome? So we have an illusion of our shield. I'm sure the enemy spies will have seen it collapse, but if it comes right back, they may believe it just flickered on and off. They may hesitate to attack. It'll buy us some time."

Ciera nods without questioning the suggestion. Nor should she—we need to act immediately, if only with a temporary solution, and this idea is as good as any other.

"I'll give the command. You need to show the folk you're alive and well. Seeing you safe will rekindle hope. Then, join us in the war room. With Rystan, naturally." The queen grins wickedly. "You children can play later."

I've always assumed Ciera Bane, daughter of Morgana Lilwreath, child of the blood of Nyx, would have a thing or two to say against my sniffing around her daughter.

I've always assumed Vlari wouldn't ever be interested in the son of pucks.

Yet here we are, in the palace that serves as the royal court of Tenebris, and the high queen is telling me I can *play* with her daughter—just as soon as she's done planning a war. With me. I am welcome in the war room, along with princes and generals.

Everything I thought I knew is wrong now. Our kingdom irrevocably changed the moment Queen Morgana and her antediluvian ways drew their last breath.

Vlari returns to the corpse next to the fireplace, and bends down to retrieve the dead fae's dagger.

She inspects it for a moment. "Human made, I think. Iron." She grimaces in distaste.

"How could he get in here?" the queen asks. "Before the shield went down."

Vlari purses her lips. "He may have been here all along, waiting for orders to act. But his clothes are wet. It's possible he swam deep under my shield, in the river. My power never quite reached the Sea Lands. I don't think an irrelevant assassin with nameless blades would have known to do that by himself, however. You've been speaking about reaching the Sea Lands in council?" The queen nods. "Did you mention you hoped to be able to see merfolks because my shields should be weaker around water?"

Ciera swears, realizing Vlari may be right.

"There may have been more than one traitor under the dome," Vlari muses.

Unlike her mother, she doesn't sound upset or shaken by the notion. As if she thought so all along.

She turns away from us to stare at her reflection in the mirror on top of the mantel. Vlari twirls one of the short strands the assassin trimmed around her fingers. "I never was allowed to cut my hair, did you know?"

I'm guessing she's asking me—her mother would have known that. "I hadn't. Why?"

She shrugs, feigning indifference, when I feel something entirely different boiling underneath. "One of the many ways the queen liked to make me understand my life wasn't mine, I suppose."

She gathers all of her hair in one twist at the back of her head, and slices the sharp dagger through it, cutting feet of silver and purple off.

I watch the tips of her squared locks darken, as if dipped in purple ink. Then she turns back to me, beaming. "Much better, don't you think?"

And it is.

She's always been the most beautiful thing in the world to me, but the long locks had given her an air of cold elegance, like that of a proper princess. A stench of court pageantry that had never suited her.

The woman in front of me looks playful, mischievous. Free. In her long pale dress, splashed with her would-be murderer's blood—or mine—she's also fierce.

I could tell her she was always the most glorious thing in Tenebris. Instead, I tease her. "Is it? I had a thing for long hair."

I'm not capable of holding a serious conversation about what she means to me. Not with her. If I ever do, she'll run screaming the other way, when she understands the depth of my obsession. Or she'll play with my heart and tear me to pieces, as is the way of the folk.

Love is the sharpest of weapons, and each of its wounds can be fatal. I need to earn hers before I reveal mine.

The queen takes her leave of us after embracing her daughter, tight and for a long moment. She places her palm on my heart, in a gesture that feels old and somewhat warm—a greeting long out of use, yet timeless. I understand it as well as words. It communicates thanks and acceptance, and something along the lines of a goodbye. Perhaps a little too formal, considering the fact that we'll see her in mere minutes.

We walk side by side through the halls. The guards must have spread the news, because none of the knights and soldiers we pass are surprised. The pairs posted at the first turn rap the hilts of their blades against their shields, hitting in sync with the beating of their hearts. And the next pair, either side of the hall, do the same, till the sound of steel crashing like a drumbeat makes the windows tremble.

As we near the entrance, my gaze wanders past the buildings, past the lines of trees, to the horizon. I see the night, dark and full of secrets. I see the stars. The dome of light that has been a constant for the last decade is no more. I never realized how much I hated it, how I missed the night.

A crowd has gathered at the entrance of the hall, their expressions full of fear and uncertainty.

They accost me first. "Drusk! The walls—"

"It's gone!"

"Is the princess—"

I suppose I dwarf Vlari. I smile, and look down at the woman next to me, inviting them to do the same.

A collective gasp cuts through their chatters, and then there's nothing but silence. They're shocked to the core.

I half expect more terror, a thousand questions, perhaps even accusations that would have me reaching for a sword. Vlari's presence here with us means the loss of her protection. But the folk erupt in a victory cry so loud all of Tenebris must have heard it—even the usurper all the way in the east.

They chant her name, bow, and beg to touch her.

Vlari has gone cold, unmoving. What some would mistake as indifference, I interpret as confusion. I remember she's not been raised for this. Never has she had any cause to believe she'd be important in Tenebris. Let alone be the savior to these thousands of folk. She has no clue how to endure adulation.

I extend my hand, inviting her to take it. She's quick to do so, crushing it in a tight grasp, as though I'm offering her a life-line. When she does, I tug her closer, and bend down to lift her up, seating her on my shoulder. A chuckle escapes her throat as I stand up, lifting her so the growing crowd can see her.

I start to make my way through the folk so she can greet them, let them see their hope. Unprompted, she reaches out, touching the extended hands of her people.

Her mother wears the crown, but there was no denying who was queen for me, even before this. Now, it's clear the people feel the same way.

By the time we've reached the closest of the seven halls—the hall of Storm, the court headed by the Frosts—musicians are in place in front of it.

They start playing with strings and flutes, an unrefined, never-rehearsed cacophony that embodies the beauty and the wildness of the fae, all over the drumming of the soldiers' shields and swords. It's chaos. It's sensual. It's unseelie, to the last string.

Vlari leaps off my shoulder, and rushes to the empty circle in front of the musicians, twirling around, her bare feet slapping the stone floor with the beat of the drums.

I'm not one for dancing. I've never been fond of the practice—though I was quick to offer dancing with her ten years ago, when presented with the opportunity. Now, I don't have a choice. I have to join her. She's the queen of the court's heart, and she's leading a true faerie dance. The kind mortals cannot be pulled away from once it starts. The kind that stays in our hearts and minds.

We all rush to follow, numb to the cold, unable to resist the pull of the age-old magic. Esea and her sister Sylph embrace the princess and mirror her steps. There's tears and laughter and pure joy, untouched by the fear of tomorrow.

We're celebrating life itself, though we're shieldless, vulnerable, and will die by morning if the invaders are clever enough to send all of their armies right at us.

Vlari's arms hook around my shoulders when I join her. Among all those gathered here, she chooses me. I wrap my hands around her waist and dance as though nothing else in the world matters. Never mind the humans. I know I'll never be able to stop. She'll have to pull me out of it.

Vlari is the one who stops first, her eyes lifting to the sky.

I follow the direction of her gaze and notice that a mockery of the hateful dome is back. It looks exactly right, though all its power has faded from it.

It may fool human eyes. It may even fool a fae or two, so long as they don't have much magic.

I doubt it'll fool the usurper, if she comes anywhere close.

Or the immortals beyond our borders.

The danger is real. The danger is close. We've ignored it too long already.

Wordlessly, we turn back to Whitecroft Hall.

We have a war council to attend.

twelve

a circle of crowns

drusk

Vlari doesn't pause to ask for directions, her purposeful steps leading us through the maze of corridors.

"I suppose you've spied on some council sessions?"

She's entirely unapologetic. "One or two, when I could."

I want to ask what it was like for her—being asleep and yet sometimes conscious of what went on around her. I don't imagine it was pleasant. She must have felt helpless.

We reach what used to be the headmaster's office when Whitecroft was our school. Professor Veret used to like his study filled with books, every window shut by blinds as he read by candlelight. The smell of beeswax is gone, as are the leather-bound volumes. Like every other chamber in the white stone edifice, it has been transformed. Now, a thick, dark red rug covers the stone floor, and a heavy table made of one tree stump dominates the center of the space. Someone painted a map of Tenebris in the middle.

My mind travels back to that fateful day in Hardrock when Vlari had looked at a map not dissimilar to this one, and asked her grandfather questions about ley lines. Now I know she was starting to devise her plan—her intent to draw on the power of each court to sustain our impenetrable wards—all the way back then. Her intent to sacrifice herself.

At any point between Hardrock and Whitecroft, she could have shared it. She didn't.

Knowing what we lost, and how close her schemes have come to costing her life, I hate the very sight of this map.

And I stiffen at the sight of one of the fourteen men already standing next to it.

Alven Oberon, the old queen's consort. Vlari's grandfather. He's stroking a bird of prey perched on his arm, his eyes set on Vlari.

I've purposely avoided him—even more so than the high queen and her bondmate. The Banes, I stayed away from for sentimental reasons. Alven I simply dislike.

He forced my silence once, demanding I not reveal Vlari saved my life. He could have *asked*. He could just have ordered me. I was a soldier, bound to listen. He could have explained the stakes, instead of threatening me and my livelihood—and therefore the livelihood of my family. I know the kind of man he is, and I know he and I will never get along.

He can still order me around. I'm a nobody from a family of servants, and he's the very opposite: a pure gentry from a grand line. A king. Though he stopped ruling it when he married Morgana Lilwreath, he is the rightful monarch of the Court of Mist.

I understand he wanted to protect Vlari. I even respect it. His ruthlessness is likely to be more useful than Ciera's gentle soul in the days to come. But I'm done with people manipulating me—except for her. Vlari, I can't avoid, she has me wrapped around her little finger. The rest of them have no place in my life.

The other lords surrounding the table, I've seen or encountered at one point or another. All seven courts are represented by their rulers. The Court of Storm technically belongs to the Stellara line, and its queen is with us, but it is no secret that Queen Luce is more interested in stargazing than the affairs of the breathing. She's looking out the window, while Genrion Frost, a duke of Storm, stands at the table on Alven's left. He is accompanied by his son, Wilden, an old friend of mine. We exchange a nod at my entrance. He now wears heavy armor, perhaps a little too heavy for his slender shoulders, which are more used to playing war among friends than risking his skin.

For all that, Wilden is one of the better lords.

Silt is a realm of barbarians. As a kingkiller may take the crown, they change monarchs too fast for any of us to bother to remember the names of them all. We've taken to calling their kings and queens the Sandman, as they live far enough south that half of their land is made up of white beaches.

The current queen should be the Sandwoman, I suppose. She looks young, which means nothing for our kind, but somehow, I sense that she is actually young—perhaps even as young as she looks.

It matters little. She's clearly a force to be reckoned with. She had the crown when we arrived at Whitecroft, and she's kept it all this time.

Ichor is perhaps the one court wilder than Silt. Traditionally, they drink the blood of their enemies to absorb their strength. Their ruler has let himself age—unusual among the folk. I wonder if he's half human. The curve of his ears, poking out of a crown of silver hair, seems rounder than the rest of ours. It matters not. The blood of the gentry is stronger than that of mortals, and this wrinkled man in a low conversation with Ciera is all fae.

The Court of Stone is ruled by a bonded pair—Queen Ina and King Liken. I'm told one negotiates with Liken, and that when no agreement can be reached, the king sends Ina, who takes care of the problem at the edge of her twin swords. Surveying them quickly, I don't doubt a word of it. Like her bondmate, she seems younger than most, but Ina's blending in far too well with the shadows. She lets her pointed teeth poke out of her lips, instead of retracting them in civilized settings like the rest of us. Most of the folk have fangs. It's simply not considered polite to show them.

Ina doesn't seem to care about being polite.

Liken is her opposite, gallant, all smiles, and well dressed in embroidered velvet, while she wears leather under her cloak.

Last, the Court of Ash, realm of fire, is ruled by salamanders. The madman settled south and only accepted gentry and lower fae with an affinity for fire in his land. When children were born with magic from another element, they were banished or killed for centuries. Eventually, there only was fire.

Ash is the only court that never condemned the merging of different classes—they never minded if a common fae married a gentry, so long as they both had fire magic. Another form of discrimination, I suppose.

Centuries later, we have a unique race, a strange court that doesn't quite belong with the rest of us. Their king is stocky, pale-green-skinned, and somewhat on the short side. I know that if provoked, he could burn half of Whitecroft before any of us could blink.

I've always been fascinated with Ash—and they don't dislike me, given that I maintain some control over fire, so long as it's in the shadows.

While not quite gentry anymore, and therefore shorter-lived, the salamanders are vicious and ferocious enough to have claimed a throne south of our land in the old days. They knelt to Nyx, as did we all, but my history lessons have taught me that Nyx saved them for last, only attacking them when she had the might of the six other courts behind her.

Of all elemental fae, the fire users are by far the most lethal.

But they're few—too few to make a difference in our forces. When Vlari sent news to all the courts, asking them to retreat to Whitecroft to protect them for the invaders, they all had mere hours to act. Being the farthest from Whitecroft, the Court of Ash had less time, and more miles to travel.

Freeing the rest of their brethren from the usurper's leash is an alluring idea. They'd make a difference in the battle to come.

My natural place should be close to Queen Luce of the Court of Star. I was born and raised in her domain, and the Frosts also should have my allegiance; Duke Genrion is the one who elevated me after finding me as a child. But I've been made part of the high court, whatever that means. Ignoring propriety, I remain next to Vlari.

"Nevlaria. We're all—" Alven looks around the table, his gaze cautioning. "Very glad to see you."

She snorts, walking to one of the free seats and taking it. "Let's dispense with lies. You're all terrified. I'm terrified. Me being here is terrible news, and bad timing. Let's move on to discussing what we're doing about it, shall we?"

The room lightens up a little. I think I hear Queen Ina whisper to Liken, "I like her."

I move to stand behind her, but she gets up, tapping her seat to offer it to me.

My jaw ticks. I want to refuse it, but every eye in the room is on us, and I feel like getting into an argument about who's sitting where isn't the message we want to give today.

I sit.

Vlari perches on the armrest, her backside resting against me.

I can smell her hair—pine wood and cinnamon, a winter scent mixed with something I can't pinpoint. I can't get enough. The things this woman does to me.

I wrap my arm around her waist and pull her closer to me.

"I think we can all agree our priority should be reestablishing the shield?" Vlari continues.

It turns out, we can't all agree.

"Yes," Ciera replies, emphatically nodding her head, while Genrion sighs.

"We've remained hidden for too long, and all the while, our people suffer throughout Tenebris. I say, let's retake the courts. If you want to play with shields, build one around Tenebris itself—don't lock us in again."

"Locking us in *saved our lives,"* the young Sandwoman says.

"Attacking when we're surrounded by seven courts, each filled with an army, is madness."

"Maybe. Or maybe we'll prevail." The salamander king sniffs in disgust. "They're just humans."

"Humans with enough iron and manpower to take us all," Alven points out.

"We have plenty of weapons in our ranks." Genrion stands a little prouder. "At least, in mine."

"You forget, Frost. The Court of Star isn't quite yours, now is it?" The Sandwoman smirks, tilting her head toward the queen, who's still at the window, ignoring us all.

It's a mess. I can't believe our survival is dependent on the power-hungry lot in this room. They'll never agree, on principle.

"Where does Stone stand?" the salamander asks, pointedly staring at Ina—he believes her more likely to be on his side.

Ina ignores him, exchanging a look with Liken.

"Stone," Liken says eventually, "has always been a pillar of Tenebris. Thousands of years prior, when Nyx came to us with a vision of a united unseelie folk, we stood with her. And we stand with the high court today."

He's reminding the rulers that the one decision that mattered was the first one they ignored: Ciera's. A statement about how little power she has.

"Thank you, Liken—and the rest of you. I have one suggestion." All eyes are on Vlari—they're done sniping at each other.

"Those of you who wish to fight and retake the courts? Go. Do it." She waves both hands, gesturing them to move. "From what I understand, each of the seven courts have about the same amount of soldiers and resources. If you think our forces as they stand are enough to retake Tenebris, then surely your own forces are enough to take your own courts, are they not?"

Silence meets her question. The tension in the room is at a peak.

"Talking of attacking at this point, without anywhere to retreat to, is madness. Suggesting that we could lead assaults at the moment ignores the fact that we have at least a thousand folk who shouldn't step anywhere near a battlefield. Cooks, children, and poets," she adds with a grimace.

A couple of lords laugh, Ina among them.

She's good at this. Taking charge, leading the conversation.

"My question was rhetorical. Our first order of business is shielding Whitecroft as well as we can. Fortunately, we have a plan of sorts in the works. Kazan, what we need from you are your best firebringers—spell a handful of energy stones at once. Understood?"

I suck in the air, half expecting the king of Ash to explode. I don't think he's ever heard an order in his life.

He looks like he sucked on a lemon, but he nods. Slowly.

"Good. Have it done by dawn. I'll see about securing a water elemental stone. Are there any other matters?"

Alven nods, and lifts a small roll of parchment high enough for all of us to see. "We've had a communique from our spy."

It's the first I've heard of a spy, but the others don't seem surprised. It's no wonder. I can't imagine such knowledge leaves the confinement of these four walls.

His piercing eyes cut to me, then rest on Vlari. "We have an asset in Violet's so-called court."

Alven passes the note to Ciera, across the painted tree trunk, letting the high queen see it first.

It never occurred to me that the man had been bowing to his wife, and now to his child—all the while our side was fighting against another one of his progeny. Being Alven Oberon may not be an easy feat. Surrounded by so much power and yet powerless himself.

Ciera curses out loud, her lovely, graceful mouth spitting out a word that would have my mother hitting the back of my head if

I'd said it. Nero extends his hand to take the piece of parchment, but the queen doesn't bother passing it around.

"What's going on?" Kazan of Ash demands.

"The usurper's army has raided the Black Woods."

My eyes widen, both in surprise and in reluctant admiration. If they dared enter the Black Woods, the human army has more courage than I'd believed.

West of Hardrock, deep in the Court of Stone, the Black Woods is the home to the untamed and shy folk who opted to remain on unseelie ground, rather than moving north, to the Wilderness. While few, they're the strongest—the wildest of us. They shoot intruders between the eyes first, and ask questions later. Or never.

"How?" Ciera asks, as startled as I.

Genrion Frost grimaces. "How do you think?"

Ciera's eyes narrow at him. His contempt might be directed toward the humans, but he's speaking to the queen. His pointed eartips redden. "There's only one way. I think they burned it down, and used their explosives to get to a village."

While it's no more than a guess, I know it to be true. There's no other way to take the Black Woods.

How very *human*.

Their contempt and indifference toward nature has rendered their once-beautiful land practically barren, hence their move toward the Alfheimr empire. I believed I couldn't detest them any more, but as usual, they've proved me wrong. The Black Woods was thousands of years old, some of its trees there for longer than any of us, and now they are probably ashes.

"The spy," says Ciera, "reports that there are a hundred captives, and that Marren is among them."

I know that name, but it takes me a while to place it. It's not the kind of name one expects to hear in conversation about living, breathing people.

Marren is a legend. A myth. One of the original travelers who'd moved from the Isle to Alfheimr, in order to leave the control of the overlord ruling us in the old continent. Mother sang some of her tales to me as a child. Some books say she is a wayward goddess, others say she's one of the very first fae to ever come into being. A mother to us all.

"*The* Marren?" I echo, feeling left out and stupid, because none of the others seem astounded.

"She leads the elven tribes," Liken casually informs me. "We've dealt with her on occasion. She's ruthless when provoked, but fair and caring. If they were attacked, I'm not surprised she surrendered to protect her people." His gaze cuts to the queen. "We need her for the war to come. If only for her healing powers."

Ciera nods. She isn't sharing the spy's note, but she tells us, "They're being transported to Hardrock as we speak, where they'll be asked to bend the knee to the usurper. If they don't..." She doesn't need to finish that sentence. The self-appointed queen is going to make an example out of the shy folk.

"Marren will never bow to a child playing queen," Genrion states. "She'll never bow to anyone. They'll kill her."

Ciera shakes her head. "They can't, can they? Marren is as old as time. She'll destroy them all."

Ina, silent until now, shakes her head. "Marren is old because she's wise and has never been one for war. She's no warrior. There's little she can do. That said, her elves are known for their ferocity. A hundred of them would make a difference among our ranks—their skills as archers could take a city. Once, we apprehended one of theirs for taking our spoils, and they practically seized my keep until we gave him back. They're that strong."

It has been too long since we've had an actual war—infighting between the courts, resolved at the point of a blade or with a challenge, is common enough, but other than the few who joined the army like me, none of the young folk had been trained for it. I may have spent the last ten years training those who want to improve, and they're stronger than any human, but none of that will be enough.

A hundred archers from the shy folk, who'd been given a bow the moment they could walk? That's another story. If the legends were true, and they can shoot farther than I can see, we need them. The thought of their joining our ranks has me salivating.

Genrion Frost leans over the central table, pointing to the map. "The Black Woods's western flank edges the Court of Mist. North, they bleed into the Murkwood, and east, the high court. It's going to be too close to Hardrock for comfort."

"Not if we move through the western flank," Vlari says, suddenly a lot more interested than she seemed to be before.

I can feel her excitement, and I don't think it has much to do with Marren or her folk, though I could be mistaken.

"Are the prisoners in the Court of Ichor now?" she asks.

Her mother nods.

"Well, to set out on the road to Hardrock, they'll take this path. The only path that can accommodate a hundred prisoners and a number of soldiers." She follows a trail with the tip of her finger, curving north close to the Murkwood. "Once they reach the capital, we have no chance, but on the road…well. I say we stand a chance."

Ina nods. "I'll lead the rescue," she offers. "Though they'll never accept it, the shy folk are part of the Court of Ichor. They're my people."

No one argues.

"We know our kingdom more than the humans, for one. That said, we have no details about the number of soldiers we'll have to face as of yet. It's a gamble, but it may be worth it."

A considerable gamble. To move a hundred elves, even bound, gagged, weaponless, and exhausted, the humans had to take five, ten times as many soldiers.

How many fae will we lose if things go wrong?

The salamander says exactly that. "It may be too much of a risk. We could lose all our fighters, all to recover a hundred archers."

"A hundred excellent archers," Vlari says. "I think it's worth it."

That's the end of it. If we have to slave over the map for hours until we have a plan, we will.

I frown, looking at the path just south of the border between Mist and Ichor. I know that place; I was sent to train there when I first enlisted in Genrion's forces. I loved it there. Freezing in the winter, enchanting in the summer, the mountains were a delight.

"What if we didn't ambush them?" I surprise myself. I'd no plan to say anything out loud. I don't even have a plan—just the shadow of an idea.

Now, everyone is looking at me, and I have to either look like an idiot, or explain myself. And probably look like an idiot either way. "That area is dangerous—hence why no one lives there. The army uses it as training ground because of the frequent earthquakes. We're trained to find shelter and survive in those circumstances, but it'd surprise me if the humans were. There are caves in these mountains, along the path where we could hide. It could be possible to start a landslide here."

The queen of Ichor frowns. "This isn't on their way. It's south of the path they're likely to take."

"A landslide up these mountains will take the entire valley," I promise. "There are spells and wards to prevent it."

I look to Genrion for confirmation. The duke nods. "It may be doable."

One of the four knights behind the king of Ash asks, hopeful, "Do we need to blow up anything?" He shrugs when we turn to him.

Vlari grins. "We'll more than likely need a few explosions."

His smile broadens, like the princess offered him a present wrapped with a pretty white bow. "It's been a few quiet years. I'll tag along, if you'll have me."

His king doesn't seem happy at all, but he doesn't protest either.

"While your plan could work, it could also endanger the elves," Nero says quietly.

His mother, the ferocious pixie my sister idolizes since she saved my family ten years ago, snorts. "Right. A landslide and a bit of an earthquake killing elves. Let the adults talk, boy."

Nero doesn't seem offended. "I'm just saying, there may be injured or weaker captives who will need our assistance."

I can't tell whether he's just naive, or willfully obtuse. Of course, not all of our people will make it. It's not expected. Whatever way we choose to do this, there will be casualties. They are acceptable losses, when the alternative is to let them all die at the hand of the false queen.

This is war, not a children's tale.

There are no miracle solutions where all of the folk end up safe, sound, and free. It's just a matter of picking the path that offers the least amount of death on our side, and the most on theirs.

Unless…

"Vlari," I say, redirecting the attention of the room to me for the second time. "You can feed from life force, and redistribute it."

The lower kings and queens exchange uncomfortable glances. None of them like the idea of a Void among us. Power over life and death is too much in the hands of one individual. Vlari can make us all kneel, regardless of her intentions, just like Nyx had. But whether they approve or not, there is no denying what she can do.

"Are you suggesting she be part of the rescue? That's out of the question. The princess needs to stay here, safe."

"She's the last of her line! If the queen were to pass, what then?"

I'm ignoring the Sandwoman and the king of Ash, my attention on the woman perched on my armrest. She grins. "Of course, I'll be there. I'll assist from a reasonable distance."

The room bursts into an uproar of protests, coming from everywhere and everyone.

It seems they still don't understand that she'll choose what she does.

She stands up and leans over the tree trunk.

"My presence will limit the casualties, and cover our retreat. I am going. This isn't up for debate."

"No." The queen straightens her spine. "We can't risk you getting involved and losing some energy in the process. Not because I want to smother you. Because you're needed in the war to come. It's too much of a risk."

"Is it?" Nero places his hand on his wife's shoulder. "We know precious little of Vlari's power. It hasn't been seen since Nyx, and it's seldom mentioned in any texts. An injection of energy could be just what she needs, and she isn't likely to feed off *us*. Facing a few enemies might be necessary."

"What if we are attacked?" Ciera argues.

"Right now, without a shield, without archers? We're doomed anyway. I'd much prefer if Vlari was north, then."

I can tell the queen hates this with a passion, but she knows we're right. If there's any way we can get an edge, we need to consider it.

"I need to go north, Mother," Vlari says, holding her gaze.

That, if nothing else, ends the discussion altogether.

The war council ends on that note, and we stay in the room as it empties out.

When no one remains, except for her family—the rest of the high court—I ask, "So where are we actually going?"

She grins. "The Murkwood."

thirteen
the queen's fool
Vlari

I've never been one to dream. I wasn't plagued with nightmares either—I just used to fall into a deep sleep. After ten years of nothing but dreams mingled with visions, I have to remind myself that this is real. I am awake. I am alive.

His presence helps. Drusk. Rystan. Having him by my side is an anchor in reality. If nothing else does, he feels real.

Rystan.

If someone had told me years ago that he was my mate, I would have laughed. Now that I've come to realize it, nothing in my life is more certain. When I'm so old that I forget who I am, I'll still know that he's mine. My mate. The man who was made for me.

I smile at him because I can't help myself. He knows me better than I would have guessed.

I don't have a thing against the shy folk, of course, but going north just to rescue them seems like a monumental waste of resources. I would have spoken against it, and refocused us on the matter at hand, had I not seen an opportunity.

I need to go north.

"And what, pray, will we be doing in the Murkwood?"

I'm amused by the fact that he includes himself in my plan. He's right to. I have no intention of leaving him behind. "Raiding Old Keep."

Old Keep is the first settlement the fae built when we arrived to this part of Alfheimr long ago. Surrounded by beasts and demons, they opted to join forces and ensconce themselves behind unbreakable walls. I've read ballads and seen paintings of the once-magnificent castle the folk lived in before any court, before any kingdoms, when the unseelie and seelie hadn't claimed their lands yet. Each stone of the castle is said to be imbued with magic, so that the castle will never be too hot or cold, too dark or light. So that no enemy can cross its doors.

It was abandoned when the unseelie and seelie parted ways, because that castle was meant for both courts, and could not be occupied by just one. They say the last to step out were the seelie king and the unseelie queen. If one had remained alone, the magic of Old Keep would have destroyed them.

I press, "If your hag didn't lie, the book on shields is there. I wouldn't be surprised—Old Keep was shielded better than any other fae land. And if I'm right, there will be more elemental stones than we could ever need there."

Every single stone in that castle is said to be an elemental stone.

I shouldn't rely on rumors and legends, but what else can we do? Appeal to the sea? We'll certainly try, but charming as Lind was, I doubt he'll offer his aid again. And even if he does, I want that book. Weighing so much on the word of a hag is madness.

"You forget. If an unseelie enters it without a seelie fae, it may fall to pieces," Drusk points out.

"Well, I'll find myself a seelie to drag along, then. Any volunteers?" I stare pointedly at my grandmother, who shakes her head.

"Oh, I think not, child. You go on your adventures. One of us has to remain here to protect your mother."

I shrug off the slight. My mother can take care of herself just fine. "Very well. There's a quarter of seelie blood in my veins. Maybe it'll do the trick."

Drusk snorts. "You're as unseelie as they come. You'll never fool ancient magic."

I let the subject drop. I have another plan at the edge of my mind—a scheme that'll take care of that little problem—but I've already said too much. While there are still spies and traitors in Whitecroft, I should keep my own counsel as much as possible.

My eyes trail across the room to my grandfather. "You did well, thinking of the heart stone in Hardrock. Without it, we wouldn't have been able to build any shield."

Alven nods, his spine stiff. "I knew it was used to anchor many a spell, offensive and defensive alike. I didn't want it in the hands of our enemies."

My attempt to smile doesn't reach my eyes. "And what purpose did you imagine we'd use it for, I wonder?"

My mother and father, Meda and Drusk, all look between us, attempting to read the room. They can feel the tension, though none of them know its cause.

I'm waiting, and Alven knows what I expect from him. What I need him to do now.

He can either be honest, or get out. Out of the war council, and out of Whitecroft.

"It's not what you think, Vlari."

It's exactly what I think.

Silence stretches. Though I don't think anyone here thought to suspect him, they're hardly surprised.

I've had endless hours to think back to that night. To the way our defenses were taken out on various fronts, and so precisely. It's clear our enemy knew just where and how to hit us, although the secrets of Tenebris aren't shared with many. The common folk don't know the army's rotation, or ways around the curses and shields of the various courts. And how had the immortals even entered Hardrock?

The obvious answer was that a traitor had whispered in the ears of the immortals, but whom? Alven was the obvious choice. I could have been wrong, but Alven had nothing to lose, and everything to gain. Besides, he was the only one conveniently away from the halls when every other member of his family—our family, I suppose—was killed.

He doesn't deny it.

For years—centuries—he's been forced to relinquish his power and dance to the tune of the queen. She chose him as her consort, forcing him away from his court, taking his power, turning him into nothing more than an ornament, and the breeder she used to father her heirs.

I understand him completely.

I can even forgive him.

I take one of the untouched glasses of wine on the tree stump. "How did you do it?"

There's no point asking if. I know he betrayed Tenebris.

"Noira," he replies, caressing the bird on his shoulder. His familiar. "She came to me one day, not long after Morgana sent our daughter away and welcomed a human pawn in her stead."

I can only nod, and take another sip.

"You're not asking why I did it."

I shrug. "That much is obvious, Grandfather. You wanted Morgana out of the way. They promised you that you could be high king if you helped take down the current government."

Alven closes his eyes. "Do you think me a fool?"

Alven is a dominant, domineering, proud gentry with a considerable amount of power, and she'd all but filed his claws.

"Certainly not. I think you were desperate." I down the rest of my drink. "And truth be told, if they'd come to me with a way to kill Morgana, I would have signed on the dotted line without looking too much into their motivations, either. I didn't even have to share her bed." I grimace, imagining what sort of a wife the old queen would have been. I sincerely doubt Alven has been given many chances to lead the dance, so to speak.

My grandfather pushes a brow up.

"I don't judge you for turning your back on Morgana, Alven." I cannot call him anything but that, not now, with everything that has passed. He isn't king consort. He isn't quite family. He's just a potential enemy. Or an asset.

"I simply need to know whether you'll turn your back on this crown. On my mother." On me.

I don't say it, but the meaning is clear.

Mother wears the crown, but I am the one who protects it from the shadows.

Alven pours us more wine. "I don't have any reason to. I am free. And Ciera is my daughter. You're wrong to think I'd destroy my family. Nothing went right, that day."

I snort. I imagine not, otherwise he wouldn't be stuck here with the rest of us.

"I never meant for Tenebris to fall. They promised to get Morgana out of the way, that's true. She refused to negotiate any trade with the west for centuries. Vikus grew tired of asking."

Tenebris and Denarhelm both adjoin Alfheimr, though some merchants are allowed to land ships on our coasts. For generations, Alfheimr has sought our business, and for generations we've refused. Opening trade routes means building roads and accepting strangers into our lands, softening our borders.

"It isn't uncommon to seek your neighbor's aid to remove a monarch. I never asked for the crown. I never wished for it. I meant for it to pass to whoever among my children was deemed most worthy of it by the house of lords." He's spoken plainly enough for me to believe him, and at the mention of his children, his sorrow is plain.

"Father. How could you think they wouldn't take advantage of the situation? Sharing details of our defenses..."

"I didn't say a word about our defenses." His shoulders sagged. "Turned out, I didn't need to. For years, for decades, I don't know, they've been scouting around Tenebris. The first I heard of it was when our friend Drusk here came back wounded, warning us of a human attack. We've had a unit or two missing in the past years—five lower fae. No one pays any mind to that. The seelie archers are quick to shoot, and soldiers defect every day. They've had their eyes on us for longer than we knew. All I offered was a way into the Shadow Peak keep."

That explains why only the usurper, Kraven Vikus, and his son made it inside, while their foot soldiers remained in the city.

I nod. Alven wasn't nearly as stupid as I feared.

"You have to believe me. I never wished to kill my family."

No. Just his wife. The wife who forced herself on him, using her title to order him into a loveless match he resented.

"I don't care about any of that. No offense. I never knew any of my aunts, uncles, or cousins. If they didn't care to know me, I'm not going to start mourning them. As for Morgana, well. I get why you wanted the bitch dead." I'm perhaps a little harsher than necessary, but at least I'm honest. "What matters to me is that you betrayed the high queen of Tenebris once for personal reasons. I understand why. It's still not exactly reassuring for my mother."

Ciera stands a little straighter, her eyes fixed on her father. "Yes. As you chose to align with Alfheimr, against your vows to protect our kingdom, I don't see any other choice. You must go."

I could groan. My mother is as straightforward and impulsive as ever. This revelation either hurt or frightened her, and her answer to that is to kick him out of Whitecroft. I understand it. I do. But ridding us of one of the best fighters we have at the dawn of a long-ass day seems like the worst idea since my haircut. Which is saying a lot, given the fact that I lived through a war council session. For one, she could be throwing him into his other daughter's arms. When the time comes, I'd much rather him bleed for us than for Violet.

"Or," I say, before Alven can accept his banishment, "you could offer Mother your oath."

All subjects of the high court have a vague duty to protect our kingdom. We swear to it under the moonlight at each solstice, but the wording of the chants is vague enough to allow for plenty of leeway, as Alven's treachery proved. A direct oath to the queen would allow no such thing. Alven would die should he attempt to weasel out of it.

I've not heard of one fae who gave a formal oath in my entire lifetime. Not to our high queen, not to any of the rulers of the lower courts, and not in the seelie kingdoms. To swear to obey all of the queen's commands till death means giving up one's freedom.

I half expect Alven to decline the offer and be on his way. Instead, he nods stiffly before dropping to one knee.

"I, Alven Oberon, King of the Court of Mist, son of Tenebris, swear my life to you, my daughter, Ciera Bane of House Oberon. I am yours to command, from this day until forever ends. May the stars bear witness."

I don't know whether the stars are paying attention, but I certainly am.

No one else is talking, or moving for that matter.

At least until the ungodly lament of my stomach breaks through the silence. I wince. "In my defense, I haven't eaten in ten years."

fourteen

starved

vlari

I eat as much as I possibly can, so fast I feel sick. I have to force food in, washing it down with wine. When I cannot stand any more, I find room for a custard torte anyway. I've never enjoyed food as much as I do on my first night back from the realm of sleep.

Ten years. I can't even begin to imagine what things might be like for the cursed prince of the wilderness, after a thousand years. With some luck, the poor fool is passed out, or dead.

I lie back on my chaise, too exhausted to even think about dragging myself all the way to my bed—some ten paces away.

Drusk, leaning against the wall in front of me, smiles in a way that's far too mocking for my liking.

"Not a word."

His grin broadens, but he remains silent, staring me down.

Part of me is glad he followed me back to my room. I would have so hated if he'd left. Yet now that he's here, I don't know what to do with him—where to put him. That he belongs in my bed is obvious, but I don't want him in there now. I don't think I could take it.

I know he's my mate, but he has no clue, and I prefer it that way. There's an army surrounding us, we're about to trek through a human-infested kingdom, and then, if we're lucky, we'll be ready for war. The last thing either of us needs is to add complications.

Our situation? It's complicated. Or perhaps, far too simple. Right now, my priority is Tenebris. I want our kingdom to return to what it used to be. I want to be able to walk through the Light Market of Hardrock. I want what's mine. What's ours. And yes, I want Rystan Drusk right next to me as I reclaim all these things, but while he's on my list—high on my list—of concerns, he isn't the main driving force in my life. If he happens to fall tomorrow, it'd hurt, but I'd survive it.

If he and I were to form a mating bond, I don't think any of that would apply anymore. If the stories are true, I'd live and die for him—with him. Neither of us can afford that. And while I was more than happy to indulge a little with him when I first awoke, I think that taking it a step further with him is a dangerous slope. If sex was on the table, he could feel our bond. He could know it. He could recognize me as his.

Part of me warms at the thought. A large part of me. But that's Vlari talking. The girl who had no one to think of but herself. The girl whose only concern was to buy and trade enough goods and favors to repair a roof.

Nevlaria Bane, crown heir of Tenebris, cannot afford the weakness that a mate provides.

I'm too dangerous, too volatile where his safety is concerned already. I haven't forgotten what it felt like to let myself take, and take and take, absorbing the life force of immortals, fully intending to consume them. And I haven't forgotten that it was seeing him in pain that triggered it.

"Do you need to see your family before we leave tomorrow?"

He inclines his head. "I'll go tomorrow. They're likely to be asleep already."

It's almost morning already. "You're sure you don't want any more food? It's delicious." He emptied a generous plate a while back, but he's just watched me eat for the last…I don't know how long. I've eaten for hours, and I feel no regret.

"Only one of us starved for years, you know."

I didn't actually starve; my system was on complete lockdown, frozen in time. It doesn't change the fact that my stomach has never been this empty—not even after gorging myself on fairy fruit and throwing it all up in the garden as a kid.

And now, it's never been so full. Our kind never needs to eat as much as I have tonight.

I manage to get to my feet and drag myself to my bed. I wince, hating the very sight of it. And the smell of it, too. The inside was stuffed with lavender, I think. I want to burn it to ashes. Tomorrow. As much as I dislike the idea of ever sleeping again, I am growing tired, and I can't afford to leave Whitecroft without all my wits at my disposition.

I drag the covers over my shoulders, closing my eyes. "Do you intend to stand there the entire day?"

"If it pleases you, princess."

I roll my eyes. Princess. When he used to call me that, I was anything but. Now, it's accurate, yet it still feels like a joke. "There's plenty of room in this bed."

I keep my eyes closed as he joins me. Feeling the warm, hard body against me, and smelling his heady scent, I decide I don't quite hate my bed after all.

A cloud of dark fur leaps on my feet, and I laugh. "Where were you all day?" I ask the fox, who fixes me with a challenging stare.

He seems to say, I don't see how that's any of your concern, and I decide he's not wrong. Being my familiar doesn't make him a pet. The wyrfox is as wild as he ever was. I wonder how he's taken to living in the castle, making a silk bed his den. From the way he starts to snore moments later, I guess he's adapted to it quite well.

I follow him into a deep slumber.

Dusk comes too soon, and with it, the buzz of activity I've heard every day for ten long years. At first, I don't move, used as I am to not being able to. But when I feel Drusk shift next to me, I open my eyes and sit up.

Sometime in the night, he must have removed layer after layer of clothes, because all I see is delicious, warm, bare skin, covered in dark ink. I gasp, enjoying the way his defined muscles flex. The marks on his back tell a story I don't know—a story of loss and friendship. My fingers trace them.

He shivers under my touch and awakens with a start. His unfocused eyes freeze when they fall on me. Then he breaks into the most open smile I've ever seen on his lips.

I could lick it. I certainly want to.

To distract myself, I ask, "When did these show up?"

He glances over his shoulder to his back. "Some, a while back, during training. I made friends with a boy who gave up the first week. When he left, I earned my first mourning mark." He reaches around his waist to touch a rose with blue lines, right over his hipbone.

"Were you lovers?" I ask, curious, I tell myself. Not jealous. I have never been the jealous type, and that won't start today.

It won't.

"Of a sort. I hadn't touched him, but we understood each other, he and I. More than anyone at the camp. When he left, I was truly alone. I learned later that he was called back to the sea. He's half mer."

That explains it. The sea folk aren't often welcoming to outsiders—and they do tend to consider half-bloods as such—but if he was asked to go back to the sea, he would have wanted to. Sea blood draws people to the water.

"And the others?"

There are plenty of blue roses at the center of his back.

"I eventually made friends, and lost them too."

His life is so different from mine. I have a few friends, I suppose, but I've never lost any of them. Before the attack, I lived in a world where young folk didn't simply die. He was already fighting a war.

No wonder my skin used to be bare of any mark.

Now I have two.

The one that appeared down my back the night I saved Drusk from the assault his friends didn't survive.

And one that crawls up my sleeve, twisting around my neck and shoulder.

Identical to Drusk's. Seeing it on his tanned skin makes me want to lick it. Nip at his flesh just there.

I wonder what he makes of his mark. Part of me wants to ask him. Ask when it appears—though I know. What it means to him now. How he interprets it. To him, it may tell the story of the battle of Hardrock. I know it's an incomplete mating ring, without any sense or structure. Unlinked filigrees trying to wrap around an untold story.

Mine, mine, mine.

He shifts on the bed, turning to face me. "Are you done fondling me, Nevlaria?" His midnight-blue eyes shine with heat.

"Not quite," I reply, redirecting my attention to his chest now. Over his taut skin, there's another set of marks, curving over his heart. I move to touch them, but he takes my wrist away. "What were these for?"

He's done sharing. He's done with my teasing, too. Drusk tugs my wrist, pulling me to him, and bends his head to mine, capturing my lips under his.

Home.

He feels like home. His kiss starts slow, soft, but when I moan, opening my mouth to his, he groans and deepens his exploration, his hands sliding along the length of my torso with a reverence

I've never felt. I'm mostly flat, without many curves, yet he makes me feel like there was never a body more sensual, more deserving of worship. I'm desperate for more. All my resolutions fly out the window when he dips his mouth to the curve of my ear and drops light kisses along its tip.

I need him. I need him like I need my own soul.

I flip over, climbing on top of him, my hands pressed over his hard chest.

In that instant, I don't care about the world. I don't care about Tenebris. I don't care about the folk. All that matters is my mate.

Then, an explosion makes the entire keep shake, and there's nothing but chaos.

fifteen
shadows at the gates
vlari

I leap to my feet and rush to the pile of clothes folded on a nearby desk. I'd prepared a pair of pants, a linen shirt, and a doublet for tomorrow. I put them on, as Drusk goes to the window.

"Southwest, close to the hall of Ash," he tells me, eyes focused in the distance. "Humans, on foot. Thousands. Too many to count." He curses out loud. "The air dome didn't fool them."

He takes his belt and weapons, I throw his jerkin to him, and we're on our way out, jogging as we head to my mother's quarters.

"That was fast. Too fast. They were ready to attack."

I can only bite my lip and nod.

My mother, father, and grandma meet us in the corridors, trailed by the king and queen of Stone.

"What's the plan?" Queen Ina asks me.

Me. Not my mother, or anyone else. Seconds ago, I was about to get impaled in the best way, and I'm supposed to come up with a plan against an invasion right now.

I've had to act like I know what I'm doing, to ensure no one questions me, but this is a bit much.

I need to think. I need…

Help.

I need help.

I only have to glance to Drusk, and he's speaking. "We can defend Whitecroft Hall itself. The children and those who can't fight should come here." Drusk resumes our walk toward the entrance of the keep. "Whatever archers we have should be inside, on windows. The guards need to protect the gates. The humans' strength is their numbers. We need to funnel them—ensure they can't surround us and attack on many fronts. If there was one magic user every two or three meters all around Whitecroft, but for an opening we choose, they'd be forced to try to enter where we can manage them."

"That won't work—not indefinitely." Liken shakes his head. "They'll kill the mages, eventually."

"Nothing will work indefinitely," Drusk counters. "This isn't the entire human army. It's a tenth, if that. Reinforcements will be on their way. Let's manage one crisis at a time."

The truth of his words makes my stomach sink.

The unvarnished truth is that we simply don't have enough mages, enough fighters, enough fae to withstand an attack by hundreds of thousands of humans.

We have to try all the same.

We reach the sculpted doors, and I finally see them in the distance.

There are at least ten thousand humans rushing down the hill, most on foot, some mounted on bridled horses, pulling machines I've only read about. Catapults. I see one working right away, propelling a fire stone right at us. It crashes against the hall of Stars. Screams, blood, and gunpowder thicken the air.

"The shield," I say, numb and cold. So very cold. "What about the shield? We could…"

"We don't have all the elemental stones—not yet," my mother replies. "The Court of Ash hasn't made one, and we're still missing water."

I'm desperate. We're all desperate and hopeless. "I'll go to the opening." I start to run.

My mother is quick to catch my arm. I turn to her, glaring up into her green eyes.

"No. You can't. If we lose you—"

"No one can kill as well as I," I point out.

"And you have the stamina of a child. Don't waste your life against vermin."

"So, I should stand back while our people waste theirs?" I'm screaming at her.

I yank my arm back, though her claws grow and sink into my skin.

But when I turn to run southwest again, Drusk stands in my way.

"Not you." There's a warning in my mind. He doesn't get to hold me back.

"We don't need you to suck humans dry. Our soldiers, our knights can manage them for a time. What we need is a water stone and a fire stone. Only one of us has a link to the Sea Court."

A link? I could roll my eyes, if I wasn't too busy fuming. I danced with one guy, once.

"I can go to Ash, and make them craft a fire stone right now. You need to get us a water stone. This is how we save Whitecroft. You aren't a soldier, princess. Let them to their work. Yours is to lead."

I want to rage, scream, and insist I rush to the front. I don't, because under the haze of bloodlust, I can tell he's right.

I nod. "All right. All right," I repeat, with more conviction. "I'm going."

Before I do, I step closer to him and get on my tiptoes. Embarrassingly, that's not high enough to reach his face, but he bends down and drops his lips on my forehead. "Go get that stone, princess."

"Right back at you."

I have a mission. It's not nearly as satisfying as cutting down a sea of humans could be, but it's considerably more useful. Though my body would have loved nothing more than to join the fight, I run to the harbor instead.

When I reach the quiet, dark shores, I don't take a moment to hesitate. I dive to the bottom of the river.

I never was taught to swim as a child. It's an activity beneath gentry folk, because running water is known to stifle our magic. It wasn't until my thirtieth year that Meda insisted I should know how to survive water. One of the many ways her seelie education differed from ours. We folk of the dark tend to shy away from that which displeases us. The seelie will always do what they believe is necessary.

I hated water then. I hate it more now, but I'm grateful. I remember an awkward stroke. I shed my doublet, letting it sink, and release my wings. They rip the fabric of my shirt at the back, but I ignore it. The iridescent, thin membranes flap, propelling me forward faster than my arms ever could.

I need to find a water folk—any water folk.

After some distance, I return to the surface, as much to breathe as to check my location. Then I sink again, and keep swimming. My eyes adjust to the darkness of the depths, yet I see no folk at all.

This can't be a coincidence. The river used to be full of nixies and other fae.

The Sea Court is staying away from Tenebris.

They know we're hopeless. They know we will fall.

I can't give up, although my limbs are heavy, my lungs begging for a break. I keep going, farther and farther, willing myself to believe those I've left behind will survive until I can help.

I have to believe it.

My family is fine. Drusk is fine. I will find help before it's too late.

Drusk

ASH IS EMPTY. There isn't a single soul alive in the entire hall. Not one sprite.

I stand in the middle of the building, letting it sink in.

They left.

They abandoned us.

More than that: they betrayed us.

I don't have to wonder how the enemies knew we were defenseless now.

I stand helplessly, letting it sink in, as the sound of cannons crashes around me.

We failed.

I turn on my heel, preparing to return to Whitecroft Hall and tell the queen she needs to call for an evacuation at once, when I hear it.

A grunt, coming out of one of the empty rooms I'd passed. I move toward it, until I stand in a messy study.

On the floor, next to a row of bookshelves, lies a familiar knight, a dagger planted in his side. The salamander who took me to the queen that first day.

I stand over him, dithering. Part of me wants to finish him off; the other knows I need to listen to him.

"What happened?"

He groans. "The king." He coughs, and the movement makes blood pour out of his wound. "He told us to move back to the Ash Court. Said he made a deal. I—" He winces, every word taking its toll. "Refused. I refused."

I stare at him, not offering any assistance.

In the face of such betrayal, I can't quite believe this. He refused, or he was left behind to keep spying on us.

"Why should I trust you? Why would you turn your back on your court if they've indeed made a deal to return home?"

The salamander's red eyes set on me. "I stand with Tenebris."

I don't want to believe it, but ultimately, the decision doesn't rest with me.

I kneel at his side and pull the knife out. I tear one of my sleeves, and wrap it around his middle, tight. It'll do until we find a healer—or decide to slit his throat.

I hook his arm around my neck and pull him to his feet. I have to support most of his weight, but we manage to get to Whitecroft Hall.

The high queen and most of the lower monarchs save for Ash are in the entryway. The Sandwoman, Meda, and Ina are notably missing. Fighting at the front, no doubt. Vlari would have been jealous.

"What happened?"

I summarize the situation as succinctly as I can manage. "Ash cleared out. They're with the usurper. He says he refused to follow his king."

Several sets of mistrustful eyes fall on the salamander, who's panting and groaning.

Ciera detaches herself from her mate's side, and stands right in front of him.

"Do you swear to serve the high court, no matter the cost, until your dying breath, Lucan?"

That's a hell of a vow for an immortal, even considering the fact that his dying breath could be in a few seconds. I half expect him to bow out.

"I swear," he replies automatically.

She nods. "Good enough. We need a salamander."

Ciera removes a charm pinned on the inside of her embroidered sleeve and presses it against his lapel. A healing charm. I don't know how, exactly, but I can tell Neb made it. It feels like my sister. It smells like her.

"Nero, can you get a healer?"

Her bondmate rushes out without hesitation.

"We need a fire stone," the queen tells the salamander—Lucan. "When you're better, do you think…"

"I can do it," he manages to croak. "Now."

"Don't be stupid," I shoot back. If he even tries to call to his magic right now, he'll be dead in minutes. "Get to it when you stop leaking."

I leave him well taken care of, and exit the hall.

I have humans to destroy.

sixteen
land of sea
vlari

The next time I emerge to breathe, my heart falls as I take in my surroundings. The ominous chain of mountains. The familiar castle that has always been a threatening shadow in the distance.

I've reached the sea. I swam through the entire river, and there was nothing at all.

If I go farther, I'll leave Tenebris entirely, giving myself to the power of the Sea Court. I don't know their allegiance. They could stand with the usurper, deliver me to her on an iron platter. They could keep me at the bottom of the sea.

And yet, what choice do I have?

I take the plunge, sinking so much deeper, into a world of corals and shining fish.

Beautiful. Treacherous. Cruel. Such is the sea. I surrender to it.

Never mind the sea folk. Tired as I am, I could simply drown out there.

I vaguely consider swimming back up to the surface, when I realize I don't need to. The air in my lungs is gone, but the burning I should feel is absent. I am breathing. I'm breathing water.

Seconds after I've realized it, I hear a laugh all around me, echoing with the waves. And the next time I blink, the water is gone. I'm standing on a beautiful beach, and the sun is shining in the horizon. I've never felt sand on my toes. I can't say I like it.

I seem to be unharmed, but none of this makes sense. Seconds ago, I was underwater. Am I dead? Is this what death feels like? It would be peaceful, if not for the panic rising in my chest.

"I've never smelled such a stench of desperation."

I turn toward the deep, familiar voice.

Him.

"Lind," I say, half fear, half relief.

He's sitting on the golden sand, his bare chest wet, a long dark skirt cloaking his legs.

"Hello, landling."

"You came."

He laughs again. "I wasn't going to, but you're so very miserable, I couldn't resist. I'm not entirely heartless, you know."

Somehow, I doubt that.

I don't waste time. "I don't know what you've heard, but the situation in Tenebris is…"

"Hopeless. Wretched. No, I know." He smirks. "Pathetic."

He's beautiful, treacherous, and cruel, just like the sea.

"I need your help. Please. All I need is a water stone. Well, one or two," I amend quickly. "A handful, maybe."

Given how much effort this trip has taken, I should stock up.

His smile is all teeth. "All she wants is a handful of pieces of my soul. Just that, nothing else."

I still.

Pieces of his soul?

"A stone imbued with my magic is a part of me, landling. Surely you know enough of elemental spells to realize that?"

I hadn't.

I bite my lip. "What do you want? In exchange."

This is the language of the fae. Deals, bargains.

He throws his head back, his bright blue hair shining in the sunlight. "Let's see…"

"We could trade for a favor," I offer, knowing nothing of more value.

He shakes his head. "Oh, I think not. You already owe me one of those, remember?"

How could I forget? He saved me, along with all of Hardrock, ten years ago.

But he hasn't refused. I hold on to that. He hasn't refused, which means that he intends to accept. It's just a matter of finding the right price.

Unless he's toying with me for his entertainment. A likely possibility, but I ignore it.

"What do you want, Lind?"

I don't point out the obvious. I am at his mercy. There is nothing I can deny him today.

"Well, you want pieces of me. I'd like a piece of you in exchange."

I blush, taken aback. Somehow, I didn't expect that.

Lind made it clear he wasn't interested in me ten years ago. Now, he is willing to trade water elemental stones for sex with me? I was offering everything—anything. I can't believe this is his price.

He'll have it, if he demands it. I don't have a choice. But Drusk. The very thought of touching anyone but Drusk makes me want to vomit.

"I don't…" I wet my lip. "I have a mate. Is there anything else?"

He laughs again. I could strangle him. All of my people are about to die, and he's making fun of me.

"Aren't you just a darling? I don't hurt for female company, Nevlaria Bane. Your body, delightful as it might be, isn't what I require." Humor leaves his sea eyes, now set on me with a harshness I didn't know him capable of. "The immortals came for your land. On the other continent, the folk are being attacked, hunted. Humans and their technology have worked out that we rule the world, and now they want a piece. The gods are on their side, as they can control mortals, but cannot hope to have us kneel at their feet."

He gets to his feet and advances toward me. "Misguided as your former high queen and my mothers were, trying to pair me with the likes of you, they had a point. We need to be linked in the only way that cannot be denied or broken. By blood. The sea, the land—seelie and unseelie alike. We need to stand together."

I'd forgotten he's a ruler until now. A lord of the sea. I won't make that mistake again.

"I will give you twelve stones, and you and I shall be allies. The price you will pay will be your blood. Your third born will be sent to the sea, raised among us, and wed into the Sea Lands."

I hate this. I hate every single part of this. He's trying to turn me into *her*. Into Morgana, who played with her children like she was their god, rather than their mother.

"An arranged marriage? I thought you didn't believe in them. I thought you said I was too weak for the sea."

He tilted his head. "I may have been mistaken, when it comes to you. But a child raised in the sea will be one of us. And you aren't arranging a thing. Give me the child. The rest is up to me."

My ears are boiling.

I'm bargaining my unborn children? I feel sick.

But truth is, without his help, I may not have any child at all. I could die with the rest of Tenebris, fading with the light at the next sunset.

"Why the third?" I may never have three children. Plenty of fae aren't blessed with even one, in all their years.

He grins, and shrugs. "I'm leaving you with an heir and a spare, landling. As I said, I'm not entirely heartless."

I would laugh if I could. "Not entirely. Just mostly."

The prince of the sea offers his hand.

I have no choice but to take it.

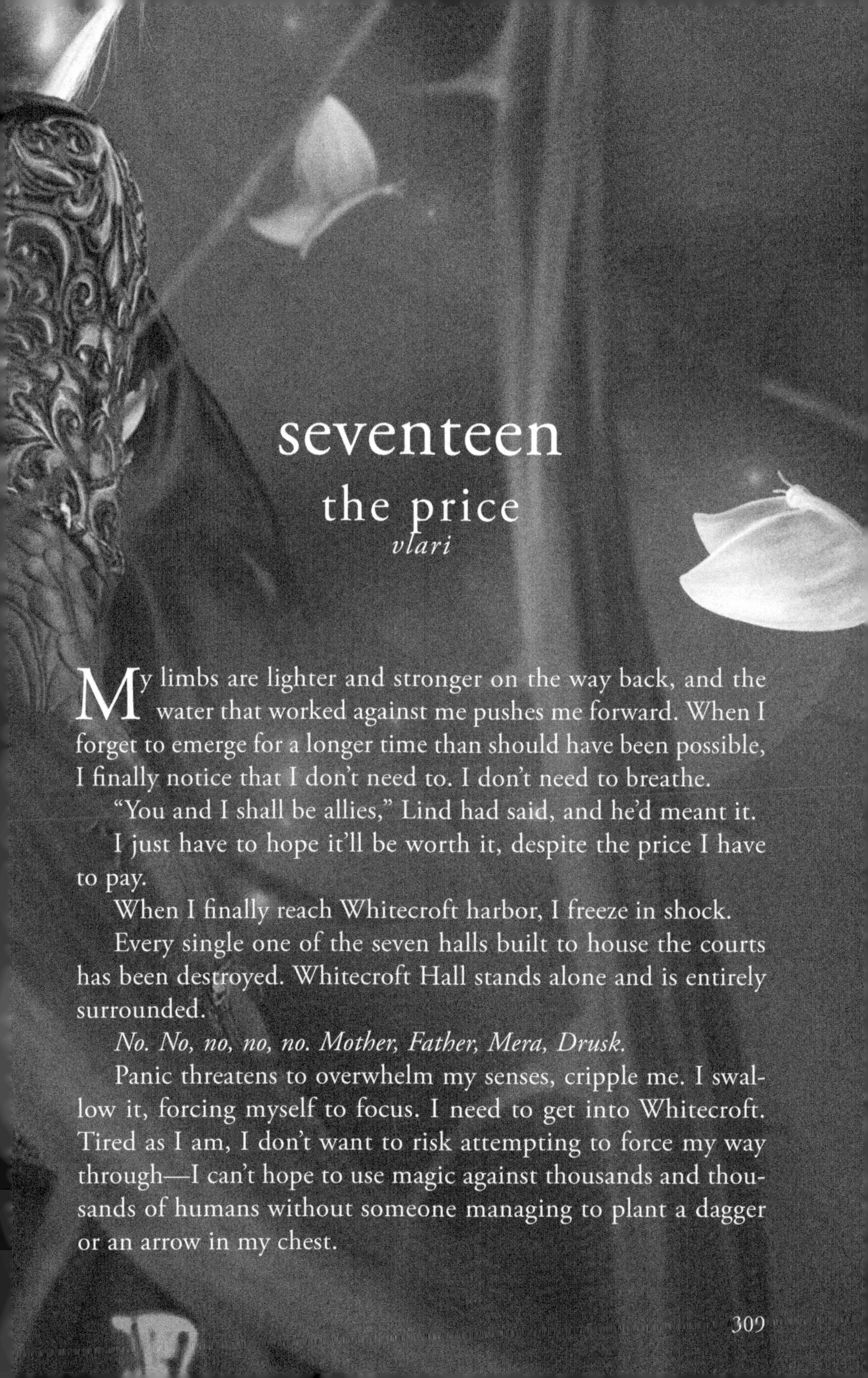

seventeen

the price

vlari

My limbs are lighter and stronger on the way back, and the water that worked against me pushes me forward. When I forget to emerge for a longer time than should have been possible, I finally notice that I don't need to. I don't need to breathe.

"You and I shall be allies," Lind had said, and he'd meant it.

I just have to hope it'll be worth it, despite the price I have to pay.

When I finally reach Whitecroft harbor, I freeze in shock.

Every single one of the seven halls built to house the courts has been destroyed. Whitecroft Hall stands alone and is entirely surrounded.

No. No, no, no, no. Mother, Father, Mera, Drusk.

Panic threatens to overwhelm my senses, cripple me. I swallow it, forcing myself to focus. I need to get into Whitecroft. Tired as I am, I don't want to risk attempting to force my way through—I can't hope to use magic against thousands and thousands of humans without someone managing to plant a dagger or an arrow in my chest.

My wings are tired; I can't count on their speed either.

I assess the rest of my abilities, and come up short. I don't think I can sass them into letting me get through.

But there's something else…

I've only been able to access it once, instinctively, without meaning to. Ten years ago, when Drusk was under duress at Hardrock, I did manage to blend into his Myst and appear close to him.

I'd be hard-pressed to tell exactly how. I was running, a sense of dread in the pit of my stomach telling me I needed to be elsewhere, or something terrible was going to happen. I entirely gave into that feeling, letting it consume me.

Right now, I'm managing my fear. Back then, I wasn't. I let it claim me.

I've changed in ten years. I may not have moved a single muscle, but my mind has grown, evolved, mostly because of my ability to think through things before I act. To talk myself out of irrational fear or panic.

For a moment, I need to revert to the old Vlari. The one who'd be crying, in pieces. The one who doesn't control anything at all.

My mother might be dead.

My father might be dead.

The few friends I have? Gone.

Drusk, my mate? Destroyed before he was even truly mine.

I let in fear and darkness, till I find it hard to breathe.

They need me. They need me. They need me now.

I feel the Myst caress my skin, wrap around me, and the next instant, I'm standing in the middle of the assembly hall Ciera converted into a throne room, my wet clothes soaking the white stone floor.

There's chaos all around me. The hall is packed. Mothers cry, hugging fae children, lords scream to the queen standing next to the throne, begging her to do something, anything. Attack, retreat, call for negotiations. At the windows, our archers launch volley after volley of arrows, and though each hits the mark, they barely make a dent in the pack of mortals attacking us.

Ciera stares in the distance, her green eyes cold. She's lost, powerless, and unable to deal with the pressure on her shoulders.

I barely pay her any attention, my eyes on one of the men next to her. Drusk. He's here. He's fine. So are my father and grandfather, but I don't even see them at first.

His eyes directly find me, and remain on me, as he gasps.

I cut through the thick pack, doing my damnedest to make my way to them.

Gradually, the shouting and crying fade, and in their place, I hear whispers.

My name. They're calling my name.

The crowd parts to let me through, and Drusk descends from the dais. I practically fall in his arms. He wraps them around me, tight enough to hurt, but I welcome it. Too soon, he lets me go. I rush to my mother's side. She opens her arms, too, but that's one embrace I can do without.

I get the leather pouch at my belt, making the stones inside jiggle. "I have the water stones. Do you have fire?"

Eyes wide, she nods and strides toward the back room, waving at us to follow.

"How did you get in?" Drusk asks, as he walks—and I trot—after her.

Where should I even start? "Long story. Did the salamander get the fire stone?"

He winces in response. "That's also a long story, but one you need to hear. Ash deserted. They made a deal to get their court back, and left us to die."

I have no words. After all I've done to get the water stone, it was for nothing?

"We have one salamander. He was wounded, but managed one stone. He's resting now."

I squint, immediately suspicious. Drusk reads my expression. "I felt the same way, but he swore fealty to the crown. He's with us. Now, we have to hope the hag's spell was accurate."

We've reached my mother's quarters. Her study is similar to the one she had in our home, the Court of Mist—filled with books and art.

Meda is standing in front of a table. At first, sensing an approach, she pulls a dagger and moves into a protective stance, but she recognizes us and lowers her weapon before stepping aside.

There are four stones on the table: an earth, fire, and air stone, next to the heart of Tenebris. I pluck a water stone out of my pouch and hand it to her.

"How did you get that many, girl? I sense a considerable amount of power in these, too," Meda says, visibly impressed.

I can't remember a day when she ever was impressed with me.

"Lind," I reply, leaving it at that.

Drusk stiffens next to me. "What did he want for it?"

I'm not going into that now. "Nothing I wasn't willing to give." Reluctantly. "What was the exact spell, again?"

"Tears of enemies, blood of friends, and a sacrifice of one the caster loves needs to be done and buried along with four elemental stones—water, earth, fire, and air. The caster needs to hold a power stone, and think about the territory they wish to shield. It has to be a territory that belongs to her—as high queen, Ciera can cast it over all of Tenebris. Right?" Alven checks with Drusk, who nods.

Silence falls around us. We have every element now. The implication is no less daunting.

Because my mother needs to choose who she will bury along with the stones.

"Drusk, do you think you could get me one of the humans from outside? I don't suppose it'll be too difficult to make them cry."

He hesitates, glancing down to me.

Ciera catches his look. "You may take my daughter, if you wish. She won't need to be part of this conversation."

In short, she isn't picking me.

Which means that she is going to have to kill one of the others. My father. Her father. My father's mother. The three people she loves most.

"I'll stay," I tell Drusk.

I need to be here for my mother.

He holds my gaze, but ends up nodding, before disappearing in a cloud of Myst.

"I believe," Alven says evenly, stepping forward, "that how you should proceed is quite clear, daughter."

Meda nods. "Yes, it is. I'm the least useful among us. It should be me."

She holds her head up proudly.

I question my impulse to remain in this room. There isn't enough air. I can't breathe. I can't think.

"I betrayed Tenebris. Without me, we'd never be in this situation."

"I'm not from Tenebris at all. I'm one pixie. A hundred of us would make a difference in a war, but me?" Meda shrugs. "I'm useless."

The woman who showed me how to defend myself, useless? The man who had my back, protecting me against his wife's whims since the day of my birth, a traitor?

Neither of them represented themselves how I see them. They are my heroes. They are my family.

I never knew I loved them—not until I'm faced with this terrible choice.

My mother will never pick my father, the bondmate for whom she'd given up everything.

It's between Alven and Meda. One of them will die.

"I could try to bring you back? After you're gone." My voice is breaking.

Alven shakes his head. "That isn't how magic works. You can recall a soul that's not been claimed. Ours will be trapped, binding the spell. If you were to undo it, it'd destroy the shield."

I close my eyes.

"To Morgana, I was a tool. A pretty tool she could use. I never had a mother," Ciera said. "Not until you."

She's talking to Meda—probably holding her hand or hugging her. I can't look.

"I always had a father. When I was banished, cast out, and cursed, you risked everything to stand against the high queen and give me a home. I love you both. I'm not strong enough for this."

No one is. No one should be.

"Maybe it doesn't have to be them. Maybe it can be anyone at all?" Nero asks.

"Who, then? Should the queen of Tenebris walk into the hall and choose a random pluck to slaughter? Who would follow me?" Ciera spits bitterly. "Besides, to be a sacrifice it has to be someone I love."

My heart breaks for her. For all of us.

She cannot choose. I know it.

Which means I must.

It will break me, but I must do it all the same.

"I need Meda." Somehow, my voice doesn't break.

Just three words.

Three words, that condemn part of my family.

I clear my throat. "If we live to see another day, I want to go north, to the border between our lands. I intend to get elemental stones from the Old Keep, but it isn't just that. I need Meda because we have to talk to the seelie courts. We have to make them understand that we stand together—our kind against mortals. No matter our differences in the past, if we're to survive when billions of humans come to our doors, it will be together." I lift my chin. "I gave my third-born child to the sea. I'll give anything the seelie demand to seal an alliance between us. Not for today, or tomorrow. So that our kind may live in a thousand years. I don't know anything about the seelie kingdoms. I think they'd shoot me on sight. Meda's from the north. They'll listen to her."

I need Alven to understand—I need them all to understand that this isn't a whim, I'm not picking a preference. I'm trying to keep a broken realm from shattering under our feet.

I haven't opened my eyes at all through the entire speech. When I feel a hand on my shoulder, I do.

My mother stands in front of me, tears in her beautiful eyes falling freely. She's so much taller than me. I've always felt like a child next to her.

Now I don't. She's the child, the one who needs protection.

"You need Meda," she repeats. Her voice has lost its heat. All I hear now is determination. "And you need Alven. My father is a king. He can guide you, advise you, and protect the crown. There was always only one disposable link in this family. I'm sorry I'm not strong enough."

I open my mouth to speak, but then she removes the intricate circlet of gold on top of her head and places it on top of mine.

Though dainty and small, I've never worn anything heavier than her crown.

"My daughter, my heart, Nevlaria of the house of Nyx, I crown you high queen of Tenebris."

I should have expected this. Ciera Oberon Bane was always honest about who she is. Honest, and cruel.

I nod, and lift both of my hands to her chin, gently.

"I forgive you," I tell her through my tears.

Then I suck the life out of her, bit by bit, absorbing her essence, ignoring the shouts and screams of my father, held back by his mother. I keep taking, and taking and taking every exquisite ounce of her power inside me, until she falls at my feet.

Empty. Cold. Dead. Sacrificed.

We bury her in the inner garden. Drusk digs a deep grave, after he comes back with a sniveling human. I suck him too, till he cries, begging for mercy.

Then, I break his neck, and step over him.

The four stones are dropped at the bottom of the well. I start to shovel. My father doesn't say a word. I don't say a word. I know I've lost him.

What I've gained in exchange is time.

The spell works. I feel the shields surround us—I've had them erupt right where they used to be, simply because I'm familiar with that setup.

The humans right next to the gates are still inside, but the rest of the army is cut off.

We make short work of them, now that we don't have to fear thousands of mortals replacing those we destroy. Besides, I'm in great form now. Matricide must be healthy.

There are no celebrations for the reclamation of Whitecroft. The only songs I allow are the odes of a soft queen, too gentle for times of war. Some of the ballads are quite good. I expect they'll outlive us.

There are no celebrations for my coronation. I've earned this crown because the folk need a monster to lead them. No one is dumb enough to think that's a good thing.

I sit on the throne, alone on the dais, and the room is silent. We've given the lower kings and queens a summary of my mother's decisions, and they watch me warily. As they should.

Ina is the first to speak. "What now, Your Grace?"

I let my eyes drag to her. "We go north as planned. You, I, whoever else has the guts to follow. We don't have the element of surprise on our side anymore. The usurper has been warned. We will go nonetheless. We'll take the shy folk. Today has proved how valuable archers are." I say nothing about my intention to venture toward Old Crest. "And when I am back, I expect each court to be prepared for an attack. We've been on the defensive for too long. I'll build shields around our kingdom, and we will take it back. But first, I will have you kneel."

I look into each of their faces.

"The Court of Ash betrayed us. Hundreds of fae died today because my mother was too soft to keep the salamanders in line. You can kneel and swear to me, or you can get out."

Empty, cold, and dead. Just like my mother is right now. Just like she should have been all along.

I stand, letting the silence wrap around me.

I've given them a true choice. They can turn their backs on me, leave and kneel to Violet. If they don't, they'll have to swear to me in a binding oath.

They all kneel.

I leave, returning to my empty room.

Only then do I allow myself to cry.

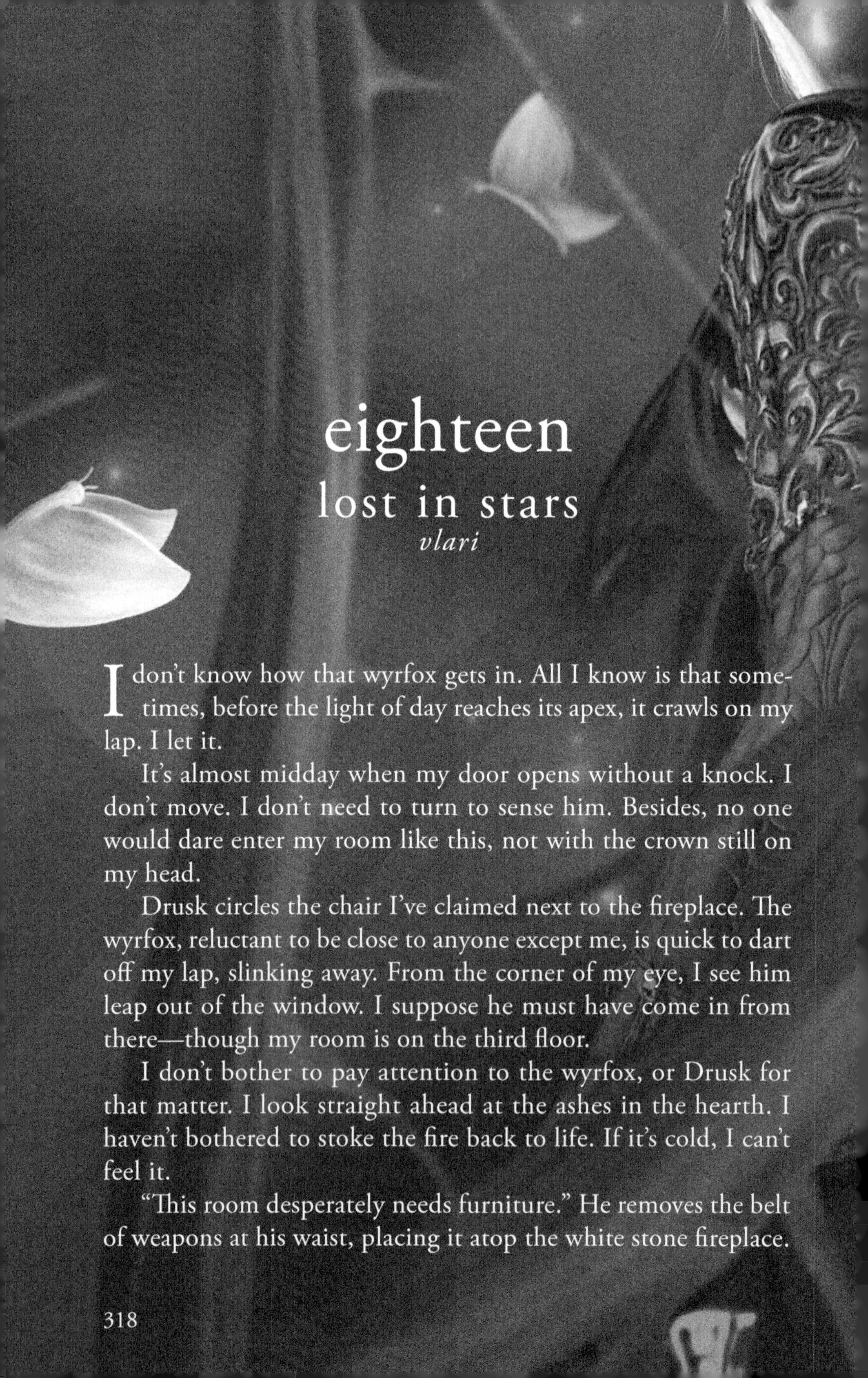

eighteen
lost in stars
vlari

I don't know how that wyrfox gets in. All I know is that sometimes, before the light of day reaches its apex, it crawls on my lap. I let it.

It's almost midday when my door opens without a knock. I don't move. I don't need to turn to sense him. Besides, no one would dare enter my room like this, not with the crown still on my head.

Drusk circles the chair I've claimed next to the fireplace. The wyrfox, reluctant to be close to anyone except me, is quick to dart off my lap, slinking away. From the corner of my eye, I see him leap out of the window. I suppose he must have come in from there—though my room is on the third floor.

I don't bother to pay attention to the wyrfox, or Drusk for that matter. I look straight ahead at the ashes in the hearth. I haven't bothered to stoke the fire back to life. If it's cold, I can't feel it.

"This room desperately needs furniture." He removes the belt of weapons at his waist, placing it atop the white stone fireplace.

"I'd request some, but it seems rather pointless," I reply. I'm relieved to recognize my voice. It isn't dark, or broken. I sound lively as ever. That hasn't changed, though everything else has.

We will head north at sundown. We'll succeed in taking back Tenebris, or we'll be buried along with my mother. Either way, I won't use this room for much longer.

"You need to get some sleep."

I would laugh if I could. Sleep? How does one sleep after killing their mother and taking her crown?

"Well, I need to rest, and I'd sleep considerably better if you joined me." Drusk removes his clothing, layer after layer—leather, velvet, and finally linen, till he stands in nothing but his breeches. His chest, sculpted by decades of rigorous training, does manage to distract me from the turmoil in my mind, and if I'm to trust his smug smirk, he knows it.

I don't want to give in. Not yet. I don't deserve to enjoy him today. I don't deserve anything at all.

I close my eyes. "I'm not tired." With Ciera's life force pulsing through my veins, I've seldom been more awake.

"Nor I. I suppose we could tire each other out."

My jaw ticks. "My mother just died. I killed her."

"Your mother killed herself," he amends. "She took the easy way out. That was probably the best decision, all things considered, but either way, it's not on you. It's on the usurper, on Alven, on Morgana. On her. On anyone you'd like, except you."

A soft thumb brushes over my lips, and finally, my eyes flutter open. Drusk's hand travels down to my chin, caressing my skin.

"And because I haven't caused my mother's death, I should be just fine?" I counter. There's no bite to my words. I've never sounded more neutral. I'm not arguing, I'm grasping for his words. Each soothes the ache inside me.

"You don't have to be fine, Vlari." Drusk tilts my chin upward so I look straight into his hungry midnight eyes. "Not today. Not even tomorrow. But I can't let you numb everything."

Is that what I've been doing? I suppose he has a point. Right now, however, with his fingertip sliding along my neck, I don't feel numb at all.

"When the sun goes down, we'll leave the safety of this haven. Anything can happen to me—to you—out there. You can't waste your last day like this. I won't allow it."

I cock an eyebrow. "And you feel entitled to dictate what I do with my time, why?" I can't help it, I always want to push him, tease him. The fact that I gave into that impulse shows that whatever he's doing is working. I'm no longer lost in grief, pain, and guilt. Part of me is right there with him.

"Because when you're being an idiot, someone must, princess."

"If you want to be technical about it, I'm queen now. Which means I could have you whipped for calling me an idiot."

"Then perhaps I should kneel and ask for mercy."

I'm about to point out he already did that in the throne room, but he moves so fast I don't even get a word in. Before I can blink, he's right between my legs, sitting back on his heels. Drusk grips my knees and spreads my thighs apart slowly. I changed into one of my mother's gowns sometime between her mockery of a funeral and my addressing the lords. It's white. Empty, numb, and cold. The seelie wear blood red at funerals, and traditionally the unseelie court is cloaked in purple when a child of the house of Nyx dies, but white spoke of my grief better than any other shade could have. I stood out, and I didn't care.

The dress is too long on me—its back follows me like a train—but the design allows me to wear it: it parts in the middle. On my mother, the slit was perhaps around crotch-height. I suppose she must have worn it over pants or another skirt. On me, it reaches the knees. Somehow, I don't look stupid. The loose, flowing fabric adheres to my body, clinging to whatever curve it found.

Drusk slides the silk along my thighs, pushing it off my legs. I don't wear anything at all underneath. I've never been one for braies if it can be helped, and dresses such as these don't allow for shifts or chemises. I refuse to feel naked—though I am from the waist down. I stare at him, my silence daring him to do his worst. He never breaks eye contact, bringing his mouth to the apex of my thighs, and closing his lips over the sensitive nub of nerves at my center.

I want to gasp. I don't. I keep my expression as even as I can manage, staring at him as he teases me, bringing his skilled fingers to my heated core and playing me like a virtuoso. Inside me, heat gathers and rises, rises, rises, always higher. Drusk knows exactly what he's doing, but so long as no sound crosses my lips, I feel like I maintain the power. Like he's losing a game we play.

I've enjoyed sex as an outlet for years, with nameless faces, and with some friends. Each time, it's been fast, simple, to the point. I'm not used to being teased like this. Drusk kisses me there like he has all the time in the world, and my satisfaction is the only thing that matters to him. He curves his index finger and rubs me softly. Then without warning, he presses his tongue against my clit, hard, and I give in. I wail. It's involuntary, insuppressible. I'm gripping the arms of my chair, claws digging into the wood. He's relaxed and aroused me like no one ever has. Now he changes his song, rough and demanding, sucking, inserting another finger. I'm whining and rocking against his mouth. My hands leave the chair to thread in his mess of blue-black wavy hair. I'm holding him right there, just in case he's cruel enough to think of leaving me wanting when I'm so, so, so very close to the edge of the precipice.

Drusk tilts his head to reach my wrist and drops his lips against it before returning his attention where I need it. He blows on me, and flicks his tongue, smirking at me.

I fall. Without warning, without control, I fall. I think I might have screamed, gripping his shoulders hard enough to make him bleed.

Oh, by all the gods in this world and the next, this man is a gift. A gift I can't believe I've ignored for years and years. I should have leaped on him the very first day and demanded he take care of me. Although perhaps not; he has no doubt learned these tricks sometime over the last decade.

I breathe harder than I do after a long, hard run, all my muscles spent. But me? I'm awake. Awake, and hungry.

Drusk gets on his feet and wraps his strong hands around my waist, lifting me up. I let him, acting like a doll in his arms. He can do with me what he wishes after that performance.

He carries me to my bed, and takes care to lower me gently before joining me, taking the side he was on so many hours ago, before we were interrupted by an army at our doors.

I shift to face him, eager for more, but Drusk is in bed, tucked in under the covers. His face is so close to me, I could kiss him. And I do just that, taking his lips, hard. He kisses me back, but doesn't give in to my attempt to deepen the kiss.

"Aren't you an eager little thing, princess," he whispers against my lips.

I am, and I'm not even going to pretend otherwise. I'm done playing for the day.

"But if you want me, you're going to have to pay the price."

I lift a brow. "Oh?"

"Sleep."

He can't be serious.

He chuckles low. "I want us well rested for tomorrow. Sleep a little, and I'll be happy to oblige in any way you could want me to when we wake."

I want to pout. "That sounds counterproductive."

"And nonetheless, it's my bargain. Take it or leave it."

He's bluffing. I'd wager almost anything that if I were to slip out of this dress, straddle him, and ride him, he'd let me. He'd do far more than let me. I don't argue, because annoying as it is, he's right. We both need rest before dusk. Before the world changes for the third time this week.

I close my eyes, doubting that sleep will ever come to me, excited and aroused as I am. But it isn't long before his scent, the rhythm of his heart beating right against me, and the arm he wraps around my middle make me feel safe, sound, and calm.

And so I sleep.

He wakes me with a trail of kisses along my neck. Sometime during the night, I turned around to face away from him. He's right behind me, the heat of his chest warming my back.

I could get used to this. Waking up every day just like that.

"It's almost twilight, princess."

"Queen," I grumble.

"Mmmh."

I suspect he's never going to call me queen. Not that I'd demand it of just about anyone else. I never wanted the crown—I'm only wearing it because I'm the one person who can. But the way he says princess has always bugged me—anything else would be better than that.

"How did you sleep?" I ask, moving to turn to him, but he laughs and grips my hips, pinning me in place.

"Small talk?" Drusk asks. "I can think of better ways to wake up. Can't you?"

Before I can think of any reply, he slides his hand between my legs, to my entrance, still as dripping wet as it was a few hours ago. Now, I can definitely think about a few things more interesting than enquiring about his sleep schedule.

The finger of his right hand curves inside me, and he slides his left arm under my torso to reach my breast, cupping it harshly. Gone is the patience and care he exhibited yesterday. His hands are rough, purposeful. In just a few strokes, a few moments, I'm desperate for more, and so, so close to the abyss.

"Please." I don't think I've ever said that word to anyone at all—certainly not to Drusk. But I say it now anyway. I need more.

"Please what, Your Highness? Do you want me to stop?" His voice is filled with malice.

I gasp. He wouldn't dare!

He laughs at me as I glare behind my shoulder, before bringing his skilled lips to my mouth. His kiss is everything I wanted earlier, when he bullied me into sleeping: deep, demanding, lustful.

I'm lost in a tumult of sensation stronger than everything I have ever experienced.

Though he's only touched me this way once, it's as if Drusk knows my body already; he presses and flicks me exactly where I need until I explode.

I've never reached an orgasm this fast, not while touching myself or with any partner. I wouldn't have thought it possible.

My mother, the Sea Court, my bargains, the usurper, Tenebris. None of it matters in this precious moment where the world disappears. There's only me and him.

I sit up and turn to him. This time, he lets me. I climb over him, discarding our bed sheet. My hands rest on his taut, defined chest, and slide along it, caressing his beautiful skin. He's glorious. And mine. Mine, mine, mine. I will never get enough.

I'm done with games for now. I need him, and I don't let anything else matter. I fumble with the string closing his breeches and free him from his pants. My eyes stay fixed on him as I lower myself onto him, moving slowly, feeling every inch of him fill me up, expand me. Drusk grasps my hips and moves to sit up, but I push him back down on the bed. He drove me to the edge of madness—twice. It's my turn. His grip on me tightens, but he lets me lead. I undulate, rising and falling, dancing on him, taking more each time until he's inside me, to the hilt. I'm teasing us both, and soon I'll need more, but the raw hunger in Drusk's eyes makes me want to keep the torture going, so I keep checking my pace, riding him so, so slowly. Each time he moves under me, thrusting deep or attempting to quicken the pace, I shush him and slow down further.

Then he's done. With a roar, Drusk pushes my hands off his chest, drags my legs toward him, and lifts them in the air under the knees, holding me hovered over him. Then, he takes me, hard, fast, punishingly, thrusts starting before the last is over. I can't think, I can hardly breathe. He's a wild beast unleashed, and I love every moment of it. I lose it. I lose it without warning, coming undone, and Drusk never stops his onslaught, pounding deep inside me while I collapse and lose my senses. I'm still a cotton ball, a doll without a spine or strings, when he shifts us so I'm under him, my hips high over my knees and my chest against the mattress. He pushes the white dress off me and enters me, resuming his relentless assault. I let him because I'm too tired to think about forming words. Part of me thinks I could pass out, exhausted, spent. Then something changes; my insides tighten, heat up again. I realize I'm not tired at all anymore. From this angle, he's too big for me, but he doesn't care: he takes, and takes, and takes, and I love it. I push my hips back to meet him and lift my chest, now on all fours. My hands reach back to part my cheeks, if only to feel him a little deeper. Drusk takes it as an invitation; his skilled finger presses me higher, probing my second entrance.

"So very tight, princess. One day, I'll take you there, too."

I scoff. "In your dreams."

He laughs like I'm silly to even pretend I'll deny him. "Oh, I will. And you'll like it. Just like you like this."

He's right, I do enjoy the ministration of his thumb in my ass. What is he doing to me?

"I'm going to come inside you, princess. I'm going to fill you."

It's a warning, not a question, and my only response is to move faster. He pants as his hips fly in and out of me, filling me deeper than ever. I feel my toes curl, and my core is on fire. Abandoning my back entrance, Drusk titillates me with his fingertips, harshly. Unbelievably, for the third time, I'm gone over the edge of the precipice. My release triggers his, and as promised, he thrusts in deep inside me one last time.

I fall forward, and Drusk joins me. We breathe in unison, lost to the world.

Then I start thinking.

I can't deny how much I like feeling him warm my insides. We fae don't reproduce like mortals; it may take a thousand days, a thousand years of him planting his seed inside me before I bear the fruits, but I still imagine my mate's child. A little girl taller than me by the time she can fly. A boy with his midnight eyes.

And the third born I will have to give to the sea.

I think I might cry if I let myself.

Instead, I get up.

"I'll call for a bath. We have to make ready to go north."

nineteen
march north
drusk

We agreed to bring two of my rangers along with Ina. I call for a meeting in front of the ruins of what used to be our base, and give my orders. I can tell the moment I see my sister's glare that there'll be hell to pay for my choices.

I left Erdun in charge of training, shadowed by Neb. With me, I'm taking Ive and Jules, because they're competent enough and they can both be spared from Whitecroft.

I'm not surprised when she follows me back home, silently fuming as she watches me pack.

I lost the right to feel protective over my sister sometime in the last decade, at least according to her. Once, the ten years between us were an ocean; now, she's sixty-three, and as capable as anyone I've ever trained. More so. I'm man enough to admit that I demand twice as much from her than from anyone else.

But she's still my sister. I remember the day she was born. Ma put her in my arms and told me she'd called her Nebula because I loved watching the void of the sky.

So when she demands to be included in our mission, I can only laugh. "You're kidding."

I don't say it as if it's a question. She must be kidding.

She plants herself right in front of me and glares. "You're the one who's kidding. You're taking Jules. Jules! I can wipe the floor with his face."

That's certainly true, and I take no small amount of pride that my sister can take a gentry twice her weight in single combat.

"Jules has been trained to follow a trail. That's valuable and relevant to the objective."

I don't add that we're going to the Court of Ichor, his home. I trust my sister, my walls have ears, and we've learned a thing or two about treachery of late.

These facts were accurate, though they weren't the reason why I'd accepted the boy and not her. Jules is disposable. Others would say otherwise; he's the son of the king of the Court of Ichor, and could succeed him. But he isn't my only sister.

"You're being sexist," she accuses me, gritting her teeth.

I have to consider her words, for a fleeting second. Then I decide she's wrong. If she'd been a little brother of mine, my answer would have been the same.

"Ive's coming, too," I point out. "So are Queen Ina, and the high queen." Nebula's eyes widen. I hadn't specified that in front of everyone. "And if another female with relevant skills volunteers, I won't turn her down. I'm not sexist. You're not qualified."

Being my sister will always disqualify her for any position that puts her in danger.

Neb crosses her arms on her chest. "What qualifications could Ive possibly have, except for an enormous—"

I lift a brow. "Who's sexist now?"

There was only one thing of Ive's that could be seen as enormous, and it wasn't her brain. The buxom half-aven had human roots that allowed for curves unusual for the folk. I'd noticed, though I wasn't interested. I'd also noticed that Ive wanted me to notice. I could have saved the girl some time and told her she wasn't going to go anywhere with me. No one was, except for Vlari. Not after today.

I've enjoyed many women of every rank, every shape and color. It's never been like that. With Vlari, sex wasn't an indulgence as much as a need. A raw need to possess and mark. She's an addiction.

"Ive is a healer," I remind Nebula. "We need her. What we need of you is to keep making those charms Ciera Bane had you sew. You know they saved lives during the attack, right?"

I'd seen it in action. Who knew whether Lucan would have survived without it? And without him, we wouldn't have been able to shield Whitecroft again. I tell her that. I can tell she doesn't believe a word of it; she knows I have an agenda.

"So, while you leave for enemy territory with two queens, to do god knows what, I'm to sew?" she seethes.

"Nebula, I don't have time for this. I was given orders: find a healer and a tracker. You're neither a healer nor a tracker. Stay and be useful, or stay and sulk. Either way, you're staying in Whitecroft."

She lifts her chin. "You're doing this on purpose. Outshining me. You always have."

The accusation stings, but I shrug it off. My pack is ready. "I'll be back before you know it. Save the insults for my return."

To my surprise, she lets me kiss her forehead despite her anger.

I walk to the rendezvous point at the edge of the marches. Vlari, Meda the pixie, Queen Ina, and Lucan are waiting, all dressed like me, in dark formfitting clothes easy to move in, and with a light pack at their sides. Vlari's wyrfox is standing at her feet, like a loyal hound.

We wait for the cover of night, as there are always scouts watching Whitecroft. We move more silently than human ears can detect, but they often have dogs trained to alert them of our movement.

The marches are northwest—a little detour, but they bleed into a wood that'll allow for some cover.

We walk in silence, as fast as we can. Vlari brings up the rear, her small legs forcing her to take two steps for every one of mine. I itch to carry her, but I strongly suspect she'd take offense. Instead, I slow down, and take her hand.

"You never told me how you got a familiar."

The wyr doesn't seem like a pet: it's as wild as they come, wary of us, reluctant to be here.

She shrugs. "I stopped him from becoming dullahan meat a while back. I'm not quite sure what to do with him, to be honest. He doesn't seem to enjoy touch, and when I try to talk to him, he ignores me. But he turns up every now and then anyway."

I lift my head to the top of the trees, where the animal is perched, following us and blending with the shadows.

I don't think I've ever heard of anyone getting a familiar while being so young. They attach themselves to kings and queens—a blessing of the wilderness.

"So long as it doesn't give away our position," I say.

To be fair to it, the wyr is even more silent than the rest of us.

We walk through the night, taking sinuous paths as far away from keeps, castles, and villages as we dare, while remaining on our way to the Court of Ichor.

We reach the path leading to Hardrock and I still, getting to a crouch, surveying the ground with a frown.

"What is it?"

I point to the flat, even, sanded path. "No force has marched in this—not since it last rained." That was weeks ago.

"They could still be in Sandovar," Vlari guesses, her eyes going south, toward the city harboring the Court of Ichor. It is but a shadow in the distance.

"It may work in our favor," Ina said. "The Ash traitor believed we intended to intercept the procession on its way to Hardrock. We could go to them, instead."

I frown. We are seven. Hardly enough to take an entire city.

"I could take us inside," Jules says.

"You're sure, boy?" Ina squints at him.

Jules has silver hair, and deep lines at the corners of his bloodred eyes. She looks younger than him—like his father, he has aged more than most of the folk do. But to her, he's just a boy. So are we, I suppose. Jules can't be much younger than Vlari or I.

He snorts. "You don't want to know how many times I snuck in and out of the keep. My father had ideas about whom I should spend my time with. Whereas I had a particular taste for dallying with peasant girls."

Ina shakes her head, though I can see she's amused.

"The humans might guard the castle more thoroughly than your father."

"You underestimate Father's fear of my fathering bastards. There were guards everywhere. But I may not have been the first in the court to have been fond of wandering off outside the gate. There's a path underneath the castle, leading outside. One has to know—and be able to perform magic—to find it." He's confident. "I can get you in. I don't know about getting us out once we're spotted, though."

"We could create a diversion." Meda tilts her head. "Set something on fire. Detonate a bomb. And while they rush to see what's happened…"

"Get the prisoners out." Ina nods, turning to Vlari.

She hasn't said a word yet. Feeling the weight of all our attention on her, she says, "It's risky."

She looks to me.

Me.

I shrug. "This mission is risky no matter what."

She nods. "Jules, you know Ichor best. Where would they keep the prisoners?"

"Under the castle, in the dungeons. The passage we'll take will come out close."

"So, we can get the folk out that way. Where could we start the diversion to draw the attention out?"

"The armory, or the watchtower."

He draws a map of his home in the sand, and as we plan, this madness almost seems to become doable.

Jules can lead Meda and Lucan to the watchtower, and blow it up with the gunpowder humans are sure to keep there. Lucan's fire will come in handy. Meanwhile Ive, Vlari, Ina, and I can lead the prisoners out. Ive will remain on the lookout to save our exit.

We walk south for the rest of the night.

We're on top of a hill when I take notice of the landscape before me—all around me. My fists tighten at my sides.

I haven't seen Tenebris from such a height since the beginning of the invasion. From here, I can see the damage. Entire forests have been razed, replaced by roads and villages. Smoke darkens the stars, polluting our land. The humans have started to reshape the unseelie realm into their ashen, barren desert.

I think about the folk. Those left outside of Whitecroft. The smart ones hid deep in the wilder woods, but if the humans have hunted the elves, I doubt there'll be anywhere safe.

My gaze darts north, past the Murkwood, to Denarhelm, the seelie lands. What do they make of our sorry state? I know they laugh at us. I laugh at us too, for once we were mighty and fond of our own importance, yet we've been vanquished by humans, who are led by a child. Denarhelm is supposed to be the weaker fae kingdom, as it's been centuries since they've stood together under one flag. Una, their last high queen, died without naming an heir. She had three children; Maeven, who already ruled the Court of Wind here in Tenebris, her twin Tharsen, cursed and cast out in the wilderness, and Fenemir, who declined the burden of the crown, content to rule the Court of Sunlight. No one insisted on her replacement—the local lords were happy to fashion thrones and call themselves kings.

And yet we, the strong, united nation, fell. I'd wager they're also worried. Once the humans have taken all that Tenebris has to give, they will no doubt cast their eyes north.

Reaching the seelie lands from the Alfheimr empire is all but impossible; the great canyons and waterfalls littering their western borders make for a better wall than any iron gates. At the first sign of an attack, they'd send archers to dispatch of the enemy army. The high ground gives them a considerable advantage.

But there's no such natural reinforcement between the borders of Tenebris and Denarhelm. The humans could march right up north if they so wish.

No doubt, the lords of Denarhelm have sent forces and spies south, watching and scheming in the shadows.

I suppose we'll find out when we get to them.

Come daylight, we agree to rest, though we're less than an hour away from Sandovar. This isn't the kind of mission to be undertaken while exhausted.

"It's market day," Jules says cheerfully. "There'll be plenty of people in the town square—we'll manage to get to the watchtower undetected."

We set camp in an abandoned goblin hole under a hill. It's far from comfortable and still smells of rotted leeches, but it's better than being exposed.

I offer to take the first watch, and Vlari's quick to say she'll take it with me.

I think I see Meda roll her eyes, but no one protests.

They settle deep in the burrow, and I sit at its entrance, my back against the wall of the cave. Vlari joins me, her legs thrown across mine.

Goblins are thieves and kidnappers, if given the opportunity; they like to dig deep walls with the smallest entrances that make them hard to find. We could have missed it if it weren't for the smell. A smell humans can't detect.

We still have to remain awake and vigilant—and watch for dogs. That doesn't mean we can't afford distractions.

I remove Vlari's shoes and proceed to massage her sore feet, my thumbs pushing deep.

Then she moans.

I didn't intend to go there today, in the wild, with five companions mere feet away from us, but that moan? I can't resist it.

I drag her hips till she's sitting right on top of me, and proceed to open her green leather trousers. I slide them past her hips, along her thighs, leaving them on her knees. My fingers skim to her opening. She's dripping wet, ready for me.

"You're going to have to be quiet," I whisper, curving my fingers inside her.

She muffles another moan, making me laugh. "Your grandmother is right next to us. Do you want her to hear you fuck me?"

"You're a rake."

"What does that make you, princess?" I ask her, opening my crotch to free my length. I rub it against her wetness, pushing it against her sensitive spots, teasing her and denying us both.

She tries to take charge, lifting her hips to impale herself on me, but I keep her waist down.

"Drusk…" She breathes hard.

"You're going to have to ask nicely if you want more."

She groans, and bares her teeth.

"What was that?" I ask. "Please, Rystan, make me cum?"

"Throw yourself off a cliff," she counters, struggling against me to get my hands off her hips.

I keep her there, and my length parts her folds at each shallow thrust, but never enters her. Payback for the way she rode me yesterday.

"That wasn't very nice. One might think you don't like me. Perhaps I should stop."

"I will murder you," she swears, her eyes flashing.

My feisty little princess.

"All you have to do is say please again. I quite liked when you begged yesterday. Is that so very hard?"

In truth, I have to be inside her, and soon. I feel myself tighten, harden, already close to losing it. She does drive me insane.

"Say it. Just one word. Say it, and I'll give us both what we need."

I half expect her to slap me.

"Please, dammit!" she practically yells.

I growl in approval and angle myself, before lodging my length deep inside her in one hard thrust that has her whimper.

We're too loud. We could be heard—by humans, and most definitely by our companions. I cover her mouth with my hand, drawing my hips out and then back inside her, back home, muffling her moans. Each thrust is deep and faster and faster. I need to get both of us there, fast, before we endanger everyone. Right then, I can't say I care if my fucking Vlari kills us all. Being inside her is more important. She rises and falls on me, taking me deeper, harder. I feel it when I hit her sweetest spot: her walls clasp around me, and she's struggling not to scream—so much there are tears in her blue eyes. So I withdraw and thrust at the exact same angle, pounding in. Vlari moves her face away from my hand and shoves it on my neck, right above my shoulder. And she bites me. Hard, deep.

Hard enough to draw blood and leave a mark.

I lose control. I throw her on her back, pushing her feet to her shoulders. Her hips are in the air. I bend to them and screw her like an animal. She started it. She bit me. It'll scar.

She's claimed me, and I'm claiming her right back with every thrust.

I want to bite her back, and the only piece of flesh anywhere near me is her ass. I'll bite that. Or perhaps somewhere else, somewhere everyone can see.

She tightens around me again, and drenches me in hotness. I hesitate, half tempted to withdraw and empty myself all over her so she smells like me, but I thrust one last time inside her.

Then I remove myself, and wrap my teeth around her left butt cheek.

I bite back, and I lick her, then bite again. I'm hard before I know it, and I do the only logical thing. I thrust back home.

By midday, I'm more or less sated. Enough to pull her trousers back up and gather her against my chest. She falls asleep in no time.

Twenty minutes later, Lucan joins us, holding his hands behind his head, with a straw of wheat in his mouth. He's the picture of casual indifference. "Maybe don't take guard duty together, yes?"

I shrug unapologetically. "No promises."

twenty
the ashes of ichor
vlari

I sleep well after our guard shift, nestled against Drusk's chest. When Meda wakes us up, she hands us slices of bread and dry meat. We check our supply and set off on our way in silence.

I don't think any of us take what we're about to do lightly. There's a high chance that some—if not all of us—will never get out of Sandovar.

"If anything goes wrong," Ina says out of nowhere, "you know what to do, right?"

Everyone else either nods or acquiesces, but I don't. A reminder that while they're soldiers and warriors, I haven't been raised like that, though Meda did teach me to fight.

I have to ask, "What are you supposed to do? Get out?"

There's a short silence, but Drusk breaks it. "Exactly. You abandon the plan and get out."

I think I've missed something. Something important. I press, "Drusk?"

Spill.

He sighs. "If we're compromised, our priority will be to get you out."

Me, not the rest of them.

"That's preposterous! I can take care of myself. We should—"

"I have a sister," Jules says, out of the blue. "Arva. Quite the clever thing—she's likely to succeed our father anyway. That savage queen has children and a husband. The rest of us…well, I like most of the people here, but we aren't relevant. You're the last in the line of Nyx. The moment you die, the usurper becomes the only person who is eligible to become high queen of Tenebris."

I hate every single word he's just said, all the more because they're true.

I cannot afford to die.

I lick my lips. "I'm going to give you one clear order. If we're in a position where we're in danger, you will get to safety. Every one of you will think of nothing but your own skin. I demand it as high queen. Understood?"

I'm met with silence. "I don't intend to die," I add. "But I'm a Void. I'm hard to take down. When I get out of there, I want you all to come out in one piece, too."

We've stopped walking altogether now.

Ina is the first to nod, slowly. "If the queen orders it."

They each give me their word—everyone but Drusk. I glare at him, demanding his submission.

He glares right back.

"I'll never swear that. Ever."

I want to throttle him, and kiss him all at once.

At long last, I give up. "Fine, be an idiot. We have to get going anyway."

We would have reached Sandovar already if we'd gone straight for the main path, but Jules wanted us to circle it to reach the doorway he used to take. It's hidden in a cave, in the surrounding woodland hills. Jules thinks another horny boy had it built; part of me wonders if it was meant for this—to get people out in case Sandovar was ever besieged or taken.

I'm reassured when we reach the cave: it's filthy, covered in dust and spiderwebs. No one has come here in a long time, which suggests the humans haven't found the path. And no wonder.

The doorway, if it could be considered as such, has no handle, nothing marking it as special. It looks like it's part of the cave. Jules calls to earth magic and a hole opens up, giving us access to a path just as dirty as the cave. While there are footsteps, they're covered by layers of dust. No one has used it the last ten years, at least.

"I suppose the boy isn't entirely useless," Meda remarks to Ina.

I'm not surprised these two get along.

They walk in first with Ive, then Drusk and I follow. Jules brings up the rear, and locks the door behind us with a wave of his hand.

"Was it many peasant women you used to visit, or one in particular?" Drusk asks the ranger.

Jules shrugs. "One at a time, many overall. I never saw the appeal of my fellow gentry. They either wanted me as a gateway to my father, or because they wanted pureblood babies—there are few enough of us that most lines are related, these days. And some gentry would rather bed a cousin than take a common fae—or a human."

"Yet your mother was human, was she not?"

"Yes, and my father's mother was, too. My father has no distaste for mortals, though he considers them inferior in many ways. Lower born, however?" Jules winced. "He swore if I ever fathered a half-sprite, he'd kill it, and the mother too."

I grit my teeth. It's not the first time I've heard such a sentiment, but it always infuriates me. I'm a halfling. So is Drusk. What do the lords of the lower courts truly think of us? No wonder Ash was so quick to betray us.

"Your father is a swine," Ina said, turning to Jules. "If he ever says such a thing in front of me, I'll open him up from one end to the next. The gentry are inbred, losing all magic because of that sort of stupidity."

"Can I watch?" Jules asks cheerfully.

Our chatter gets more subdued as we approach the city—I can hear activity above us. Footsteps and talks.

Jules grows quieter, and jumpier. At one intersection, he stops us. "Hang on a minute. Something's wrong."

I turn to him, alert.

"We're close to the surface. We should be hearing things—people outside, shopkeepers, soldiers marching—even if it weren't market day. It's too quiet."

He tiptoes to the path on our right that looks a lot dirtier than the one we've taken. "We should be able to peek into town from here."

We follow him, careful not to make a single noise. Soon, the path ends with another blocked exit—he magics it open, and light floods our tunnel, bathing us in warmth.

We're at a window inside the outer walls surrounding the city, with a view to what looks like the town center, right in front of the stronghold.

There's something blocking the path. It's dark, charred black. At first, I don't understand what I see. Art, perhaps? If one can call it that. I never understood human tastes.

"By the gods," Ina whispers.

I hear Ive retch behind us. I can only stare once I realize.

The charred statues at the gates aren't a mortal's poor opinion of art. They're people. Folk. Shy folk, burned to a crisp, and displayed right here.

They were all thrown together in chains, and then the humans had them set on fire days ago. It can't have been recent, otherwise there would be smoke, and a stronger smell.

This was left as a message. A message for us.

For me.

I lose it.

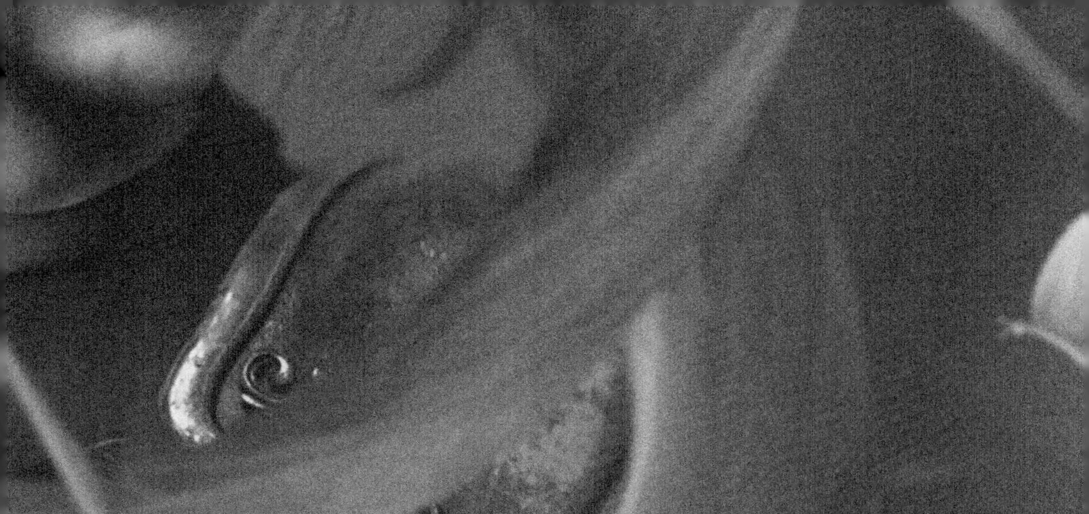

twenty-one
darker woods
drusk

I can tell what Vlari is about to do less than a second before she moves to leap out the window, rush to the middle of Sandovar, and kill everyone in sight. Just in time to catch her hands and pull her back.

She kicks, swears, and throws punches, screaming at me to let her go. I cover her mouth, and drag her back through the tunnels.

This was exactly what the humans had intended, and I can't give them the satisfaction. I can't risk losing her, either. So I drag her kicking and screaming, taking each hit, keeping her as silent as I can until we're out.

I only let go when Jules closes the path behind us.

She punches me. I let her have the first hit, but I counter the second. "Not even you can take thousands of humans at once, Vlari. One would get to you. An arrow. A lucky dagger. Are you selfish enough to condemn your kingdom?"

She yells and launches at me. I pull my sword, and block her with the blunt side. I know this is about releasing her anger more than hurting me, or I'd be dead by now.

"We have to go. She was too loud," Jules urges us.

I nod. "After you."

He starts to run, and the rest of our company follows him. Vlari is still glaring at me, bloodlust brightening her gaze. "Are you done, or am I going to have to throw you over my shoulder?"

I treat her like a child to make her realize she's acting like one.

"They deserve to pay. They deserve to burn."

I nod. "Certainly. And to see to that, we'd better be alive."

She's shaking with rage, but I see her claws retract.

"Come on. Jules was right, we were probably heard."

We follow after the others, prioritizing speed over silence this time. They find us anyway.

When I hear the dogs barking as they hunt us, I grab Vlari and place her over my shoulder as I promised I would. She's the slowest among us.

"Wait!" I only have time to scream before the ground collapses beneath our feet, and the air crackles, propelling us with a terrible force. My head hits the ground so hard I feel dizzy, and I can taste blood in my mouth. All around me, there's nothing but chaos. I have to blink several times before I understand the issue isn't my vision. We're engulfed in a storm of dust.

A bomb. One of us stepped on it. I've heard about them, of course, but it's the first time I've ever experienced one.

"Ive?" I can barely hear a word I'm saying. I must have ruptured an eardrum, or hit my head too hard. "Ina, Jules, Lucan?" I call everyone one by one, hoping their hearing's better than mine at the moment. "Scatter. You go back to Whitecroft. We're making a detour. Meda? With us."

Through the dust, I spot the pixie. She nods, understanding me, and follows after.

It doesn't matter whether the landmine had been planted specifically for us or if it's just coincidental we set it off; everyone a hundred miles off has heard it, and knows our location. I have to hope that, if the others haven't heard me, they're smart enough to get the hell out of here and return to Whitecroft.

That is, assuming they're still alive. I don't let myself think about it.

The first part of our mission was a phenomenal failure, but it doesn't mean that we have to give up on the second. Especially now that we know what the mortals are capable of.

We're veering to the north when the first arrow flies past me. Then, there's another, and another after that. They're shooting blind, in the dark, but it's a volley; many come close. I hear a grunt, but I can't stop.

"Meda." Vlari's alarm makes me turn.

Her grandmother's some paces to our left and a footlong arrow sticks out of her shoulder.

I dart to her side, and pull her on my shoulder, too.

Running at full speed while carrying two pixies, I tire faster than I would like. When the arrows stop for a moment, I take cover behind a tree, and kneel on the ground.

"Now isn't the time for a break, boy," the pixie barks at me, before groaning.

Vlari hops off me and moves to her grandmother, pulling the arrow out without any warning. She rips some of her undershirt off and ties it around Meda's shoulder while I do, indeed, rest. And calm down.

It takes a few breaths to feel in touch with my magic. Myst gathers around us, faster than I remember it ever coming to me.

"Your hands," I ask, removing my gloves to touch them skin to skin.

Vlari and Meda take my offered palms, and I pull them along with me, leading my Myst as far north as I've ever gone, then farther still, as deep inside the Murkwood as any fae can venture.

I only let go when I feel my magic straining, taxing me too much. The Myst is a dangerous tool, but an endless stream of clueless tutors had shown me how to harness and control it at

Whitecroft. The first lesson was to never push past my limits. Unless I want it to kill me.

We're all out of breath, tense, and filled with ire.

But we're safe, for now.

We landed in a glade, so deep inside the Murkwood we could be on seelie territory—or at the borders.

"These hills," Meda says, with a wince, waving to the elevations in the distance. "I know them." She's struggling more than she should be after one shot. Getting hit by an arrow is never pleasant, but there's something else going on.

The moment I start to suspect it, the stench of poison hits my nostrils. The arrow was iron tipped, and laced with something.

"Her wound," I say.

Vlari rips Meda's sleeve off, and we can see dark, almost-black blood ooze out of the cut, drenching the makeshift bandage.

Meda swears. "Salt and bane."

Vlari's eyes widen. "How will it affect you?"

Poisons would only weaken me or her for a time, but pixies are not gentry folk.

"Depends on how much they used. Help me up."

The last thing she should be doing is getting up. "You need to rest."

"What I need," Meda replies, getting to her feet, "is to reach those hills. They mark the start of the Darker Woods, which belongs to the Court of Sunlight."

Seelie land.

Vlari and I glance at each other.

"Do you think they'll help you?"

"I know they will. Let's go. Before something worse than humans catches our scent."

twenty-two

fair folk

vlari

I grin as my boots hit the mossy ground.

Drusk is quick to catch it. "You know, most people would be trembling at the idea of approaching the seelie folk when they hate our guts. Not to mention that we're in the land of the wild folk."

"Most people aren't me."

When I ran through the Murkwood last, I was anxious. Ten years ago. A few weeks ago, to me. The passage of time is written over the forest; there's no denying that it's changed in a decade. I feel fewer creatures roaming around us. They've retreated north to the deepest part of the woods, in seelie land, away from the human settlements.

The human presence has affected the entirety of Tenebris, not just the courts.

The thing that changed most in all this time is me. I don't fear anything here. Not the fachan, not the headless huntsmen, not the nightmares. Not because the wild folk aren't terrifying, ferocious, and bloodthirsty. There is no doubt that each and every one of them would delight in claiming a chunk of flesh from a high court urchin. But the last time I came here, I was another person. Vlari the small. Vlari the inconsequential. Vlari the shadow cursed, under Morgana's poisonous spells.

That girl no longer exists.

I don't know how, given the fact that I never noticed him until now, but the wyrfox rubs his fur against my leg, demanding my attention. I rub his mist-covered head. "That's right, boy. It's where we met."

Drusk hands me one of his knives. "Here? What were you doing in the Murkwood?"

I don't think there will be any need for it, but I greedily pocket the blade and wink at him. "I'll tell you if you're good."

"I'm never that. You'll tell me anyway."

He may have a point.

If there was ever a path through these woods, it has long been overrun by crooked branches, rocks, and mushrooms. The shy folk of the woods know how to walk without disrupting nature—or leaving tracks for a hunter to follow.

Reaching for the hills Meda bid us to get to, we head farther north, past the mirror lake that was frozen long ago and remains that way through all seasons, until finally, we see it in the distance. The Old Keep.

"Part of me wishes I had the skills to compose a song," I sigh. "Or sketch a pretty picture."

Unsurprisingly, Drusk laughs at me. "When the gods were distributing abilities, they took a good look at you and decided your art was painting the land red with the blood of your enemies instead."

I smile. I'm not sure he meant it as a compliment, but I choose to take it that way.

"That, and driving me insane."

Not long after, I bristle, my senses alerting me to the presence of something hostile. "Feels like we're going the right way."

Drusk only nods, walking closer to me. I see his eyes take in our surroundings, leaving nothing unnoticed. He and I are so different. He's controlled, careful. He's borderline seelie at heart. I grimace in distaste at that notion.

In the old world, the fae were ruled by one unseelie and one seelie monarch, married to keep the kingdom united. People could choose their allegiances at any time, standing with one court or another depending on their nature. I've even read about those who chose one side, and then the next a century after, only to come back to their first allegiance later on. It sounds messy. I can't say whether our solution is any better, though. People born in Tenebris are unseelie and those of Denarhelm are seelie, by default, regardless of their nature. Some eventually travel away from their native home, but it's rare.

I undoubtedly belong to the unseelie court. I'm fine with plans that are more of a vague outline, happy to take care of issues when they arise. There's nothing wrong with a little chaos. My amusement takes precedence over many other concerns—such as my survival, sometimes. I may very well die, but I sure will give the best jibe before I go. Drusk thinks a lot farther ahead than I do.

I glance at him, musing about how his nature and mine fit. He might just keep me alive, for one.

We're not unlike my mother and father were, I realize. Ciera is—was—all wants and needs, quick to dismiss anything that she didn't like the sound of; Nero considers his duties, the greater good. Thoughts of my father snuff out whatever joy I regained. My father, whose daughter killed his bondmate. He hates me now, no doubt. I haven't seen him since we buried Ciera.

I force myself to return to my former train of thoughts. Seelie, unseelie. I wonder if all mates are shaped that way, similar enough to fit, different enough to complete each other.

"What?" Drusk asks, without watching me.

He must have felt me looking at him.

I smirk, thinking about his reaction if I give him a real answer. If I told him what I've realized: that he was made for me. Or, I suppose, I was made for him, technically. I'm the younger one.

He likes me. He even wants me. It may confuse him, given that I'm not much to look at, too short to be graceful, too prickly to be pleasant, and unlike the rest of the ladies of the court, not fawning all over his delicious muscles. I would, but his ego doesn't need it. But for all the likes and wants, Drusk is nowhere near accepting that fate has tied his life to mine yet.

I came to that conclusion by myself, and he should have the chance to guess it too.

"Nothing. I was just wondering if you were trying to signal your presence, or if you're just that bad at stealth. Is this what you're teaching the folk in your classes?"

He rolls his eyes, exasperated with me. "Not all of us can be three feet tall, pixie."

I walked into that dig. "Five, I'll have you know."

By midnight, I hate to admit it, but I start to tire. Endurance has never been my strength, and I've kept up with Drusk's pace for miles—one of his strides is about three of mine. I don't complain, though. Meda's a lot worse off than I am.

Just as I open my mouth to suggest taking a break, Drusk bends down to my side and wraps his arm around me. Almost automatically, I leap, and he catches me, to perch me on his shoulder. Considering his hulking build, I fit. The protective padding of his coat even makes it comfortable.

I choose to be offended nonetheless. "I'm not that slow. You should take Meda."

"I'll pass," she shouts without turning back.

Now that he's holding me, though, I can tell he was slowing down for my benefit before. We're moving at a much faster pace, gliding through the forest almost as fast as a cloaked shade.

Damn him.

"Sure." Sarcasm drips from his words. "I figured you'd want us to get to the border before next year, though."

I'm mad, but not mad enough to give up my seat, so I just zap him with a burst of Void, fast enough to avoid any damage, but getting drained can't be pleasant either way.

He says nothing to indicate he felt anything at all, not even a grunt. I'm considering doing it again, but I smell Drusk's retaliation before I feel it, a distinct stench hitting my nostrils. Then my neck's suddenly uncomfortably warm. I tap at the back of it, putting out a flame.

My eyes take in our surroundings with one glance, but we're still entirely too alone, without so much as a rabbit in sight.

When it hits me, my jaw drops. "My hair. You burned my hair!"

I feel him shrug under me. "What's left of it."

"Do you remember what happened to the last person who did something to my hair?"

"If you can't handle the consequences, may I suggest you refrain from testing me?"

I may murder him. Gleefully. The only person allowed to attack my hair is me.

I kick the back of my heel against his chest, and try to jump back on the ground, but he just laughs it off, keeping me in place with one arm around my thighs.

"Calm down."

As though that phrase has ever worked on any woman. "I'm going to—"

"Vlari." His tone has changed. Gone is all amusement; I catch a layer of alarm underneath.

I stop wiggling and look around.

We've reached a valley. I can't be sure, but given the direction we've been going, I think we may be at the very edge of unseelie territory. On the right side stands the last of the Shadow Peaks, and on the left, the Dread Hills, at the edge of Darker Woods.

In the darkness, I can't see much ahead, but we could finally be on seelie land.

"Do you see anything?" My voice has fallen to a whisper.

"I don't need to. They're in the darkness."

Of course. I try not to feel too jealous at the fact that his power allows him to sense anything hiding in darkness.

Out loud, I call, "Come out! We've come for a chat, not a stabbing."

Meda, who no doubt had a much better speech ready, sighs, but my words were efficient enough: I see shapes approach from either side of the woods, surrounding us.

The first creature I can distinguish is a hag, older than anything I've seen, if one is to judge by the thousands of folds around her beady, pearly white eyes. Her teeth are filed into points marred by fresh blood, and she wears nothing, other than her veil of thin silver-white hair. Her clawed feet support scaled legs so thin I don't know how she stands upright.

"Truly, no chance for a little stabbing?" she croaks, her grin terrifying.

"It has been long since we've tasted gentry blood," says a voice full of longing, coming from the other side.

I turn to see a fachan, fixing me with a stare.

"Enough, Gridi," Meda chides. "It's my grandchild you're threatening."

The hag lifts a hand, and a sphere of light bursts out of it. She squints, and then gasps. "Well, my old bones! If it isn't the great Meda. The king will have a thing or two to say about you showing your face here, after everything you did."

Meda did something to the king of the Court of Sunlight? This doesn't sound good. At all.

"You know he'll want to see me." She narrows her eyes. "Without delay."

The hag snorts. "That he will."

twenty-three
salt and iron
nebula

I'm stitching yet another damnable charm to another identical doublet when the high-pitched horn of an alarm resounds through Whitecroft.

I abandon my work and leap to my feet, rushing to the closest window. There's nothing wrong anywhere. The earth folk are redoing the foundations of the halls. For now, we're stuck in Whitecroft Hall, but we're rebuilding six of the seven halls.

"Here!" Poera calls from the other side of the room. She went to a window, but it faces west.

Ronda and I join her, and I curse.

There's an army approaching from the west, led by salamanders. They're coming at us through the Arm of Sea. They know about the weakness under our shield caused by the water.

I don't hesitate, putting on one of the doublets I was working on over my silk shirt and rushing downstairs.

I have to be useful. I know how to fight. Whatever my brother says, I can fight for my people just as well as he.

I reach the entry hall, presided over by a lord I recognize as the old queen's consort, Alven Oberon. He gives orders. Long-range archers to the upper floor; every builder to reinforce the gates; those who can't fight, inside; those who can't do magic, outside with steel and bows; those who can, at the gates.

I take a sword, a bow, a quiver of arrows, and head out, closing my doublet.

I can do this. I can do this. I have to do this.

I follow a company of guards and soldiers to the waterside, and stand guard.

I wait. For what seems like an endless amount of time, I wait. They must have been an hour away when I saw them upstairs, but we have to be here, ready to push them back the moment they appear.

So we wait.

I need to pee. This doesn't seem like the sort of time when bodily functions would constrain me, but here it is. I rush back to the castle and find an empty corner where I can relieve myself, before returning to my position.

By the time I return, the first humans have reached us.

They take to the river, swimming deep under the shield. I extend my bow, aiming for the sea. Archery isn't my specialty, but I'm good enough for this. Good enough for picking off humans.

The first few die before they can hope to reach the shores, but there's so many of them. So many.

We kill hundreds, thousands. Some do make it to the riverbank, and now the first line of fae against us must abandon their bows for their swords. More humans spill into our territory. Their bodies fall at our feet. We have to step on them. It's awkward. The smell of blood clogs the air, making me feel sick. I'm getting tired and my arm aches, but I never stop slicing whatever my blade can reach: throats, shins, the weakness in their armor between their shoulders and their necks. Anything I can do to hurt. To kill.

I will protect my home.

And then, the first salamanders reach us, and there is fire.

Vlari

I DON'T HAVE to ask where these woods got their name. There are so many trees, all clustered together, that the abundant foliage covers the sky—we can't even see the light of the moon. These woods must be dark even during the day.

Within less than an hour, we've reached the head of a fortified stronghold. The woods mustn't be very extensive. I suppose "Darker Grove" doesn't sound quite as dramatic.

Everything about the seelie castle is alien, different, other, and yet, so very fae in nature.

At the gate, the two knights wear the exact same uniform, polished to perfection. They're even the same height. Both are dark-haired. I wouldn't be surprised if they were twins.

We're admitted inside, and everywhere, there's symmetry, perfection. The white stones of the path are polished, square, smooth. In the distance, I hear a chant similar to our winter songs, but peaceful, slow, tender, caring.

I want to vomit.

I've only taken a few steps inside their world and already, I'm bored.

The rose-stone castle is bathed with light inside—its high walls boast hundreds of humongous windows. Along the walls, there are statues and paintings of mournful maidens and still lifes of flowers.

"Do they ever have fun?" I wonder, whispering to Drusk.

He chides me with a look, but I see him wince as he takes in the gigantic painting of an apple. A boring apple.

We're led to a vast chamber where dozens of gentry are gathered around a table drinking wine as musicians play the most lifeless song of all time.

I guess I have my answer. Fun isn't their thing.

"My king. Apologies for the interruption." The hag bows deep in front of the last man I would have guessed was king, among those gathered here.

It's a boy with red hair and an easy smile that reaches the corners of his moss-green eyes. "What do we have here?" He sends Meda a wicked grin that makes me think that he, at least, does know exactly how to have fun.

His gaze takes us all in, but soon returns to Meda.

He gets up, leaving his companions without so much as a glance. He takes his goblet of wine with him, though.

"Come on, old friend. Let's get you attended to."

Although Meda stood tall and proud, never giving off that she was in any way injured throughout our walk, one glance and that man knew there was something wrong with her.

She gestures for us to follow, before setting off after him.

After walking through many corridors and up several flights of stairs, we reach what can only be the royal chamber—a vast room, larger than the entire throne hall of Whitecroft—filled with plush velvet-covered chairs and cushions, and a bed large enough for ten people.

I am guessing that it occasionally fits as many, from the king's vibe.

"Come, old friend. Sit, sit. I'll get supplies."

He disappears into a side chamber.

Meda drops on the sofa he indicates, and removes her cloak, shirt, and chemise, till she stands topless.

I stare at her. "You know him well, then?"

Meda shrugs. "You never asked about my life before I came to you," she points out.

She's right. I've always been too intimidated by her to do anything but obey her—or fight her when she demanded it. Meda wasn't an easy person to get close to. For me, in any case. She got along with my mother.

"I was the captain of Titus's guard."

My jaw drops.

"That's right!" the king chirps, returning with his hands full. "And one of my closest friends, too. Which is why when you promised to return, I believed you."

While his tone remains light, the accusation is unmistakable.

Meda smiles up at him. "And I'm here, aren't I?"

King Titus laughs, throwing the mess of things he's fetched on the rest of the sofa. Clean cloth, flasks, gauze, needles. He proceeds to unwrap Meda's wound. I wince along with Titus when I see its state. It's clearly infected. The skin along the edges of the cut is raised and greenish, the blood pitch black.

I want nothing more than to take a step back. Titus leans in and licks it.

"Just salt and iron. You've survived worse."

He cleans the wound carefully, and when he's done, places his hand over it. I can feel magic pulse through.

"I can probably speed that up, now that it's clean," I offer.

I couldn't think of healing her while she had poison inside her. Closing off the wound over salt and iron would result in pain for the rest of her days, and maybe kill her in the end.

The king directs his attention to me for the first time.

"You're the granddaughter, then?" he guesses.

I nod, joining them. I place my fingertips at the edge of Meda's collarbone and transfer some of my energy to her. I'm tired, but I haven't tapped into my magic at all recently. I barely feel the strain. The wound closes up in front of our eyes.

"Fascinating. You're a Void, are you not?"

I nod, tenser than I'd like.

"I've read many books on Voids. We haven't had one for a while—they're rarer than most powers. I think the last student we saw came to us some fifty years ago."

I'm speechless.

Drusk says it for me. "You had a Void fifty years ago? We haven't seen one since Nyx in Tenebris."

Titus laughs. "Unlikely."

I frown, confused.

"You may not have had a gentry, noble-born Void who can be recognized by anyone of importance in centuries. That doesn't mean that a random sprite may not have possessed such a power, without having the means to recognize it. And it's also possible that some are fully aware of their ability, and choose to conceal it. Who's to accuse them of murder if no one knows they can kill with a touch?"

I can't deny the truth of his words, yet I want to argue.

"Though clearly, you're rather powerful. This little exchange would have cost the last Void I knew all her strength." I can't tell whether he's honest, or wants to make me feel better.

"Do you have Mysts?" I ask.

He tilts his head. "Far fewer. They're native to your parts, the children of the Court of Mist."

Drusk and I exchange a glance.

His power is native to my court?

"I see you don't know your history. Your kind, south of the border, has never been fond of recording what you consider boring."

Touché.

"Some five or six thousand years ago, Denarhelm extended to the southwest, but a few unseelie folk had a mind to take it. To do so, they called to a sacrificial magic that let them blend in with darkness. Some of them were fire users, others air mages. They abandoned their link to the element in exchange for control over darkness. Regardless of how many battles we won, they'd destroy us in the night. We had no choice but to flee. These unseelie took the Court of Mist. Their leader fathered the line of Oberon, but all who followed him were Myst. As the power wasn't natural, as such, it was only rarely given to their descendants."

In just a few minutes, this playful king had turned everything I knew on its head.

I think I could stay here and hear him talk for years and not realize any time had passed.

Before I let that happen, I straighten.

"King Titus, with your leave, I humbly request your assistance. I only have to listen for a moment to realize your people and I would benefit from standing together. Denarhelm and Tenebris, we have a savage, bloody history that links us all. But we're falling, and you still stand. Help us fight the invasion, and we'll build a future between the two realms of the folk."

The king watches me, and his green eyes aren't playful or kind at all. They're probing, assessing, weighing.

He smiles without an ounce of kindness. "Oh, I see it. The rage, the darkness. The madness. I see it buried within your pretty eyes." He turns to Meda. "Your granddaughter truly is an Evergreen, is she not? Beautiful, hard, and filled with bloodlust."

I'm taken aback when he steps in and appears right in front of me. Drusk is on me immediately, but I lift one hand to hold him back.

Titus's eyes aren't green at all at this moment.

They're amethyst. Violet. Just like Morgana's. Just like my hair.

I know my history better than most after reading Nyx's journal. My ancestor was the daughter of Maeve, child of Queen Una—the last high seelie queen. Maeve had a twin and a little brother. I knew her line hadn't ended, but I'd had no clue who were the descendants. We know little of the seelie courts.

There he is. My cousin, though the thousands of years separating us ensure there's little to no blood in common between us. Yet we're the same. One thing on the surface. Something else entirely underneath.

twenty-four
the last stand
vlari

We ride.

Our horses are nothing like the indolent mares we used to keep in my youth. We were given the fastest horses bred by the kings of seelie. They practically fly. My legs and back hurt, as I don't think I've ever used the kinds of muscles it takes to gallop this fast for hours on end, but I urge the horses farther still, ignoring the pain. I'm not about to delay our arrival.

We take the fastest road to Whitecroft, uncaring about any human spotting us. They'd never catch up with us if they tried. If they dared. Something tells me they won't.

Drusk grins back at me, the wind teasing his messy hair. The beautiful jerk is enjoying this torture—unlike me, he's used to riding faster horses. I have to grin back. I'm glad one of us is having fun at least.

It takes half a day for us to reach Whitecroft, with only one break so the horses could drink and rest. When we first see the dome of light in the distance, my heart leaps in my chest. We made it. Everything is going to be just fine. I let myself believe the three days we spent away have changed nothing. But whatever lie I tell myself dies as we approach.

Far to the east, on the other side of our haven, I see them. Thousands upon thousands of vermin dressed in black and gold, holding a mockery of the flag of Tenebris: the signet of a golden stag on an amethyst backdrop. Only their stag is young and pretty, while ours has longer horns wet with blood.

They're trying to take everything from this land, down to its very soul.

Our enemies are laying siege to Whitecroft, entering through the river. The opening doesn't allow for the full bulk of their army to get in at once, thank heavens, but they're still getting in. I can't see inside the walls, our shield preventing me from distinguishing anything, but I don't doubt that our people are in trouble.

I see the red flames of the Court of Ash mingling with the mortals. We should have guessed they'd shown them the one weakness in our defenses.

"Ash will pay for this. If it's the last thing I do, I'll hunt down every salamander and destroy their history."

Drusk has the gall to laugh at me. "Every one? The children, and the poor soldiers who had a choice between following orders or dying, too?"

I glare at him. He should know that sometimes, I can do without a taste of reality. Wrath is far more palatable. "They may kneel and beg. But the crown of Ash is mine to destroy today."

To that, Drusk finds no objection.

"Such bloodlust, cousin," Titus drawls, catching up to us. "You'll have to learn to share. We wouldn't want my riders to have nothing to play with, after all."

Drusk rolls his eyes. I have the distinct impression he dislikes Titus. I don't—and not only because he gave us an army. He's a mirror. The reflection of what I may become, if I live to see as many centuries as he. Powerful, cold, and ruthless? Yes. But also clever, jovial, and softer among my inner circle. He's overcome the blood of the monster within, and so can I.

Although he is a little too dramatic for my taste. He made me sweat bullets yesterday.

"Oh, I see it. The rage, the darkness. The madness. I see it buried within your pretty eyes." He turns to Meda. "Your granddaughter truly is an Evergreen, is she not? Beautiful, hard, and filled with bloodlust."

He's discerned everything I try to hide about me. He knows who I am inside. The person who wants to keep taking, and taking, and taking lives. The monster.

"What benefit would there be for my people in helping you?"

My jaw ticks. "If humans settle in Tenebris, they'll look north next. To you."

"And if you're settled in Tenebris, you may look north, too."

"Not if we were allies."

He laughs. "Let's be honest, alliances last as long as whims to your kind. I'll need considerably more than that. I'll need blood."

"You'll have it." I don't hesitate. "Aid us, and I'll swear that as long as my line lives, the unseelie kingdom will come to the aid of the seelie land when they need it."

Here I am again, swearing things for my children, and my children's children.

But at least this vow, I comfortably stand by.

The king steps back. "Mmmh."

He returns to Meda's side. "I see why you had to stay. It can't have been easy to whip this one into shape. She's strong-willed."

My grandmother sighs. "And then some. I didn't do half bad, I reckon."

That's almost a compliment.

We may all die after all.

"Very well, child of darkness. You'll bleed and swear, and we'll march south with you in the morning."

Meda blinks. "You think you could call the forces so fast? It'd take a month for the riders to gather and join us."

Titus winks. "I had them come ten years ago. It took your little queen long enough to swallow her pride and come."

I am entirely speechless.

He had an army on standby, ready to march to us?

And more importantly, would he have ever gone south if I hadn't come?

I know the answer to that.

No, he wouldn't have. He would have let us burn.

The seelie aren't unlike us at all, it seems.

"To be fair," I say, "I was asleep for the last decade."

Come to think of it, I understand exactly why Drusk can't stand him.

"There'll be plenty of slaughter for all of us." I point to the path past the marches. "If we follow this road, we'll get to the other side of the river. There's a stone bridge to get us where we need to go. Some of us could cut off their exit."

"Unless they blow the bridge," Drusk replies. "I say we face them head-on. Most of them are human soldiers, on foot."

I turn to Titus, soliciting his input. His eyes flash purple as he focuses on the battle ahead. "That tent," he says, tilting his shield. "How do we reach it?"

I saw no tent at all, focused as I was on the swarming soldiers at my gates. I follow his gaze, looking past the army, far in the distance.

"On the hill, in the woods," he says.

I finally find it: a large cloth tent, dark brown, almost indistinguishable from the trees of the Silent Orchard. It's perfectly positioned to have a clear view of the entire valley where Whitecroft has been built.

"Violet." I say her name softly, like a spell or a promise, and my teeth flash.

I didn't expect her to show. In the last ten years, all we learned of her suggests that she's remained hidden behind the walls of the Shadow Peaks, and let mortals fight her battles. But she's here, today, because she believes she is winning. That she'll finally take us down.

"If we want to cut off the head of the snake, that's where we need to go."

I nod. "And fast. Before she flees." I have no doubt that the moment she sees the seelie forces, she'll rush back to her hole. "We can reach it from the southern river flank."

"I'll lead most of my men directly to the river. You can take the path to the bridge—whether it's destroyed or not matters little. Once you're at the bridge, my men can cross it to cut off the army if they're able. And you can reach the hill on foot, so she doesn't see you coming."

I bite my lip. If I'm to walk from the bridge to the tent, I may arrive too late. Violet would spot Titus and flee.

"You'll need to wait it out. Give me time to get there before you descend on Whitecroft. If she retreats to the Wicked Court, she'll be as shielded as we were in Whitecroft. There'll be no reaching her there."

And I need to reach her. There can be no peace while there are two queens in Tenebris. The Court of Ash has proven that. If they disagree with one monarch, the minor lords could defect to the other until the end of time.

Drusk glowers. "Every moment we delay our attack is a moment the folk of Whitecroft are suffering. We have to get down there right now."

These are the words of a soft heart, a beautiful soul.

Not the words of a ruler.

Titus ignores him entirely. "We'll give you till sundown." He tilts his head, and wordlessly, one of his commanders moves his horse right behind mine. "Use the time well."

I nod, and turn to Drusk. He looks beyond mad, understandably. I don't ask him to follow me. He won't. His place is right here, with those who'll help the folk. He needs to get to his sister, his parents.

I have no one to save.
I have everyone to save.
I bring my fingertips to my lips and blow him a kiss.
"Stay safe," he tells me.
"Always."
Then, I ride at the head of a hundred knights.

twenty-five
tastes of power
vlari

I should have taken exercise a lot more seriously.

After we reached the bridge—thankfully not blown up yet—I took Samel, the commander, along with two knights he picked with me, and I struggle to keep up with the three of them. Though my limbs ache, my lungs burn, and my throat tightens at each breath, I push forward.

At sundown, Violet may flee. To truly end this war, we have to get there before. Red and gold already strike the horizon in the distance.

I push harder and harder, half wishing I could call to Drusk's power, but firstly, I'm not trying to reach him for once. I don't think I could make use of his power when he isn't in the vicinity. And mostly, I know I'll have to save all of my energy for facing my aunt. Physically, I'm not at my strongest. I can't afford for my powers to be depleted, too.

We reach the bottom of the hill in time. To my relief, Samel stops, concealed behind a tree rather than racing forward and forcing us to attack before I recover.

Silent as shadow, I join him, and drop on the floor, spent. I breathe in and out, forcing myself to slow it down in order to control the rhythm of my heart.

Without a word, the commander hands me a flask. I frown at him; I have water with me. I'm waiting before drinking so I don't puke it up. He takes it back, pressing it against his lips and taking a long swallow to show me it's safe. Reluctant to offend my new allies by declining some custom I don't know about, I do take it, and drink.

The moment the clear liquid crosses my lips, I feel all pain, all exhaustion, all heaviness lift and dissipate. I've never been more awake, more vibrant.

I blink. "What's that?" I murmur.

Samel tosses the flask to his knights. "A dangerous tool. Highly addictive, and harmful in greater doses. It's ambrosia. A recipe that belonged to the ancient gods. We only use it when in dire need. It tricks your mind into believing you're well. You aren't. It'll only work for a time."

I nod, understanding the peril in such a tool. But today, I don't care about the repercussions. All I ask is for that sip to fool me for the next hour.

Samel peeks behind the trunk of our tree. "I sense the presence of several. And considerable power."

I nod. It's hard to miss.

I've only been in Violet's company once, and she was flanked by two gods back then. I don't know what her presence feels like. Yet, the aura I sense is somewhat familiar. And as Samel said, powerful.

"There'll be guards," I say. "I'll try to slip by them to get to her." The sooner I kill her, the sooner this will all be over. "Can you handle them?"

"I suppose that remains to be seen." The commander is matter-of-fact. He may die and he doesn't seem to care. Seelie might as well be another species, after all.

"Let's see, then."

To my relief, we don't race up the hill. We saunter, to draw the guards to us. And they come at us. A dozen humans rushing out of the immense tent. Lords, I'd guess, from their rich clothes and great swords. The three seelie knights raise their swords, ready for the onslaught. Leaving my sword at my side, I raise both arms instead. All men stop, then scream, then drop at my feet.

Samel lowers his arms. "Why, exactly, aren't you in the battlefield at the moment?"

I shrug. "A few of them, right in front of me, is easy. I can't engulf an entire army at once."

Humans are too weak to feed the Void, but sucking on them didn't cost me any energy either. And a good thing too: I know this is just the aperitif. The amount of power I sense radiating from the tent hasn't changed.

The next person coming out of the tent is a looming shadow that has haunted my nightmares these few years. A dark-haired immortal with a cruel beauty. In my dreams, I taste him again, and I can't let go. In my dreams, I kill him and lose myself in the process.

Samel steps forward, but I hold his sleeve. He's not ready to face him. None of us are.

I don't know why I didn't expect the gods to be here. I thought they would have taken Tenebris and returned to their empire. Why are they still at Violet's side? It doesn't make sense.

"Didn't I kill you once, little Vikus?" I ask.

He bares his white teeth. "You failed in this, as in all things, child."

I take one step forward. "Oh? The way I see it, I got my people out when you meant to kill or control them. For ten years, I kept them safe, and you failed to make Tenebris yours. I can't imagine your daddy took that well. Is that why you were banished, forced to babysit our little kingdom?"

I'm baiting him, because right now, I feel layers of shields around him. He needs to attack me; to do so, he'll have to lower his defenses.

"I'm exactly where I want to be," he replies, unbothered.

I tilt my head.

This continent was meant to be ours. When our kind grew tired of the old world and moved here, we were supposed to claim all of it, hence why it was called Alfheimr, home of the elven folk—the fae. But the immortals accompanying us took one look when we landed and decided they liked it. Their empire is built in their image, with all the entertainment, all the pleasures they require. I'm not surprised they want our land, if only because our magic makes it beautiful, abundant, rich. But immortals cannot be satisfied here in Tenebris. We don't worship them, we don't sacrifice in their name, we don't line up to participate in their orgies. Humans consider them gods—we know that the immortal descendants of the old gods aren't very different from us. More powerful, perhaps, but they can bleed and die just like the rest of us.

"Oh? Color me surprised. Tonight will be a full moon. Aren't you missing a hell of a party?"

His eyes narrow. He doesn't like that I know of their custom. And I'm right. He wants to be there, in his capital, gorging on wine, lust, and blood.

"Let me guess. Daddy dearest told you to remain here until you've gotten rid of me. He's too frightened to face me himself after last time and, well, you're expendable. You must have a sister or brother better suited to the throne."

I can tell from the darkness creeping in his eyes that I'm right again. "I was given Tenebris. This is my land. I'll have my pleasures right here, with your people, every full moon. Just as soon as I've destroyed you."

I laugh out loud. "You truly are insane."

If he thinks the folk are going to lick his boots—or anything else—he's certifiable.

"And you're as good as dead, vermin," he retorts.

It's all the warning I get before the hill collapses under my feet. I leap in the air, letting my wings push through my reinforced tunic. I can feel Samel and the two others do the same behind me. At least they have wings; not all of us do. A flock of humans bursts out of the tent, bows ready, and shoot at us. The speed of my wings serves me well. The paper-thin membranes infused with magic are so fast that to an untrained eye, I disappear and reappear at another place. My companions aren't pixies: I hear them scream as arrows hit their wings, their most vulnerable features. I manage to fly to the border of the precipice, landing too close to the Vikus boy.

I try to spring back, but he reaches for me, grabbing me by the wing. Then he rips it off. My scream cuts through the valley, piercing the air. I've never known such pain. It's not just that he's ripped away one of my limbs—he's also taken part of me. A magic that makes me Vlari. I fall and try to crawl away, but he draws his foot back and kicks me so hard I'm propelled backward. I hear his delighted laughter as he hovers over me, grabs my throat, and knees my stomach firmly enough for bile to rise to my throat. Never letting go of me, he keeps hitting me—knees, feet, punches. He's gleefully knocking me around like I'm a ragdoll. He's not using any of his power, keeping his shield firmly in place. Part of me wonders why he doesn't just finish it. He has me. I can't get away. I'm no use at close range against an immortal twice my size. But I know why he's taking his time: he's enjoying it.

I tortured him. He's going to kill me with his bare hands.

In the distance, the sun goes down. I have just enough strength to turn toward Whitecroft. The seelie riders have attacked.

I try to find peace. At least Titus will see that my people are freed from this monster. He'll take care of them. He'll take them north and reinforce his borders—I don't doubt it for a moment.

I think about my mother's death. Pointless. I think about Meda, who sacrificed so many years to try to shape me into something, someone who could fight. She threw them away.

I think of Drusk. I promised him I'd be careful. I suppose fae can lie, after all. I need him more than air, more than the sky with all its stars, more than life itself, and he never knew it.

I can't get away from the immortal. I can't…

I see steel flash through the air. A dagger.

A dagger I recognize.

It almost killed me once. Now it's aimed at the Vikus's throat.

The immortal catches it midair, turning in the direction from where it was thrown—behind me. He rises, letting me go, and I don't hesitate to crawl away.

When I'm a few paces from him, I rise, wincing.

The Vikus ignores me, eyes behind me. I dare a glance back.

Drusk.

Drusk is standing right behind me, his dark wings expanded behind his back. He flew to me, leaving Whitecroft, right in the middle of a battle. There are arrows sticking out of his back, but he ignores them all, ignores everything but me. Or rather, my back. At first, I think he's paying attention to my broken, ripped-off wing. It can't be pretty. But his eyes are set on something else entirely.

The mark running over my skin. The mark he has on his shoulder, too.

I feel the Vikus's magic before I see it: he's throwing destructive magic at both of us. Now we're two, he's done playing.

One of Drusk's wings wraps around me and pulls me to him. With a nonchalant wave, he molds Myst into a shield.

Now that I'm close, I reach around to pull out each arrow and start to heal him. He takes my wrist, shaking his head. "Not now. You have somewhere to be," he reminds me. He turns his attention back on the Vikus. "I'll take care of this."

I want to say no. He can't face an immortal by himself. Last time he did, he almost died.

The Vikus is striding toward us.

We should take him together. If Drusk can keep him occupied, I can attack when his shields are down.

Before I can say a word, Drusk kisses the side of my cheek. "Let me do this, princess."

I hear it in his voice. The raw need for blood and vengeance. I'm his. He didn't know it before, but I'm his and the Vikus was hurting me. He wants blood for it.

I nod, and rush toward the tent. The immortal tries to launch himself at me, but Drusk places himself in his path. The impact as they collide sounds like a roar. I don't give them another look, because if I do, I'll remain behind.

And I have my own war to wage.

I enter the tent.

twenty-six

secrets and lies

vlari

My blood is ice.

For a long moment, I don't understand what I see at all. It can't be real. It must be a nightmare.

My personal nightmare.

The tent doesn't look like anyone's idea of a queen's war council. There's no map, no plan, no table. Just one throne, and in a corner, one large bed with red covers and silk cushions. A lovers' nest. Except the girl on it has been bound at the ankles and wrists, to be used as the Vikus saw fit, no doubt. She doesn't even move at my entrance, so still one might believe her dead.

Violet is a broken slave.

And from the one throne in the room, Morgana Lilwreath smiles down at me.

At her side, kneeling on the floor of the tent, there are four women, all naked, their heads cast down. They do not move. I don't think they can. They may as well be made of stone.

"You're dead," I reason. "I saw you burned to ashes."

As the words cross my lips, I know them to be a lie. Not the kind of lie I cannot say: I've seen a woman burned to ashes, and I believed it was my grandmother. It'd been a decoy, a fake.

"And you're incredibly gullible," she says, bringing a bloodred grape to her mouth.

I can't make sense of it. Whatever way I try, I just don't get what's going on.

So I give up. I just ask, "Why are you doing this to her? She's your daughter."

Morgana chuckles. "Yes, I suppose she's that. But I've no use for a treacherous worm, let alone an incompetent one. If she'd come to me in peace, I'd have pitied her and given her some land to lord over. Instead, she intended to take my kingdom. We can't have that, can we?"

I nod. So, Violet schemed without her knowledge. One small piece of the puzzle, but I still can't see the full picture.

"Why didn't you come to Whitecroft? Reveal yourself? Your people would have welcomed you with open arms. You're high queen."

She rolls her eyes. "Yes, that I am. High queen of Tenebris, a broken, poor kingdom that can't rival the northern fae, or hope to take any land to the west. Let's face it, the bright days of our history are in the past. No one would have remembered my name if things had gone on as they were supposed to. Now, I'm not saying my consort's betrayal was welcome, but it's certainly opened up some opportunities."

I can't be hearing this right. "You allied with the Vikus boy?"

She shrugs. "He wants to take on his father. I want to be right next to him when he does. And, well, if a sharp knife finds its way into his heart after the wedding, all the better."

"I see." I blink. "Where does this come into it?"

I gesture to the poor, broken girl on the bed.

Morgana smiles at me, batting her long lashes. On the floor, her snake slithers to circle her throne. I note her other familiars aren't here—away, or burned along with the decoy, I don't know.

"Well, he certainly can't marry me. I'm taken, remember? By my traitor of a husband. I suppose I could dispose of him and take Ceron myself, but I'm fond of Alven. I'll retrieve him, make him pay for his betrayal, and have him back at my knee, where he belongs. I've given Violet to Ceron, to bed and wed."

Ceron. That must be the Vikus's name.

I make my way to the bed and look at the girl. Her lips are chapped, her wrists and ankles raw. She must have fought against the bonds. Her wide eyes are red, as though she's long shed her last tear.

If someone had told me I'd pity Violet a few hours ago, I would have believed them mad.

I take her hand and heal her wounds, one after the other.

I am not one to show kindness. Not without a price. I feel like she's already paid it in full.

"Oh, Nevlaria. Don't be foolish. She would never have done the same for you. This girl has wanted nothing but to destroy our entire family since the day she learned I cast her aside."

I let go of her hand. "Why did you? Cast her aside," I clarify.

Morgana grins. "I can't have too many wolves around me, now can I?"

I frown, not understanding her.

"It's easy to see from the very start. Who our children become. Some are meant to remain in the shadows. I like them most of all. Others have a strength of sorts. They're to be watched. Occasionally, a child is born with enough power to make me wary."

"Like a Void granddaughter," I glean.

"If it had been up to me, I would have sent you away, too. But as your mother had already left court, I thought you'd stay out of the way. My mistake." Morgana stands up.

She's dressed in a stunning black gown with a gold breastplate against her chest. On either side of her wide hips, she has a dagger with a silver hilt and an iron blade.

I've never seen her fight, not once. But I don't doubt for one moment that she knows how to make use of them.

"If you're after the continent, you could go with your Vikus, and leave Tenebris to us," I say, knowing exactly what she'll reply.

She isn't one to share power.

Morgana tilts her head. "And why would I give you what belongs to me?"

I close my eyes. There is only one way this ends. I lift my hands and start absorbing her power.

At least, I try.

She doesn't have any shield, any protection against my Void, and yet, I don't manage to.

She laughs at me, positively delighted.

Then, she draws one of her two swords in her left hand, and reaches out to me with the right.

And she sucks *me*.

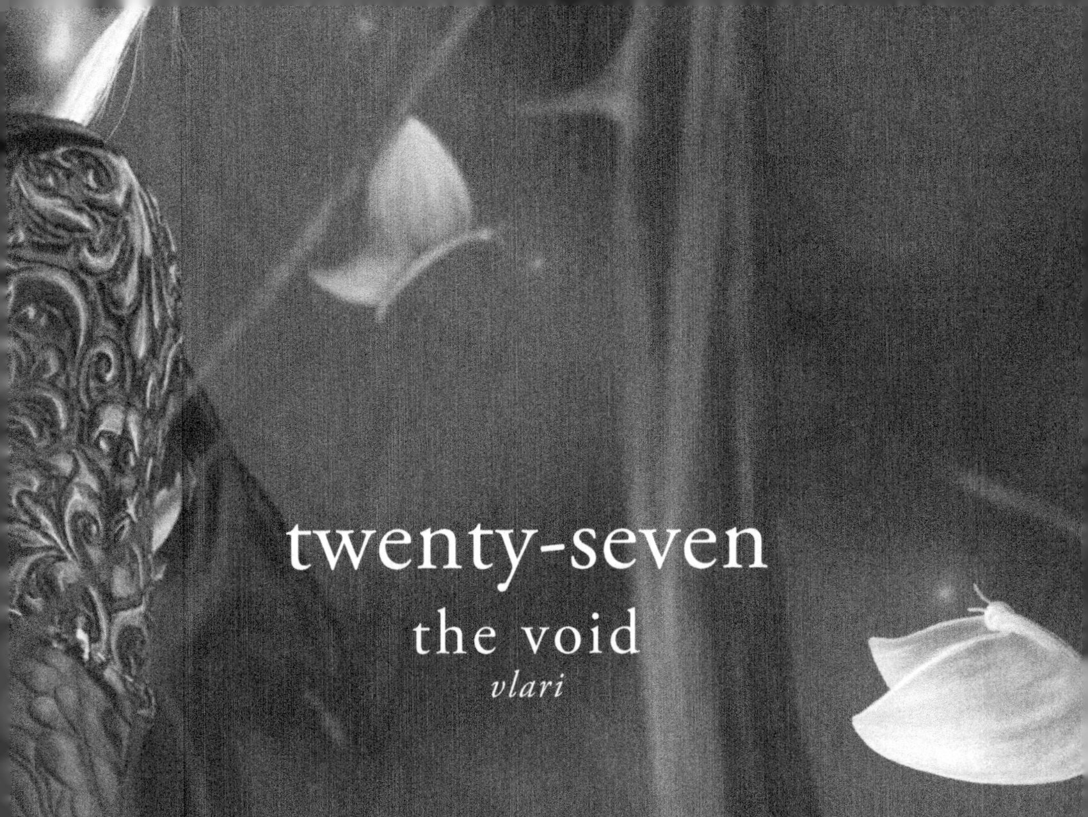

twenty-seven
the void
vlari

A Void. Morgana is also a Void. It makes no sense at all. If that was the case, surely people would have known it. And yet, I feel my life essence draining, drop after drop, and I scream. I don't know how to stop it. I've never had to.

The very thought that I'd caused such suffering to others, even my worst enemies, makes me feel sick. This is worse than any torture, worse than getting kicked and punched by Ceron.

Suddenly, I understand the women at her side. I understand why she kept so many familiars back in the Wicked Court. I even understand her fascination with Alven. She was sucking on them all, increasing her power by taking theirs, little by little.

Blinded by pain, weaker than ever, I try to lift my hands anyway, and suck her right back.

Morgana's blade is at my throat, pushing through.

"Oh, I don't think so, pretty thing. If you want me to allow you to live, you're going to do exactly what I say."

I spit on her.

Morgana draws her fist back and punches me. I fall back, out of breath, out of everything.

I retch, but there's nothing for me to vomit.

She pulls me by the hair, and drags me to Violet. "You know, I think I never taught you any lessons. It's past time I got involved in your education, don't you think, granddaughter? Firstly, don't waste your time on kindness. It's never worth it."

She throws me on the bed, next to her daughter. Pulling a set of golden keys out of her neckline, she unlocks Violet's wrist, and tosses her the key. "Be a good girl, and untie yourself. Then, you can bind your niece to the bed and get out of here."

Violet's eyes widen. She glances back at me.

"You would have done as a decent secondary prize, of course, but Ceron always wanted her." Morgana grins wickedly. "He has a taste for revenge that makes him positively unseelie."

"I'd rather die a thousand deaths than let that pig touch me."

"That could be arranged," Morgana says. "But you and I both know you're weak as a kitten. You'll lie there and take whatever your future husband wants to do to you."

I try to get to my feet, but Morgana blasts me again, and I fall backward, twisting in pain.

Violet's awkward and slow, but she unlocks each of her three remaining bonds. "I'm sorry," she tells me.

I don't have the strength to form a response. I don't have the strength to do anything. I let her bind my ankles. I let her take my sword out of my belt, and then, I let her bind my other wrist.

Morgana circles the bed. "See? This is the woman you wasted precious energy on. Not that you could have taken me on with it, but still. You'll remember this lesson, won't you, granddaughter?"

I only wish she were close enough that I could spit on her again.

All I can hope is that Drusk manages to overcome Ceron, somehow. But I've fought against him. He's too strong. I managed to get the best of him last time because I took him by surprise.

I close my eyes. There is no hope. There is nothing I can do.

I am Nevlaria, daughter of the Void. Always powerless against the true queen. She owned me from the very beginning.

I catch movement from the corner of my eye. A girl. One of the four. To my surprise, I recognize her. It's not the first time I've seen her naked, after all.

Rose.

The human girl Morgana took in exchange for Violet when she turned her daughter into a changeling. At her feet three other naked people sit. Two fae, and a human. I am shocked to recognize the lone male among them—Dekren. He's lost so much weight I took him for a girl at first.

I force myself to ignore them, focusing on Morgana, waiting to see what'll come next. More torture, no doubt.

Then, Rose lifts a knife in her hand and shoves it down, aiming for Morgana's shoulder. Instants before the blade can find its target, the queen catches her wrist, twists it in the air, and plunges it down, forcing Rose to stab herself in the stomach with a cry.

Another girl I've never seen tries to fight her, too, but Morgana is as well trained as she's ruthless. Her body's a beautiful, merciless weapon. Watching her fight is like watching a dancer. Every girl tries to attack her, and all fail, so quickly their attempt is pitiful.

I'm slow to notice whatever hold she had on me is gone. I'm so drained I almost can't tell the difference.

I crawl on top of the bed, and reach toward her before taking her energy. To my surprise, it works. Not well. I feel like I'm only absorbing tiny droplets—she's guarding the rest. Somehow.

Morgana is far more skilled than I've ever been.

No wonder she never allowed me to be trained. She wanted to keep all the power to herself—and it is.

My wrists, I note, are unbound. Violet must have freed me. I lift my other hand, and grunt as I suck her in. I'm too tired. My mind and body don't want to do it, but I force myself to keep taking her in.

All three girls and Dekren are on the ground, bleeding out or already dead. The fae lasted longer than the mortals, but Morgana won.

The queen's snake unfurls from her throne, and slithers to her shoulder. Only when he touches her do I understand his purpose.

He's feeding her his energy. He's granting her power. Yet I don't sense that he's losing any of his own.

When she's sufficiently restored, she turns to me, her cruel eyes filled with rage. She raises her hands, and I brace myself for the oncoming onslaught on my soul.

On shaking legs, Violet steps between her mother and I, my sword in her hand.

Morgana stills.

"You know what your problem is, Mother? You like wolves to kneel for you. You should have put us down when you had the chance."

Violet disappears, and reappears behind Morgana. The first flick of her wrist cuts the serpent's head clean off. Morgana screeches in fury. Her daughter's blade already found another target, slicing her back. Morgana moves to counter the blow, but already Violet's on the other side. Her swordsmanship is poor—worse than mine, and I am no expert—but I've never seen speed like that. Not even when I have my wings have I ever moved as fast as she.

I don't need to wonder why she never used her ability before. She didn't have the strength, depleted as she was, and there was no hope of taking on Morgana when she could just drain her life force. Now while I'm draining Morgana, she can't use Void, just like I couldn't when she was taking me in. And that leaves her prey to Violet's strikes.

I finally feel some part of myself awakening. Morgana's life force is feeding mine, giving me back some strength. I use it to drain her faster, harder. Soon, I see fear in those hateful eyes.

Keeping one arm outstretched, I reach for the key on the bed, and unlock my ankles, before standing up to join the fight.

I catch Violet's eye, and tilt my chin, gesturing for her to take Morgana's back.

Then I let go of the Void.

Morgana is quick to turn to me and bombard me with the full extent of her power. She's taking her daughter's advice: this time, there's no teasing. This time, she wants my death.

I fall to my knees, and she smirks, victorious.

Then blood spatters, showering my face. Violet plunged my sword right through Morgana's throat, screaming.

I gasp, falling back as Morgana's power suddenly flickers out.

Her body drops to the ground.

There's nothing but silence in the tent, save for our breathing.

Then Violet screams again, lifting the sword for the second time, and stabbing the cooling corpse, over and over.

I get to my feet, and join her.

Soon, we're laughing like children. I've never known a more entertaining game.

Then I swear. Drusk!

I rush out of the tent. I'd know if he was hurt. I'd feel it. But that doesn't mean he isn't in trouble.

I freeze as soon as I get out of Morgana's stuffy chamber, laughing out loud.

Flanked by Samel and his two knights, he's dragging Ceron uphill, bound like a hog.

I rush back to the tent, kneeling in front of the four brave, brave souls who took on Morgana for us. Without them, who's to know what would have become of us? I have little strength left to me, but what I have, I give. I give, and give, till all four are breathing.

Only then do I let myself collapse, knowing I'm safe with the girl who a day ago was supposed to be my worst enemy.

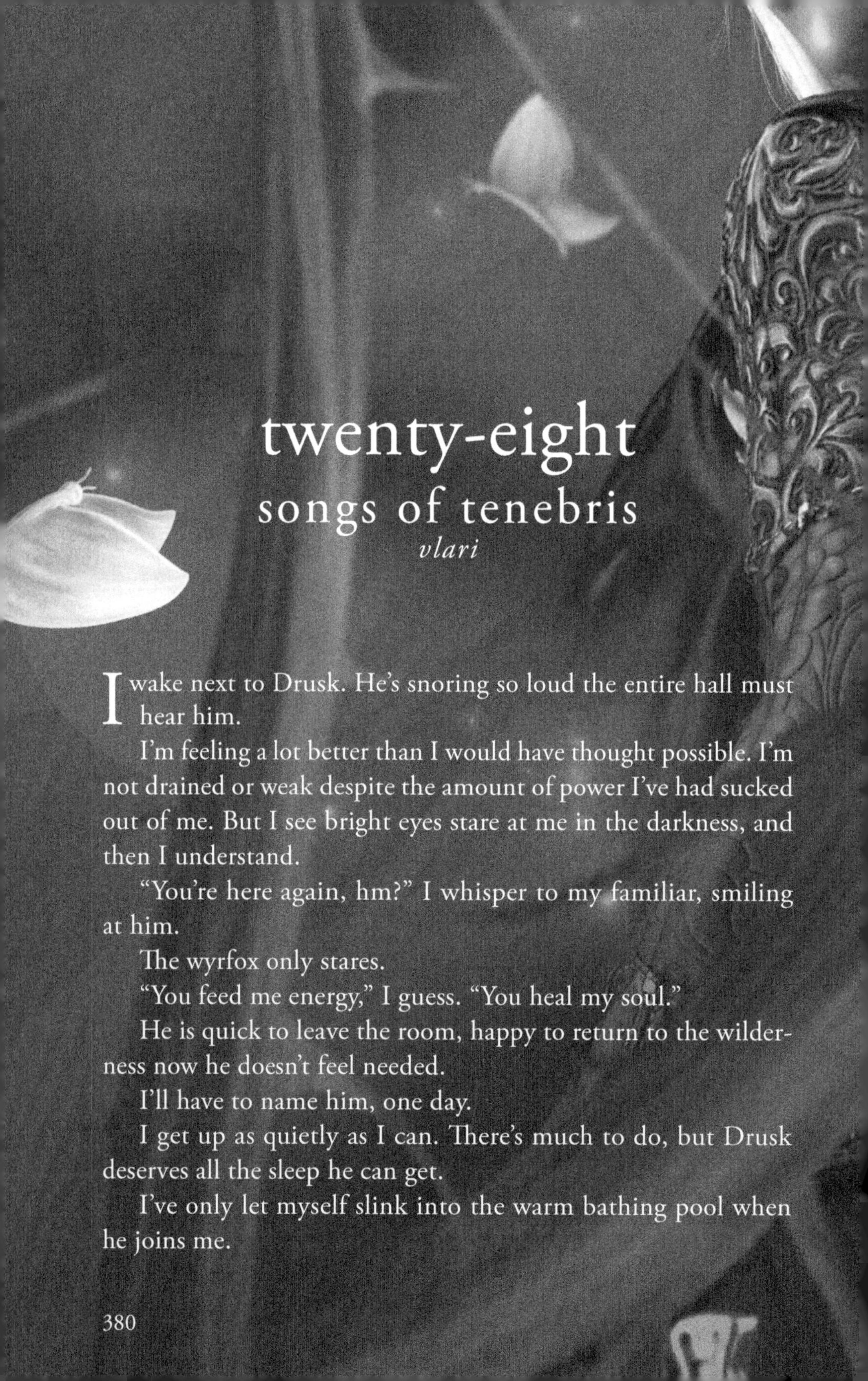

twenty-eight
songs of tenebris
vlari

I wake next to Drusk. He's snoring so loud the entire hall must hear him.

I'm feeling a lot better than I would have thought possible. I'm not drained or weak despite the amount of power I've had sucked out of me. But I see bright eyes stare at me in the darkness, and then I understand.

"You're here again, hm?" I whisper to my familiar, smiling at him.

The wyrfox only stares.

"You feed me energy," I guess. "You heal my soul."

He is quick to leave the room, happy to return to the wilderness now he doesn't feel needed.

I'll have to name him, one day.

I get up as quietly as I can. There's much to do, but Drusk deserves all the sleep he can get.

I've only let myself slink into the warm bathing pool when he joins me.

We don't talk. We could have lost each other a night ago. We could have lost everything.

But we're here, we won.

We saved our kingdom.

Words are useless. I let myself drown in him, for a time.

Then I dress, brush my hair, and set my crown upon my brow.

There are dances and songs despite the terrible losses. We've burned an army of humans, but over a thousand folk are gone. Great folk, gentle folk, soft, sweet folk. Friends and foes. Every single one of them will be missed. We celebrate their lives and scream their true names to the stars.

I dance with my aunt, I dance with my seelie cousin, I dance with my friends, and of course I dance with my mate.

My Drusk.

"You knew," he accuses me, glaring, though there's little heat in his eyes.

I don't have to ask him what he means. "It's not my fault you were slow."

"When did you guess?"

I shrug. "Ten years ago."

Drusk and I sway to the beat of the drum Titus plays better than any unseelie I've ever heard.

"You're wretched. You could have told me."

I shrug. "You like wretched."

He pulls me till I'm plastered all over his hard, bloodstained shirt. "I like nothing about you, princess. I like sunset. I like starlight. I like diamonds and wine. You, I adore."

I get to my tiptoes, and he lifts me the rest of the way, to reach his mouth. I wrap my legs around him and let him carry me to our bed.

Though it isn't quite ours. Whitecroft was never our home. Hardrock could never be either. The Wicked Court of Morgana will be destroyed along with the entire Shadow Peaks, if I have my way.

And I shall. I am high queen.

For one night, I let myself forget about it. I forget about the survivors from the Court of Ash, that I will have to send to trial. I forget about the immortal rotting in my dungeon. Violet is having her fun, torturing him, but she doesn't want to take his life, and for that, I'm grateful.

The last thing we need is to destroy a Vikus and give Alfheimr reason to launch an open war with us. This time, they used humans as proxies, but if we were to kill Ceron and attack first, his father could come at us with all his might.

If war comes to our gates, I'll be there to wage it, but I don't want to risk my people's blood again so soon.

For one night, all that matters is feeling my mate inside me till neither of us can move. And we do just that.

WE DRAG HIM to the border, bound and blindfolded, and let him go without any supplies. He can beg or barter for them beyond the border.

When we reach Mirthgrath, I kick Ceron to the ground, and remove his blindfold so he can watch me.

His eyes are a storm of fury.

"You came for my world and you leave with nothing. You tried to destroy me—us—and you failed."

He holds his head high. "I will kill you, little girl. All of you."

He's encompassing Drusk, Titus, and Violet in one sweeping glance.

I bare my teeth. "Let me make you a promise. If you ever lay a hand on my family again, we will take yours. Not just you. Your children, and grandchildren, and their children, too. This is your last warning. Stay away from Tenebris."

He gets to his feet, tall and proud as ever, though I know Violet cut him down a thousand times, waiting for him to heal before cutting again.

That enrages me. I can't help it: I suck on his soul one last time, making him scream.

He never begs, and I hate him for it.

"There," I say. "Now your hair matches Daddy dearest's."

It's silvery-white, rather than dark. I've drained almost every drop of his life, and the man has the gall to laugh.

"We immortals are patient," he tells me. "And one day, we'll take your pitiful kingdom."

He turns around, walking away like a king.

And we let him.

"That promise of yours was careless," Titus tells me. "You spoke for both of your bloodlines. You may have linked your fates."

I ignore him. There are more important matters to attend to.

As soon as the Vikus prince disappears in the darkness, I start the second ritual.

The tears. The blood. The stones. The sacrifice.

It is my grandfather I set to rest today.

And with his death, Tenebris is once again land of the unseelie fae.

epilogue

Vlari is the worst at keeping secrets. From me, in any case. We have a tradition of sorts, she and I. Every year, she does her best to hide her presents and party planning for my birthday, and every year, I figure it out. The first few times, it hadn't been on purpose; I just came across whatever gift she'd stuffed in a broom closet. I must admit that the last few years, I've sniffed around for it, knowing how it infuriates her when I find her presents.

I haven't found anything this year. Not in the lily pond, not on the roof, not behind the paintings in the armory.

She knows it, I can tell. The way she smirks when she enters the hall of crowns shows she knows she's victorious.

I try not to pout.

The fact that she's particularly gorgeous tonight, wrapped in one of Ma'am Rolo's long gossamer gowns, so delicate I almost see through the blush fabric, would drive any man to distraction.

"Do you truly need to look at her like that?" Dornant asks, grimacing.

Dornant despises any show of affection, from anyone at all—Vlari and I more than the rest.

I ignore him. He's a hundred and fifty now, twice the age Vlari and I were when we saved Tenebris from the human invaders, but in his entire life, he has known no sorrow, no hardship. We've built a world where our children have the luxury of being spoiled and naive. It's our grandest accomplishment.

"Oh, leave Father alone, grumpy." Rulla yet again confirms her place as my favorite child, slapping the back of her twin's head.

I can admit that. Dornant is Vlari's boy. Rulla's my girl.

Dornant glares at his sister. "Just because I have to accept Mother and Father must have had sex at one point doesn't mean that I need visual reminders."

"One day, you'll fall in love, and then I hope you know Father will exact his revenge."

I grin, imagining it. I'll embarrass the hell out of him if the day comes that he sets his eyes on anyone.

Vlari reaches us on the dais, but instead of joining us, taking the ornate throne at the center, she turns to face the court.

All fall silent as she raises her hands, palms up.

I frown, confused and on alert. I don't know of any announcement scheduled for today, of all days. My birthdays are nights of mindless celebrations, much more casual than that of the queen. Hers are political affairs gathering the lords of all of Alfheimr.

"Lords and ladies, kings and queens." Her crisp voice fills the still room, and the folk silently bow before her. "For one hundred and thirty years, I've ruled our land as best as I could. I have weighed your complaints, I have quelled your anger, I have shielded us from our enemies."

"Praised be the queen!" Titus yells, raising his golden goblet.

He's a frequent visitor now that we've moved to the Old Keep, deep in the Murkwood, so close to the seelie border.

The court echoes him, drinking to Vlari's health.

She waits for silence before continuing. "What no one has ever said is that I wouldn't have been able to do any of it without those who stood by my side, now and then. My mother, my father, my friend, my sister." She turns away from the court, and faces me now. "And you, Rystan."

She uses my name so sporadically, particularly in public.

"Thirteen decades ago, you reclaimed our country with me. Then, you raised our children, advised me, consoled me on my darkest nights. I may hold the crown, but you're the pillar of the realm."

"To King Rystan!" Meda toasts, followed up by the rest of the court.

I grin, accepting their ovation with a bow.

I'm not used to it; my role as Vlari's consort is to stand in the shadows. I understand how her grandfather ended up resenting it. I don't. I'm happy taking care of my family. Of Vlari. But Alven never loved the late queen; he was trapped out of the sunlight, condemned to exist in her shadow.

"Today, I considered giving you a spelled cloak, or a pretty ring, or a dagger that turns any heart it pierces to ice."

My mate has good taste.

"Then I realized you've had that and more, these one hundred and thirty birthdays. There's only one thing left for me to give you."

She nods at the children seated either side of me. They rise and move to stand next to her, both facing the crowd.

Whatever is going on, they're part of it, the two traitors.

To my shock and dismay, Vlari gets to her knees and bends her head.

"Nevlaria Bane, High Queen of Tenebris, do you recognize your heir?" Rulla asks, her clear voice as eloquent as her mother's.

"I recognize my son, Dornant Bane, as my heir."

We've talked of this. I believe Rulla is better suited to politics than Dornant, and Vlari agrees, but our daughter is seelie to the core. She's always had her eyes to the north. Binding her to Tenebris would be unkind.

Whenever we talked of succession, I imagined it would occur in the future—in hundreds, if not thousands of years. Not now.

I search her eyes. She can't mean—

"High Queen Nevlaria, do you consent to surrendering the crown?"

"I consent," she replies, without a moment of hesitation.

Just like that, it's done. She's no longer queen. Rulla takes the dark crown on her head, into which the green heart stone of Tenebris has been set, and Vlari rises to face the stunned court. My mother hugs her grandmother. The folk murmur amongst themselves, as stunned as I.

Vlari's giving me the one thing I wouldn't have asked for, the one thing I truly want. Herself. Her time, her priority. She's given up all of her power for me.

Rulla strides to her brother, and Dornant kneels to receive his crown.

"Long live the high king!" she bellows.

There's silence at first, but all, puck and pixies, elves and gentry, come to their senses and exclaim as one. "Long live the high king!"

I woke up believing the rest of my life was going to be meetings and festivals, parades and war councils. I woke up knowing that I had to compete with the rest of Tenebris for my mate's time. Now, we have our entire lives before us to do as we please.

For the first time in centuries, I'm free. We are free.

I wish Alven were still with us, little as I liked the bastard. Vlari cared for her grandfather. He's gone, too. I wish Nero had shown his face sometime in the last century, but since his bondmate's death, he's retreated deep into the Wilderness, like so many shy folk. I wish my sister were here with us, but she's one of the names we shout at the sky every year, in remembrance of the battle of Whitecroft.

They should have enjoyed today with us, but they can't, and I have to make peace with their loss. The one true shadow that can never heal from my heart is the absence of Cissa, our third-born daughter. A child of the sea who hardly knows us. I don't doubt that she was invited, but she never comes to us.

I stride to my mate and wordlessly lift her, throwing her on my shoulder.

I know just how I want to spend the next hours, and that's not playing nice with a court that's no longer ours to rule.

"Revolting," the high king states, glaring at us.

I wink at my son, dragging his mother to our bed one last time, before we vacate the royal rooms that now belong to him.

To be updated about more stories in this world, you can join May Sage's Coven or subscribe to her newsletter.

May Sage writes about various worlds and prioritizes those with a high number of reviews and ratings. If you enjoyed Shadow Cursed, don't forget to leave a review!

next in alfheimr

The Cursed Crown

My lips hitch up an inch as the hulking, slender man bends down to whisper in my ear. "A divided kingdom without a leader is weak. You will fall. You will fail. You will all die without my kindness, little girl."

He expects me to falter, shiver, and drop my gaze to the ground like the flock of gentry buzzing around him.

My eyes widen in feigned dismay. "Kindness? Why did no one think to tell me you had any?"

I have to allow him that one concession: Rydekar is fun to tease.

He doesn't even smile. I don't think anyone has taunted him. "I have none. You will beg nonetheless."

I just may, in his dreams. And in my nightmares.

NO ONE WAS ever born less suited to ruling than Rissa, the thorn of the seelie realm—a half-fae so wild she's spent the better part of a hundred years in the woods.

For all her flaws, she's the last of the high court bloodline, and the southern king seems to think that's reason enough to slap a crown on her feathered head. He needs her to unify the seelie forces. She needs him to forget about that nonsense.

In an effort to aid her people without condemning herself to a lifetime of misery, she sets off on a journey to find the one person with a stronger claim to the throne than hers: the cursed prince.

Sealed in the mountains of the Wilderness, under many spells, the heir of the first seelie queen is the only royal strong enough to protect the fae lands from their immortal invaders.

Surviving the untamed tribes and awakening a thousand-year-old prince seem a lot easier than ruling an entire kingdom where everyone hates her very nature.

And her choices won't come without consequences.

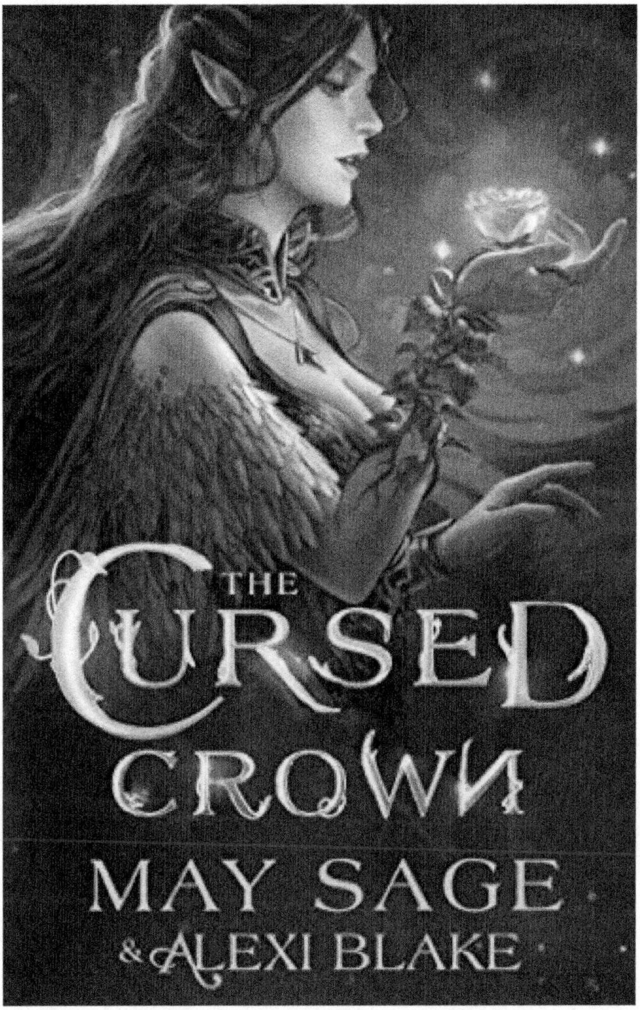

Available on Preorder on All Retailers
out in december

Songs of Tenebris

A Series of Novellas

More soon in the Coven and on May Sage's Newsletter!

An Arrow In the Mist
A Noblesse Oblige Trilogy

Hayden's life as a diplomat's assistant used to be simple, but the untimely death of the emperor of Alfheimr throws the entire realm into chaos.

The throne collects dust and blood while the crown heirs settle their differences at the point of a cursed blade.

Everyone in the Inner City has picked a side.

Except her, the young woman whose choice will define the fate of the realm.

No heir thought to court a simple sprite, but Hayden's past holds the keys to a treaty the future ruler will need to keep their crown on their head—or their head on their shoulders.

One treacherous friend, one irresistible foe. How could she possibly favor one over the other?

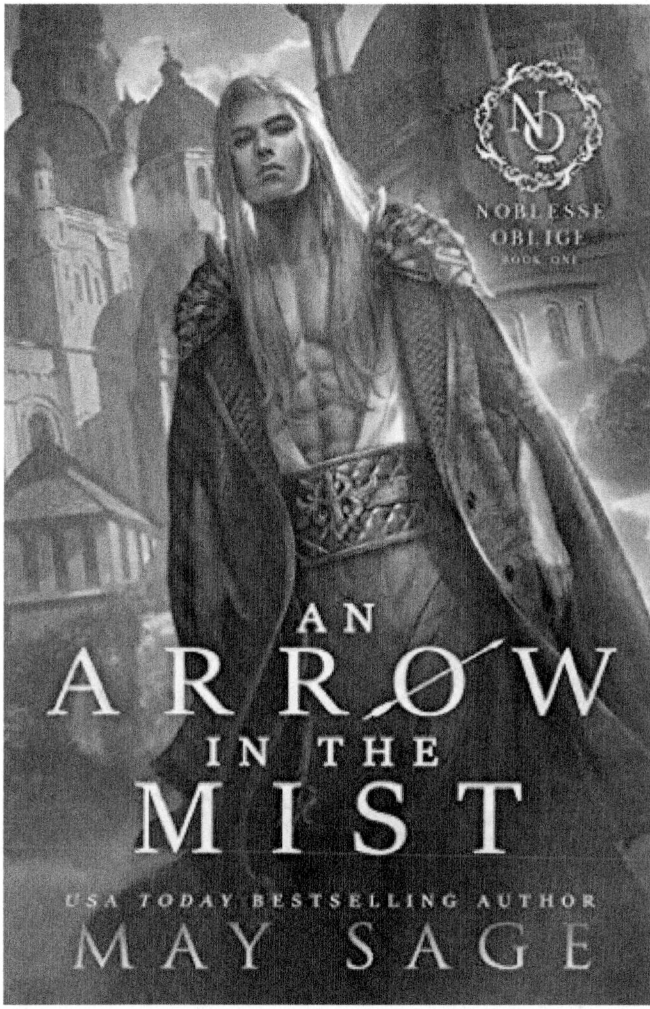

On Preorder Now

Masters of Alfheimr

Twins. One girl, one boy, both destined to rule the empire.
Lenka and Nikandre are the two sides of the coin that will dictate the fate of the world.
Only, fate hasn't yet chosen heads or tails.

Masters of Álfheimr is a Noblesse Oblige Trilogy prequel novella.

Available Now

also from may sage

I set out across the lawn, to the woods, moving at a brisk jog. My muscles immediately protest against the unfamiliar exercise. It's been a while since I've run. Back in middle school, I used to be part of the track team, but I've since given up on anything even resembling team spirit. My father insists that I keep at least one extracurricular activity, "for my future". I've chosen chess.

I've vaguely thought about running through the woods, simply because they're right there at our doorstep, and pretty enough, but I don't think I'd truly meant to do it. Now, with my lungs burning, my shins weighing five tons each, it's a matter of pride. I haven't even cleared a quarter of a mile. As a kid, I used to be able to run four or five without straining. *I feel like I'm dying!*

My ears ring, and my breathing gets so uneven, I have to stop. I bend forward, holding my knees. Damn. I'm going to start working out. What if a murderer was running after me? I wouldn't last five minutes.

I calm down enough to start appreciating the view again. Sometime in the last quarter of an hour, dawn rose in the horizon. The sky is all shades of blood and water over the line of trees surrounding me.

To my surprise, I have to admit I like it here. It's peaceful. Quiet.

And I haven't felt any itch, any pain.

Not since I left the house.

Not since I woke up, actually.

I'm fine.

I haven't been fine for such a long time, it's a little odd to me. Fine feels uncomfortable on my skin.

Then I see it, right in front of me, almost close enough to touch my nose. A little folk of some variety. Three feet tall and purple-skinned, creased like that of an elephant, and covered with a soft layer of white fur. It's fluffy enough to be cute, although I don't think I've ever seen a face so grisly. Its droopy, beady eyes are surrounded by a million wrinkles, and it has no nose—just two slits, farther apart than that of a snake. It licks its lipless mouth with a long, serpentine green tongue that looks slimy.

I lift my torso abruptly, eager to keep my face far, far away from it.

"Sorry," I say impulsively, like the well-bred girl I'm not.

I freeze, the realization dawning on me.

It's the first word I've ever said to one of *them*, and with good reason.

The folk of this world glamour themselves to be invisible to mortals like me when they roam our world. Animals see them, or at least sense their presence, hence why cats and dogs sometimes stop dead in their tracks, staring at what seems to be nothing. Humans cannot see them, and therefore, I act like I don't.

There's safety in feigning ignorance. I'm just another girl, if I'm not aware of them. I can't see them? They don't bother to see me.

Aunt Julia told me that from the moment she started to interact with the folk, her life took a turn for the worse. They started to tease her, play with her, to catch her attention or ask for favors.

In my childhood, I think I used to wave at them, but they don't pay attention to little boys and girls. Most children can see the folk, until they grow to believe there's no such thing as fairy tales.

I've been so, so very good, for years and years.

And now, I've spoken.

To my surprise, as I stare at the creature with dismay and fear, it stares back, and it's terrified.

What could the likes of him have to fear from me? I'm one hundred and fifteen pounds, soaking wet. I took self-defense lessons, but I'm aware I'm lacking in the threatening department.

The strange thing doesn't agree. It's shivering from head to toes. "I beg your pardon, my lady. My *queen*!" it squeaks, bending at the waist, so low it's shoving its face on the muddy ground.

By then, it's quite clear that this is a case of mistaken identity. In a split second, I decide to ensure the creature keeps mistaking me for whoever he thinks I might be.

Did he say queen?

I don't have much to work with, but I stand upright, throwing my shoulders back and lifting my chin in what I imagine is a queenly way. I'm ridiculous, sweating, out of breath, and imitating Lady Di.

"You're pardoned. Now, go, I need my privacy."

There. Not too bad, right?

The little folk pops its head up, suspicion written in his puckered, leathery skin.

Dammit. I gave myself away, somehow.

"If I may, why is Her Majesty so far from the bright lands, and at such a time as this! Should they find you here, on unseelie soil—"

The words make little sense to me. I think back to Julia's tales, trying to decipher its meaning, so that I might give a convincing answer.

I settle on sticking to my guns. I am queen. He's…whatever he is. I doubt he can be very far up on the food chain. "Tell me, since when do I have to justify myself to you, exactly?" There's a threatening edge to my words.

At first, it works. The little folk is trembling and shivering, reacquainting its face with the moss.

Then I hear a low, rumbling laugh, followed by a pointed slow clap. I turn to the sound, and freeze.

He stands feet from me, leaning on a black oak tree. The man from yesterday, still in black under the coat. Now that he's ten feet away, I can tell it's forest-green leather, stitched with gold embellishments. Trees and leaves, birds and hearts, follow the edges of the garment.

I concentrate on it, studying it in great detail, if only to avoid looking at him directly. I've had a glance. It's enough. Enough to realize my terrible, terrible mistake.

I should have locked myself in yesterday. I should have convinced my family to pack up their bags and move far, far away.

Run, run, run away.

I don't. I don't move at all. As much as I want to flee, I obviously suck at running. Besides, I can tell. He'll enjoy the chase.

The fae is the most beautiful thing I've ever beheld. There's no need for any posturing on his part. I itch to kneel. To bare my throat to him, like a spineless bitch.

Come, come, come closer.

His dark eyes whisper promises of pain and pleasure, wordlessly beckoning me, but it is his mouth I fear. His playful, full, bloodred lips have no business on the face of a man. I note the delicately curved point to his ears, poking out under his waves of black curls.

Screw it. I need to go, and I do just that, willing myself to ignore both of the folk as I storm past them, sprinting in the direction of my home.

At least, I hope it's the right direction. Suddenly, I'm not sure at all.

A laugh follows me. I don't stop, concentrating on one single goal. Getting back home alive. And whole.

Part of me wishes I were religious. I could pray right now, if I knew how. I could swear to be good. I could swear to be a better person, a better daughter and sister, so long as a higher power intervened, ensuring I got home in one piece.

Please, please, please.

One moment, there's nothing but the muddy ground in front of me. The next, a root lashes like a whip, curling under my foot. I see the ground approach, and wince in anticipation. At my speed, the fall is going to hurt.

I close my eyes, willing reality away, but the pain never comes.

Instead, I feel something much worse.

Warm, soft hands holding my middle. The scent of wood, blood, musk, and ashes hits my nostrils. I open my eyes to see the fae right under me, lying on the ground, his elaborate coat stained with mud and moss. He doesn't seem to mind at all. He's smiling as though he couldn't be more pleased.

Run, run, run away.

I don't. I know it's far too late for that.

On Preorder Now

Printed in Great Britain
by Amazon

87350204R00237